TASTE

TERRAWAY
BOOK ONE

MARY E. TWOMEY

MARY E. TWOMEY, LLC

TASTE

BOOK ONE IN THE TERRAWAY SERIES

By

Mary E. Twomey

COPYRIGHT

ACKNOWLEDGMENTS

Special thanks to Ruth Gross and Bailey Soper for editing this book, and not judging me on my typos.

Super Duper special thanks to Jen Like, who gave me a quiet place to write, and listened when I couldn't be quiet anymore.

DEDICATION

For my mom and dad.

For sacrificing, for loving and for praying.
Somehow, the four of us kids turned out alright,
thanks to you two.

FREDDY KRUEGER, BUGS AND WOLVES

Ollie's laugh was a welcome sound, warming my heart as my brother's familiar cadence reached me through my cell phone. "What if I give you a million dollars? Will that get me out of meeting Bev's new boyfriend?"

"Not even if you offered *ten* million," I replied with a smile on my face. I loved it when my brother laughed. "Had you said you'd buy me a pack of gum, I'd have let you out of meeting the man who could turn out to be your future stepfather, no problem."

Ollie let out a dramatic groan, sounding eight years younger than me, even though he was really eight years older. "Don't say 'stepfather'. You know he won't last. They never do."

"That doesn't sound like ideal stepson talk," I scolded, pretending to be the adult, so at least there was *one* present for this conversation. "This is important to Bev, so be a good son for her. Try to be pleasant."

Ollie sighed, and I could picture his hazel eyes that matched mine rolling back at the very notion he should be seen as a son to our mama. "Yeah, fine. I'll bring my best fake smile and I'll even say nice things to him like, 'Please, do tell me about your criminal record,' 'Wow, you still have some of your own teeth', and 'How fascinating you don't have a job. Think of all the free time!'"

A chuckle escaped before I could suppress it. Then the deeply programmed guilt rippled over me that rose up whenever we poked fun at Bev's expense. "Be nice, now."

"I'm only coming to hang with you. How about I skip the new guy meet and greet, and just catch you after?"

My tone turned southern and bossy as I tucked a stray auburn curl behind my ear, using my knee to steer the car. "Oliver James, if you ditch me, I'm pretty much going to crazy murder you. You haven't seen Bev in years. Bite the bullet."

I could hear the fondness in my older brother's voice. "Ah, but you're the good child. The blessed child. October Grace: the daughter who stayed in Georgia to look after our psychotic mama. You know very well you should've moved away, like Allie and I did." He paused for a beat at the mention of our estranged sister, but then sniggered at my threat. "'Crazy murder'? Well, I should hope you don't opt for a regular, run-of-the-mill offing. I'd at least like my death to make the front page."

I scoffed good-naturedly. "What are you, the mayor? If you want the front page, I'll have to break out the fancy tools."

I spotted a large abomination of dust on the dashboard. I'd just detailed Terence, my Taurus, but there the dust sat, mocking me and throwing up a middle finger that it wouldn't be banished. I swiped it away, wishing again that all the dirt and dust in the universe would just stay out of my car, my house and my world. I mean, is that too much to ask?

"I don't want to go to this thing," Ollie whined.

"Ditch me, and you'll regret it. I know all the good places to dump a body if you leave me to go meet New Boyfriend alone."

He let out an audible shudder. "You creep me out when you say stuff like that, because I know it's true."

I gave Ollie my best evil villain chortle. "I was thinking we should have a *Nightmare on Elm Street* marathon when you come into town next week. All Freddy, all night. Sleep with one eye open, if you dare."

"I'm just happy you're willing to entertain a movie marathon that doesn't star Bruce Campbell. I can only watch him in *Evil Dead* so many times."

"Do you have a problem with my first love?"

"No, I have a problem watching *Evil Dead* for the hundred millionth time." He cleared his throat, and I could tell he was gearing up to say something he was reluctant to voice. "I'm staying at Gabby's the first night I come into town, and maybe the night after, too. Freddy Krueger will have to wait."

I whispered in my creepy witch voice, "Freddy waits for no one!" I shook my head at my brother's old habits. "You're back with Gabby? Do I need to tell you that you're a masochist? How many times are you going to get together and break up with her?"

"I dunno. Maybe ten?"

My attention was distracted when something black skittered across my dashboard, drawing my eye, and making my spine tingle. "What the..." I scratched the back of my hand and grabbed a wipe from the package I kept in my glovebox. Still steering with my knee, I smashed the trespassing ant, keeping an eye on the road as best I could. The trees and grass that dotted the side of the road would have been a much better home than my car. Poor ant didn't have a clue. I longed to wash my hands, but suppressed the urge as best I could.

"What's wrong?" Ollie inquired, noting my diverted attention.

"A bug in my car, right after some dust on my dashboard. I just detailed it, too."

Ollie's pause was not unexpected, nor was the parental mode he slipped into without missing a beat. "You alright?"

"I'm fine, just annoyed. It's like, one of the two places I like to keep clean."

My brother's response was quiet and controlled. "Life is messy, October, and that's okay."

I sighed at the mantra he'd drilled into my head, wishing that one day I'd get to a point where I didn't still need to hear it. I was about to concede that he was right, that dust and one single ant was nothing to be concerned with, but my hackles rose when a line of ants marched out from under the passenger's seat. They traipsed up the console just to stare at me, repeating the speedy path of the damned onto my dashboard, drawing my focus.

They stared at me, paused between my steering wheel and the odometer, studying me with their beady little eyes that had intention. Bev's trailer was always filled with a wide variety of bugs and critters, but these ants had marched with purpose in my direction.

I let out a noise of distress when a row of cockroaches followed behind, facing me on the dash to make up a second row of gawkers. "What the..."

"What's up, kiddo?"

I tried to keep my eyes on the road, the city giving way to thicker smatterings of trees that dotted the landscape. The cockroaches were starting to freak me out, not because I was scared of them, but because cockroaches were naturally afraid of daylight, and these guys were out on their own free will in the late morning sun that shone through my windshield. *Weird.*

I needed to scratch the back of my hand, but gripped the

steering wheel tight and clutched my cell phone to keep myself from slipping into bad habits. When a small army of furry, black caterpillars inched out from under the passenger's seat and climbed up the dash by the dozens, I let out a shriek, sweat breaking out on my forehead. They looked like a line of mobile Groucho Marx eyebrows, moving unapologetically into my view. "Gross! Get out!" I kept a steady hand on the steering wheel, willing myself not to lose control of the car. I tried not to think about what kind of filth I must've somehow missed that had attracted these creatures to me in droves.

"October? Hey, what's wrong?"

"I... My car is dirty!" I screeched, not ready to admit to my brother that I was so filthy, apparently, that the car I'd tried to keep immaculately clean was now infested with bugs that inched closer to me, like I was their target. I could practically feel them crawling on my skin, so I scraped at my arms again, hoping to alleviate some of the tension that was building to blow the top off my stress volcano. "Ollie!"

Ollie's voice tried to calm me through what he probably assumed was a freak-out over a few dust bunnies. "Life is messy, and that's okay," he repeated. "After this stupid dinner next week, I'll clean your car myself. You'll see. We'll get all the dust out, and it'll be good as new. I'm here, kiddo."

That would've been comforting, but a rattling noise sounded in the front of my car, making me even more apprehensive. My car was perfect. It was supposed to be perfect. It was only a year old, and I took meticulous care of it. What could possibly be wrong with the engine?

I let out a horror movie-style scream and dropped the phone when a zillion tiny white moths flooded the interior of the car through the vents. They pelted my skin and fluttered their germ-filled wings in my ears. I let my foot off the gas, swerving in and out of oncoming traffic as I tried to get a grip on my panic. My heart pounded in my chest as a flash of my body, fresh from a car wreck, surfaced in my imagination. They'd haul my carcass out of the bug-infested wreckage, no doubt disgusted to see someone driving with a car that was overloaded with insects. I was filthy, as I'd always suspected, and tried so hard not to be. My brother would come to collect my bug-spattered body, wondering how it all went so wrong.

Air was suddenly difficult to suck through my lungs. I needed to find a safe place to pull over, but the moths were in my face. I thought it couldn't get any worse, until something slimy slithered up my pant leg. I shrieked and kicked my right foot without thinking, slamming on the gas by accident. The moths began to flutter around the car, giving me a glimpse of the road I was swerving down more precariously than Evil Knievel had a right to.

I hadn't seen the half-naked, brown-skinned, mid-thirties dude standing in the middle of the road next to a gray wolf.

Like, a legit wolf.

My brain processed things in the wrong order when I

caught sight of what looked like hundreds of fat worms crawling all over the man's muddy skin. My foot scrambled for the brake, stomping down too late, I was certain. Without meaning to, I screamed and shut my eyes like a baby, praying I didn't hit the guy and fling his bug-riddled body into a swift death.

I braced myself for the crash, but it never came.

When Terence the Taurus screeched to a halt, it took a solid three seconds before I could open my eyes to take in what damage I'd done. Quick as I could, I pulled off to the side with shaking fingers and a scared whimper, grateful the road was fairly deserted at this time of day.

I scrambled out of my car and crashed through the green and brown bramble that lined the roadside, leaving the door wide open to escape the bug-stuffed vehicle. It was either that I permitted the bugs to infest me or that I let the wolf eat me, and I was too turned around to make anything like an educated decision. I had to locate the dude I'd almost hit and make sure he was okay. Before I could turn my head to the street, I closed my mouth through a terrified scream when bugs poured out of my car, flying and scurrying toward the open road. The cloud of insects dissipated out into the sparse bits of nature behind me and across the street. The creepy-crawly army was now cloaked behind trees and a few knee-high bushes.

The dude was gone. I mean, simply vanished, as was the wolf. They'd been in the middle of the road, plain as day, but looking around now, they were nowhere. The man's brown skin, tall physique and broad, naked shoulders should have been easy to pick out, especially factoring in that he'd been covered in streaks of mud and worms. And how exactly was a large gray wolf supposed to up and disappear, like some kind of twisted magic trick? They were gone. I mean, just utterly nowhere.

I clawed at the backs of my hands as my anxiety hit a new level. My perfect car had been polluted so horribly, and I almost killed someone in the mess of it all. I sunk to my knees, hugged my middle and rocked myself on the side of the road. "I'm not crazy. I'm not crazy," I chanted over and over to myself. The fear that I was insane was never all that far off, but hallucinations were a new one. Usually it was only my OCD that kept me dosed with a healthy fear of being hauled away if it all got to be too much.

If *I* got to be too much.

I took my sweet time calming myself down. I focused on steadying my breaths and summoning up all the mantras my brother and sister had drilled into my head over the years. They'd done everything so I wouldn't be the crazy girl, rocking herself on the side of the road. I didn't have it in me to tell them they might've failed.

When it dawned on me that there was a wolf roaming about, my trembling legs finally found their way back into my car. I looked around, noticing with surprise that the interior was shockingly clean. There was no trace of the insect invasion anywhere. I knew my meds didn't have anything resembling a hallucinatory side effect on the warning label, but the whole ordeal was so confusing; I was starting to wonder how much of my spluttering brain was firing correctly.

"October!"

I scrambled to retrieve my phone, wiping it down first so the floor germs didn't attack my face when I pressed the device to my cheek. I didn't know how long my brother had been calling for me. "Ollie?"

"What happened?" he thundered, fear controlling his oft-swinging temper.

My eyes darted to the road nervously, as if I was hiding a dime bag under my seat. I didn't want the world to know I was dirty, that bugs had crawled in my car. "I, um, I saw a bug. A few bugs, actually." I swallowed, not wanting my brother, of all people, to think I was filthy. "I dropped the phone because I had to slam on the brakes real quick. Something was in the road." Or *someone*.

Ollie calmed with my explanation. "You scared me. Are you alright?"

"I think so." My voice came out pinched as I worked out the next words I couldn't keep from spilling out of me. "I don't want you to ever send me to a mental hospital, Ollie. Promise me."

My brother's reply came out slow and practiced. "You know I would never send you away. If you feel yourself tipping over the edge, I'll come get you, and you'll stay in

New York with me. Nowhere safer. Then we can be crazy together."

I breathed a gust of relief that the world was still spinning on its usual axis. There were no more bugs, no one who was almost murdered by my mid-motor freak-out, and my brother was coming home next week for a visit. Everything would be alright. I had plenty of sanitizer in my glovebox to clean up the mess I'd managed to escape. "Okay. Thank you. I think I'm alright now."

Ollie was patient with me, and never condescending. "October, your car is clean. You don't need to worry about a little dust and a couple of ants."

I pinched the bridge of my nose and let out a steady exhale. "You're right. Tell me you'll be there for Bev's special dinner next week."

I could hear the softness that only came when Ollie smiled. "Are you kidding? You're my favorite person. I wouldn't miss it for the world."

2

BEV'S SPECIAL THINGS

"October Grace, could you stop being useless, and pass me that clip?" Bev looked at herself in the sliver of mirror that was visible through the mountains of clutter. There was a coat hanging on the edge of the broken profile-length glass, and a pink hat with a coffee-stained, crumpled flower on the brim that had seen better days. Something had nested in the brim, and left a brown trail behind as a sweet, sweet memory of what the hat could've been.

I looked around my mama's mobile home for the clip she wanted with the practiced patience of the dutiful daughter I was. If there was a superhero outfit for shutting up and smiling, I would have it in five different colors, with a cape or something, so everyone would know of my shutting up powers without me having to say a word. Some people were good at weightlifting; I was good at smiling through the discomfort.

"Which clip do you want, Bev? They're all so pretty." It wasn't easy to find a clip in the chaos. Each one that littered the thigh-high pile to the left of the door in Bev's bedroom was in a state of disrepair, or had been covered in some sort of animal mess. I kept my fingers tight inside my hospital gloves, my face composed through my internal wince. Nasty as she might turn, I just couldn't let Bev put rat feces in her hair, no matter how pretty her clips were once brushed "clean".

Most nurses didn't feel the need to have their own box of rubber gloves to carry around in their car, but most nurses didn't have a mama like Bev.

Bev teased her thin blonde bangs so they had a little life in them. The rest of her hair had endured a good brush-through at the insistence of her comb that was missing about nine teeth. She held out her hand expectantly to me without moving her gaze from the mirror. "Grab me something pink. There's a rose-ish one with pearls I was looking for the other day. Can you find it?"

I gave a good representation of searching for the accessory. I breathed through my mouth to avoid the sharp sting of ammonia that permeated my pores from all the rodent and feral cat excrement. I looked toward the mountain of clothing that stretched to the ceiling. To the left of it was the pile of torn and ratted towels that were precariously perched atop a busted record player Bev had sworn that she was "just about to fix" ever since I was a kid. I fished through the sea of garbage at my feet that climbed up to my thighs in spots.

I reached past the doorstopper that was actually just a large white rock. The rock was older than I was, but it still lit up when I touched it. Bev could never get it to light up, but swore it was still a good doorstopper. Try getting her to put the doorstop outside with the other rocks, and she'd throw the biggest Southern Belle fit you'd ever seen. So the light-up white rock with jagged edges stayed put in the doorway of trash. Well, to me and everyone else in the world it was garbage; to Bev it was all her "special things".

I had an affinity for lavender-scented antibacterial hand sanitizer, so to each her own, I guess.

I cast around the larvae-infested area that had her discarded yogurt containers. "No, I don't see your rose clip. How about this one? It would look pretty with your shirt." I lifted a gray clip from the mess, swallowing my creeping anxiety at the maggots that squiggled and squirmed when my gloved hand swept near them. I knew how to approach the wildlife that had taken up residence in Bev's singlewide mobile home. Give them a good warning, and they scattered for fear of being taken away from their golden opportunity. No one tried to kill them here. No one bothered. For each cockroach, maggot or spider extermi-nated, there were hundreds more to take their place. It was the best life ever for them. Not so much for humans.

I made the mistake of drawing in a breath through my

nose and winced. It wasn't the stench – which was abominable, make no mistake. The thing that stung me were the memories that swirled up inside of me like vomit. Every can of rotting tuna, cat food container, aerosol can and broken bathroom fixture swelled together to sing me its symphony of neglect.

Pungent neglect smelled like childhood, and I wanted no part of that.

I exhaled out the stink my memories clung to before I was paralyzed by the mental image of my four-year-old self in the refuse. Ollie and Allie had waded through the chaos to play hide-and-go-seek with me when I was little, and they pretended to be young for my sake. My older brother and sister, I loved. But Bev and the ammonia that rotted my soul and turned my stomach? Not so much.

I sucked down the sour memories and reached for Ollie's mantra that never failed me: *keep your chin up, take it slow*. This was second only to the ever-helpful: *life is messy, and that's okay*. That was enough to keep me rooted in the waste, not abandoning Bev to her devices, as Ollie and Allie had done long ago. If I were a manipulative hoarder, I would need someone to not ditch me. I would want someone who knew my secrets but didn't run. I couldn't control Bev, but I could control myself. I had to live with myself every day, and I knew I couldn't do that if I turned my back on my mama, mentally ill as she was.

Today the cockroaches weren't prone to scatter. Instead, they inched toward me, like they were listening in on our boring talk. There were two neat little rows of them watching me, just as they had been doing last week in my car. I'd tried to write that off as a bad daydream, but here it was, happening all over again. My head whipped around in paranoia to check for a row of ants or eyebrow-looking caterpillars, but there weren't any in sight. The cockroaches barely fidgeted in the normal insect way, but instead stood still, like watchful little soldiers waiting for me to do or say something interesting.

These cockroaches weren't afraid of the bare bulb that shone overhead. For some reason, that little tidbit made a whimper catch in my throat. Usually they scattered like cockroaches are supposed to from any kind of illumination, but these ones, like the bugs last week, seemed sentient, controlled somehow.

Cinderella got birds that braided her hair. I apparently got cockroaches watching my every move. *I rock.*

My body wanted to shiver at the disgust coursing through me, but my brain had suppressed the need for that particular release. It had been too many years. The carpet in Bev's room had been a dusty rose color once upon a time, but now was a squishy brown underneath the piles of things, trash, newspapers and animal droppings.

Bev stabbed the gray clip into her perfectly poised blonde hair as if she hated her skull and wanted to inflict pain upon it. She tilted her head and admired her colorful and precise makeup job in the smudgy mirror. She wore her usual Barbie pink eyeshadow, bright pink lipstick on thin lips, and complimented the look by applying thick, black mascara to convince herself she had long eyelashes, like Allie and I had gotten, but she'd never had. I don't know how she always managed to look so put together, when she could barely see her reflection. "Wow, you're right. That does look pretty. I'll have to find that pink pearl one, though. If you see it, let me know."

"Will do."

Her voice turned sharp, as she tended to do on a dime. "Don't steal it, now."

I chewed on the correction I'd never needed from her. "Of course not, Bev. No one's going to steal your special things. Can we go?" I had someone to see, and every minute spent waiting in the mess felt like twenty minutes wasted.

"Now, now. Hush up, October Grace. Your brother's traveled all the way from New York to see us. He ain't going nowhere." She adjusted her pants that I still couldn't believe were stark white without noticeable stains on them. "In fact, for staying away for three years, let's say we make Ollie wait another fifteen minutes."

The stubbornness was already starting. I knew it would. There was too much baggage to be discreetly shoved under the rug. Not that there was a rug visible, or that another piece of crap could fit in the mobile home, but you get the picture. "Ollie's already on his way there, so we've got to get going." I'd been standing in the one clear space that was exactly large enough for one twenty-two-year-old woman, if she kept her arms at her sides and didn't move much. I feared the massacre a sneeze could do. In fact, I feared breathing at all, but gave in to the hazardous habit with a grudging grimace.

A line of ants skittered across my black sneakers. Someone new to the dysfunction might have made the rookie mistake of shuddering, and thus, would bring more rubble down upon her head. I knew to let the ants pass as I choked down a whine. I had tucked my jeans into my socks, so I knew the damage was only psychological.

Luckily, I'd been bred for enduring psychological damage. It was one of my many superpowers.

Today, much like the cockroaches, the ants stopped their progression, formed two rows, and paused to stare at me, as the ones in the car had done. There wasn't accusation at me being associated with the clutter. They merely looked at me with curiosity, as if studying my mental state.

I was personifying insects, so I guessed my mental state wasn't all that great. I had a good many patients at the prison I worked at who saw things that weren't real, but as I looked down at the ants tilting their miniature heads up at me, I knew I wasn't imagining things. Finally they seemed to confer with each other about something and went on their merry way to the never-ending pile of garbage for their day's feast. One woman's trash is an army of ants' treasure.

I wondered, not for the first time, if my doses of crazy

were from my father's genetics – whoever and wherever he was.

"I can't stand that he's meeting us there and we have to drive ourselves the whole way." Bev spoke the word "drive" like it'd been rude to her. I started to worry that our long-awaited reunion would devolve into the cattiness that usually exploded once Bev decided she had good reason to be offended. It was that stellar Southern pride that she wore like a County State Fair blue ribbon on her chest. Her self-importance always managed to annihilate even the most perfect days. "I don't know why your brother doesn't come here. I mean, this was his home, too."

I knew better than to answer the obvious. Bev didn't see the chaos; she only saw a sea of treasures. Growing up with next to nothing made Beverly Jo Reese that much fonder of the things she could now afford on her meager salary as a receptionist for the smallest real estate office in northern Georgia.

"I don't know," I lied. "But Ollie hasn't come to see us in years, so let's try to get along, okay? Just for one day, Bev."

Okay, that was another lie. Ollie came back at least twice a year to visit me. But Bev didn't need to know about that. It would only hurt her, and I didn't want to do that.

"When am I not nice? Honey pie, I'll have you know that Jeanie came out of the bathroom with the back of her skirt tucked into her hose, and I didn't say a thing." Before I could comment that any friend would've told Jeanie to her face instead of talking about it after the fact, I remembered that manners like those were lost on Bev.

"Did you leave your change of clothes in your car, honey pie?" Bev tore her gaze from her reflection and zeroed in on me. I gulped, understanding a cornered animal's urge to bolt by any means necessary. "Well, go ahead and get changed, October Grace. I'll wait."

I looked down past my unzipped lavender hoodie to my "I heart Pee-Wee Herman" blue fitted t-shirt. I'd worn the jeans without holes in the knees in anticipation of not being at the prison, stitching up inmates for a whole weekend. There was really no point in having pretty nails or fancy hairstyles, pulling the hours I normally did. Since I had very little life, I worked ten-hour shifts six days a week. Or maybe that was why I had very little life. I couldn't decide which was the chicken and which was the egg at this point. The job kept me occupied, and more than paid the few bills I acquired. However, I had precious little need for nice clothing, so I wore what I liked in the few moments not clad in blue hospital scrubs. "I'm already dressed, Bev. This is what I'm wearing."

Bev wrinkled her nose in distaste. Her home did not offend her, but her daughter's lack of social propriety always did. "You and Oliver are meeting my special guy today. Could you put in a little bit of effort? A ponytail? Really? When's the last time you got your hair done? I'm just saying."

Bev was always "just saying."

"And maybe try to do something about your face. No makeup? Really? Maybe you could get away with that when you were eleven, but you're in your twenties now. Your skin tone's uneven. Makes me absolutely cringe when I look at you too close."

My cheeks heated, but I kept my mouth shut and my eyes downward. I tried to soothe the sting her words left me with by reminding myself that Bev had a problem, and there was nothing to be done about that, other than to be kind and try not to piss her off too badly.

The swarming flies congregated nearby for their afternoon meal of putrefied food and animal crap. When I shifted too near their treasure, a handful of flies landed on my forearm, watching me like a dog watches its master. The little guys were also somehow too focused on my every movement, which freaked me out a little bit. I didn't want to be queen of the flies, but I didn't have the heart to shake them off. They weren't being annoying. They couldn't help how they looked. You know, totally gross. I would need a ton of hand sanitizer after this.

Bev was still ramping up on all the things she hated about me, which I guess I asked for by not looking nice. "If you don't wear any rings or jewelry at all, you're never going to catch a man. They're going to think you're simple. No man's going to spend money on a simple girl. Is that what you want? Are you simple, October Grace? And what did I tell you about wearing jeans?"

"That my butt won't attract a husband if I insist on

covering it up." I sighed, staring up at the ceiling. "You're right. I'm sorry, Bev. But you know, your new guy's going to want to see you. The rest of us are just there to shake his hand and sit in the background. You're the one he's been emailing and dating for six months. Hopefully he doesn't care about my butt."

Her tone was a knife cutting on the edges of my psyche. "Well, if you don't throw your boobs in his face like you did Gideon, then that'll be true."

I cringed, but didn't bother to correct her. Instead I crossed my arms over my sizeable breasts and hoped Pee-Wee Herman could de-amplify anything that might stand out. Pee-Wee Herman was good like that.

"And people say you can't find a good guy online. Do you know how many profiles I had to wade through? I don't want to speak ill about people I've never met, but there's some real trash out there."

I was good at not saying what I was thinking, which was usually the perfect thing to say around Bev. "He sounds nice."

"You'll love Ezra. He's wonderful. Handsome, loaded and holds the door open like a gentleman. He'll probably be too polite to tell you that you look like a slob in that outfit. He won't even tell you not to stand like a man or to stop slouching." Her tone cracked me like the sting of a belt. "October Grace, if I've told you once, I've told you a thousand times; stand up straight!"

"Yes, ma'am." I obeyed immediately, but the onset of

her fight voice made the backs of my arms start to itch. "Ezra sounds great. You should be with someone who makes you happy."

She deflated at my compliance. "Ezra's wonderful. He bought me this." She displayed the gold necklace with a floating ruby that hung just above her obvious cleavage. It was more tasteful than her usual jewelry, which often sent oglers straight to her bounty like a giant neon sign that flashed "Eat at Joe's".

I'm not sure why, but every time she said his name, all I could picture was a stooped elderly man with his hooked nose in a dusty book. Bev was nearing fifty, but Ezra sounded like an old guy name. I truly hoped he was close to her age. The last one she'd been taken with had been in his late twenties, and had graduated high school the year before Ollie. Ollie was eight years older than me, but even at my younger age, I knew that was weird. Bug carcasses I could suppress my shiver through, but Gideon? Dude still gave me the creeps. Gideon worked at a fast food joint just outside of town, that now I made sure to avoid. He'd asked me to call him Big Daddy once.

I hadn't meant to punch him, but that was the last of the Big Daddy talk. It was much harder for him to stare at my boobs with one eye swollen shut. Yet, I learned, still not impossible.

Bev turned from her precarious perch in her garbage utopia to examine me with a discontented sigh. It was laden with all the things her pageant failure of a daughter could've been, but wasn't. You wouldn't think those pageant judges would frown on seven curse words in the middle of your stars and stripes song, but apparently that was the quickest ticket off the pageanting circuit. Mission accomplished. I'd lost the pageant, but I'd won my freedom from being a six-year-old girl teetering precariously in high heels and smeared in what felt like clown makeup.

"Well, I guess your outfit will have to do. I hope Oliver didn't wear jeans. Ugh, you kids. I have to do everything for you. I don't want Ezra to think we're trash."

I climbed over the mountain of clothes, ducked under the overhang of drying newspapers, squeezed through the two walls of debris in various shades of decay and rot to the door – otherwise known as the escape route. My own personal ticket to paradise.

3

BEAUTY TIPS FROM BEV

The fresh air hit me like a slice through my lungs. I could smell earth, tires and trees through the clean breeze that chased away all the horrors I'd grown almost immune to.

From the neighbor's yard, my favorite pit bull bounded up to me, tail wagging and janky teeth smeared with drool and blood from a dead bird he dropped at my feet. Most people were afraid of Sandy because he attacked a few people. Okay, more than a few. But he was a sweetheart, loveable and cuddly if you could get past the drool and the teeth. And the scars from fighting other animals. And the teeth. Sandy sat in front of me and wagged his tail, yipping like a puppy, though some of my earliest memories were of playing with him when I was a girl, pretending to be a dog so I could scamper alongside him.

I hoped the wolf I'd accidentally almost hit was okay.

"Hi, baby! You doing okay out here?" Sandy's barks seemed laced with a warning, but I couldn't decipher anything more specific than that. "Man, I missed you." Sandy always appreciated the hearty scratch behind his ears.

"October Grace, get up and stop playing with that mutt! Git! Git!" She swung at Sandy with her purse. Luckily she had terrible aim. Sandy had never attacked my family, which I appreciated, even though he had every right to defend himself against Bev's purse.

"Bev, it's fine. He just wanted to say hello." I buried my face in Sandy's neck, and for a second, I heard him sigh contentedly, as if he needed the contact as much as I did. Some weeks, Sandy was my only hug. Some months, even. "I missed you, boy."

I kissed Sandy on the top of the head, giving his neck a hug that didn't make me once think of the germs I knew were crawling all over him. I loved Sandy. Love was funny like that – erased a myriad of otherwise insurmountable obstacles. One more kiss, and I led him back to his yard, retying the useless rope that never held.

Bev sniffed at Terence the Taurus as she slid into the passenger's seat. "I don't know why you had to spend so much money on a new car. Such a waste. I drive past half a dozen used cars being sold on the side of the road for probably a fraction of what this set you back. Do you know how many things you could've bought with the difference? You could've bought nice pants, for one. Perhaps a pair of shoes that aren't tennis shoes? Maybe some makeup to cover over all that?" She motioned to my face that was always a bother to her. I didn't mean to shrink, but my neck disappeared into my shoulders like a turtle. I don't know why I let that dig cut me, but Bev didn't miss a beat. "What you really need is a total makeover. Honestly, it's like you want to parade around your worst features. I'm just saying, is all." Then she turned to me with a syrupy expression after buckling her seatbelt, and I knew she was going to ask me for something. "Honey pie, I'm a little short on the lot fee this month. Any chance you have a little extra?"

I shrugged apologetically, balling up my toes in my shoes to hide my discomfort. Loaning Bev money was against the rules. Ollie, Allie and I had concrete laws we'd agreed to, and no matter how much I didn't mind helping Bev out, I couldn't disobey Ollie like that. "Sorry, Bev. I wish I could, but I'm tapped out."

"What'd you spend all your money on? I hope it was something good, if you can't spare a couple hundred bucks to help out your mama."

"A harmonica," I lied, reaching for anything at all. Obviously, the wrong thing. I wasn't great at lying on the spot to Bev.

"You spent hundreds of dollars on a harmonica?"

I swallowed. "It was a really nice one. And it wasn't hundreds. I just don't have any extra this month. I really am sorry." The being sorry part was true. I wished I could manage Bev's finances and help her when she was short, but Ollie and Allie had been firm. No money to Bev. I cleared my throat. "Um, so your new guy sounds great. You haven't been this excited about anyone in a while."

She clasped her hands together, temporarily forgiving me for blowing my life's savings on my fictional harmonica. "Oh, I can't wait for you all to meet Ezra!"

In her girliness, I forgave her for the slight on my wardrobe I had bought because I loved. I forgave her for talking down about Terence the Taurus, who'd been faithful to my butt when Bev couldn't be because she is who she is. She was happy, and despite all the crap she'd put us through, I wanted a slice of girly fun for her. One of us should be young. She'd always been better at being young, anyway.

As I started down the dusty street, Bev pulled down the visor to make sure the slight breeze didn't dare rise up against her perfect hairdo. "You know what you need? A boyfriend. How's that little Mexican boy you see on and off? Juan? Pedro? Jose?"

"Beto," I reminded her. "He's Puerto Rican, and we're off again."

"Oh, well that's what happens when you wear jeans that don't give the poor boy something to look at. I'm not sure how you managed to keep him for so long in the first place."

"I dunno. I'll have to take notes from you, since you seem so over the moon with Ezra." It was always safest to switch the conversation around so Bev was the star. I liked to watch her shine anyways. She had a bright smile that, when it wasn't vindictive or phony, was actually very pretty. By the number of sincere grins of anticipation she'd worn this morning alone, I could tell she was really into this guy.

Bev was fussing in the mirror with her hair, and wondering aloud when I would consider getting highlights to get those "disgusting brown notes" out of my hair so it could lean more toward my auburn tones. "But then you might look too red-headed, and we can't have that, either. Blonde. Blonde's safest. What man can't keep his hands off a blonde?" She laughed, and I tried to get my smile in place for her. She liked me best when I laughed at her jokes.

Man, I prayed they were jokes.

Bev's pinched nose wrinkled as she eyed a piece of hair that inched out of place. She snuck up on the errant hair like a ninja and stabbed it with a spare pin from her pocket. "October Grace, could you be a love and see if you have any more pins in your purse? I need another."

"Oh, here you go." I pulled one from my hair and handed it to her. Each half mile of distance from the trailer calmed my unsteady heart rate by a necessary degree.

Bev pointed out each used car by the side of the road on the hour-long drive east, mentioning how much better a buy they would have been than my new car.

I scratched the back of my hand as I drove, taking out my stress on my skin, as usual. I'd discarded my gloves on my way out of the hoard, so they weren't there to save me from germs, or from myself. The scrapes had healed since I'd checked in on Bev last week, but they opened afresh after only an hour spent helping her get ready. Pinpricks of blood started to show on the back of my hand, and somehow the red felt good. Right, in a way. It was the one thing that felt like breath in the familial land of suffocation I had yet to figure out how to extract myself from. Ollie and Allie were smart. They got out. Every time I told myself something Bev did or said was the last straw, my conscience tore at me and brought me back. Bev had no one. She needed someone to take care of her. Ollie and Allie didn't see it that way. They had this notion that the parents should take care of the kids. Maybe in a perfect world, sure.

"Why do you need all those buttons on the dash? I feel like I'm riding in a rocket ship. I bet you don't know what half of those do. I'm just saying. I could've gotten you a better deal. Then you would've had money to help me out with my lot fee. Some kids care about their parents, is all."

"I'm sorry, Bev."

I had a lot on my mind, so after a few more criticisms, I went to that happy place where Bev's voice turned to white noise. I knew it was best to ignore her instead of hope or expect some sort of change.

My teeth were on edge, but it wasn't from Bev's home, her mouth, or her erratic pffts when she saw something she didn't like out the window. I was most anxious to see Ollie.

Oliver Reese hadn't been home in months – though if Bev asked, it would be years since he'd ventured back to Georgia. The three of us used to live together – my brother, sister and me. Then it got to be too much for Ollie and Allie. My big brother left Bev and her house of hoarding for the fresh air in New York. Really the fresh air could've been blowing any which way, so long as it was a plane ride away from Bev. Ollie had a harder time letting go of the little things than I did. Now he was an investment broker, and a good one at that. He was always throwing around words like IRA, Roth, and compound interest. I pretty much just wrote him a check and let him invest it however he felt like.

"Now when we get inside, it would be helpful if you didn't call me Bev. I know that's how we work, but I think it would put him off if my own daughter didn't call me 'Mama'."

Considering coloring my hair was one thing, but she'd never liked being reminded that she was a mother, or that I was her daughter. "Um, I guess that would be alright. Just for today?"

"Just around him. I don't want to be a Mama unless it's around him. He likes that kind of thing."

Yes, Ezra likes that whole being a parent thing. What an oddity. I tell you what, the second he asks me to call him Big Daddy, I'm heading home.

"Okay, *Mama*," I forced out. "You look real nice." It was true; she always put herself together like a beauty queen. I took a deep breath and donned a pleasant smile that I tried to feel. I knew I shouldn't let Bev get to me. She didn't know any better, and I did.

My GPS gave me another robotic command, which I obeyed. I don't know why the female robot voice always struck me as funny, but I giggled under my breath at the serious way she mispronounced the name of the highway. My smile was too quick, my chuckle too audible. I swallowed the sigh I wanted to exhale when Bev started harping about too much technology making a person sterile. "Not that you've got to worry about that. I mean, you'll probably be old and gray by the time you find someone who'll settle down with you. It's all about hiding your flaws. You just flaunt yours," Bev scolded me with a tsk at my outfit. "I mean, just look at your clothes. Do you want people to think you're simple, colorblind and poor? Honestly, it's like you want to die alone."

I swallowed down the thing I'd come to terms with long ago, but never loved when it was voiced. "That's good advice. I'll try harder next time. Maybe I'll wear something pink." I played hardball with her favorite color, hoping it would alleviate the tension only I could feel as I scraped at the skin on the backs of my hands.

4

EZRA'S HUGS AND KEEBLER ELVES

I wasn't sure what I expected of Ezra. I guess my mind went to an old, lonely, short, squat unshaven troll who peruses online dating profiles using a picture of his years-old high school face photo-shopped with Channing Tatum's body instead of his own.

Ezra Manaul was nothing like I anticipated, which I guess was a good thing. In fact, from the time he greeted my mother with a hearty hug and a respectful kiss to the cheek, he did nothing but surprise me.

My mouth dropped open when we walked over the threshold and into the residence. To call it a residence is like referring to Scarlet O'Hara's house as a cute colonial. Ezra had a lavish house to rival Tara set on at least thirty acres of rolling greens.

Ollie and I exchanged looks that spanned every emotion from confusion to hope to utter dread that Bev would be found out to be the griping hoarder she was. She was good at putting on the normal for a crowd; I only hoped I could do the same. I stood up straighter and brushed my face with a pleasant smile, trying not to run from this place where I clearly didn't belong.

Ezra had the air of Father Christmas to him, wrapped in the body of a sandy-haired, well-built, late-forties magazine model for golf clubs and teeth whitener or something. He kissed Bev's cheek respectfully, a glow of adoration in his eye when he greeted his girlfriend. It was sweet, which was a new thing for me to see on Bev.

Ezra refused Ollie's hand on principle, instead engulfing him in a hug that made my brother's eyes bug out. "Oliver! I've heard so much about you." His British accent threw me, even though Bev had mentioned it a few times. "Beverly talks about how proud she is of you constantly. I feel as if I know you already."

This was news to Ollie, since Bev had never once told him she was proud of his choices, but used his preferences to berate him at every turn. The hug lasted two seconds, and I could see Ollie turning purple with confusion and a distinct get-this-person-off-me plea. "Really? Wow. Well, it's nice to meet you, Mr. Manaul. Or is it Manuel? It wasn't clear over the phone."

"It's whatever you feel like calling me, including 'your servant', which is what I am for the three of you tonight." Ezra was overjoyed to see us. His blond hair was well-groomed, short on top and brushed to the side. He was dressed in country club best. His nails were manicured, and his face was lined in that handsome way that only the wealthy manage to age. Then, just when I thought he had to be too perfect, he shot Ollie an "I'm really not a pretentious tool" conspiratorial look and said, "My friends call me Ezra, if you're looking for a straight answer. And I do hope we become friends."

The house had marble half-pillars built into the walls of the foyer we stood in. For some reason even this small detail made me nervous, reminding me how completely out of my element I was. The polished floors shown like Cinderella had just waxed them herself. The vaulted ceilings seemed to reach up to Heaven to thank Ezra for being such a cool guy.

I'd been content to lurk in the background while my mind continued to be blown in the fireworks that kept erupting. I mean, the man had an oil painting of a horse in his foyer, for crying out loud. Well, a centaur, I guess. Or a reverse centaur. The creature had a black horse head with a man's body, and he was depicted fighting in a battle against evil Goblins, who had their claws raised before their inevitable defeat at the reverse centaur's mighty sword.

So not only was Ezra loaded, well-mannered and kind, he liked fantasy fiction, and didn't care who knew it. I couldn't help but take a shine to the guy.

For the first time, I agreed with Bev. I was way underdressed and totally out of place. Even Ollie wore gray dress slacks and a lavender button-down shirt to try and look presentable. His auburn hair was short, but properly styled to make him look like he could fit in anywhere. I prayed my simple ponytail said the same thing about me. I shoved my hands in my pockets and hunched my shoulders inward. That was how I went invisible in my mind. It totally worked, too. People's eyes tended to pass right over me when I looked at the ground and kept to myself.

Ezra had other plans. "October Grace!" he crooned, as if my name was a song. The way he beamed when he said it, I wouldn't much mind at all if it was. I'd never heard a Brit say my name before, but when Ezra did, I appreciated it anew. "You're even lovelier than your pictures! Absolutely beautiful. You take after your mother in only the best of ways."

He was too perfect, which made me want to distrust him off the bat, but when he drew me in for a bone-crushing hug, I let go of one card in the deck I'd stacked against him, stiff though I was in his embrace. I didn't so much like the germs, but I gritted my teeth through the slow death most people called "affection", so as to appear normal. "I... Thanks, Ezra."

"Ezra!" he barked out a genuine laugh that filled the vaulted ceilings with levity as he released me. "I love it. I can tell we'll be good friends already." He motioned to the reverse centaur oil painting. "I see you're admiring my art collection. Do you know much about Tikbalangs?"

"Huh? No. I'm more of a vampire-werewolf-zombie-whatever's-on-my-recommended-list kind of fantasy fan. Is a Tikbalang the reverse centaur guy?"

Ezra seemed over the moon delighted that I was taking an interest in his fascinations. "Indeed, it is. This is the Battle of the Dark Hills in a magical land called Terraway. The Tikbalangs vanquished the last of the Elves and utterly devastated the Goblins, though the Goblin race managed to survive." He pointed to the smaller, wrinkled creature with his claws raised. "That there's a Goblin."

I nodded, impressed by how into his paintings he was. "What kind of Elves? Are we talking Orlando Bloom, Christmas or Keebler?"

Ezra quirked his eyebrow at me, and then let out a laugh that told me I'd said something hilarious that caught him by surprise. "Beverly, you didn't tell me what a quick wit your daughter is. Come in! Come in! You must be exhausted from the drive. Keebler Elves." He shook his head and chuckled again.

I wanted to blanch at the shmoozy words, but he looked so kind when he said them. I didn't notice any hint of agenda poking through his broad smile. It had the air of a weather man's charm mixed with the sincerity of a priest.

Ezra proffered his elbow to Bev, and then offered his other to me. I'd not been led anywhere by a gentleman since I was a kid, and even then, I'm pretty sure Ollie had been doing it as a joke. I was anything but a proper lady. I was my guy friends' dude friend, and my girlfriends' nonthreatening pal who never stole the spotlight from them.

I took Ezra's arm, shrugging at Ollie's wide eyes. Ezra wasn't a figment of Bev's imagination, and he was most certainly a hefty step up from our world.

"Let me get you something to drink. Sweet tea? Lemonade? Arnold Palmer? Something stronger?" He winked at Bev, who actually blushed. I'd never seen Bev properly happy, but this was it. I could tell in the way he lit up when she touched his arm that he was smitten with her just as much as she was taken with him. I began to understand that the charm that had wooed Bev didn't just emanate from Ezra's wallet. I treasured a small smile when I realized that perhaps Bev was growing – wanting what was good for her, instead of seeking out train wrecks.

If it wasn't so weird, I'd have been more verbal with my joy. As it was, Ollie and I were dumbstruck mutes Ezra led around the corner to the grandest living room I'd ever been in, complete with a fireplace. He handed us drinks that the maid – an actual maid – brought in for us. I felt sorely out of place, but Ezra didn't seem to mind. In fact, Ezra treated Ollie and me like we were celebrities. Mute celebrities, but celebrities nonetheless.

"The big apple, eh? You must be very good at your job if you're working in an office there. Beverly tells me that you're a junior broker?"

"Yes, sir," Ollie croaked out.

"A junior broker after only three years at the company?

Good for you. I admire a man who knows how to seize the best out of life and still manages to keep his head in the end. As your head's firmly attached, I can see you're doing a brilliant job."

I watched Ollie's wide eyes and confusion give way to a perplexed nod and a humble "thank you, sir." It broke my heart how unused to praise Ollie was. I tried to stuff kindness and adoration in the crevices of his personality whenever he wasn't looking, but for the most part he managed to fend off compliments with a flip of a hand and suspicion that kindness usually came with motive. Ollie shifted on the oversized white leather couch next to me, radiating equal amounts of discomfort and surprised pleasure at the verbose accolades.

After another ten entire minutes of singing Ollie's praises, Ezra turned his attention to me. I wanted to fake that I had to run to the bathroom just to escape the sincerity in Ezra's eyes and the thoughtfulness in his words, but thought panic might not bode well this early in the getting-to-know-you stage of things.

It was a thing of luck that the maid came back into the living room, her wrinkled hands and face putting her age at right around seventy or so. She wore a simple black dress with the sleeves rolled up, and a white apron that didn't dare have a stain on it. "Dinner's served, Ezra."

"Thank you, Lynna. Lynna, this is Oliver James and October Grace, Bev's charming children." Though she looked like a servant, I noted that Ezra introduced her as if we were meeting a new friend, which endeared me to him even more.

Lynna inclined her head to us, but her gaze fell on me, taking in more detail than I felt comfortable doling out to strangers. I straightened my shirt and lowered my chin as I stood, introverting afresh.

5

PAINTER, PLAYBOY AND VAMPIRE

e followed Lynna to the dining room, where two men were sitting at the table with a slight waif of a woman. One of the guys had a square-shaped head and looked like he'd never smiled a day in his life.

Bev beamed at the three. "Well, I didn't realize Ezra had company hiding in here. I'm Bev."

The surly square-headed dude dipped his chin to Bev. "I'm Danny." He introduced himself to us with no further explanation or interest in learning our names. Danny's look of calculating disdain told us he didn't want to be here, and knew our family didn't belong with the Manauls. Couldn't blame the guy for hitting it dead on the nose.

The second guy was a toothpaste model or something that didn't belong in real life. He set down the paperback he'd been leafing through and stood from where he'd been sitting across from Danny at the long table. He had a broad chest, messy black hair, angular features, high cheekbones, a chiseled jaw, and too many handsome things about his face for the rest of the world to have a fighting chance. As he looked over at us, I noted he had one cool blue eye and one gold eye that shone against his tousled black hair.

I couldn't stop staring. He was the caliber of sexy who could play a vampire on one of those teen television dramas. He wore a crooked smile that pulled up at the side when he saw us. It was the dimple in his left cheek that got me, making him look boyish, despite the fact that he was clearly several years older than me.

Putting his book down, he extended his hand to Bev politely. "Pleasure to meet you, ma'am. I'm Von, Danny's older brother. Ezra's told us so much about you."

Of course they were both British. That sealed it. Von was the best looking guy I'd ever seen in real life. Add that to the fact that he'd been reading a worn paperback at the table, and I knew he'd be dangerous to any girl with a pulse. I kinda wanted to run very far away so I didn't do something stupid. I settled for keeping my distance and lowering my chin to study my hands.

Bruce Campbell was my favorite actor in the best movie of all time, and I knew if he could see me now, he would cringe at my bashfulness. Bruce Campbell would never shrink away from whatever cutie caught his eye.

Give old Bruce two minutes, and she'd be laughing at one of his jokes, completely had by the twinkle in his eye.

No, I was no Bruce Campbell.

Bev produced a coy smile and shook her hot pink painted fingernail at the late twentysomething hottie. "Now, don't you go starting with that 'ma'am' stuff. I'm not that much older than you."

Von inclined his head to her politely. "Indeed, you don't look a day over thirty."

Ollie and I exchanged a "barf" expression and exhaled a familiar sigh of practiced patience. Bev was always on. It was the difference between introverts and extroverts. And the difference between Bev and us.

Von wore jeans and a red t-shirt stretched across his lean but toned muscles that read "Nothing Tops the Hops". "Pleasure to meet you all."

Danny grumbled as he placed his napkin on his lap. "Go back to your stupid book, Von. That'll get the job done."

Though Von's smile was light and his words entertaining, I could see a flicker of... something behind the song and dance. There was a tired edge to his grin, a shade of distance in his eyes that was palpable. I wondered if that was what I looked like when Bev cut me down and I pretended I didn't hear it.

Danny felt no such need to perform, and in fact looked allergic to smiling. I could only guess he was a bodybuilder around Ollie's age. His short, cropped black hair made him look like military on leave. He had a thick neck and huge biceps. He clearly spent every available moment in the gym, and looked like he had never once cracked a joke in his life – only skulls. I decided to give Danny a wide berth.

The girl next to Danny was a frail little thing, maybe only a couple years older than me, but the haunted look in her eyes made her appear like a little old lady, despite her youth. She had skin so pale, it appeared translucent, revealing blue veins under the paper-like skin. Her black hair was straight as a board and cut at her shoulders. I guessed from my years of sizing patients up with a look that saw past the lies people told all medical professionals, judging by her pallor and sunken-in dark eyes, she was a very sick woman.

She wore an expensive pink dress that reminded me of the good old pageant days, only this was the sleeker young adult version I'd flunked out of. I noticed she was wearing nylons and heels, and sincerely felt for the girl whose dainty hands were clasped in front of her with a hopeful look on her face. She looked just as nervous as I'm sure I did. My own hands were gripping each other and tearing at the flesh on my knuckles. She shot me a small smile, which I returned before looking down at my hands again.

Ezra motioned to the girl with a sweeping arm. "This is Mariang. My daughter's the most beautiful twenty-four-year-old in all of Georgia, yeah? And Danny's her boyfriend. He's a brilliant groundskeeper. One of the best." I could see the glint of nerves in Ezra's eyes and posture. His voice went a little higher as he introduced his daughter and her boyfriend, and I realized that we weren't the only ones who were anxious to make a good impression. That made me relax a little. We were perhaps still a stone's throw away from playing board games together, but with the right aim, a stone's throw isn't all that far.

"Shall we?" Ezra said to the room, pulling out the seat at the foot of the table for Bev like a gentleman. It was a nice thing to watch. An odd thing, but a nice one. Her ex-guy Gideon had never even taken her on a real date (he was more the straight to the bedroom while leering at Allie and me kind of jackhole), but with Ezra, it seemed he knew the steps that needed to be taken to secure a prize.

Despite everything, I wanted Bev to be with a man who saw her as a prize. Maybe then she'd start treating others with that same kind of respect.

Dinner was roasted goose with a cranberry reduction served alongside roasted garlic-laden vegetables. I'd been planning on slapping together a sandwich for my dinner, so this was definitely a step up.

Ollie was better at being social, so he fielded most of the questions, letting me enjoy my dinner. Ollie was on my right, and Von at my left, with Mariang and Danny seated across from us. Danny kept shooting me calculating scowls that erased my appetite, though everything looked and smelled amazing.

I'd watched Lynna pour red wine into my glass without touching the stemware, so I knew that didn't have finger germs on it. Von was drinking what looked like a frill-less Bloody Mary. When he caught me studying the glass, he put it on his left next to his book, further from my view and cleared his throat.

Bev narrowed her eyes at me, warning me not to blow it all for her. "Honey pie, Ezra was talking to you."

I turned to look at the kindest aqua eyes I'd ever seen. Ezra made me want to confess all my secrets, which on instinct told me to keep my mouth stapled shut. "I'm sorry, sir. What were you saying?"

"I was wondering if you wanted different silverware."

My eyes widened as I plopped down the fork I'd been polishing without realizing it. I'd only cleaned it twice, which I knew wasn't enough, but I didn't want to tip my crazy hand too soon. "No, sir. I think I'm just nervous, is all. I'm sorry."

Ezra relaxed, now that he knew I wasn't upset. It was the first time I actually felt bad for my OCD inflicting itself upon someone else. Usually I only made myself miserable. "Oh. Well, we're no one to be afraid of, I assure you."

Von pointed his fork across the table. "Now that's just not true. Danny's plenty terrifying. Breaks rocks with his teeth just for a laugh, he does. At least he balances it out with the Mr. Rogers sweater. Fetching, yeah? I was thinking of getting one for myself."

I shot Von half a smile, doing my best to relax and just be myself. "You might need to bedazzle yours. You've kind of got a flat personality. The rhinestones will help you stand out more. You're just too shy."

"So she speaks." Von squinted his golden eye at me, sizing me up.

"I was planning on answering everything in song for you, but I wouldn't want to make Danny dance at the dinner table. He looks like a *Macarena* type of guy."

Von smirked at me. "I like you."

I didn't miss a beat with, "I don't blame you," which made Von throw his head back with a throaty laugh.

I'd made the hot guy laugh. I win all the points ever. I could practically feel Bruce Campbell smiling, chucking me on the shoulder with a proud, "There's my girl. You finally stopped hiding."

Danny clenched his fist around his fork, which flexed his swollen forearm muscle, earning a whistle from Von and a hoot from Bev. "How's that for unintimidating? Does it look like I dance for a laugh?"

Von turned his attention back to me. "What do you think? Am I as intimidating as Danny? I mean, if you were walking down the street and saw the two of us, which one would you be more afraid of?"

I bit my lip at being put on the spot. "Oh, um probably you, but only because I'm not afraid of anyone who wears a cardigan on principle." I pointed to Danny's brown sweater that had a button missing near the top. Now he had an odd number of buttons. I didn't much care for odd numbers.

"Well spotted, new girl. Danny's an utter love bug. Only you were wrong on the *Macarena*. Danny's strictly into the ballet. You should see his pirouettes."

"Are they as graceful as yours?"

Von's dimple winked at me. "Almost."

I switched to Ezra to avoid incurring Danny's wrath, which didn't seem all that hard to do. "You have a gorgeous home, Ezra."

That's right. I'm being social. Better late than never, I guess.

"Thank you, October Grace."

Bev spoke up from the queen's place at the end of the table. "Honey pie, would you be a love and pass me the rolls when you're through with them?"

I looked around for the rolls, but Bev wasn't talking to me. She held her hand out expectantly to Mariang, and my jaw dropped.

Bev only ever called *me* honey pie. Granted, I would rather any other nickname, but it belonged to me. Aside from life, it was the only thing she'd ever given me. The wind felt knocked out of my lungs. I struggled to be cool and not let anyone know I had a gaping chest wound that was bleeding all over the table. It was my fault, really. I'd given Bev a small amount of power. I'd let the name mean something precious to me, and now it was common.

Ollie could always feel the daggers in my chest. I cleared my throat when he tapped his foot against mine under the table, straightening so I didn't let anyone else sniff out my heartache. "Ezra, that's a lovely painting." I pointed to the grand oil masterpiece of a mud-soaked landscape with a few rural huts off to the right. The framed canvas stretched across the entire wall behind Mariang and Danny. On the top corner of the frame, I noticed a small movement drawing my eye. There was a yellow caterpillar perched there, just staring at me.

Like, staring at me. *What is it with the bizarro bugs lately?*

"It was painted by our very own Von Vandershot." Ezra tipped his head to Von, who waved at the crowd like a prom princess.

Oh, come on. Stop being so sexy. Painter, reader and looking like that?

"Do you study art?" Von inquired conversationally.

I shook my head as the dessert was brought out. "No. I'm more of an 'if it's there and it looks nice, I'm cool with it,' kind of girl."

Danny snorted in that condescending way art students did if you mentioned you liked Norman Rockwell. "Figures."

I let the jab roll off my shoulders. No way was I ruining

this pot of happiness for Bev over something stupid like not being super into Picasso's left toenail.

"Oh, and you're all about culture and art?" Von challenged his brother, leaning forward with his elbow on the table. "Sod off and leave the girl alone. She's just being polite."

It was kind of precious to watch Ezra squirm as he shot Danny and Von looks of warning. "Language, gentlemen."

Von straightened. "Very well. *Lay* off, then, Danny."

"'Lay off'? How about I lay you out?"

Mariang's dainty hand rested on Danny's arm. "Danny, please. Just one dinner where you two are civil. That's all Dad asked." Her voice was so bell-like and gentle. With her British lilt, she sounded exactly like Julie Andrews, complete with a welcoming smile. She was delicate in that way that made you want to speak softer for no apparent reason.

Von was unperturbed. "I already have plans to get laid out tonight, thank you, though by someone even more fetching than you, Danny old boy, if you can believe it." He rolled back his shoulders and feigned ease, as though Danny being blatantly aggressive wasn't vexing at all. "Red-head from the pub I went to last night," he explained to me, though I'm not sure why. Von held up his hand for a high-five for me to congratulate him on his conquest.

Let me tell you a little something about disease control. You high-five the wrong person and you never know what kind of bird flu/swine flu/meningitis/lizard tail disease you'll contract. However, it was a necessary gesture to sustain normal behavior in popular society, so I indulged Von in a high-five, my palms crawling with discomfort when they rested back in my lap.

In my experience, this high-five downgraded me from woman of possible interest to little sister or dude friend. It had taken less than an hour this time around. I was getting quicker at being friend-zoned. *Score.*

I had recently split with my on-again off-again casual guy Beto, and during our off periods, I migrated to kid sister with him, too. I'm not sure what I was doing to make that happen, but I think it had something to do with high-fiving guys for screwing random women.

Ollie caught my eye and smiled reassuringly, taking a deep breath to remind me to relax. The germs would not get me. They would not multiply and infest my largest organ.

Yes they would, but I was practiced enough with it all to produce a convincing smile and not run off to the bathroom to scrub my hands. *Yet.*

Four seconds.

Eight seconds.

Ezra cleared his throat and cast another warning look at Danny and Von. "Gentleman," he emphasized, "feign an upbringing I can present to a fine lady." He motioned to Bev, who smiled demurely at him, her blonde hair still perfectly in place.

I counted four more seconds, and the germs climbed onto my wrist.

At twenty seconds, they were on the back of my hand, making it itch something terrible.

Ollie reached for my hand under the table to keep me in place, but he waited two seconds too long. I burst out with, "Do you have a restroom nearby?"

Ollie's shoulders deflated, and I knew he was disappointed I wasn't further along in my progress than I'd been on his last visit. I felt terrible for letting him down, but there wasn't much for it now. My hands were literally crawling with spider-like stranger germs.

"Of course, dear." Ezra tilted his chin toward Von. "Will you show her?"

"Not a problem." Von stood and led me down the hall that connected the kitchen and the foyer, opening the door to the bathroom I really could've found on my own. "Don't get lost now."

"I'll do my best." I shut myself inside and turned on the tap, waiting the obligatory few seconds for the hot water to live up to its name. I scrubbed the sexy guy germs off my hands, soaping in between my knuckles just in case anything had festered there. I washed and rinsed three times for good measure, and dried my hands on the towel.

I was about to turn the knob when I heard a low murmur of voices just outside and a few steps down the hall.

"I don't think it's her," Danny grumbled.

"How would you even know that? Mariang said she was sure. She had the vision. Do you trust your girlfriend or not?"

I paused, confused at the strange conversation I guessed I wasn't supposed to be overhearing.

"Of course I trust Mariang. I just mean that maybe she was mistaken." There was a pause, and then Danny said, "We need to have Mason test her bones."

Von's tone turned livid with disgust. "Are you having a laugh? Please tell me you're absolutely barking mad. Mason doesn't like coming Topside, for one. And if he tests her bones and she's not Matruculan, then he breaks them! You want to send that poor girl home with a broken arm? You want to ruin this for Ezra? Ezra truly loves Bev. You have Mason break her daughter's arm in Ezra's house, and no way will they bounce back from that."

My heart rate picked up when I learned they were talking about me. I leaned my ear to the door to get a better listen.

"I'd watch Mason break a thousand women's arms if it'd give us just one more Omen. This is the problem with you; you won't do what it takes."

"Oh, Danny," Von muttered, sounding disappointed. "This is your whole problem; you'll throw anyone under the bus for the job. Listen to yourself. You'll not summon Mason here."

"It's already done. I've had him watching her on and off for a week now."

My palms started to sweat and itch simultaneously.

Von's tone grew distraught. "Are you completely mental? Where's your sense of humanity?"

Danny scoffed. "I don't need a vampire to lecture me on the shiny thing that is humanity. No one cares what you think; you stopped being a person the second you started craving blood more than beer."

6

OCTOBER GRACE, VAMPIRE HUNTER

I sat at the table with clammy hands that had forgotten how to use a fork without dropping it after every fifth bite. I didn't know how much of the conversation I'd overheard was real – how it could be real – but I sure as Sunday understood that if a dude named Mason showed up, I was making a quick exit. I'd never broken a bone before, but I'd reset plenty. *No, thanks.*

Ezra turned back to me, but after that I was a turtle in a shell. "Your mother tells me you're a nursing assistant. That sounds like a fascinating job."

"Yup." I'm sure that's exactly what Bev told him, since she didn't know much about my life. I sat up straighter and tried to appear normal, like I wasn't freaking out. Like I wasn't sitting across from a guy who'd just hired someone to rough me up, and a potential... I couldn't say it. I know vampires aren't real, but by the way Von and Danny were talking, it sure didn't seem like a myth.

My succinct answer annoyed Danny, as evidenced by his rolled eyes. Not sure what crawled up his butt, but I knew it wasn't the yellow caterpillar, which was still observing me with a curious tilt to his head.

I decided to name the caterpillar Wilbur, since I'd never been intimidated by a Wilbur before. I was still pretty sure my OCD medication didn't have any hallucinatory side effects, so I tried to keep my cool and write it off as a big, giant whatever.

"Correctional nurse," Ollie interjected politely. "October's not a nurse's assistant. She *has* an assistant so she can write up reports and make recommendations for psychosocial support." Ollie stopped only when my heel dug into his foot to shut him up. Ezra didn't need to know more about me; I was on the periphery of his goal to get to know Bev better. Sticking to the basics was a better tactic. Nurse, age twenty-two, high-fives strangers without having to wash her hands, doesn't have bugs looking at her like they want to sit down to tea and have a chat. Also, wooden stake-flinger, because everything I knew about vampires came from *Buffy the Vampire Slayer*.

Ezra looked truly upset that he'd gotten a detail wrong. I was worried about bone-breaking Mason showing up, and of course the alleged vampire on my left, but Ezra was concerned about social graces. It was actually kind of sweet.

Ezra frowned. "Oh, I'm sorry. And I had a premonition I would muck something up. I do apologize that it was something concerning you, dear. Tell me, what's the difference between a nursing assistant and a correctional nurse, so I can properly remember the right one for next time?"

My voice was small, and I wished Ollie hadn't said anything. "The kind of nurse you're thinking of works in a hospital or does homecare, while a correctional nurse treats only inmates. It's really not anything you have to worry about. It's almost the same thing. People get it mixed up all the time."

Wilbur took notice of my cordial response and nodded twice at me, as if to let me know he approved of the succinct breakdown. Or maybe he was thinking my hair looked weird. It was hard to understand Wilbur, but he looked lonely up there, so I tried my best.

Ezra regarded me with a hint of confusion and worry. "That seems dangerous."

Mariang nodded. "Indeed. Aren't you frightened going to work every day?"

I shrugged, casting her a small smile. "There's plenty of security. It was a little intimidating at first, but now it's just like any other job. Overwhelming some days, boring on others."

Mariang looked at me as if I was Wonder Woman. "Well, I think you're quite brave."

I blinked at her, stunned. "Wow. Thanks, Mariang."

Von sized me up in a way that made me bristle. "You're just a little pixie, though. Are we talking juvie?"

I didn't care if Von was a vampire or not, I didn't prefer to be judged on my size.

"No, though the inmates sometimes act like juveniles." I was perplexed by their concern for me more than anything. "Crossing the street can be dangerous if you're unprepared." I noticed Danny and Ezra exchanging wary conspiratorial glances. I bent my head down to look at my plate, effectively putting an end to any further dissection of my life choices.

Ezra was in on it. Though I couldn't be sure if he'd sanctioned the bone-breaker to come, I knew by the look he'd exchanged with Danny that something I'd said meant some kind of confirmation to them.

I scratched the back of my hand under the table. Ezra was strange to me. I didn't understand his game. The whole kind eyes thing really threw me.

I cracked into my crème brûlée, expecting vanilla pudding made to look fancy. What greeted my taste buds set my eyes rolling back in my head as I moaned. "This is amazing, Ezra. Did Lynna make this? What's in it?"

Ezra smiled that I was participating in conversation. "It's lavender. She loves cooking with fresh herbs. Utter gem, she is."

I turned to Ollie, who was smiling at me, relieved I hadn't gone completely into my turtle shell. "Dude, try yours. It's unreal."

Ollie and I moaned in unison, forgetting our table manners in the wake of the ecstasy from the amazing dessert we couldn't put down. Von, Ezra and Mariang chuckled in amusement at our dramatics. I'm sure they were used to such fanciness, but I was blown away.

Bev was not amused. "Honestly, you'd think you two were raised in a barn, carrying on how you are. October Grace, you're making a pig of yourself."

Ollie's head swiveled to Bev, his eyes zoning in on her dangerously. "That's one," he warned her, quiet in his controlled fury. I reached over and snapped the rubber band on his wrist that his Anger Management counselor had given him to center himself, reminding him that now was not the time for a family fight. Ollie didn't like it when Bev slid in the fat jokes. She'd done the same thing with Allie until my big sister had stopped eating.

Screw Miss Manners, I was in Heaven. I decided to try and play ball with the troubling conversation I'd over-heard in the hallway, and just be myself – weird as I was. "Ezra, this is only the most perfect thing I've ever eaten in my life. Scratch that, most perfect thing I've eaten in all my lives, including the one where I was a vampire hunter." I took a drink of water, meeting Von's eyes in a playful chal-lenge. Von swallowed hard, his gaze darting toward Ezra and Danny in silent alarm.

"Even that one?" Ollie asked, grinning. "Ah, yes. We had that leprechaun meat dipped in a vampire blood sauce in the underworld hunter life. That was to die for." He played my game as if it was a game, and not a mental arm-wrestling match between myself and the new guys.

My nose scrunched while I danced around the V-word, as if I wasn't aware it was a hot button that shouldn't be pushed. I walked right up to the taboo and banged it like a friggin' gong. "Nah. Vampires taste like beets, no matter how you sauce them." I winked at Von to let him know I'd heard his little conversation in the hallway – for better or worse.

Von snorted through a smirk and started coughing, swallowing down his bite with a few gulps of water. "That caught me by surprise. Haven't had this many genuine laughs over dinner in ages. How many lives have you had, little peach?" Von asked me, wiping his mouth on his red cloth napkin.

"Ten, obviously. I mean, I've got about a medium amount of wisdom. Been around the block a few times, but I'm not all jaded yet. It's a delicate balance. I was on top of my game when I trained with ninjas to punch out the fangs of vampires. See, a few troublesome vampires and their buddies tried to break my arm to test the strength of my bones." I tapped my chin as if in thought. "What was that guy's name who tried to rough me up? I think it was Mason or something like that."

That's right. Cards on the table, people.

Danny, Ezra, Mariang and Von all stiffened, but Ollie laughed while Bev rolled her eyes. Ollie didn't miss a beat, and glommed on to my oddball jokes. "Sure, but that life where you were a chimney sweep in the Charles Dickens era wasn't so bad."

Mariang cast me a meek smile. "Luckily you made it out with your sense of humor intact."

Von cleared his throat. "Did you get to meet Ebenezer Scrooge perchance?"

"Meet him? Who do you think taught the old grouch bookkeeping?" I pointed my spoon at Ollie, who tipped his head in Von's direction.

"You seem to have led quite the interesting life, November," Von remarked as he finished off his dessert.

"My name's October," I corrected him, not unkindly.

"I know." Von picked up his Bloody Mary and swirled it around in the glass, letting it coat the sides in a way tomato juice couldn't. It was as if he wanted me to see the horror he'd hidden in plain sight.

Von was screwing with me. He knew I'd overheard, and now he was taunting me with his inclination to suck down a little O-Negative. Von took a sip and smacked his lips. "My, that is refreshing. Fancy a taste?"

I cast him a dubious look, not sure if I was more put off by the fact that there was blood in the glass, or that he'd sincerely just offered to share his germ-infested drink with me.

7

EZRA'S SURPRISE

"Tell us about yourselves," Ollie said between bites. "What do you do?" he asked Danny.

"Groundskeeper," Danny replied without looking away from me. His eyes narrowed in a silent threat not to out Von for the... vampire? Yeah, for the vampire I was pretty sure that Von was. "Ezra already told you that."

Von whispered to me, "Groundskeeper by day, salsa dancing jazz singer by night." Von had a way of making me laugh, of making me forget he might actually be a real live vampire. I caught a glimpse of Von's canine teeth when he smiled. They were slightly longer than I deemed they should've been.

Ollie pursed his lips through a tight smile. "That's nice. The property here is amazing. That's your doing?" Ollie was best at being polite to prickly strangers. He was used to out and out hatred from Bev, so the lesser antagonizers were a fun challenge.

Danny harrumphed. "Well, it's certainly not Von's hard work. Layabout just lays about all day. Idiot."

Von deflected the dig with a well-practiced grin. I knew that grin, and wore it almost as convincingly when Bev was being herself. "That's the benefit of being a layabout. You don't have to mow the lawn." He tapped his temple. "Idiot, or genius?"

"You work here?" I asked Von.

"I do. Security for Ezra." At Von's answer, Danny scoffed.

"What's your favorite part of the job?" I asked Von, ignoring Danny's obvious opinion.

"When pretty girls ask me a hundred questions about it." Von grinned at me, so I looked away. He was one of those way too handsome to look directly at kind of guys. I knew if he called me pretty again, I'd start to develop a crush on the guy who screws random women and high-fives me about it. *Not again, October. Not again.*

Ezra wiped his palms off on his pants, and I caught a wavering in his voice as he stood and walked over to Bev's chair, where she sat like a queen. "Now that we're all here and we've met each other with no catastrophes, I have something I'd like to say."

I choked on my water when Ezra Manaul lowered himself to one knee and pulled a small box out of his pocket. I could feel my heartbeat in my cheeks as Bev started shrieking and crying like a woman in the front pew at church.

"Beverly Jo, ever since I read your profile, I knew I'd found someone I'd never want to stop learning about. From the very moment I saw your face in that restaurant where we had our first date, I realized there was no point in going to a restaurant unless you were there to share every bite with. From the first kiss, I knew my heart wasn't mine anymore. I love you, Beverly. Will you be my wife?"

I assume Bev said yes. She was screeching like a cat, waving around the biggest rock I'd ever seen, like she'd just won a lifetime supply of Rice-A-Roni on the *Price is Right*. She hugged Mariang with what I could tell was too much force for the girl's frail body. Bev cried and whooped like she'd just won the lottery, which I guess she kind of did.

I was a statue, frozen to my seat amidst the chaos. Bev jumped up and down in Ezra's embrace, her big boobs bouncing every which way as she danced. I shouldn't have been focusing on a hope that one of them wouldn't pop out of her hot pink blouse and knock Ezra unconscious, but that was all my mind could process. Her breasts were known to make appearances at the most inopportune times. My kindergarten graduation feels like the worst one, but really, there were so many surprise appearances; it's hard to choose the blue ribbon winner.

I could tell Von hadn't been starved for second-base fun. It was obvious he'd had his pick of the bounty. He was appreciative of the set that bounced right in his eye line, yet unimpressed.

Bev wrapped her arms around Danny, who looked like he was just as apprehensive about his girlfriend's new mom's breasts popping out and smacking him in the face as I was. He sat back down, his thin lips stretched in a frown as he watched the hoopla around him with only a passing interest.

Ollie was pulled into a tight hug by Ezra, which I knew made him uncomfortable. "Oh, I know you're much too old to need a new father, but can I just say that I'm over-joyed to have a son?"

"Congratulations, Ezra," was all Ollie could manage through his haze of shock.

Ollie handed Ezra off to me to rid himself of the affec-tion that only confused people like us, but I was still frozen in my chair, stunned. Wilbur was shaking his head at either the scene or me, I wasn't sure.

I managed to offer a congratulatory nod to Ezra, who couldn't stop grinning. The newly engaged man hoisted me up out of the chair and wrapped me in his strong arms. The hug felt like warmth, comfort and safety all wrapped tight around me. Too tight. I couldn't breathe. His unfath-omable love for Bev was one thing, but being this nice to Ollie and me? I kept looking for the angle. He was rich, so he clearly wasn't trying to get at Ollie's money.

Ezra held on for two seconds.

Three seconds.

Four. When his grip tightened further, I yelped and pulled a ninja move to extract myself, ducking from his grip and pushing my hands out between us. I popped the flat of my hand to his chest to smack the kindness away, forcing the nicest man on the planet to stumble back several inches, clutching his sternum. I didn't mean to clench my fists as they bobbed defensively. It was all instinct. I hadn't been hugged by anyone except for Ollie, Allie or the McCray family as a kid, and they knew better than to hold on that tight.

"October Grace!" Bev shouted, her face twisted into that I'm-about-to-beat-you expression that made me flinch.

I dropped my fists, my face pinker than Bev's shirt. "I'm sorry! I wasn't thinking, and I just... I'm sorry! Ezra, I'm sorry." I buried my face in my hands, ruining Bev's perfect moment. Years from now, this would make it into the proposal retelling. The man on bended knee, the diamond the size of a watermelon, and October Grace throwing her dukes up at the most polite man she'd ever met. Despite my move to a home in a quaint suburb, part of me knew I'd never get the trailer groomed out of me.

Ezra was still coming down from his high, his expression a mix of elation and devastation. "My fault entirely." He extended his hand to me, being the polite adult in the situation when I'd devolved into a chagrinned child.

I shook his hand, loathing myself with each bob of our wrists. I tried not to recoil from the hand-to-hand contact I usually tried to avoid. "I'm so sorry. It's not you. You're all perfect. It's the hugging. I'm not used to... I promise, it's not you."

"Bev, show us the ring again," Ollie said in a loud voice meant to distract from my disgraceful behavior. I loved my brother, but winced on his behalf when Bev shot him a glare at calling her by her first name.

The others were ready for champagne and celebration, but I was ready for an escape. I excused myself for the bathroom, and by "excused" I mean I bolted out of the dining room like a total coward. I couldn't help it; I needed what I needed. The hug was still on me, so I knew the germs couldn't be far behind.

Pulling my bar of soap from its tin container in my messenger bag, I began washing the ick from my skin. I lathered in between each finger, then started the row over again. I clawed at the backs of my hands through the suds, scraping the flesh in ways that felt good for a second, and then not so good when the sting got to be too much.

After I rinsed, I started all over again, but this time I scrubbed up to my elbows, scraping at the skin to really get it good and clean. My unzipped hoodie's sleeves were rolled up to my biceps, exposing the lurking germs that were invisible to the untrained eye, but completely obvious to me. I'd studied them under a microscope, so I knew they were there, eating at me while I slept and multiplying with every brush of human contact I had to endure.

Ollie called to me from the other side of the door on the third round. "You alright in there?"

"Yeah. Just dying of embarrassment. But that's not a bloody death, so I won't leave too gory of a mess. I'll be out in a second."

"I'm coming in." Ollie let himself into the emerald bathroom with bronze fixtures. Everything was regal, gawking at me like I didn't belong. "Hey, it's okay. No one's even talking about you trying to punch out Ezra anymore."

"I didn't take a single swing at him!" I argued with the smirk in my brother's voice, scratching my arms to rid them of the germs that were being particularly stubborn today. "Any chance you want to drive Bev home? Take one for the team? I don't think I can make it through an hour of her yelling at me. I didn't mean to push Ezra. He's great. Honest!" I was miffed that Ollie was chuckling.

"Oh, I know. Ezra's fine. Bev's never going to let you live this down, though." He stared up at the ceiling. "I guess I can do my duty as your brother and spare you. You've taken the last three years. What's one hour?" He said it like he was trying to convince himself. "But in the next life, you owe me something awesome."

"Like a bag of only yellow Skittles?"

"A big bag of all yellows, without a single purple one anywhere around me. Like, not even in the universe where I might be traveling for at least a week."

"I'll see what strings I can pull." I exhaled, rinsing off once I was certain the germs were gone. "You're a lifesaver.

Thanks, Ollie." I went to reach for the door, but jumped when Wilbur caught my eye on the frame at the top of the doorway.

Ollie's eyes fell on Wilbur. "Oh, it's just a little thing. Don't tell me you're scared of a little old caterpillar all of a sudden."

"Huh? No. I just wasn't expecting him to be there, is all. Hush up, you." I shoved my brother and grinned when he mussed my hair. "You two go on home. I need a minute before going back out there and facing Ezra again. I'm so embarrassed."

Ollie nodded. "Yeah, that's probably best for me to get Bev gone before you come out of here. I'll calm her down on the way home. Don't worry."

"Thanks, Ollie. You're the best. You know that, right?"

"Only when you tell me, so never stop." He gave me that paternal smile I'd been going too long without, and left the bathroom to give me a moment to gather up my scattered bearings.

8

CHANGING TIRES AND BONDING
OVER LIARS

I didn't get to see the rest of the gorgeous mansion, but the quick exit was worth it to leave without further incident. I all but bolted to Terence the Taurus as soon as I could make a seamless departure. I tossed a polite farewell and another apology to Ezra, which he waved off with a benevolent smile I knew I didn't deserve.

I noticed a problem before I started up the car I loved. I was leaning to the right as I sat in the driver's seat. The whole car was leaning, in fact. I got out, praying I'd parked on a slight hill, but hissed out an unladylike swear when I saw I had two flat tires. Of course this would happen. Of course I'd given Ollie a ten-minute head start.

I leaned closer to examine the damage, expecting a nail or something to clue me in as to how this bucket of nonsense had rained down on me. My breath caught when

I saw two violent slashes marring both tires on the right side of my car. I couldn't imagine what I'd driven over that had done that without me noticing.

No sooner had I pulled out my phone did Danny and Ezra come trotting out in my direction. "Oh, no! What happened?" Ezra asked, eyebrows furrowed.

I waved off their concern. "It's alright. I've got a spare."

"Two spares?" Danny pointed to the second flat.

"Just the one. But I'll call roadside. Hopefully they won't take too long. Don't worry about it. It's not a big deal. You can go back to your evening. I can wait in the car."

Ezra looked at me as if he thought I might burst into tears at any moment. "You poor thing. Don't bother with a tow, yeah? My car has a spare Danny can replace yours with. Danny?"

Danny was already on his way to the four-car garage that looked big enough to house a family of five. I lowered my forehead into my hand, exasperated with myself. "Really, it's fine. Seriously, I'm like, ruining your life all over the place."

Ezra looked like he was holding himself back from hugging me again, which was probably best for all involved. "Why would you say such a thing? You're not ruining anything at all. You're giving us a little adventure to liven up the evening. Danny hasn't changed a tire in quite some time."

"I'm sure he's got better things to do." I popped my trunk, put on a pair of size small hospital gloves I always traveled with a box of, and hefted out the spare tire I'd hoped I'd never have to use. The jack and travel toolbox came out, and I set to work unscrewing the nuts as I knelt by poor Terence, my beloved Taurus. His headlight seemed to look at me like, "Dude, this is totally embarrassing."

"Really, October Grace. Danny can do that. You don't need to bother with it at all."

The fact that he was such a nice guy and still volunteered Danny's services told me he had no idea how to change a tire. It was sweet. I jerked my chin toward my wrench. "Do you know how to do this?"

Ezra chuckled with chagrin. "I confess, I've never changed a tire before. You've found me out."

I waved him down, smirking when the perfectly dressed country clubber knelt next to me, his unwrinkled khakis giving me the finger that I was making them ruin their perfect crease. "See that? These nuts need to come off first. Easy enough, right?"

Ezra smiled at me, like we were doing something audacious and fun he just knew we'd get in trouble for. "You're really teaching me how to change a flat?"

"I really am. Ollie wouldn't let me get my driver's license until I could change a tire, change my oil and knew how to give my car a jump."

"He's strict. I had no idea Beverly's children were so very capable."

"Well, after today, you'll be the same amount of

impressive." I slid the jack under the car and started pumping until poor Terence was slightly raised.

"Should we wait for Danny? I feel like the car will come crashing down on your hands or something."

"Nah. The jack does what it does while we do what we do. Now we take the good-for-nothing off the axle," I instructed, pulling and twisting until the ruined rubber broke free of Terence. We were cozied in between the two rows of topiaries lining the long driveway. For that stretch of time, there were no distractions as I worked under the fading light from nature and the answering illumination filtering through the tall bushes from Ezra Manor. "Now we put on the new one. Easy-peasy."

Ezra helped me lift the tire in the early twilight, and together we angled it correctly so it slid on. I handed him the iron, and he looked at it with wide eyes. "I'm afraid I don't have much aptitude for cars. I'm strictly a drive-it-until-it-doesn't-drive sort of bloke."

"I'm watching you. Don't worry. Righty-tighty. You know the drill. Put the nuts back on and tighten them, and you'll be good to go." I bit back my smirk when Ezra looked mildly flummoxed by the few things he'd been presented with. He set to work with hands meant for swiping credit cards, his humble attitude playing in his favor. He wasn't too bad at it, and took my gentle guidance with grace until the job was completed. "Wow. You must really love Bev to let me make you help change a tire. That's real cool of you."

"I do love your mother," he said, turning to look me in the eye. "I would do anything to make her happy, including learn to change a tire just to bond with her daughter."

I swallowed, unsure what to do with this guy's constant sincerity and kindness. "Well, now I know she'll be okay if she's out with you and you get a flat."

"She doesn't know how to do this? Where did you learn, then?"

"Ollie. Ollie and Allie taught me everything."

"Allie?" He quirked his blond eyebrow at me. "Is that a girlfriend of Oliver's?"

"Huh? No! Allie's our sister."

Ezra stared at me, as though certain he'd heard me wrong. His hand was frozen on the tire. "But Beverly told me she has two children."

I had little issue lying for Bev to cover over whatever she needed extra strength concealer smeared on. I sucked it up when she needed me to call her "Mama". But *this*? I couldn't gloss over this offense. It was too hurtful. Too mean. My tone came out clipped, though I didn't mean to sound short to the poor guy, whose only crime was falling in love with Bev. "Allison Mercy Reese is her second-born child. Bev has three kids, whether she wants to admit it or not. Allie's twenty-seven, and she lives in California. She's got hair like me and freckles like Ollie. She's got a biology degree and works as a researcher for a chemical supply company." I was hurt that Bev dismissed my Allie so rudely. Allie filled the role of mother in my life, and I was loyal to her as such. "Allie and Bev didn't get along, but she doesn't deserve to be erased like that."

Ezra's fingers pressed into his hairline as if holding too many things back so they didn't spill out all over the pristine driveway. "I don't understand. Why would Beverly keep that from me? I'll have a third daughter? I should like to meet her straightaway."

I was glad we were closed in by the green topiaries that were taller than a person. It made the confession feel like it was safe to give, though I knew there was no chance of things turning out alright after I pressed further into the wound. "Allie asked Ollie and me for some space. She wasn't mad at us or anything; she just wanted to start over in California. She didn't feel she could do that if Ollie and I were still around. So she left two years ago. Promised to call twice a year. Once at Christmas and once on Ollie's birthday, but she forgot this past Christmas. I haven't heard from her since Ollie's birthday last year." I tried not to let the constant stream of unrest well up in me. I'd tried her number the day after her missed call on Christmas, but it was disconnected. I knew she'd given up a lot to raise me, but to cut me out completely hurt worse than I could put into words.

So I never discussed it. If Ollie ever started, I gave him one warning and then hung up on him if he kept at it. He wanted to hire a P.I. to find her to make sure she was okay, but Allie had been firm before she'd left that she would contact us, not the other way around. She was my mother, more than anyone else, and I respected her as such.

"This is... I'll have to talk to Beverly about this. I don't understand why she wouldn't tell me she had a whole other child."

My conscience tugged in my chest. "Look, I'm sorry. Maybe I should've let that slide. Your relationship's none of my business, and you should be happy. You seem like a nice enough guy. I just don't like when Bev tries to erase Allie like that. I won't stand for it, and if you don't mind me saying so, now that you know? Neither should you."

Ezra stood, posturing as he pulled me up off the concrete. The air was just starting to get nippy, so I hugged myself. "Of course I would never try to erase a family member. I'll speak with Beverly about this, and we'll get to the bottom of it. I'm sure it's just a misunderstanding." He stared at my car with a tight frown and furrowed eyebrows, mulling over the extreme ups and downs of the night.

Danny came down the drive with broad shoulders and empty hands. "I thought I had a spare, but no dice. Sorry about that. Did you..." He pointed to the freshly changed front tire in confusion.

"Actually, Ezra helped me. He's got a real future as a mechanic ahead of him, if you ask me."

Danny grimaced and turned to the man who was still reeling. "Truly? *Ezra* changed your tire? I cannot picture that." He picked up my shredded tire with one strong hand. "I called a tow truck for you. It'll be about an hour."

"Thanks, Danny. I'll wait in the car. You two have a good night."

Ezra turned to me, blinking a few times before he found his words. "Nonsense. You'll come wait inside."

Before I could argue, Ezra was already several steps away walking toward the house. Danny kept a respectable distance behind us, but I got the uncomfortable feeling that I was being corralled.

FRIGGIN' CHIROPRACTOR

The hairs on my arm stood as we neared the front door. It had been left open, but before Ezra could pull me behind him to shield me from things I surely wasn't meant to see, I glimpsed the upturned bare, muddy feet of a woman, sticking out over the threshold. "What the..."

My exclamation was cut short when the door swung further open to reveal a cloaked bodybuilder with dreadlocks. He was standing over the body of an unconscious woman with his dark hood pulled back, revealing a fierce and determined face. He had a half-inch short brown beard cropping his stern jawline, thick eyebrows, and an unyielding gaze that seemed to see nothing but my horror. The down on her luck woman sprawled on the floor at his feet was dressed in what looked like a tattered gray wizard's robe. Her brown skin was covered in mud.

I wanted to take a look at her, to see if I could help in some medical way, but the dude standing over her was no joke.

"Mason! Good to see you, son." Ezra forced a smile, but I could tell he didn't want me conversing with whatever Elf-Vampire-Viking dude Mason was.

Six and a half feet of solid muscle greeted me with a cold stare. I took in his cool gray eyes that studied me every bit as much as I scrutinized him. Dude had hairy forearms thicker than even The Rock had a right to walk around with. He had seven long dreadlocks tied together with a leather lace, holding his hair back from the face that was handsome in that I-just-ripped-open-a-lion-with-my-teeth kind of way.

My spine tingled with an ominous desire to bolt. Delusional or not, Danny had invited this Mason guy here to try and break my arm. I didn't think I believed in vampires, but I sure as Sunday believed in oversized bodybuilders who might attack me.

Mason motioned to me as I took a step backward. "This is her? This is the new Omen?"

"Mason! This is not the time. We're handling it," Ezra barked, turning from the British Ward Cleaver to... I dunno. Someone meaner. I took another step back, almost to the edge of the porch.

Mason smelled my flight seconds before I bolted. The only advantage I had was that I was still outside of the house, but I decided that was the only advantage I needed.

I turned and leapt off the porch, hitting the concrete walkway at a run I was well prepared for. I was a decent sprinter – even speedier when I was being chased.

I'd watched my fair share of horror movies, so I knew better than to look behind me, but the desire was there when I heard Ezra shouting my name into the early graces of the evening. My arms pumped when I heard the heavy footfalls of a two-person stampede coming up behind me.

I didn't know where I was going. I had no car and no knowledge of the area – so I ran, kicking up the dust behind me, hoping they'd choke on it.

I charged down the open road, wishing I hadn't been fooled into thinking the fact that there were no other mansions on the street was impressive instead of ominous. There was no one to help me, no one to call the cops, no one to see Danny grab at my arm, brushing his fingers to my skin to warn me that he was closing in.

So I did what any normal person would do in such a situation where escape was impossible. I let out my air in a gust, stopped dead in my tracks when I felt his arm again, tucked down slightly, and braced myself for the impact.

In my imagination, I would be low enough and Danny unstoppable enough that he would fling over my body and slam himself onto the pavement. In my imagination, I'm also nine feet tall and built like a truck, which isn't totally true to real life. As it turns out, getting hit by Danny was much like getting smashed by a freight train, given his considerable bulk. I was jolted more than I anticipated, but managed to hold my ground as Danny toppled over my hunched body. The fall knocked a defeated "ooph!" out of him when he hit the pavement with a thud.

I couldn't even work out a triumphant "Suck it!" to Danny, since Mason was only a handful of paces behind him. I didn't have time to build up enough speed to escape the Viking. His seven dreadlocks flew out behind him like flags of doom. I didn't have anyone who might come to my aid – all I had was me, and I wasn't sure that was enough, even on a normal day.

Instead of running, I kept my knees bent and body-checked Mason's pelvis, lifting his legs when he collided with me. I dug my shoulder into him as he doubled over, and used his forward momentum to launch him over me in a midair somersault. It was the classic using his size against him tactic, and Mason was a big fella.

That seemed like the appropriate time to work out a good dig, but Danny was starting to assemble his bearings, so I took my head start and bolted for the open road.

Stupid Danny for latching onto my ankle just enough to make me stumble like a dummy. Stupid me for going through all that trouble of throwing them both down, only to lose it in the final inning by tripping over a technicality.

My hands kissed the concrete, but Danny still didn't let go of my leg. I rolled onto my back and kicked at him, cursing internally when Mason rose to his feet, fixing me with a glower that told me Daddy was tired of playing around.

"Don't break my arm!" I shouted, holding my loose fists up to block whatever blows might rain down on me.

Mason was unwashed and looked like a mountain man or Viking warrior or something. Mason's fingers curled into a tight fist, and my heart raced. "I won't leave this place until I can bring good news back to my father's people. We can't wait any longer! If it's you, you'll be awakened this very night."

"Huh? Dude, I don't know what you're talking about! I'm already awake. Let me go, and we're cool."

Mason towered over me, and the intimidation factor I tried not to feel hit me at a new level. "You're not going anywhere." The hairy arms that reached for me were too strong for me to win against, but I wasn't about to quit now. I punched and kicked even as Mason's thick hands wrapped around my left wrist, lifting me to stand.

It wasn't my first time being grabbed at by a huge man. It wasn't my twentieth time. I didn't pull my punch when my fist flung out and clocked him with my right hook. Fear rose up in me, but I punched him again in the same spot twice more before I debated the benefits of cowering. I knew what cowering got a girl. I spat in his eyes, which was the only way I could get him to loosen his iron grip on my arm that made my wrist feel like it might splinter.

Danny's arms wrapped around me from behind, securing my thrashing body while Mason wiped my spit from his eyes. "Would you hold still?" Danny gritted his teeth through my stomp on his instep.

Mason wrested me from Danny, flinging me over his shoulder like a sack of potatoes. "I hate this maneuver!" I raged, pounding on Mason's lower back with my fists. "This is humiliating!"

Mason's voice was steady. "Now, now. You were such a sweet little thing last week when you rolled out of your car, all scared. I don't know where you get all this rage from."

"From you! You're taking me against my will with the purpose of breaking my arm, you jackhole! You want me to just go quietly so I can still be a 'sweet little thing'?"

Mason and Danny set back toward the mansion, their contraband immobilized. They marched down the street and up the driveway, not stopping until they crossed the threshold. Danny locked the front door as Mason deposited me with surprising gentleness on the floor of the foyer, ignoring Ezra's warnings of them going too far. Mason's voice was low and even, not even out of breath, the jag. "This ends tonight, Ezra. I'm not leaving until we know whether or not you've finally found a new Omen for us." Mason met my glare as I tried to right myself. "Are you quite finished trying to dodge your duties?"

"What are you talking about? Dude, you carry me like that ever again, and you don't want to know the problem I can be."

Mason tilted his head to the side. "She's a feisty one. Almost got away from me." He held up his hands to try and convince me they were innocent, when we both knew they were not. "Alright. I won't need to grab at you if you stay where we can see you."

My mouth popped open as I gaped at him. "I think you've got me confused with someone else. Someone you can try to intimidate and jerk around." The exit was only a few feet away, but Viking Bob was standing like a linebacker, blocking it.

Ezra pointed to the front door, his upper lip curling in a faint sneer that made me recoil. "You'll not put your hands on her, Mason. I'll handle this in my own way, in my own time."

I wasn't sure what my plan of escape should be, but I knew I didn't want to stick around to see which of the two men had the biggest temper. I slowly inched away from the argument, hoping I could find a backdoor and slip away out into the night.

"I warned you!" Mason called out, and in the next second, his hands turned into weapons again. "We're doing this now, Ezra."

I was wrestled to the floor, screaming when Mason kneeled with all his weight on a sensitive spot on my spine. "Stop it! Stop it!" I wailed. He had my hands behind my back and jerked on them with brutal force. "Ow!" I kicked to no avail, trying to turn myself over so I could get him off my spine.

Mason's voice was deep and steady, as though he was walking through the steps on how to change a tire. It was his calm that made me panic the most. That he could pin a girl to the ground with all the inflection of a patient flight attendant made my blood run cold. I fought with everything in me for an escape. "I know this feels like a hot knife in your spine, and I don't want to hurt you, but you can't go anywhere."

Ezra's voice rose above the others'. "Not her spine! What if you're wrong? Her arm, Mason. Try breaking her arm if you must."

I fumed at Ezra. "I knew you were too good to be true!"

Mason was unperturbed, focused only on breaking my back like the worst friggin' chiropractor in the world. "You'll stay here, or I'll make this even more painful. Nod if you understand."

"Bite me!" My face was red with fury at being dominated by the mountain man. I squirmed as best I could, but he had me so pinned that for all my thrashing, I barely moved. My eyes locked in on the woman in the gray tattered robes who was still lying on the hardwood floor, eyelids shut, as though in a deep sleep. The gashes and bruises peppering her body were what I feared might be in store for me next. I bucked with renewed vigor, hoping my inner Bruce Campbell would save the day.

"Have it your way."

"Mason, stop! You'll kill her!" Ezra commanded.

Mason didn't stop. He dug his knee deeper into the side of my spine and then jerked my chin upwards with his free hand.

I like to pretend my job's no big deal, but working in a

prison comes with a certain level of danger you just plain get used to. I've been stabbed twice while on the job, and I'll never forget the feeling of the shiv slicing into my thigh, or the one that cut my arm, forcing me to never wear tank tops in front of Ollie ever again so he didn't find out and freak. I still recalled with perfect clarity the sharp pain that started at the entrance and echoed up my body long after the shiv was removed.

The lasting agony of those stabbings paled in comparison to Mason playing a game of chicken on my spine. White-hot torment ricocheted up my back and spread out to each connected nerve ending. He had my chin jerked up so I couldn't take in a full breath. While I tried to gasp out a scream, he was slowly suffocating me. I knew beneath the never-ending torture that the pain was a tool to asphyxiate me, at least enough to deflate my fight. So I gritted my teeth through the pain, praying no lasting damage would be done to my spine.

Mason kept my wrists confined with one of his too-large hands at the base of my spine, while the other thumbed my chin in a "hang in there" kind of way that utterly confused me. "You're a spirited one. Are you ready to calm down yet?"

"I'm ready to kick your ass!" I shot back, my intimidation factor compromised by so many things in that moment.

Danny and Mason exchanged a look of doom, and I

knew Danny was giving Mason silent permission to mess me up a little more.

"Von, no! He's got it under control!" Danny shouted, and before I knew it, a red t-shirt came whipping by my blurred vision. Mason released me, and my chin cracked into the hard floor, making my eyes water. Von and Mason were scrapping on the floor, with Mason being the clear victor only a few seconds later, though it didn't look like either competitor really wanted to hurt the other.

I tried to army crawl away with shaking arms, but I was in too much lingering pain. Ezra rolled me over and scooped me up in his arms like a baby, bending my spine back the right way, which somehow started the ripping agony all over again. "Danny, get Mason out of here!" Ezra called over his shoulder. "I'm the Ambassador to the Topside. *I* decide how quickly things get done, not you. I'll not be bullied by the council!"

Mason was irate as he shook Von off him. "The people are dying! You can't keep ignoring them! Danny, make him understand! Hayop is going to cave and consent to using Sama's rations if something doesn't change soon! It's only a matter of time before we bow to Sama! Is that what you want?"

Ezra whirled on Mason, making me seasick as I fought to take in a full breath without crying or letting my misery be known. "Do you think I take lightly what the mantle of the Omen has done to my daughter? Everyone's so quick to sacrifice someone else's child, so long as it's not their own.

How about this one? Will you sentence her so easily?" He gripped me with what could only be described as a protective hold, cradling me midair like I was five and skinned my knee, and he was Ollie come to rescue me. "I'll not force her into anything, and I'll not show her the heartlessness of our world until I'm sure she's the one."

Mason shook his head, the ends of his long dreads swinging out to shame Ezra. "You've lost sight of what's important. One life is nothing compared to the hundreds of thousands she could save. And I just tested her spine. If she were a normal girl, it would've snapped. She's the one, Ezra. You're just stalling because you're afraid to drag her into this life."

I was still debating between clocking Ezra and clinging to him as my only beacon in the sea of insanity that was storming around me.

"'One life'," Ezra simpered. "Please! How many Omens did the last Topside Ambassador go through before there was only Mariang left barely standing? How many daughters have died? Mine won't be next!" he roared, vicious in his fury. "And this child won't put her name on that death certificate until she understands what she'll be getting herself into."

Mason was livid as he gestured to the supine form of the woman he'd dragged into the mansion. "I brought her a body from Terraway so the girl could be awakened. Let's get to it!"

Ezra ignored Mason and turned to the others. "Von,

take October Grace to the living room and see that she's okay. If she needs a doctor, call one."

Danny stepped forward. "I can take her."

"You," Ezra sneered, looking down his nose at Danny. "Like you can be trusted when it comes to Mason. The two of you... In this, I trust Von more than I do you. Think on that, young man."

Danny clenched his fists and stepped back.

Von was hesitant. "Are you sure you trust me, Ezra?"

Ezra nodded once. "She's not bleeding. You'll be fine."

Von smiled at me like the whole thing was a shrug-worthy offense. "Little tense in here, yeah? I've got you, November." Ezra handed me off to Von. It was bad enough I'd indulged myself as long as I did in the fatherly protection, but I wasn't about to be helpless in Von's arms to boot.

"No more men are carrying me, you hear?" I stated my demand.

The second I put weight on my legs, my knees began to buckle. I hated myself for the whimper that escaped my lips, and even more when Von caught me and hefted me up in his arms like a damsel in distress. "How about just this once," Von offered like a gentleman.

I was no damsel. I was humiliated, so I buried my face in his shirt to hide my shame. I could feel the hot sting of tears rising up in me, and knew I could never live with myself if I cried in front of the brutal men. "Bathroom," I requested.

"Anything you say, darling."

CONFESSIONS OF A HALF-VAMPIRE

*V*on went toward the emerald and gold bathroom in the hallway between the foyer and the kitchen. The last time I'd been in there, I thought the worst thing to happen in this house was when I'd shoved Ezra. Now I'd gladly make that my screensaver to escape this. Von lowered my feet gingerly to the floor and let me into the bathroom, closing me inside. Though I knew he was right outside the door, the few inches of privacy permitted me breath as I did my very best not to cry, scream in horror, or lose my mind. I inhaled through the physical, mental and emotional misery, trying to come up with a plan to escape the men who no doubt had Mariang locked up in the bell tower or some crap. Too many questions zoomed through my mind for me to reach out and pick just one to address.

I washed my face in the sink, pursing my lips through

the sharp sting in my spine from the workout Mason had given it. I knew I couldn't start washing my hands until I got home – *if* I got home. If I started here with all the things that scared me piling up, I knew I'd never stop scrubbing. I looked at my face in the mirror, biting my lip through the painful act of merely raising my arms to redo my ponytail. I couldn't let them dishevel me. I knew domination was half about appearance, so I tried to erase the visible damage, so Mason couldn't think he'd won. My spine still rang with vibrations of torture, but I exhaled through it, willing the horrors away as best I could.

"Hey, Von?" I called through the door.

His British lilt came back tender and laced with concern I could feel through the door. "You alright in there?"

I swallowed, feeling stupid as I closed my eyes and put words to one of my many concerns. "Are you a vampire?"

"No." Von's swift response made my shoulders relax, but then tense up again when he added, "I'm a half-vampire."

I swallowed the lump in my throat. "Is that like, half a serial killer?"

Von's explanation came to me with the controlled air of a teacher explaining gravity to his student. "I'm not a full vampire, but I was bitten by one last year. I crave blood like you wouldn't believe, but every bit of human blood I drink gets me closer to the transition. Then it's goodbye sun for me, no more sleeping at all, and I'm left a scavenger who feeds on humans instead of the roast goose we had earlier. I'd be more rabid animal than man. No soul, and no conscience. The bloke who bit me didn't even know his own name. Did you see my eyes? They used to both be blue, but one's gold now. If I transition into a full vampire, they'll both be gold, and I'll be gone forever." He sniffed the air like Allie used to do when I'd had the crockpot going. "So if you could do your best not to bleed, that would increase both our chances of survival quite a bit. I don't want to bite you any more than you want me to."

A loud bang from out in the foyer area made me jump, and I couldn't tell if it came from a gun or something less harrowing. The scuffle sounded like it was still near the front door, but I knew the wind could shift at any moment.

I cleared my throat and tried to stay in the conversation. "This is... This is a lot. You're really a vampire?" I pressed my hand to my forehead, trying to keep up.

"Half-vampire, yes, but you can't let me drink your blood."

I threw out my arms in exasperation, even though he couldn't see my wild gesticulation from the other side of the closed door. "Well, obviously I don't go around letting strangers suck my blood."

Von shuffled forward, and it sounded like his hand was pressed to the door in earnest, his voice inches from my ear through the wood. "Look, you want to leave? The quickest way to make that happen is to stay put, so we can secure the house from an attack. The muddy woman lying in the foyer out here? Her name is Tanga. She's a messenger sent by King Geon to search for a new Omen. King Geon wants his hands on an Omen, which would be very bad for you, if that's what you turn out to be. He's bent on kidnapping you, and as much as you hate us, Geon and his messengers are far worse."

"Okay. I barely get what's going on, but whatever gets me home fastest."

"Atta girl." Von exclaimed when another loud bang sounded, followed by a crash. These were the kinds of horror movie tricks I hated – when they tried to make you jumpy by using sudden loud noises right when you were trying to have a moment. Bruce Campbell would never have jumped at a cheap stunt like that. Bruce was amazing, but I was a big chicken. "Are you almost finished in there, Peach?"

"That depends. Do I need to run from you?"

"That depends. Are you bleeding anywhere?"

"No, but I still want to go home."

Von paused, and my heart dropped into my stomach. "You might have to stick around a little while longer. I know that's not what you want to hear. This all must be pretty confusing, but I promise you, I want you to come out of this unscathed. I'll have a talk with Mason; make him see reason. He's really a decent bloke. Truly one of my best mates. Sometimes people get a touch of madness in them when they're at the end of their rope."

"Yeah? Well, madness just so happens to be my

specialty, but I've never tried to break someone's spine before."

"I'll make sure he doesn't do that again."

I looked at my reflection again, but this time something caught my eye. Behind me on the emerald wallpaper was a long black diagonal mark that was throwing off the perfect order of the bathroom. I gasped when I saw it was a line of cockroaches climbing down from the ceiling. When I glanced up, I saw dozens more coming out from the vent above my head. "Um, Von?" The cockroaches came skittering down the walls in thick rows and pooled at my feet, congregating around my shoes and covering the floor. "Von! Something's happening!"

Von flung open the door, surely not expecting the sea of insects that were lapping at my skittish feet. He swore loudly and gasped at the hundreds of shiny black bugs that were now assembling around me, encasing me in my own private island of horrors. They weren't in perfect formations like the ants were, but they were standing around me with purpose. The truth was out: I was Pigpen from the *Peanuts* cartoon, only instead of dust, I traveled with a cloud of bugs. I stood in my shame, unsure how or why the bugs kept flocking to me. Maybe they knew I was trash, or had been raised in it.

I was horribly embarrassed. First I almost punched Ezra seconds after his engagement, and now I was surrounded by bugs like a filthy soon-to-be stepchild.

"Okay, love," Von said in a soothing tone, his hands

raised with a forced smile to calm my anxiety. "I want you to jump to me. Can you do that?"

My back was still throbbing, but I moved to obey. My foot scooped up dozens of little trespassers, drawing out a frightened whimper that pulled Von closer. His gaze was filled with kindness, which, given all the other emotions that could have been controlling his features, said a lot about him. I met his gaze, not holding back the distress that choked me. "Make this be over," I begged, meeting his compassionate eyes with fear I didn't bother concealing.

Von postured, and then nodded, taking charge when I was on the verge of falling apart. "Don't worry, little peach. I'll get you out." He charged through the sea of bugs and scooped me up like a friggin' fireman on a mission, carrying me out into the hallway. He spent an entire three seconds letting me cling to him like the child I was, cradling me without a hint of judgment or impatience.

Von kissed my forehead, and then gingerly set my legs down so he could slam the bathroom door shut. Then he snatched up my hand and bolted toward Ezra and Danny, who were still arguing. Mason was nowhere in sight.

"Tanga!" Von announced, his panic clear. "Tanga's starting to wake up! Her minions are in the bathroom, gunning for the girl."

Ezra clenched his fists, not panicked, but pissed. "Brilliant. Von, take October Grace to the panic room with Mariang and Lynna."

I knew enough about solitary to know I sure as Sunday

wasn't going to get locked up by these loons. I bolted for the front door, ignoring the shouts of the men that echoed around me. Danny lunged for me, but he wasn't fast enough.

I flung open the heavy front door, not anticipating a cavalcade of moths a zillion strong waiting for me in a veil stretching from the porch to the overhang above. They were so thick, I couldn't see anything beyond them. Not the expanse of the front lawn, not the moon, not anything. I screamed as they whipped past me in a white blur. They flew with purpose and speed, using haphazard strokes of their soft wings.

Mason charged past me and slammed the front door shut. My ears heard nothing but my own screaming and the flapping that sounded like a million decks of cards being shuffled at once. "I've brought the Omen a sacrifice, and that sacrifice is about to wake up and put up a fight. We're not waiting on this, Ezra. If you think I'm the worst thing that's coming here tonight, you're dead wrong. Tanga's no doubt already sent a message using her minions to tell King Geon we've found the next Omen. He'll send soldiers here to take the girl and test her!"

"Let me out of here!" I shouted.

Mason whirled on me as the moths flew through the house, dispersing in the air as if they were on a single-minded mission of doom. One of his dreads whipped me in the face, and his upper lip curled behind his short beard in a scowl. "You can't leave! It all hangs on you!

Don't you see? If King Geon takes you, it's over for the rest of us. We don't know who's in Sama's pocket! Geon could take you straight to Sama, and then where would we be?"

"Um, how should I know? I don't know King Geon or Sama or you!" I spat out a few moth wings that had turned to powder on my lips, increasing my panic. "I just want to go home!" My arms flew out to punctuate my point, but Mason must've thought I was trying to fight him. His burly hands found my wrists like heat-seeking missiles, clutching them between us so I was right where he wanted me. "Let me go!"

Mason's voice was calm, but his grip was punishing. "The sacrifice I brought you isn't dead yet; she's starting to rouse. You think you hate me? All I'm doing is keeping you inside the house. If King Geon's working for Sama, he'll steal you and lock you in his dungeon, testing you using unspeakable means. I know the king's mind. I know the danger. I'm trying to protect you!"

"Hurting me isn't protecting me!" My tone was a mixture of angry and mournful. I struggled against him like a butterfly caught in a net as hundreds of moths exploded themselves into me like so many miniature kamikaze flyers.

Mason pulled me closer so I was looking into his eyes in a way that felt intimate. I didn't do well with intimate, so I focused on his nose. His voice was solemn, and his gray eyes earnest. "And I'll do it all over again if you try to escape. You'll get yourself killed out there, and I won't have that. Being hurt is better than being dead."

Before I could spit back a response, there was commotion coming from the direction of the kitchen. Von darted to the back of the house to check it out, and then whipped toward us, a Biblical plague of flies on his heels. "We have another visitor! King Geon's second lieutenant's trying to break in through the back door. They know you abducted Tanga, Mason! Did you think he'd just let that go?"

Ezra closed his eyes like someone had just farted in church as the flies swarmed the foyer. "This is why, Mason. This is why you need to let me handle things. Now you've brought international war on my home! And Tanga's waking back up!"

Mason gestured to me. "Then have the girl kill Tanga now before the lieutenant breaks in!"

I gaped at him, accidentally letting two more moths into my mouth. I spat them on the floor with the others, shuddering through my internal freak-out. "What? No! You're crazy! I'm not a killer!"

Bugs in my mouth. There were just *bugs* in my *mouth.* The *life is messy, and that's okay* mantra didn't extend to bugs in my mouth. I let out a pathetic whimper I despised myself for, but that was the most I would allow myself to carry on about it in mixed company.

Mason let me go, warning me with a finger not to try any funny business. When he pulled a machete out of his cloak with what looked like perhaps too much experience wielding it, I decided maybe this time it would be best for me to obey, since I was unarmed.

Ezra yanked a knife from the dirt of the tall plant near the front door, casting me a look of apology when I gasped. A Viking wielding a machete was alarming enough, but the modest knife in country club Ezra's grip broke my perception of him anew. It looked so vulgar in his manicured hand. "It's necessary. Stay where you are, and we'll protect you."

Mason charged toward the back of the house where the flies originated from with his machete drawn. The flies followed him, thank goodness. In the chaos, I backed into the wall of the foyer near the hallway and away from the front door. I clawed at the skin on the backs of my hands to relieve a little of the stress that scraped at my insides. I bit my lip as I reached for the touchstone that kept me from screaming like a mental patient in the middle of a Thorazine withdrawal. *Bruce Campbell wouldn't cry right now. You can get through this.*

The men scattered like, well to say they scattered like cockroaches would probably be poor form. I assume they went to look for a big old can of bug spray after they fended off whoever was trying to bust in through the back of the house. I took a few breaths that were moth-free, and the freedom of that particular drag into my lungs was a relief. My aching spine was pressed to the wall as I scratched at my skin, silent in my cyclone of distress. Small beads of blood rose to the surface, and then started to drizzle down the slope of my arms.

They were crazy. They kept knives and machetes around for after-dinner fun. I knew there had to be a catch to Bev finding such unadulterated bliss.

They were all in the kitchen, fighting who knows what kind of magical creature King Geon's lieutenant might be. It was my one chance to escape. I scrambled around Tanga's stirring body toward the heavy front door. I didn't know what damage a jillion moths could do to me, but I sure as Sunday knew what a machete could do.

No sooner did my fingers brush the brass knob did Ezra come barreling towards me, his knife dripping with the fresh blood of the intruder. "No! October, stop!"

My hand slipped on the knob, but the door was dead-bolted now, so it didn't much matter. "I have to go home!" I shouted, turning for the bolt.

It was at that precise moment Tanga broke free of her bindings and snatched at my ankle from her supine position on the floor, knocking me to my knees. She stood in her tattered gray wizarding robes, and I shrieked at the too-tall woman with razor-like teeth. She had fingernails adorned with attachments that were just as sharp, looking down on me like I was a juicy burger. She had brown skin and long black hair that was matted with knots and mud in parts. Her injuries seemed an afterthought as she cracked her neck with a sinister smile. "At last," she said as her bugged black eyes fell on me.

11

SWITCHING SIDES

Tanga looked wild, and totally unperturbed by the patches of mud and dried blood caking her dark skin. She was focused on me, but my attention was only set on escaping Crazy Town. I tried to right myself from my hands-and-knees position on the floor to escape, but one of her hands swung down and caught my arm. Her metallic nail attachments sliced deeper than a finger had a right to. I hissed in surprise as blood pooled at the cut and began weeping down my arm.

I snarled, fed up with the fight I didn't understand, but somehow found myself smack in the middle of. I leapt to my feet, returning her slash with a punch to the throat, since she was much taller than me. I straightened while she choked, her eyes widening and then narrowing as she recalculated the threat I was to her. I punched her three more times in rapid succession, not holding back any of my rage. "Back up, you assjack! I don't even know you."

When Tanga was doubled over and in too much pain to fight, Mason positioned himself between Von and me, growling I swear like a dog. I didn't understand why it seemed like he was protecting me from Von, of all people, but I wasn't about to complain. Mason was switching sides, protecting me when he'd just been twisting my spine like a jerk.

Ezra wasted no time wrestling a frenzied Von in the foyer, the two locked in what looked to be an emotionally painful struggle. It seemed Von wanted to lose as the two scrapped and tumbled. When Ezra finally pinned Von to the floor, still somehow flawlessly unruffled, his voice was gentle. "Easy, son. Easy now. It's just a little blood. Breathe through it."

"I think I'm alright," Von said, as if he'd been the one to get cut. "I'm sorry, October!"

"I've got her, Von. Go get some air." Mason inched closer to stand at my side. His hairy arm wound around my stomach and yanked me away from the gasping Tanga, flinging me behind him and smacking my back to the foyer wall.

The filthy bug woman had only just recovered from my punches, but Danny and Von were already wrestling her to the floor, binding her hands with a few zip ties. She seemed happy to let me escape those few feet in the same way hunters get excited talking about Bambi when it gets close to open season. "King Geon sent me for the Omen," she growled, her stomach pinned to the hardwood by Danny and Von, who wouldn't negotiate. "All he wants is her, not anyone else. You'll be spared if you just give her to us!"

Mason spat a thick wad of grossness on her face, making me cringe. "That's how I found Tanga. I heard you were narrowing down on locating the Omen, Ezra, so I came to offer my assistance. Intercepted Tanga on my way here when I learned her plan was to abduct this one," he said with a thumb jerked in my direction. "I think Tanga will make an excellent sacrifice."

Ezra's voice was grim. "King Geon's overstepped before, but never so clearly as this. Sending someone to steal the Omen?" He shook his head in disgust.

"Then let us send a message, Ezra." Von finally regained his composure, standing with Ezra when it seemed Danny had Tanga under control. Von's shoulders tensed slightly in front of the man I could tell he was viciously protective of. Though Mason was burlier, the fire in Von's suddenly malevolent eyes reminded me of the inmates who would smile kindly to lure everyone into a false sense of security, only to slit someone's throat if they took cuts in the chow line. I plastered my shoulders to the wall to distance myself from every freaky brand of psychotic surrounding me.

Von's voice had an edge to it that belied the smile he had in place. "Does King Geon really think so little of

Ezra's security that he'd send you here to take what doesn't belong to him?"

"The Omen belongs to all of us!" Tanga screeched.

Von tsked her like she was a petulant child. "Aw. I almost want to let you escape so you can go back to your almighty blowhard of a king and tell him a sweet little teenager beat you up."

I wanted to correct him and mention that I was actually twenty-two, but now didn't seem the time for semantics.

Von met my eyes and gave me a nod of solidarity that served to center me in the midst of the insanity. I couldn't speak, so I bit down on my lower lip and nodded my compliance in return. I decided that of all the monsters I was surrounded by, the vampire was the least terrifying. *Half-vampire*, I reminded myself.

Danny caught our little exchange of trust, and I could see the wheels of a plan turning in his head. He picked up Tanga's head and slammed it hard to the ground, knocking her out in one fell swoop. "I know how to prove October's an Omen. If I can do that, she can be awakened today, yeah?" he asked Ezra.

Ezra rubbed the back of his neck. "I suppose. But I need more proof than just her bones being harder to break."

Danny rose from his perch atop Tanga and moved past Mason to face me. I was expecting a conversation or something, not his stupid giant muscles slamming me back against the wall in the foyer. I let out a scream when Danny pulled a knife from his belt and pressed it tight to my throat.

"Danny, stop!" Von and Ezra cried in unison.

I expected the tip of the knife to puncture my skin as Von lunged for Danny to get him off of me, but Danny didn't cut me. Instead he reached for a trickle of blood on my arm, dabbing a little on the tip of his finger. "Smell that?" Danny taunted his brother. "You're a sick man, Von. You want to drink her blood, don't you?"

Now Von was trying to get at me, his eyes wild with fight as he tried to push Danny out of the way with his fangs bared. He'd gone from the only one I could kind of trust to ravenous for my blood on a dime.

"Danny, no!" Ezra cried, trying to separate the brothers.

Danny held his red-painted finger out to Von. "How about just a little taste. Tell us if she's part human and part Matruculan. It's better than Mason trying to break another of her bones, yeah?" Danny looked unperturbed at Ezra's shouting, addressing only his brother with a look of faux sympathy. "You've been so good, abstaining as you have. Tell me what she tastes like – pure human? Or a little something extra? We need the confirmation. You'd be doing us a service by just having one little taste."

"No!" I screamed, afraid of the monster I could tell Von didn't want to be. "Von, you don't want to do this!"

Von lost his mind and threw Ezra to the ground with an inhuman roar, popping Danny's finger into his mouth.

No one expected Danny's right hook, least of all Von. Von hit the ground and stayed there, though I knew he could've gotten back up to return the punch. "She's both!" Von choked out. "She's half human and half from Terraway. Definitely Matruculan." He writhed on the ground, fists clenched in his hair as he gnashed his teeth. "How could you do that to me, Danny?" he roared, utterly beside himself. "More! Now that I've tasted her, all I want is more! No, Danny!"

Now Danny's body acted as a shield to keep Von off of me as the vampire leapt to his feet and lunged for more of my blood. I'm pretty sure I screamed as I closed my eyes to brace for the end of it all.

Ezra's arms went around Von, jerking him back. "Son, remember yourself! You don't want to do this!" When that didn't seem to deter Von from reaching for me again with frenzied fingers, Ezra shouted, "There are extra blood bags and honey bottles in the kitchen. Run!" As soon as Von fled the temptation, Ezra whirled on Danny. "Have you no pity for your own brother? He's doing his best, which is a far sight more than you're doing to help matters."

"I don't care what you think. I care that this one's awakened. I care that Mariang gets a break! If Von can help, it's the least he can do."

I felt for Von, who was trying not to be a monster, and despised Danny, who didn't care that he was. I hissed at the sting of the cool blade that returned to my skin. Danny pushed the tip to my jugular, glaring into my eyes that refused to shrink. I would not be small in front of these psychopaths. If they wanted to keep me here, it would be the worst decision of their shortened lives.

This was not my first time being held at knifepoint. It was my tenth, at least. The first time was a teenager who took my backpack on the way to school, the dummy. All I had in there were books and homework. I ended up failing that American History assignment though, and was convinced that "My dog ate my homework" might've held up better than "A knife-wielding thief stole my homework, I swear."

I hadn't cried then, and I wouldn't crack now. Danny was tall and muscular, but I was scrappy. I held his venomous gaze and returned it with one of my own. "Don't move an inch," he seethed.

Mason swore. "Danny, stop!" His burly arm wrapped across Danny's shoulder to cuff his hand over Danny's throat. "If she bleeds, you go down, brother. We need her alive."

"Do it," I dared Danny. "You want to cut me open? Do it, you pansy!"

"Don't tempt me!" Danny's thin lips snarled at me. He had a square-shaped head, and when he was livid, he had a passing resemblance to Frankenstein's monster. I could practically see the bolts in his neck. "You're lucky I actually need you alive, or I'd have handed you over to King Geon for testing. You think you hate Mason and me? Geon's far worse."

Ezra and Mason were shouting for Danny to drop the knife. "Danny, don't! We need her alive! That's the whole point of all of it!"

My back was still aching, but I muscled through the sting, glaring into Danny's blue eyes with just as much hate as he focused on me. "Why are you hesitating? You've got me right where you want me. Do it, you wuss!"

Mason hissed at me, "You're not helping, kid."

Danny released a little of the pressure when Mason's grip tightened around his neck. As Danny's knife pulled away, Mason's arm retracted so Danny could swallow again. I knew I had exactly two seconds before Danny convinced himself my head would look fabulous mounted on his wall. I pulled the cheapest (but most effective) shot and kicked him straight in the groin, ducking to the left just in case he came back for a stab. As he doubled over in throbbing pain, I grabbed the back of his head and slammed it down into the wall above the baseboard, kicking him in the side for being a jackwagon.

Tanga's nails sliced through the zip ties I'd known couldn't hold her for long. She was on her feet and lunging for me, as if I was the one who'd kidnapped her.

"October, run!" Ezra shouted, his knife raised as he readied to defend his home.

Instead of running for the front door, I bolted toward the back of the house into the kitchen, certain I could find an exit somewhere. The flies were everywhere, and Von was heaving in big gulps of air as he sucked on a juice pouch. He paused his drink and motioned me toward the pantry. "Hide in there until we get this all sorted."

I didn't bother arguing, but shut myself inside. I heard shouting that told me the fight wasn't a clear win for us – though really, I was still trying to figure out whose side I was on.

I grabbed what I needed from the pantry in case I was brought back into the fight. It wasn't my best plan, but I'm no Bruce Campbell. Homeboy would've had his boomstick in hand and a five-part plan he'd execute with a roguish smile on his face. I was just trying not to break down into tears.

I pocketed what I needed before the door was flung open, a bloody razor-clad hand reaching in and gripping my arm, slicing deep enough to make me stop thrashing so she didn't hit an artery and cause a real mess. "Finally," she breathed. "King Geon's going to have fun with you now, after all the trouble you've caused me." I could tell she was summoning up gumption or serenity or magic or something ominous to start the next phase of her plan. She opened her mouth, and hundreds of white moths flew out like vomit, encircling us in a cloud of white.

12

BLIND AND BLOODY

I began to understand why animals peed themselves under extreme duress. I was on the verge.

Von attacked from behind her, and Ezra flew in from the foyer. The two pummeled Tanga's tall form to the ground with many manly grunts, pinning her down on her back. Leaping out of the pantry, I ignored the guys' protests for me to stay put and ran toward Tanga's head through the angry flock of moths that exploded on me in little annoying puffs. They seemed to be controlled by her rage, of which she had an endless supply.

Tanga opened her long razor teeth and uttered an ominous, "*Gumising, anak na babae ng kamatayan!*"

I loved the horror movies that had evil spells in them, and she was totally ruining it for me. "Whatever," I murmured as I popped the top off the tub of cayenne pepper I'd stashed in my pocket.

"Get back!" Ezra shouted to me. He tried to stab Tanga without getting pierced himself with her armored nails. She swiped at Ezra's face, gouging him across the jaw. He fell back in shock, holding his chin. "Ah!"

I punched Tanga hard on her nose, doing my part to keep her away from Ezra. I assumed he was the good guy in this situation, though really, it was anyone's guess.

The kitchen was in pandemonium as moths swarmed toward their master, pelting us like tiny dust bullets that exploded all over in a haze of disgusting chaos. They tried to somehow help their master by pissing us off, and darn it, it was working.

"Hold her head down, Von!" I yelled, trying to stay on point even after seven moths flew in my mouth. I spat them out, refusing to freak out until it was all over. I centered myself as much as I could with the mantra Ollie had made me say over and over. *Life is messy, and that's okay.* I knew for sure there were no moths in my bedroom back home, so I forced the germs and the powdery guts from my mind and put myself back in the action. If that one room was clean, then the rest of life could be a little messy, and I could deal. That was the theory, anyway.

The second Von slammed Tanga's other wrist to the linoleum, I dumped half the contents of the bottle out over her black eyes. On instinct, Tanga blinked, just as I'd wanted her to. The powder settled itself into her eyeballs, forcing a terrified scream to erupt from her mouth. I took my opening and dumped the other half of the tub into her mouth, wincing as her razor teeth snapped at me like a shark as she choked the hot spice into her lungs.

Von was sweating, and his hands were having a hard time keeping the witch properly pinned. The moths were pelting us, making me blanch. Tanga was on the defensive for the moment, but I guessed the small advantage I'd bought us would be short-lived, not unlike us if we didn't hold onto our upper hand.

"Here, I can help." I knelt on shaking legs to the bug-littered floor of the kitchen, holding one of Tanga's razor hands down with my knee while I pinched down on a pressure point between her shoulder and her neck. She screamed impossibly louder, and Von shot me an appreciative look.

Despite the confusion and chaos that had stolen my sanity, Von gazed at me like I was something amazing. "Did you just blind her?" Von asked over Tanga's screams.

"Temporarily. I bought you two some time, so sort out your shiz!" I motioned to Ezra, who had blood dripping down his chin.

Ezra's face was awash in horror and regret at seeing me kneeling atop the writhing bug witch's arm on the floor, while Von wrestled the other half of her.

Mason barreled in like a Viking, ready for a whole mess of killing. He clutched a long knife in his hand that was already dripping with thick, red blood. "Move back, girl."

Von groaned. "So much blood!"

Ezra held out his palm to me, his hand steady, though his breathing was not. "October, close your eyes, dear."

"A little too late for that," I chided the grown man. "And if I let her go, she'll come after you, Mason. Do what you gotta do and be done with it!"

"*You* have to do it. I can help you," Mason explained. I let out a pathetic noise of distress when his hand molded mine around his weapon. Mason caught my eye and nodded as he raised the long machete he had clutched in our joined hands. "Thank you for your sacrifice," he said to Tanga in what could only be described as a respectful tone. Then, before I could run through the list of life sentences this would get me in a court of law, we plunged the blade downward into the thrashing woman.

I whimpered, and the sound rang of inexperience. I'd witnessed a great many crapfests in my day, but I'd never held a woman down while a Viking and I stabbed her through. I didn't totally understand why I was helping them. Or maybe I did, but didn't want this to be how it all went down.

The moths swarming around us started flying as if they'd had one too many at the bar. Their drunken flight paths were easy to intercept with a bat of a hand, and many started to flop to the ground in defeat, now that their leader was on her way to her last breath.

Sure enough, the red came bubbling out from Tanga's crusty gown, spilling out onto the floor of the kitchen, staining the linoleum.

That was the tipping point for my whines of distress to mutate into screams of horror.

13

AWAKENING AN OMEN

"*D*anny, phone the Academy! Mason, secure the doors and make sure no one else is coming for her," Ezra commanded as he bolted into the foyer with Danny to handle whatever needed taking care of out there.

Mason ran out of the room, leaving Von and me to hold down Tanga as she bled out, still fighting with unsteady limbs.

Von eyed the thick blood with longing, biting his lower lip through the desire to shed his façade of humanity in front of me to become the beast he was. "Well, do your thing, Lestat! You can drink non-human blood without transitioning, right?" I said to Von, motioning to the thick crimson pool that was toying with his stability.

Von shot me a grateful look and bent down over her torso, opening his mouth wide like he was about the chomp down on a salami sub. I winced at the sound, trying to imagine that he was biting into an apple, and not a person. The gratuitous slurping as he stuck his mouth to her gushing wound and sucked like a nursing baby gave me the creeps. He let loose gluttonous noises that made me want to ralph all over the place.

I watched, my mouth twisted in disgust and horror as Von pulled back, whining, "For all this that she's got spilling all over the place, the only thing I smell is your blood!" He licked his lips, fixated on my smaller injuries. "Your young, healthy blood."

"Stop freaking me out! And FYI, it sounds pervy when you say I'm young and healthy like that." My little gouges were nothing to Tanga's stab wound, but Von eyed my arm with longing. I pointed my finger in his face and leveled my most no-nonsense stare at him. "Don't you even think about it." I tried to reason with the beautiful beast, knowing my threats would do precious little if he decided his willpower wasn't as appealing as the turkey dinner I had swimming around in my veins. My voice changed to a softer pleading, as if talking down a jumper. "You said my blood would get you closer to turning into a full vampire, right? That you don't want to only come out at night? That you don't want to live off of humans?"

Von nodded, looking pitifully at me. "But I want it," he whispered.

I leaned over Tanga and gingerly picked up his wrist, touched his finger to the sticky blood, and then lifted it to paint his lips with the crimson. "Drink this. This is the feast that's on the menu, so knock yourself out."

Von gulped as he nodded, bowing down to indulge in his degradation, his lips suckling like a sweet baby as Tanga tried to fend him off with one of her weighted hands. Though I knew he was a monster, my heart did an upside-down ballerina spin for him, wishing I could do something to help (other than offer myself up). It seemed to be the equivalent of craving a filet mignon, but only being granted a Big Mac. After a few seconds, Von contented himself with the endless supply of Big Macs. I softened when he reached across Tanga, gripping my wrist in desperation to keep himself centered. I could tell that he loathed himself as he drank, and though I understood precious little about the situation at hand, Von needed me to stay with him, strangers though we were.

"I'm sorry. I'm so sorry. I know how this looks. I wasn't always like this," he pled between slurps.

My heart tugged in my chest at his self-loathing. That was an emotion I completely understood. "Hey, I'm not going anywhere. I'm right here," I offered.

Von let out a whine of distress as his hand pressed to the pantry door. "The blood! I can still smell it. You tasted so fresh. Ripe as a peach. I've been so good! This is torture!"

"It'll be alright, Von. Take a breather." I closed my eyes and tried to think of anything else to block out the sounds of Von glugging blood. I wasn't generally a "the sky is falling" kind of girl, but I'd read enough Anne Rice to know a vampire when it licked the blood off a person.

Von lapped audibly, and I cringed. I didn't care for the sound of people sucking soup off their spoons, and it turns out I was even less endeared to the sound when Tanga's blood was the tomato soup.

Mason came into the kitchen and knelt next to Tanga, watching her wan face as she struggled to breathe. He'd been gouged by her long nails on his bicep, and a trickle of red oozed out of him as he came down from the fight. The nurse in me wanted to treat it. I knew Von wanted to help in his own disgusting way.

When Von's gaze fell on me as he pulled up from his dinner, he forced a serene expression into place. He moved around Tanga and knelt next to me across from Mason, his one blue eye and one golden eye staring deep into my hazel to force about a calm neither of us felt. "I need you to try something," he whispered.

Mason sat up straight, his head whipping to Von. "Shouldn't Ezra be here for this?" I could hear Ezra and Danny's mumbled arguments coming from the living room area.

"I thought you came here because you wanted things to change. You know Danny can't be the Reaper for two Omens. If you really do love Danny, you'll see how bad that would be for him. And for Mariang, come to think of it."

Mason checked to make sure Danny and Ezra were

still in the other room. I got the feeling we were about to do something we weren't supposed to. "Do it quickly, then."

Slowly Von reached for my wrist, giving me time to pull away. I considered it, but since he was gentle when he brought my hand to rest atop Tanga's chest, just to the left of the sticky wound, I allowed it for the mere reason that I was curious. He seemed to know what he was doing, while I was still trying to catch up. His voice was quiet when he spoke to me, as if we were about to share in some grand secret. "If you're not an Omen, nothing will happen, and I'll drive you home myself. If you are an Omen, you need to be awakened. Reaping the life of a dying citizen of Terraway is how that's done."

I shot him a look of concern. "All I heard was 'Blah, blah, blah, you can go home after this.'"

Von smirked, ignoring the two men shouting in the next room. Danny and Ezra were really getting into it. "That's spot on." He brought the crown of my head to his chest, his fingers sifting through my disheveled ponytail as if he actually cared that this was a massively confusing day for me.

"I just killed someone," I confessed, my guilt palpable. "I'm a nurse. My job's to heal people, not kill them."

Von shushed me. "Tanga had her own evil plans for you. Now close your eyes and concentrate. Can you feel something cold flowing through her skin?"

"I, um... No. Her body's still warm."

"Keep searching. Find the thing that's cold and try to suck it into your skin. Like inhaling with your hand, yeah?"

"Huh? I don't know how to do that." I wished I didn't have to be in a situation where I had to remind people that I was a real live person, and not a vampire-unicorn-centaur or whatever they were.

Von gripped my ponytail with his sticky, wet hand, making me shudder. I wanted to run for the nearest shower. I let out a choked whimper that had just as much to do with the dying body as it did the blood and germs in my hair. I sucked in my impending tears when Von's calm voice broke through my fear. "Listen, I know this makes no sense, but trust me. This is what you were born to do. Forget that it's impossible. Breathe with your hand. Find the cold and draw it into your palm. If you don't, Mason will just bring another Mambabarang body in here for you to kill."

I had too many words, but none of them were what I wanted to say. I kept my mouth shut and swallowed the bile that rose in me at touching Tanga's filthy robes while she struggled through her last breaths. I gripped Von's bicep with my free hand, silently begging him not to leave when things were so confusing. I did my best to suspend reality and let my heartbeat flow through my hand like a breezy breath in and a breath out. I willed myself to feel anything like what he'd described. I closed my eyes and concentrated, urging whatever cold was in Tanga to come into me. I could feel Mason and Von silently begging me to hurry, to fulfill whatever box they needed checked so I could go home.

Nothing happened at first, but after a few more seconds of ignoring Danny's shouts and Ezra's angry retorts coming in from the living room, I stumbled upon a small reprieve from the confusion. "Huh." My fingers fumbled across her torso as I clutched for the chill. "I think I found it!" I gasped, holding tight to Von's arm with my free one.

"Are you certain?"

"It's happening? It's finally happening?!" Mason moved to my other side. His rough hand was on my shoulder as he watched the weirdness with wide, boyish eyes.

"Brilliant! Now drink it into your palm. Like, will it into your body."

"O-kay?" The slippery cold was like a slow-motion fish, twitching this way and that as it tried to squirm away from me. I tried to be gentle as I coaxed it with silent words, drawing it further into my hand. *Come on, little buddy.* The chilled fish tried to swim away, but my will was stronger, absorbing the cold until it filled my fingers and wrist. "I did it!" I pulled my hand from Tanga, grimacing at the amoebas that were no doubt skittering all over my skin.

Mason gripped my shoulder. "You actually did it?"

Suddenly I felt cold all over. My insides turned to ice, and I shivered at the painful sensation. "Ow!" I shouted, breaking our whispered exchange. "Ow, ow, ow, ow! Oh, something's wrong! Get it out of me!" I yelled, grabbing

Von tighter as the ice began to feel like knives shooting into my belly and spine. My joints grew rigid, and I began to panic. "Help!"

Mason and Von moved my stiff body away from Tanga to sit a few feet from her, staring with trepidation and wonder. I was a popsicle, and I had 007 holding onto one of my arms and a Viking holding onto the other. So, you know, I was pretty well freaking out.

Von was urgent now, his sweetness turning into a sharp command. "Now put the cold into my hand. Like, release it into me. Hurry!"

"I c-can't! It's s-stuck!"

I started to sway, but Mason caught me and put his arm behind me so I could anchor myself using his shoulder. "Do it! Give the soul to him!" Mason cheered me on. "I've never seen an Omen awakened before." He let me lean into his burly side, which was warm when I was freezing. He held onto my free hand, squeezing gently to communicate solidarity. "Von, come closer. Focus, both of you!"

Danny and Ezra ran back into the kitchen, identical looks of horror and astonishment painting their faces as Von took my trembling hand and pressed it to his cheek. "No!" Danny shouted, lunging for me with wide eyes.

The invisible fish finally wriggled toward the exit point without me needing to tell it to. I gasped when I felt it split into two, part of it ricocheting into Mason's hand that held onto mine, while the other half slid into Von by way of his cheek. Mason and Von fell away, writhing in choked agony as Danny tackled me to the floor, knocking the wind from my lungs.

The cold had gone, so I was about fifty-fifty as far as pain versus elation. I felt lighter somehow, and the things that bothered me and taunted me slowly lifted like balloons being untied one by one so they could fly up and tap on the vaulted ceiling. My problems and fears seemed distant, as if there was a glass wall between me and my awful day. Even my OCD seemed placed on a shelf. The world looked different, though I had no idea how or why.

"No! No! Give it here!" Danny demanded from his perch atop me, searching my hands for signs of the phantom chill. When he didn't find it there, he felt all over my body, squeezing too roughly as he searched for the invisible fish. I struggled to catch my breath as I tried to sweep his hands off me, kicking and punching at random to fend him off.

Before I could brace myself, Danny's sweaty lips crashed down on mine in the most confusing kiss of my life (not that there were a ton to choose from). I screamed against him, my hands scrambling to extricate myself from the most unwelcome advance. He pulled away and called out in a mournful wail, "It's not here! Von, no! What did you do?" Both Von and Mason had fallen back and were clutching their chests like they'd just come in first and second place at a marathon.

I sat up and socked Danny across the face. Using my

brief window, I took my advantage and ran for the front door, not caring what lie in wait for me out in the night.

I bolted for my car, ignoring that Terence the Taurus was covered in a thick layer of bug sludge, and was still in need of a spare. The goo was slick and clear with a brown tinge that made me gag – but it would take me home, so I swallowed my scream and clutched the slimy door handle with the sleeve of my ruined hoodie.

A low voice I'd never heard before sent a chill up my spine. "I knew it was you."

I looked up and saw a man covered from head to toe in mud walking toward me from the other side of my car. It was the same man I'd almost hit last week, who'd been standing in the middle of the road with a wolf. He wasn't covered in worms this time, but he was no less forbidding. His black eyes gleamed with defiance in the glow of the porch light. While Tanga had looked beaten and bedraggled, this guy had an upright posture, and though he was covered in mud, he somehow struck me as more upper crust than her. A smear of mud obstructed part of the design of what looked like a geometric facial tattoo on his cheek. I was irate that I couldn't get away from these guys. "I've hit my limit with mud monsters today, dude. Get away from me!"

Ezra's voice was stern as he sidled up on my left. "She's our responsibility, Prince Langgam. She's barely been awakened half a minute. You can report back to King Geon that we're in process. We'll handle any other soldiers he sends for her with the same final blow we dealt Tanga. Any attack on her henceforth will be met with the full force of Terraway. She's under my protection now." When Ezra's hand gripped my shoulder, I whirled on him with a swift left hook and an uppercut that felt right deep down in my soul. He'd tricked Bev, sure, but he'd hoodwinked *me* into thinking he was this great guy, too. I hated being wrong.

"Handle your Omen, or I will!" Prince Langgam threat-ened Ezra, who was shocked I had that much oomph in my punch. "Father sent me to retrieve her, but I'm on your side, Ezra. I know you can do more with her than Father can. Let me help you!"

Danny was on me from behind in the next second, and fear like none other lit me from the inside as I struggled to get him off me. I kicked my leg back to try to knock his shin, but despite his battle wounds, he was just plain stronger than me.

Danny's bicep wrapped around my neck in a choke-hold I was all too familiar with. I'd had to use it on a few patients who attacked me for various (crazy) reasons. I knew I had precious few seconds before I lost conscious-ness, so I made the most of them by plunging my elbow into Danny's stomach to try to dislodge myself from him. "Stop fighting me!" he growled, jerking me away from my car. "Man, you're strong!" His fingers dug into a nerve on my side, purposefully inflicting more pain so I would run out of air faster in the struggle. I hated fighting people who knew what they were doing. I let out a scream I prayed anyone would hear.

I was seeing spots now. I reached up and tried to claw at Danny's eyes, but missed. He was so friggin' tall. Ezra's horrified face was shouting something at me, but I couldn't make it out. The muddy Prince Langgam came into my blurred vision, his brown lips drawn in a tight line of disapproval at my fight.

Then my world faded to black, and I lost all hope of finding my way home.

14

TIED TO A FRIGGIN' CHAIR

I awoke the next day with a pounding headache in a place I'd never been before. I was upright in a sturdy chair. Correction, my wrists and ankles were *tied* to a sturdy chair with plastic zip ties that mocked me with how easily they kept me immobilized. I blinked as I surveyed the space, wondering what my next move should be. I wiggled my arms as best I could to test how much give I had, but it wasn't enough to be of any use.

The windowless concrete room was large and the air was stale, so I guessed I was in a basement. There were a few boxes, a large black safe, and a chair stacked in the corner for storage, but other than that, the long room before me was empty and unadorned. I couldn't see what might lie behind me.

The slashes on my arm were bandaged, and my hoodie was missing. Poor Peewee Herman on my t-shirt was splattered with blood, but at least we were still in this together. Other than that, the blood and the mud from the battle had been wiped away.

I would not cry. Even as my chin quivered, I sucked in any traces of tears, determined that no matter what, I would go down swinging – or more likely, tied to this stupid chair. I recalled shoving loose change in my pocket earlier that morning, and a last ditch idea lit my brain. If I could slide a quarter out of my pocket, maybe I could use the serrated end to file the edge of the tie away. If only I could bend my hand enough. My hips hadn't been secured, so I had at least some grace for motion. I rocked my pelvis forward up off the seat and shifted my hips so I could make a grab for my pocket, but my best gyrating accomplished absolutely nothing. I was about to let out a scream in my frustration, but an unwelcome voice cut through my haze of rage.

"I can't watch this anymore. I didn't expect you to try so hard." Danny walked around from behind, where he'd been lurking in the stairwell that wasn't totally visible to me. I hadn't known a second person was in the room. He stood in front of me, his arms crossed over his chest. He had a bandage on his forearm, and the thin gashes on his face had been treated. He held up a hand to calm me. "Relax, relax. You're only tied down so you don't try to escape again."

I spat in his face in lieu of a verbal response.

Danny wiped the gob of my DNA off his short hair.

"Yeah, that sounded dumb when I said it. What I meant was that we're not going to hurt you. We just need to explain things, and you seem bent on escaping and fighting."

I would not speak. I was being held against my will, so they could make me listen, but they couldn't make me talk.

"Yeah, that was the wrong thing to say, too. We did hurt you, but we didn't mean to. Ezra and Mason were trying to keep you from leaving so you weren't abducted by King Geon's soldiers." He rubbed the back of his neck. "I'm no good at explaining all this, but Mason's in shock and Von's getting reamed by Ezra still, so we're stuck with each other." Danny pulled a chair from the area with the few boxes in the corner and dragged it to sit across from me. He sat back with his hands folded across his toned stomach, his boot crossed over his knee. He took a generous few beats to decide how best to communicate with me, the wild animal. "You're not talking?"

I snarled at him.

"Maybe that's for the best. We're the good guys, despite the whole tying you to a chair thing. We weren't expecting an attack last night. Tanga's a Mambabarang, which is a race of people who live in Terraway. The Mambabarang population is angry with Ezra because they're starving to death. Most of the creatures in Terraway are starving, actually. The suns there are powered by reaped souls, and the useable supply's been dwindling." He scratched his dark, military cut hair, and I wondered when the last time he'd showered was, or how clean anything was in this enormous place.

Danny was waiting for my meltdown, but I wouldn't give it to him. I'd just fought my way through a bug storm and helped incapacitate a monster woman, stabbing her through the chest. Anything was fair game. Oh, and I'd punched my future stepfather in the face, which I'm guessing vented a little of my daddy issues and bought me another couple years before I had to look too closely at that old scab.

Danny fiddled with a string on the hem of his jeans, addressing it instead of me. "You know, I'd untie you if I could trust that you wouldn't run away, but I don't believe you won't bolt again."

My answering glare confirmed that I was a flight risk, but I didn't care. He already knew as much, and I wanted him afraid of setting me loose on them. I wouldn't go out a shrinking violet. I'd worked too hard for that. My job was physical, and holding back only ever got you shanked.

"Let me see if I can explain this all to you without making your head explode." He rubbed his hand over his face. "Ezra oversees the food supplier. That's Mariang. There are seven nations in Terraway, each with its own set of suns. Each nation needs one reaped soul per day to keep the crops growing so its people don't starve. Affects some nations more than others, but that's the rough spot we're in."

I'm not sure what he expected me to say to that, so I said nothing.

"There used to be more Death Omens, but Mariang's the last one. It's hard work, carrying the weight of seven nations on your shoulders, but she's been doing it beautifully." I could tell by the admiration in his words that he was wholly devoted to his girlfriend. Good for him, though she could do better.

"Even so, Ezra's been searching for a second Omen to take some of the burden off his daughter. Working as hard as she does takes its toll. She's been getting weaker in the past couple years, and far worse in the last few months. If she dies, the whole of Terraway goes with her. If she takes a sick day, tens of thousands go hungry. And since they're already stretched thin as far as famine goes, one missed day racks up quite the body count." He waited for me to respond, but honestly, what was I supposed to say to that? "Nothing? You don't have any questions about any of it?"

"Just get on with whatever it is you want from me." *Crap.* I hadn't meant to speak.

He fastened the middle button on his brown cardigan. "You have the genetics to become a Death Omen, just like Mariang is. We've been searching for a long time for someone to lighten her load, to shoulder some of the burden. It's grim, kid."

My nose scrunched. "What the flip do you know about my genetics? Sure, Ezra's engaged to Bev, but that's half the family tree. *I* don't even know the other half. Are you telling me Bev's part Omen?"

Danny was patient – something I didn't think he was capable of. "An Omen happens when a Matruculan from Terraway successfully mates with a human." He used a crude hand gesture to unnecessarily illustrate his point, as if I didn't know what "mating" meant. "Bev's the human in that equation."

My fight left me along with all the blood in my face. "Are you telling me you know who my father is?"

"I don't, but it's no matter. Mason tested your bones. Matruculans have stronger bones, so he was able to tell that you're part Matruculan, like he is. Von tasting your blood confirmed it. Your father was Matruculan, whoever he was."

"Stop!" I cried out, my voice breaking and turning hysterical. "Look, I've been attacked who knows how many times, bathed in bugs, held a woman down while Viking Bob, Lestat and I killed her, and now I'm tied to a chair! A person can only take so much."

Danny's thumb stilled over his abdomen, perplexed that this was the thing that finally pushed me over the edge. I could tell my threat of tears made him uncomfortable. "Alright, alright. It's okay. We don't have to talk about that. We can talk about Prince Langgam, who's upstairs messing about with Ezra. We always suspected he was on the side of the council, but you can never be too certain.

That he showed up last night to help us and not to abduct you solidifies it."

"I don't want to hear about that. Tell me something good. Something not this."

Danny frowned as he thought. "We didn't lose the fight. The charms around the mansion are back up again."

"Try harder. Something *I'll* think is good."

"Um, well, you've now got job security for life. That's pretty great. Mariang's a rare breed. That you're here, and you've already been awakened is a very good thing."

My shoulders slumped as I shot him a look filled with attitude. "Oh, you're hopeless."

"'Rare breed'. You make me sound like a horse," Mariang said as she flitted down into the basement with footsteps lighter than a ballerina's. Her eyes fell on me and she gasped. "Danny, what have you done?" She ran to me, each step a graceful dance. Her translucent skin made her dainty frame seem like it moved through water. She had changed into a simple pale blue dress that made her skin seem that much more opaque. "October, I'm so sorry. Danny, give me your knife!"

Danny stood, but didn't hand over anything that might set me free. "Sorry, but I'm the head of your security, so what I say goes."

Mariang fumed, looking like an angry pixie that might start farting fairy dust. "October's not a danger to me. She's going to be my sister! Let her go!"

Danny pointed to his chair, and though she was still angry, Mariang sat down. "Your almost sister blinded and reaped a Mambabarang, punched your father, your guard, and nearly took Mason down. If you want her untied, help her to calm herself. Explain to her what you are. What she is."

Mariang's thin black eyebrows pushed together as she considered this. "Fine. What do you want to know? What'll help you settle down?"

Blame it on sisterhood, but I actually believed that she wanted to help me. I took a chance and answered her with a question. "Who are you?"

15

OMENS, REAPERS AND
MAMBABARANGS, OH MY!

Mariang nodded, her posture more perfect than a doll's. "I'm a Death Omen. Do you know what that means?"

I shook my head, my mouth dry as sand when I spoke my concern. "Danny just barfed a bunch of words at me that barely make any sense. Start from the beginning. Are you here to kill me?"

She hung her head, saddened at my logical assumption. "Of course not. I don't bring death. It's more like I recognize it. I give death a purpose. I even take a little of the suffering if they're in pain." She soaked in my forlorn expression with a sympathetic tilt to her head. "It's not as bad as it sounds. All I do is find someone living who's close to death. I shake their hand, take the cold soul out of them and feed it to Danny. Much the same as when you fed the energy to Von and Mason. The dying person doesn't even feel it. Then a few hours or so later, they can die peacefully and painlessly with their soul at rest."

"Oh, that's all?" I quipped, for lack of a better response. I guessed nonstop screaming wouldn't be the big girl way to handle all of this, though it was a tempting option. Still, I felt quasi-guilty doling out my attitude onto the girl who'd actually been kind enough to explain things to me. "Sorry, I'm having a hard time wrapping my mind around everything."

Mariang softened. "Not at all. I was raised knowing about Terraway, and when I was awakened, it was a sharp turn for me, as well." Her fingers twiddled slowly in her lap as she pressed onward. "Von said that you helped Tanga pass on."

I nodded slowly. "Von told me to feel around for something cold and suck it into my hand. Then it turned my insides icy."

Mariang shivered, her bony shoulders so dainty, I worried about damage the simple movement might do. "You'll get used to that. Best exchange it quicker next time."

"Next time?" I recoiled, my nose wrinkling. "What are my options? How do I make this be over?"

"You'll stay here," Danny stated, not like a request, but a command.

I shot him a withering glare. "Pass."

Danny's hand cut through the air diagonally across his torso. "That's it. That's your only option."

Mariang waved Danny's bossiness off and cast me a conspiratorial "these stupid boys" look, which endeared me to her a little more. "That's quite impressive that Von and Mason were able to talk you through it, and even more incredible that you were able to pull it off with no training. No one has that ability anymore except for me." She looked down at her thin, fragile hands. "Dad's been waiting for a second Death Omen to come along. He suspected it was you, but we couldn't be sure. That Mason offered Tanga up as a test subject was excellent timing. Unfortunate for her, but I never did care for her temper. All the Mambabarang messengers, really. They're always coming at an issue with weapons blazing instead of solving things with a simple conversation. It's exhausting." She pointed to the ceiling. "Prince Langgam's still here, waiting to see how well you comply. He's a Mambabarang prince. Probably my favorite person in the whole nation of Sakuna. He can actually be reasoned with, unlike his father, King Geon."

My voice was hoarse as I tried to wrap my mind around the fact that I'd just killed someone I didn't even know. "I'm a Death Omen, then?" I felt hollow as dread crashed over me. "I kill people now?"

Mariang's aqua eyes were compassionate as they observed my despair. "You killing Tanga was only so you'd be awakened. You won't have to actually kill anyone after this."

Danny was standing next to Mariang with his feet shoulder-width apart and his arms crossed over his chest. "Terraway depends on these souls being reaped. There are seven nations, so we have to reap at least seven souls a day, plus one if we want things stable for an entire twenty-four hours. That's eight souls a day. It regulates the suns in Terraway, makes their crops grow, and keeps their land fertile. It goes on a chain, and Prince Langgam's nation is the last in line, so when Mariang's short for the day, they're the ones who suffer most. That's why he's here, demanding you start your post immediately."

I shook my head slowly as the too much crashed over my head. "I don't think I can do this, guys. Wherever and whatever Terraway is? It's not my fight."

Danny leaned forward and gripped my knee, squeezing a pressure point. My breath caught in my throat so it didn't birth into an obnoxious scream that would accomplish nothing. "I expect you want to live. This is me being patient. I suggest you not test my limits."

He finally released my knee on Mariang's command. Danny and I scowled at each other, but we said nothing. Mariang's voice was small, but full of conviction and a calm I wished I could feel. "There was no one else for Terraway, so I was brought into the job far too young. I didn't have a proper Puller the moment I awakened, so it took its toll on me." She lifted her arms and frowned at the translucent skin with veins that looked labored and faintly bluish.

"It felt like a cold fish trying to escape," I agreed, making sure we were talking about the same thing. All this noise about souls and Omens was way out of my league. I felt like I was stuck in a science fiction movie with only a map of Hogwarts and a locked wardrobe door to Narnia to get me out. I clutched my metaphorical crystal ball and plunged deeper into the strangeness. "So Tanga was on the edge of death, and the soul inside of her knew it, so it was freaking out and turned cold. Is that right? Then I pulled it out of her and fed it to Von and I guess that Mason guy, and then, what?"

"It's a peaceful death for Tanga, and the soul fuels one of the Terraway nations' suns for one more day."

"But how? How does the soul get from the guys to Terraway?"

Mariang gave me a patient smile, not irritated at all by my curiosity, the gem. "The Pullers are tied to Terraway, so the soul goes directly from them to the suns with no additional effort on their part."

"That's incredible. So Von and Mason can do that now? I'm an Omen?"

Danny threw out his hands in exasperation. "That's what I've been explaining this whole time! But she says the exact same thing, and all of a sudden you're not daft?"

Mariang nodded, ignoring Danny's outburst. "That's right, October. That's why you need a Death Reaper. Danny's my Death Reaper, or my Puller. He's equipped to deal with the corroding soul in ways I'm not. You and I are uniquely equipped to extract the corroding soul, but it's poison to us if it stays in us too long. That's why we need a Reaper to pull it from us. The problem is there's a sea of ready and willing Reapers, but only me as an Omen. And now you, of course, if you choose it."

"*If* she chooses it?" Danny guffawed. "Don't give her the option. We're grasping at our last hope, Mariang. There *is* no other choice."

Mariang addressed only me in her delicate Julie Andrews British accent, her hands folded in her lap. "This job is difficult. Each time I do it, it takes a dreadful toll on me. I very much like you, despite what you must think of us. I wouldn't wish this on anyone. It'll always be your choice to help us or not." Her voice quieted. "But make no mistake, we need you. I *will* die if I keep up at this pace. If I die, Terraway goes with me. That's millions of men, women, children and babies."

I stared at her a few moments, watching her face for tells to be absolutely sure she wasn't pulling my leg. I deflated at her kindness, my shoulders relaxing. "Thank you. Thanks for treating me like a person in this. Now, how come your boys don't look starving? I thought the famine was across the board."

"That's an excellent observation. It is, but Duwendes

aren't technically citizens of Terraway. They live here mostly. They can survive on human food just fine. The rest of Terraway survives on a crop called *buhay*, which needs the sun if it's to grow. Even the Duwendes who live in Terraway don't suffer the same as the others, who starve. Danny, Von and Mason are Duwende. Well, Mason's half-Duwende, half Matruculan."

I jerked my chin in Danny's direction, but directed my question to the only person I would speak to. "How come his skin's not like yours?"

"He's lucky," she answered, and I could hear how forlorn she sounded.

Danny did something I didn't expect. He placed his heavy hand on Mariang's shoulder, giving her a squeeze of solidarity. "There's nothing wrong with your skin," he told her quietly. It might've been sweet if I didn't hate him so much. He glared at me. "You shut up about it. She's lovely how she is. I should ask you why you're so puny."

I bristled, hating it when people remarked on my stature. I'd always been behind on the growth curve. Ollie and Allie had done everything to make sure we'd had enough to eat, but some nights, there just wasn't anything there. Now that I was an adult and could eat when I needed to, I'd earned a healthy amount of muscle and curves. A slam on my body felt like a slam on them and their efforts to keep me healthy, which was one thing I wouldn't stand for. "Shut your blowhole, dude. I clocked you one just fine with my puny arms. Untie me and I'll do it again."

I'm not sure why I thought it was a good idea to taunt Danny, but I quickly remembered why I hated him. The back of his hand flew out and knocked me across the face, snapping my head to the side.

"Danny, no!" Mariang cried as my head bobbed and lolled downward. Sparks went off in my vision as I blinked away the pain that echoed through my face. I tasted blood in my mouth and felt a little dribble onto my lip.

Mariang was on her feet, moving the bear of a man back with her wide eyes and stricken expression. "You can't do that to her! She's going to be my sister!" She pointed to my slumped posture and messy ponytail that was half pulled out of the rubber band from all the chaos. "Apologize to her, Danny! I'm serious! I can't have you fighting with her. This has to work."

Of all the things that left me speechless about that day, Danny actually muttering a grudging, "I'm sorry," was in the top ten of my "most confusing" list. Though he was the one with the muscle, she was clearly the alpha. He was the pit bull who submitted only to the kitten, and even when she purred, he responded to the roar lurking beneath.

Mariang ignored both of our seething and resumed her place in the chair, sitting like a lady amongst wolves. She covered his large mitt with her dainty one and looked up at him with a gentle grace I was sorely lacking. She picked the conversation back up as if there had been no interruption. I could tell the girl had been bred for politics. "Danny won't strike you again. Do you have any questions, October?"

I digested this while something burned in me that I needed to say. "I have to talk to you," I said to Mariang. "But only you. Can you tell your Reaper to give us a minute?"

"Good that you're learning the proper terms." Mariang looked up at Danny, who scoffed.

"Not a chance. Say what you have to. She doesn't do a thing without me."

I fumed at having no space and no privacy. "Fine. Have it your way." I hoped my tone sounded apologetic when I said to Mariang, "Your boyfriend pinned me down and kissed me. Just thought you should know. I socked him for it, but it happened."

Mariang nodded, unsurprised by what I assumed would be a devastating blow. "It was a desperate attempt to suck the soul out of you. He shouldn't have done that, but he wasn't thinking straight. That's how I sometimes feed it to him when he takes the corroded soul from me. In the last day of a human's life, their soul begins to rot, like a quick-acting poison. It's what makes it so cold during that final day. It's dangerous to us Omens if it's in us for a prolonged period of time."

I wasn't sure how to process the whole poison bit, so I put it on a shelf in my mind as I glared up at Danny. "Don't try anything like that again."

Danny addressed me with a similar dose of hatred. "I won't be able to do it now anyway. Von and Mason are your Death Reapers because they got to you first. Von shouldn't've done it, but he did. And Mason assumed he was too old for the soul to go into him at all, otherwise he wouldn't have touched you while you were being awakened." He wiped a hand over his face. "I thought Mason was too old, too. But Von should've known better. I could've handled two Omens, or at least talked you through suppressing the chill yourself until a trained Reaper could be assigned to you. The list of Reapers is a mile long, and Von's not on it."

"Why not? If he can't do it, then how did he?"

Danny clenched his jaw as he spoke. "Oh, he can do it, but he's not supposed to. He was banned from ever being able to serve his post a few years ago. Never graduated from the Academy."

"Is that important, graduating the Academy?"

"I don't know," Danny simpered. "Is having a nursing degree important, or can anybody off the streets do it?"

Mariang waved her hand, as if to excuse Von's expulsion from their wizard school of death-chugging. "Von's impulsive. Got into a bit of trouble when he was younger. He's learned his lesson. He's fine now. A lifetime ban was too harsh. It's why Ezra hired him to work as a secondary guard for the household. Poor dear couldn't find a job otherwise after it all hit the fan with the vampire attack."

"So you started the party without me? You have to know that's a mistake." Von's voice reached me before he did. He descended the stairs, taking in my panic that was laced with anger. "Give me a few minutes with the girl, mates."

Though I loathed Danny, I had been well introduced to the danger Von presented. I swallowed hard and kept my head down, praying he didn't smell fresh blood on me.

16

LESTAT'S CRAVINGS

Mariang stood and moved toward the stairs, but Danny was stubborn as he spoke to his brother. "It's not a good idea for you to be alone with her. She's clearly unstable. Where's Mason? He can handle her if she mouths off again."

Von glanced at the ceiling. "Mason is... dealing with his new life. It was a bit of a surprise that the soul split and went into the two of us. That's never happened before. It's always been one Reaper per Omen." Von was sporting quite a few bruises and scabbed-over lacerations from the fight.

Danny grumbled, "It probably knew you couldn't handle the job, so it took the next available person." He jabbed his finger at me. "You'll calm down and listen to Von, or I'll be back down here to punch you for real."

Von sniffed and then took a good look at my face with a heavy sigh. "Why is she always bleeding? I want some sort of gold medal for making it through this without gorging myself on this little thing's blood."

Mariang rubbed her forehead, mildly exasperated. "Von, please. Attempt to be a gentleman. You'll scare her."

The only thing I despised more than being called little was being referred to as a thing. I fumed silently as I watched the couple disappear up the steps while Von observed me with hesitant eyes.

When the door at the top of the stairs closed, Von studied my lips with too much desire. It would've been sexy if he actually wanted me, and not my blood. He rubbed his forehead to snap himself out of the trance and addressed me directly. "What happened to your face? Why is it red? Is that blood on your lip, November?"

"Your brother's a jag," I explained.

Von moved to a spot a few feet back, and we both breathed a little easier. "I'll cut you loose in a moment. I seem to be... Just a moment."

I cast around the empty basement. "Not for nothing, but you seem like the worst person for me to be alone with right now, and that's some steep competition, what with everyone here bent on messing me up right good."

"I can control myself. I'm not hungry at all," he lied, eyeing my lip. "If I'm to be your Reaper, I have to be able to handle your blood without pouncing." He let out a few deep breaths before he carefully knelt down in front of me, taking out his knife and cutting the tie off my left ankle.

Blood rushed through my left leg in a painful relief. I pursed my lips to keep my whimper behind my teeth, but the muted sound escaped into the air, informing him that my bindings were too tight.

Von was watching my reaction with a genuine look of concern lighting his eyes. He bit his lower lip when his gaze trailed to the thin red trickle I could feel oozing down onto the side of my chin.

"Don't," I warned, though really I couldn't do anything to stop him if he wanted to suck my blood.

Von tore his gaze from the crimson and stared up into the stern warning radiating from my eyes. "You're not afraid of me, are you? You look more angry than anything else."

"Well spotted, dick."

Von looked at me, amusement poking in his dimples. "You know I'm a vampire, yet you're not afraid of me?"

I kept my chin raised defiantly. "You being immortal just means that I get the joy of kicking your butt over and over again if you mess with me."

Von pointed to his mismatched eyes. "I'm still half me, not a full vamp. I'm not immortal. So be careful how hard you kick my arse, tied up as you are." Half a smirk tugged the corner of his mouth upward.

Darn that dimple in his left cheek.

My nose scrunched. "Not immortal? I'm pretty sure

that's against the rules according to Anne Rice, *Twilight* and *Buffy*. You drink blood, so that's normal."

"Yes, I'm a very normal half-vamp. I drink blood, age like anyone else, and do everything in my power not to transition. Vampires are very different than the movies. They're rabid, usually used for sport or attack, roaming around on all fours like a beast. They have no reason, no conscience and no soul. Every ounce of human blood I drink gets me closer to the transition. That's why you can't let me drink your blood."

"Oh, that's why?" I rolled my eyes. "I'm glad you spelled that out for me. I was about to slit my wrists and ask if you had a glass handy."

"You're funny when you're up against the wall."

I shook my head. "What a raw deal. No immortality? No mind control? No super powers?"

"Well, I've got a heightened sense of smell, though that only means I'm constantly aware of the temptation surrounding me just walking out of the mansion." He examined my lower lip again. "And I assume you know that vamps can read minds."

My eyes widened as I tried to scrub out how attractive I found him. My cheeks turned rosy as I looked away in chagrin, my neck shrinking into my shoulders.

Von clapped his hands and laughed. "Oh, that was borderline adorable. I can't read minds. Honestly, this isn't a carnival."

I shot him a scowl. "Silly me."

"Yes, you do seem to be a silly one." He spoke to my lips, so I sucked my lower lip into my mouth, licking the blood off it.

"If you kill me, I'll haunt you right good. You'll wish the worst thing in your life was being a little thirsty every now and then."

"You'll haunt me, eh?" Von's teasing smile brought about the levity both of us needed to make it through this... whatever this was. The meet and greet, I guess.

"Nair in your shampoo, salt in the sugar bowl, destroying all your paintings. The works."

"My, you are an evil little ghoul. Best not pounce yet, then, yeah?" Von reached out from his kneeling position in front of me and touched the blood on my face, hissing at the desire this visibly brought about in him. I could see the debate in his eyes, the torture that being so close to his own personal pecan pie brought him.

There was something ethereal about Von's touch. Though I'd been on a mission to make their lives miserable seconds before, as Von's other hand brushed my cheek, a ripple of tranquility echoed through me, calming my fury.

"Incredible," Von whispered, as if he'd felt the strangeness in our contact, too.

Von's finger hung between us with my blood painting the tip. "That doesn't belong to you," I whispered.

The tension was building until he blinked, and then he

seemed to breathe normally again. He popped his finger into my mouth, and I sucked until I was sure I got all of it off him, laving my tongue around his digit.

I knew the germs were there, but for some reason I didn't feel them crawling inside of me and all over my face when Von touched me. That same wave of acceptance and peace brushed through my body, and my OCD seemed to shrug, as if it couldn't be bothered to throw a fit. Some part of me was perplexed, concerned that my brain was processing things so very differently than it usually did. The other part of me was elated that a well-adjusted life just might be in the cards for me after all. I'd worked so hard to appear normal, but somehow Von's touch brought me to a plane of existence where I could actually *feel* normal, instead of pretending to be so.

"I'm not hungry at all. I'm not hungry at all." Von's eyes rolled back into his head as if in the throes of pleasure that was mingled with a wince from pure torment. He leaned forward on his knees, resting his forehead to mine. "Peaches, you're killing me."

"You're not hungry at all," I reminded him in a gentle whisper. I closed my eyes as his nose brushed from side to side against mine. My mood began to shift when I recalled the various crackheads who had been cold-turkey detoxed prior to being put in the system. They needed a fix, and those with a conscience hated themselves for the need they couldn't control. The hopeless ones had no higher thoughts in sight, but constantly craved and did anything they could to satisfy that desire. Von hated himself for lusting after my blood. As much as I wanted to cling to my anger, I knew there was hope for his redemption because he had a conscience still. "You're alright," I whispered. "I'm not afraid of you. You're not a monster."

Von nodded against me, his eyes closed. "You're only half-right on that." He pulled his head back, feigning ease through his cocaine itch. "Look. You calm down, and I'll undo all these. They look uncomfortable, and I want to let you go."

I was so close to getting him to cut my remaining three limbs loose, but the sound of two whips cracking straightened our spines in unison. Von rose to his feet, his upper lip curled in a snarl. His shoulders tensed and hands raised for a fight. "You have no business here."

A voice that was alternately squeaky and gravelly replied with a sinister, "We's has business wherever wees pleases. Your wardses can't keeps us out."

A second voice added an enraged, "Our king doesn't obeys Topsider ruleses. We heard wordses you might has the new Omen."

I couldn't see who was talking, since they were behind me. I struggled in my chair, panicking anew that a fight might go down with me offered up as a sitting duck sacrifice. Von's hand lowered, his knuckle brushing over my cheek to sweep away a layer of anxiety. "It's alright, love. It's just a couple of pesky Goblins." His voice sharpened when he addressed the two intruders. "It's a wonder your race is still allowed breath. Get out, before Ezra finds you've broken into his home."

One of the Goblins laughed. It was a high-pitched, evil witch cackle that made goosebumps erupt up my arms. "The half-vamps is thinking he's scarings us. Pretty little abominations, he is. Wees should adds his teeth to our collection."

In the next breath, Von lunged across the basement. Try as I might, no matter how far I turned my head, I couldn't see the brawl that went down, or who was winning. I let out a loud scream, hoping someone would hear it and come to Von's aid. I was terrible backup, tied up as I was.

There was a series of punches, someone choking, and then a body that skidded across the concrete floor and landed to my right. I let out a noise of distress until I realized it was a Goblin who was staring up at the ceiling with glazed over eyes, and not Von. The creature was no taller than three feet, had skin like a wrinkly old potato. He had bugged eyes that didn't seem to see me, even though I was close enough to touch. The scuffle went on behind me between Von and the remaining Goblin as the one at my feet blinked, slowly starting to come to.

I struggled with laughable progress, wishing Bruce Campbell could hear my cries for help so he could come down into the mess and save me already. The Goblin on the floor cracked his neck before he took me in with wide eyes. His surprise gave way to a calculating smile that made my blood run cold. "What has we here? All trussed up for me, are yous?"

I didn't dare answer him. I knew nothing I said would help my situation.

With surprising dexterity for someone who'd just been thrown across the basement after being knocked unconscious, the Goblin stood, and then climbed up to sit on my lap like a child, ignoring the scuffle behind us. I expected some kind of attack, helpless as I was, but instead the Goblin rested his head on my chest, sighing contentedly like a toddler. "So softs." He called over my shoulder, "Fergo, you has to come feels theses."

I struggled to knock him off me with my pelvis, but he responded by grabbing hold of my left breast and squeezing, like he was testing the ripeness of a tomato. I'd been groped a decent amount of times, given the job I had, but never by hands so small and greedy. "Ezra!" I wailed, knowing Von had his hands full with Fergo. Bile rose in my throat as the tears welled in my eyes, but I refused to let this be the thing that broke me.

Hard footfalls were already slamming down the steps. It wasn't Ezra, but Mason who answered my cries for help. His look of surprise at the intruders told me the basement had decent sound insulation, but the shock didn't deter his fight. Mason ripped the Goblin off my lap without hesitation, and didn't waste a second asking for explanations. With hands too well-versed in violence, Mason snapped the gropey Goblin's neck, and then threw his limp body against the wall.

Von finally won the fight against Fergo, turning the small body into a tasty beverage.

17

STUCK WITH VON AND MASON

They left me with Danny, of all people, while the cool kids in the know went upstairs to discuss the break-in, and what to do about it while I remained tied to a friggin' chair. "I fixed the hole in the charms that they broke through," Danny offered by way of an apology.

I didn't speak, for fear of tears bursting out of me if I opened my mouth.

"Nothing? You're not talking to me now? I guess that's a relief. Mariang's the one you can talk to about..." He mimed having breasts with his hands, as if that encompassed all the things it meant to be a woman who people felt they could grope just for the heck of it. "You know, lady stuff."

I glowered at him in response.

Danny cleared his throat. "You're holding yourself together pretty well, considering. Mariang was an absolute wreck when one of the Goblins tried that on her a few years ago."

"Not my first pervy rodeo, chief." Danny met my hard gaze, and I tried to keep a level chin up through the emotional wounds I was sure were stamped all over my breasts. I had a small frame and a decent set, which made me a target for men with no self-control. "I hope you made the dude who touched Mariang pay."

Danny nodded, as if in promise to me. "I cut off his hands, and then made him watch while I fed them to a stray dog. Then I killed him."

My mouth dropped open at the unemotional recount of the brutality. "Well, that'll solve it. All I do is get to file a complaint with HR. Not as fun." I don't know why I was confessing the assaults to Danny, of all people. I didn't even tell Ollie about most of them.

"You seem like you could break a few hands that roam where they shouldn't. I'm surprised you bother with the paperwork."

"Well, if I fight back and cause damage, I'm the one who has to patch them up, being the medical professional and all. Then I have to dodge being grabbed at while I'm treating them. Like I said, not as fun as the perks of your job. No HR for you. Lucky duck."

His arms were crossed over his broad chest, and he looked at me with the air of a vow in his firm gaze. "You don't have to worry about stuff like that anymore. I'll be around, and so will Von and Mason. We don't let that sort of thing fly around here."

"You left me tied to this chair, so the Goblin took his advantage and felt me up. That's on you."

Danny paled, but said nothing to defend himself or apologize. In fact, Danny decided against talking altogether after that bitter dose of truth.

It was a thing of mercy when Von finally jogged down the steps however many agonizingly long minutes later, cleaned up from his bloody fight. "Sorry about that, mates. I'm back. Nothing like a good fight to start out the evening."

Danny stood and left without a word to either of us. I couldn't tell if he was upset, or if that was just his way.

"Still sitting down on the job, are you?" Von kidded, and then slapped his knee like he'd made a hilarious joke.

"It's a good thing you're pretty. Help a girl out?"

"Of course." He pulled out his knife, but before he cut me loose, he lowered his voice. "Are you... Are you well?"

I didn't know how to answer that, so I swallowed the lump in my throat as I fought for the truth. "I can't remember the last time that mattered. I'm fine."

"I thought he was knocked out, and then when he got to you, I was wrapped up with Fergo and couldn't help you in time." He knelt down before me, gazing up into my eyes with too much regret and empathy.

"I know. It's really fine. I'm holding it together."

"I can see that." When Von released my right leg from

the tie, I felt blood flow through properly again. I hissed my relief while my head lolled back. I hadn't realized how much it hurt until then.

I expected Von to move to my other bindings. I did not expect him to rub the spot where the tie had bit into my skin. My leg tingled all the way from his fingers on my ankle up to my belly, that same freaky peace calming my anxiety when he stroked my skin. "That feel better?"

"Yeah." I bit down on my lower lip to keep it from trembling, my emotions swinging like a yo-yo on a frayed string. As he looked into my eyes, I felt like I could tell him the truth – that someone here might actually listen. Von was my only shot, so I took it. "I don't like this."

Von gazed up at me with understanding I didn't expect to see burning there. "I get it. So let's take it one step at a time. This was all a little much, yeah?"

"Yeah," I gulped, turning my face away from his. The golden and blue eyes were too earnest. The face was too handsome. I wasn't used to gorgeous men being that close to me or paying me such focused attention, unless I was holding a beer they coveted. "You can start with my other ties, and then tell me how I got here. I mean, from the beginning."

Von tried to hold my gaze, but I found I couldn't look at him for too long. It was like staring into the sun. He had the kind of face that made a girl want to spill all her secrets, and then regret it in the morning. I couldn't live with another regret, so I avoided his blue and gold orbs like the plague, focusing my eyes on my lap and ignoring the heat that came from being watched so closely.

Von broke the tension with the tone of a patient educator. "Ezra's been searching for a long time for you, scouring websites and medical records, hoping for something to turn up so his daughter could rest for a day."

"Well, I've got to hand it to him; he sure fooled me. Not easy to do, so you know, congratulations to Ezra on being a super amazing liar." I couldn't keep the misery of betrayal from my voice.

"I know he must seem a monster to you." Von turned my chin so I was looking into his eyes. The contact gave me that same almost high that erased my need to shirk from the simple touch. When he removed his hand, I quickly glanced downward. It was too intimate – too intense to have eye contact like that. "But we'll all gladly be the monsters if it gives Mariang a fighting chance." Von placed his hand on my knee and shushed me as if he was calming a wild animal. He tried to get me to look at him, but I remained stalwart. "It's been a day, and believe it or not, you'll want us to get along."

"*You* want us to get along. *I* want to leave." Sure, I was being bratty, but I was their captive, so I didn't feel too bad about that.

Von examined my face as he rubbed the grooves on my right ankle left from the zip tie again. "You and I've got a long road ahead of us, yeah? Best not jump ship till you know which ocean you're about to drown in."

"Dude, I've got no idea what you're talking about."

Von's hands were deft and strong, massaging my right calf in ways that made me moan pornographically. When my eyes met his on their way down from rolling into the back of my head, he was smirking at me. Of course I stiffened and kicked out at him to shake his hands off me and knock the smug off his mug. "If you want me to undo your arms, best not kick my best feature." He cut the ties from my arms, and it was as if I could breathe again.

On instinct, my arms moved to cover my breasts, as if that would erase the pervy Goblin's touch. "What happens now?"

Von glanced up to the stairwell behind me when he heard footsteps. "Ah, just in time, Mason. I'm getting to know our new charge."

Mason's thick eyebrows were pushed together as he took in the bindings on my arms. "I thought you'd wait for me before you took her bindings off." He stood next to Von's chair, observing my discomfort as he crossed his arms over his burly chest. He'd taken off his cloak and was dressed in a simple black t-shirt and black cargo pants that were tucked into his sturdy boots. He looked like a military renegade with his dreads pulled back in the leather string.

"You'd rather I leave her tied up longer? She's clearly not a flight risk anymore." Von was settled back in his chair across from me, but his eyes sparked with new life at having made a little progress. He pulled a cigar out of his pocket and took his sweet time lighting the tip, turning it slowly as he watched me sit there and do friggin' nothing. He took a few puffs, and then finally spoke. "I felt her panic. You?"

Mason nodded, his expression grim. "I didn't hear anything, but felt it first. Like something was wrong. I was already coming down to investigate when I heard her scream." Mason actually looked guilty when he spoke to me. "I didn't mean to bond with you." It was odd to see the big, burly man appear a mixture of contrite and upset while he stood at attention before me, like a soldier.

"I get it. How about you let me go home, and when you all need me to mind-meld someone who's on their deathbed, you can hitch a ride and meet me there. I can still keep my job. I can still have my life."

Von let my hope simmer for a few seconds, considering the validity it held. "It takes eight souls per day to power the seven nations of Terraway, and we're painfully behind on that quota. So much so that people are already dying all throughout Terraway. Have been for months now. Some of the nations are quite desperate, actually."

My heart sank. "I'm guessing this job will be more often than the once a year I can stomach dealing with it all?"

"You guess right. It's more than a nine-to-five. Mariang and Danny are at it from seven in the morning until the sun goes down." Von lowered his voice and winked at me. "Then they really go at it."

"That wink better have been Tourette's," I snarled at

his casual address. "You don't know me well enough to wink at me. And I don't care what Mariang and Danny do. It's no business of mine."

Mason gripped the back of Von's chair. "Be professional, Von. This is already a bigger mess than it needed to be. One of us is going to knock you out sooner or later."

Von tsked Mason. "Some best mate you are. Temperamental, as always." He turned his head to me while jerking his thumb toward Mason. "It's the Matruculan temper. Only Ezra's managed to master it." He puffed on his cigar. "Well, Mariang's going to be your sister. Thought you'd want an in on her life."

My hands felt dirty, and I needed to wash them like I needed to get the crap out of there. "Please, like that marriage is happening. Ezra just wanted Bev so he could find a Death Omen. Now that he's got one, he won't go through with the charade."

"You call your mother by her first name?" Mason inquired, tilting his head at me. "I haven't been Topside in a while, but I don't remember your kind doing that."

"You're welcome to call her 'Mama' if that helps you."

Mason stiffened, his upper lip curling. "I've done nothing to earn an attitude from you. It was a simple question."

"Hello! Every second you stood there while I was tied up, you let it happen. When people stand by and do nothing while someone else is in trouble, it makes them just as guilty as the jackweed who tied me here. And you really hurt me upstairs! So yeah, nice as you're trying to be now, you're on their team, not mine."

Mason rubbed the back of his neck. "Oh, right. I forgot about the whole beating on you thing upstairs. I had to be rough to see if you were Matruculan. If you were a regular human, your spine would've snapped."

My mouth dropped open, and I wanted to call down all kinds of murderous wrath upon Mason. "So if Ezra had happened to be wrong about me, you would've paralyzed me, or worse?" I shook my head. "Like I said, you're on their team, not mine."

Von rubbed his palms together as he leaned forward, resting his elbows on his knees. "Ezra didn't have to propose to your mum. He could've just stopped by, asked a few questions, ran the basic litmus tests and been on his merry way. He's tested hundreds of young women who were potential Omens. Didn't flirt with or propose to a single one of their mums. Make no mistake, he's sincere about yours."

My lips were pursed as I contemplated this new information. "What if I say no to being your new poster child for death?"

Von pretended to consider my question. "Lady Mariang would die, and with her, most of Terraway." His voice lowered to a grave tone. "Mariang can't keep up with the workload. She'll die within the year if she doesn't find relief soon, if she even makes it that long."

"Well, I don't want that," I offered lamely. I liked Mariang, despite the chaos that came with her. Of all the people I'd met at Ezra's mansion, she was the one I least wanted to bite it prematurely.

"Indeed. Mariang's falling behind. That means people are dying who aren't at rest. Their soul is corroding inside of them, which makes for a painful death. But forget about the humans. Mambabarangs in Sakuna control insects. If the Mambas starve to death and start dying off, the insect population will die, and your whole ecosystem will pay for it. And that's just Prince Langgam's nation."

"Serious? That's... Wow, that's a lot to process."

"Indeed. No matter how you slice it, you're needed. Whether you stay for us or stay for the humans, I don't care. But unless you want to watch your planet and the people around you slowly wither away in their pain, then you have to step up."

I lowered my head, trying to wrap my mind around it all. "There's no one else?"

Mason closed his eyes. "You're going to be the death of me. This is why. This is why I don't live around other people. Selfish to the last drop."

"Selfish?" I postured. "Wanting to live a normal life without tearing people's souls out of their bodies isn't selfish."

Von scoffed at his friend. "Were you sunshine and roses when she accidentally bonded with you up there? You punched a hole in Ezra's wall! You were positively distraught over having to give up your life for this. It's not selfish to ask if there's a way out of giving up your life for a cause you didn't even know about a week ago. Ease up, Mason. You haven't been around sentient people in a while, and you're coming across like an arse."

Mason exhaled and rubbed the back of his neck, losing a little of his bite. "I guess that was a little harsh."

Von sighed, and it was a weighted sound that made me pause my anger to listen. "Look, like it or not, we're going to be stuck together from morning until night. We have to get along, or we're going to make each other miserable."

I nodded, rubbing my temples to try and put everything in the right order. "How long was I out before? Last thing I remember was Danny putting me in a chokehold in the driveway."

"It's been nearly a day. Duwendes have the ability to shoot peace into people. It's called pulling. Danny pulled a bit too hard when the two of you were having your row out by your car. I'll make sure no one does that to you again so much that you pass out."

"Is that what you were doing when you touched my cheek a little bit ago before the Goblins showed up? You were pulling?"

"I was. It's part of my job, now that I'm your Reaper. Omen work is stressful, so Mason and I will make sure you aren't too worked up. Otherwise Omens burn out all too quickly. All Duwendes can pull like that, but Mason and I are the only ones who can also yank a soul out of you."

Well, that was troubling for many reasons, one of

which being that my OCD meds only stayed in my body for a day, day and a half max. I was surprised I wasn't climbing the walls by now, actually. I wondered if Von's pulling had something to do with calming down my impending crazy.

I glanced around the half of the basement that had been behind me and out of my range of vision. My skin went cold when I saw a square cell in the corner. The tall steel bars and cement floor let me know that I wasn't the first they'd held prisoner. "Why do you have a jail down here?"

Von waved off my concern, puffing on his cigar. "Oh, that's not for you. That's mine. It's for when I get out of sorts, like when delicious peaches come waltzing into the mansion, bleeding all over the place as you are now." Von displayed his cigar to me. "These help. I don't know if it's the oral fixation, or that they relax me, but I'm not going to bite you. I'm eighty percent certain. Seventy if you keep up that bleeding you're so stubbornly fond of doing."

Mason groaned while I narrowed my eyes. "Hilarious. You know, I can feel her anxiety building from here. I'm not sure your jokes are helping much." His large hand swept out in my direction. I hadn't realized he was about to say something and was only gesticulating, so I flinched at the close proximity of a hand flinging out toward me. Mason stopped, taking in my obvious mistrust. "I wasn't going to hit you. Honest." He wiped his hand over his face. "Believe it or not, I'm not the bad guy."

I shot him a dubious glance. "You tried to snap my spine. Spin that abuse-excuse garbage elsewhere."

Instead of arguing his point, Mason surprised me by hanging his head in shame. "You're right. Ezra wasn't pleased with my methods, either. Terraway is desperate, and I'm afraid I've become the heartbeat of my homeland. I should've explained things to you first. It does nothing now, but for what it's worth, I'm sorry I hurt you."

I shot him an appraising look and a nod as I mulled over the apology I hadn't been expecting. "Now *that* I'll accept. Can you keep your Hulk rage under control?"

He seemed confused at my terminology, but understood the spirit of it well enough. "Absolutely, milady. As you command it." He tucked his arms to the small of his back, his feet shoulder-width apart and his chest puffed like a soldier facing his commander.

My eyebrows furrowed at suddenly having a soldier address me like I was someone in charge. I acknowledged his professional address with a wary bob of my head. "Then we can be cool. I can let it go, and we can start over. No more hurting me, and no more tying me to a chair. Those kinds of things should go without saying." I watched them give their consent, relieved we seemed to be making progress.

Though I'd been fighting to get out of the chair, I felt like I needed to remain seated to collect my thoughts and rest my unsteady legs. I pursed my lips as I thought over how to word my next fear. I leaned forward, resting my elbows on my knees. Von mirrored my body language as he waited for me to speak. "Danny, you know, he kissed me when he was trying to suck the life out of me." My face soured. "That sounded bad. You know what I mean." I cast them both a sidelong glance that held too much apprehension in it. "We're not doing that."

Mason looked horrified. I mean, he had to have been a decade older than me. But still, I felt like it needed to be said. "Of course not. You're practically a child."

I glared at Mason. "I'm twenty-two, I'll have you know. What are you, like forty?"

This brought about a miffed look from the Viking. "I'm thirty-one, and much too old to bother with children."

Von's laugh started at his toes and traveled up his quaking body until it birthed from his sculpted lips. He threw his head back and palmed his stomach as he leaned back in the chair. "Oh, I needed that. Thanks. It was getting too serious in here." He winked at me, and I wanted to slug him. "We're going to have some fun. I'll remember you said that when you're begging for a kiss once we get to know each other better."

I mimed barfing on the floor between us. "At least I know you're a happy delusional loon. Much better than the unhappy kind."

"You'll be my work wife. I do what I want when I'm off the clock. You can, too."

"Be my guest. Just keep your STDs on that side of the room, and we'll get along swimmingly." I pointed to his eye with a shaking hand. "And that had better be a seizure, that wink. I thought we talked about that."

Von blew me a kiss, and I wondered if this kind of "charm" served him well in the past. He certainly seemed married to his rakish personality. "Oh yeah, we're going to have some fun."

I heard heavy footsteps behind me descend quickly in our direction, followed by a hoard of flies that made my heart race anew. I stood to make sure no one got any bright ideas about tying me to the chair again.

It was the mud man, still bare-chested and barefooted. "This is taking too long," he bellowed, standing between the two guys and me. Prince Langgam ignored Ezra's shouts of caution. "I knew it would be you. Let's go." Langgam yanked me forward by my arm and put his slimy hand on my forehead.

My skin crawled from head to toe. Stranger germs were the worst. I could feel them eating away at my epidermis. "Get off me!" I shouted, breaking his hold and backing up.

Langgam pointed at me in triumphant accusation. "She has the sagrado stone! My minions saw her touch it."

Von and Mason both gasped and backed away from me, as if whatever stone I was supposed to have made me an instant murderous villain. *So dramatic.*

Langgam jerked me by my arm so I stumbled toward him, and then he wrapped me in a headlock. "You! Which one of you is the Duwende? Which one is her Puller?"

Von stood, chest barreled. "We both are. And I'll thank you not to damage your food supply."

Lang snarled. "That's impossible. She can't have two Reapers. And you're too old, Mason."

"Let me go!" I stomped on his instep, body-checked him and tried a few more tricks, but nothing was working.

Mason lunged for Langgam like the wild man he was, but the mud prince held me tight and reached out to grab Von's arm before he shouted "*Alis na!*" before Mason could pummel him.

I screamed when the floor collapsed beneath me. I disappeared through the concrete with Langgam's hand on my forehead and Von reaching out to me as the two of us were pulled under by the mud man.

18

OCTOBER GRACE, QUEEN OF THE MUD

I landed with an ungraceful thud on squishy mud and immediately began to sink several inches. *Mud.* Mud between my fingers. Mud all over my clothes. Mud seeping into my shoes. Mud covering my open wounds.

Langgam said something to me, but my ears felt filled with cotton, so overwhelming was the state of my shock.

My breath caught in my throat, choking me with terror. All the dirt in the world I'd tried to avoid seemed to have congregated here, and turned itself into mud to bathe me in my own personal hell. "No, no. No, no." I chanted the one word over and over as often as oxygen would permit it. I didn't have to look at myself to know I was rocking back and forth. I couldn't feel my body anymore, but I knew my patterns of destruction. The poor dummy who abducted me didn't know the crazy he'd brought into his world.

My mind was paralyzed in a state of shock I hadn't been confronted with in a while. I'd been doing so well, but half a day off my meds didn't help me fend off the crazy I knew was always waiting to take me over. I couldn't get up. I couldn't feel my face. I couldn't feel anything through my craze of OCD terror.

I'm pretty sure someone was talking to me, but I couldn't process the garbled words and turn them into language.

My body started to melt from its rigid hold when I felt that same warm touch I'd been introduced to in the basement. My chest began to contract again, and I felt the relief of my many issues with dirt and germs taking a full step back so I could breathe. My neck was granted flexibility again, so I craned my head up to find Von checking my arms and legs for a reason why I hadn't picked myself up yet. "V-Von?" I worked out, my voice uncharacteristically tremulous.

"There you are. I was afraid you'd gone batty for a second there. Are you hurt?"

I didn't think so, but I was covered in mud from the waist down. Germs skittered all over my body, infiltrating my pores with who knows what kind of Leprechaun flu.

"I can feel all of this, you know. When I touch you, I can sense your anxiety. This seems to be registering worse than being tied to that chair, yeah? Let me take some of it away, or we'll never make it through this."

"I have to wash my hands!" I fretted, though I was

covered in mud, so really I needed an antibacterial shower of some sort. I wasn't sure if I consented or not, but suddenly Von's filthy hands were touching mine. The squish of the mud between our fingers made my neurosis flare up before he sucked a little of my alarm out. Then finally my shoulders slumped, and I began to see a little more clearly. My chin started trembling, but when Von saw this, I bit down on my lower lip to try and appear mildly put out, instead of as if I was on the brink of a panic attack. Von pulled a little more, and I was able to exhale a few of my demons. "Wow, that's insane. I actually feel a little better. You should bottle that magic. Thank you." I looked down at my ruined jeans in disbelief. *If only Ollie could see me now.* "I'm filthy," I remarked, startled. *I'm filthy, and lucid. That's a first.*

"It's just a spot of bother, nothing more," Von assured me with unswerving kindness in his eyes. "I've been in rows far tougher than this, and I always manage a way out. We'll be alright."

My head whipped around as I tried to catch up and put any measure of sense to being sucked through a concrete floor into... another dimension? An alien planet? I looked around at the rural huts to my right and began to wish for David Duchovny and a roadmap. All I had was that Prince Langgam jag who abducted me, and was staring at me like *I* was being the problem because I wasn't on my feet yet.

Terraway, I guessed.

We were near a village of thatched-roof huts. Prince Langgam was standing a few feet from us, agitated that his captives weren't moving fast enough for his liking.

Von's closed expression showed no signs of playfulness. "Up you get, then. Not to worry; I'll get us out of here." He held tight to my gloppy hand to ensure we endured the alternate universe together. "It's okay. We're just in Sakuna." He hoisted me up, leaving one arm around my waist to support me as my limbs took their sweet time recalling their usefulness. Normally I would shy away from such intrusive and intimate contact, but as I looked around, I knew that I needed something to hold me upright.

The entire vast world was covered with deep mud so that there was nothing green in the rural area that I could see. I looked up and gasped at the duo anomalies hanging low in the sky with horror. Under better circumstances, I would have been enraptured with wonder. *Two suns.* This world had two suns.

It looked to be early evening here, and I wondered what kind of time zone difference we were dealing with. Because, you know, when you get abducted, time zones are the only thing you should be worrying about. I internally shook my head at my scattered brain.

"Do you have the sagrado stone?" Von demanded, his voice turning sharp.

"I don't even know what that is, so I'm guessing that's a big, fat no."

He deflated, his shoulders relaxing. "Figures." He cast a look of loathing at Prince Langgam. "You would've said anything to throw me off my guard, yeah? She doesn't have it. All this was for nothing. The Omens aren't your jurisdiction. You're stepping on Ezra's territory, and he won't take kindly to that. If you're taking her to King Geon, she'll not move another inch."

"Let Ezra punish me, then. I don't care anymore. I can't wait another day for her to get on the job! And of course I'm not taking her to my father. I'm not insane. I want her to actually work."

"Dude, I was unconscious!" I countered, affronted at the slam on my work ethic.

I stumbled in the muck that was seeping into my shoes and polluting my socks. When I looked up, there was an ocean in the far distance that lapped against the muddy shore under the setting suns. Their suns were two slow-burning flames that licked the spheres with white, blue-tipped tongues, making the atmosphere unbearably hot with a thick layer of sticky humidity.

The oxygen was thin – too thin to take a deep breath. It felt like the density of the air atop a mountain. It was oppressively humid, and the air itself was laced with too much heat to feel refreshing when I sucked a heavy drag into my lungs.

There were trees with brown leaves around us, but they were gnarled and bent at odd angles, looping through each other and pushing through the thatched roofs of the huts.

I scratched the backs of my hands, terrified at being taken to a place not of my own choosing. Von kept his arm looped around my hips and clutched my hand with his to stop me from hurting myself. It was... decent of him. Of all the strange things in this new world, that one was up near the top. Despite the kindness, I tugged my hand out of his grip. "I don't do hand-holding."

Von molded my arm around his waist and kept his arm tight around me to hold me close. His head lilted to the side to speak low in my ear. "You're going to break the skin if you keep scratching yourself."

"Oh, right. I'm sorry." My neurosis I'd never managed to get under wraps was now a life or death vulnerability. I clung to Von's belt, wanting this whole thing to just be over already. I tried not to enjoy the strange feeling in my stomach at being tucked into Von's side so intimately.

Von reached into his boot with his free hand and pulled out a knife, like being transported to another dimension was nothing he hadn't prepared for. His voice was filled with edge and bite when he finally spoke. "What was your plan, mate? Abduct your food supplier? How's she going to help the kingdoms down here?"

Langgam turned to us, his black feathery eyebrows furrowed as dozens of flies buzzed around him. "She has to see who she's doing this for. Lady Mariang hasn't seen our

devastation in years. My people are dying while she rests."
He stomped off through the sludge, expecting us to follow.

Von's upper lip curled. "Mariang rests *because* she's dying. You know that. You're just being impatient, taking the new Omen before the rest of the council even have the chance to meet her." He clutched my hip and moved us forward, our shoes sticking in the sloppy mess. Bile rose up in my throat, but before I could vomit out my anxiety, I felt that same slow trickle of Von draining the worry out of me. Von didn't seem to need to focus all that much to help me out, and didn't miss a beat of his argument with Prince Langgam. "You've got mere minutes to return us Topside. You know Ezra will send in soldiers once he's figured out where you've taken us."

"That sounds like a threat," Langgam snarled, casting Von a sidelong glance. "You should know better than that."

"And you should know better than to wage an attack on Ezra's home, steal an Omen and expect everything to turn out fine just because you bloody say so!"

I wanted to voice an opinion as we all trudged forward, but I had no words. I decided to keep my mouth shut and gather information as Langgam spoke. "I'll return you both as soon as this girl understands. Words mean nothing. Seeing is the motivator." He narrowed his eyes when he saw Von's knife still drawn. "You'll put that away, half-vamp. Are you trying to make your life expectancy even shorter?"

"Living just long enough to see you beg for mercy is plenty of time for me."

I winced when seven cockroaches climbed out of Langgam's mouth and skittered down his body into the muck. "Do it. Run me through. You bleed me, my family will see to it you're drawn, quartered, and then hanged just for the fun of it. We'll send the pieces to your family one at a time so they have plenty of opportunity to miss you."

I popped my hand to Langgam's chest, satisfied when he moved back a step. "Quit trying to get in the last threat or the biggest threat. Be nice, or I'll be less than cooperative."

Von squeezed my hand in solidarity. "It's alright, love. Prince Langgam's just jealous. See, if I cut him into pieces and sent them to his family, they wouldn't shed a single tear. Ezra cares for him more than his own father does. And how does he repay Ezra? He abducts his future step-daughter right out of the man's home. Genuine, that one."

Langgam fumed, his fists clenching in anticipation of throwing the first punch. I worried what the outcome might be if the two came to blows. "It's fine, Von. Let's just get this over with."

We made our way to a cluster of huts nearer the shore, pausing when Langgam bent down to snatch up a yellowish shoot growing up out of the mud. He displayed it to me, and then chomped down on it. "This is what we in Terraway survive on. It only grows here, and only if the suns don't scorch it the second it springs up. A few years ago, the *buhay* would grow taller than me. Now we can barely get it to sprout more than a few inches." We passed another small shoot, and Langgam pocketed it, saving it instead of shoving it in his mouth.

When we reached the huts, I waited while Langgam bellowed for the people inside to join him. I gasped when painfully thin, bronze-skinned people trickled out. There was a family with a young child whose ribs were sticking out. Next to them stood a man and his pregnant wife whose hips were too bony to support the added weight of a fetus. A handful of men filtered out, all bare-chested and in filthy shorts to combat the heat. They saw Langgam and bowed on both knees – even the pregnant woman, who needed her husband to support her as she pressed her knobby knees into the muck.

Prince Langgam motioned to the growing crowd that was around thirty people now. "These are some of the citizens of Sakuna. One soul is enough to regulate our suns, giving us enough *buhay* for the day to sustain our whole country. It doesn't take much, but without it, we starve." Langgam put his filthy hand under my chin and jerked it up so my shocked eyes bored into his. "Are you understanding any of this, tiny human?"

I twisted my face from his grimy grip. "Don't touch me."

Langgam's glare was fierce, and seemed almost on par with the heat from the suns. I knew I was supposed to look away and cower, but I didn't. I couldn't. I'd done enough cowering in my childhood. "On your knees, Duwende!" Langgam commanded Von.

Von didn't move, so I stood with him, unsure what I was supposed to be doing. "Don't you dare kneel, October. Your station is above Prince Langgam's. Don't let him make you feel otherwise."

I glared at Langgam. "Wasn't planning on it."

"You should kneel," Langgam growled at Von.

"You should make me. I'm her Reaper, so my station's not quite so lowly anymore."

Langgam snarled at the two of us and turned to his people, who were now forty strong on their knees. "I want you to remember the faces of my people when you want to complain about the toils of your new post. Lives depend on you doing your job." He nodded to the citizens, who looked up at him with the hope one might save for their white knight. He reached into his pocket and pulled out a *buhay* shoot, handing it to the pregnant woman, who took it with a sob of gratitude.

"This is the new Omen?" One of the men asked, his voice gravelly.

"It is. I brought her here to show her the people she'll be saving, and so you all could see the woman you owe your gratitude to."

At this, they bowed their heads to me, bobbing them up and down as they thanked me for work I didn't even fully understand yet. My breathing was already shallow. Filling my lungs was an arduous task with the oppressive heat and the thick air. "No, please don't do that. Get up. Honestly." My fingertips and lips started to tingle, and I knew I couldn't deal with all this much longer. I absolutely refused to pass out in front of the dangerous prince and his subjects. I glared at Langgam for putting me in such an awkward position, trying not to lose my nerve at the flies that began to swarm around him, ready to obey his commands. Bev's trailer had trained me well not to fear bugs, so I let Ollie's constant wisdom of *Keep your chin up, take it slow* hold me in place. "Take us home, Lang."

Lang gritted his teeth at my command. I could tell that my lack of a "please" or "you're the handsomest, strongest prince in the world" grated on Lang (as did the shortening of his name), so I made sure to treat him like an equal even more just to piss him off.

Flies buzzed around us, a few landing in Von's hair. I brushed my filthy fingers through the tousled follicles, softening when Von leaned his head into my muddy palm. I was shocked at my own daring, braving the innumerable germs that crawled around on a person's head just so Von wouldn't be so uncomfortable. I was starting to like this whole pulling thing. It was like I could almost feel Von's unspoken needs more than the foghorn that was my OCD. That kind of clarity felt like a fresh breath, and Lord knows I hadn't breathed in a long time.

Normally I wasn't a big public display kind of girl, but this whole world was turning me upside-down. Von's arm curled around my waist, bringing me tight to his side to ensure we got out of this mess together. Whatever percentage of vampire he was, I could tell he didn't want to be here any more than I did.

When Langgam didn't respond, my tone turned sharp. "Take us home now."

I heard a barking in the distance that I assumed was a dog fighting with its chew toy. When I saw the terrified looks on the people's faces, I knew something was wrong.

"Into your huts!" Langgam cried, his tone laced with a note of worry. "I didn't realize it was that time of evening yet. Hurry!" The people scattered, grateful they were about to escape whatever fate awaited them if they stayed out in the open, you know, like we were.

"The Omen!" cried a little boy who looked no more than five. He was all bones with big eyes, wearing only shorts. "Your majesty, she can hide with us!"

Langgam gave the boy a grateful nod and shooed Von and me off to follow the boy. The animal's barking grew louder, and soon grew into grunts and throaty growls that were too vicious to be playful. Before we reached the hut, I turned and saw Langgam helping the pregnant woman to her hut with her husband. They were only halfway there when the beast in question came into view.

This was no dog. I couldn't tell if it was a hornless, hairless misshapen goat or a large reptilian-crow hybrid. Its forelegs were five times as long as its hind legs. It had giant green, scaly bat wings, goat ears and a long, pointy chin with a bauble of hair hanging from it. The teeth were long and sharp – like if Edward Scissorhands had snaggly, jagged teeth to match his hands. Instead of hooves, he had claws that looked ready to tear off the pregnant lady's head. He sort of looked like a janky miniature dragon – totally precious in his weirdness. He had a rope around his neck with sacks of something hanging from it, banging into his scale-covered chest with every bound.

"Get in the hut!" Lang called to us. I could see genuine fear for the pregnant woman and his people on his face, and knew he was the kind of criminal who regretted the kidnapping and reneged halfway through.

I wasn't totally sure what the plan was. I mean, I'd never seen anything like it. I knew Langgam wouldn't be able to get the woman to her hut in time, so I ran back out toward the open land, ignoring Von and the little boy who warned me to come back. I'm not sure if I was hoping Edward Scissorteeth would eat me instead; all I knew was that I couldn't sit back and watch a pregnant woman get attacked. I snatched a two-foot long stick off the muddy ground and ran at Edward, holding the stick like a bat. I was ready to do some serious damage.

"No! Get back here!" Von shouted from the doorway of the hut.

Bruce Campbell wouldn't have run. My favorite movie star would've faced the demons head on, boomstick in hand. I summoned my inner monster slayer and gritted my teeth against the attack, wishing I had good old Bruce by my side.

Lang turned his head in my direction and gasped, his eyes wide. He abandoned the pregnant woman to her husband and charged toward me – The Rock, albeit the muddy, dirty, slimy version, in slow motion. Lang's voice boomed across the expanse with a panicked, "No!"

19

EDWARD SCISSORTEETH

My heart thudded unevenly as I watched Edward Scissorteeth come charging toward me, his fangs bared. I screamed in my head, but was determined not to let my fear be known. I looked dead into the beast's eyes, trying to communicate that he didn't run this show.

"Don't you dare bite me!" I warned the beast. "You know I don't want to hurt you, boy."

Then something strange happened (as if all of this wasn't odd enough). Just before Edward lunged for me, he stopped short, as if confused. His gurgling bark was vicious at first, letting me know he was pissed I was cramping his homicidal style.

"I'm telling you, if you bite me, it's going to be a short trip to the end of this stick for you. Best calm yourself down, young man."

Edward dropped his growl and sneezed like a puppy several times as he sniffed the air around me. He smelled like rotting hard-boiled eggs, so how he was getting other scents beyond that was a mystery to me. His bat wings wafted the egg stench toward me, making my eyes water and the limited oxygen I could take in even less beneficial.

Edward watched me curiously, circling me as Langgam reached my side in a blind panic. "Get in the hut! Are you so bent on making my life harder that you'll throw yourself to the *sigbin*?"

"Oh, quit worrying about nothing. He's just curious. I didn't even need this stick."

Von sidled up beside me, unsure if he should attack or wait out the strangeness of what I'm assuming was a scary monster to their land. I exhaled a gust of gratitude that Edward stopped before the easy kill.

"Here, puppy. Come on. I won't hurt you." I held out my hand, not totally sure if I'd finally cracked, or if I was onto something. I was used to being the strange one. While the cool kids bought their lunches with money or had moms that loved them enough to pack a brown bag, I had a government stamp that stood out like a red beacon of poverty. In the eighth grade, I'd had exactly one pair of jeans that fit me, and I had to wear them the whole year, ignoring the looks that people give those who never change their clothing. Had someone – anyone – been cool to me, I would've dropped my bite and purred like a kitten. But they scattered. They always scattered in junior high. I was grateful I'd only had one year of high school to endure before I was allowed to take my GED and get the flip out of there.

I kept my hand out to Edward, beckoning him forward. It was obvious he was a wounded outcast who clearly hadn't been taken care of. Langgam put his body between us, growling at the monster who just wanted to sniff me out. "Get down," he ordered Edward, snapping his fingers. "They've been trained to only obey the royal family, and sometimes they can't manage even that. I don't know what luck you seem to have, but the second it runs out, this *sigbin* will attack you. They kill on sight. I don't know what's going on with this one. Defective, I guess."

Von stood next to Langgam to shield me, but the danger didn't seem to be all that harrowing anymore. I knelt down and reached between Langgam's legs, handing the puppy the stick I'd gotten to defend myself with, just so he'd have something to play with. "Here you go, baby."

"Honestly!" Langgam huffed. "Get in the hut!"

"Peach, slowly back away and come with me."

"Do you see him hurting me?" I motioned to Edward, who was playing with the stick like it was a chew toy. "He's a puppy."

"Do you see what's hanging around his neck?" Langgam pointed to the rope collar with the five misshapen, shriveled sacks hanging down from it. "Those are hearts from Sakuna's citizens. There's a curfew here. If anyone's caught outside at this time of evening, the *sigbins* have been instructed to tear out their hearts. It's my brother's way to thin the herd."

"Your brother's a sick jaggoff." I looked behind me and saw the entire village standing in the doorways of their huts with mouths agape. Apparently no one had ever tried being nice to poor Edward. My breath was so shallow now, I feared what might happen if I tried to stand.

Von reached down and placed his hand atop my shoulder. "Careful."

I ignored Von and cooed to the puppy, "You don't want to hurt anyone, do you? No. That mean old brother has you doing things you don't want to do. My brother would never do that to you." I paused before crawling between Von and Langgam, forcing myself to get disgustingly muddy for the good of the people in the huts still gawking at me. "Come here. I won't hurt you."

Langgam's voice was level, but weighted with fear for me. "Lady October, you'll slowly back up and stand behind us. How you haven't been torn to bits yet is beyond me."

"I've always had a thing for dogs. They get me." I reached out and beckoned the creature closer. "Is everyone in their hut yet? Did the pregnant woman make it there?"

Langgam softened, and I could hear a note of wonder in his voice. "They're safe. You're doing this for them? You're risking your life for *my* people?"

"I don't give a smack in the face whose people they are. I won't sit back and do nothing while a pregnant woman gets mauled by an animal who doesn't know any better. Your brother's a sideways jackfish, Lang."

I looked up and saw Von crack half a smile before stuffing it away so he could be on guard in case my puppy decided to eat me.

Edward inched closer, sniffing the ground before he gave in and buried his muzzle in my palm. I would have cringed at the germs if he'd been a person, but I'd always had a pass for animals, not caring how filthy they got. Animal germs had never really bothered me. Plus, you know, I was queen of the mud by this point.

Edward purred like a cat when I ran my hand over his scales, petting him behind his goat ears and smiling through my fear and curiosity.

I stiffened when an arm wrapped around my stomach protectively. The cologne, cigar scent and firm abdomen told me it was Von kneeling in the mud behind me. "Okay, love. It's time to say goodbye to the terrifying monster. Prince Langgam can handle the *sigbin* from here." He tried to pull me back, but Edward compensated and came toward me, craving the contact I could tell he'd been living without.

He was me. I shied away from touch because I didn't understand it. I hadn't been raised with a whole lot of the good kind. Judging by the scars on Edward's face, he hadn't been treated to a Brady Bunch life, either. I wanted that life – the Brady paradise. Five brothers and sisters who never left, two parents who loved me and ate dinner together around the dining table, and a house that never got dirty. Shoot, their lawn didn't even have dirt beneath it. It was too good a dream to be real, and wish as I might, I knew something as perfect as that would never happen for me. So I held Edward, smiling as he snuggled into my lap. He folded down his hind legs so he could lie across me, his head outstretched so I could tickle under his goat's chin. I smoothed the scales that had flecks of blood on them, wishing he'd lived a more peaceful existence with plenty of dog treats.

Langgam and Von were watching with unconcealed fascination as Edward purred in my lap. Von's arm was around my stomach still as he knelt behind me, eyes wide at the *sigbin* who was close enough to touch. I could tell he wanted to reach out, but possessed a healthier fear than I did of the beast. I reached to my right and pulled his free hand forward. With my palm guiding the back of his hand, Von gently stroked Edward's scales, shocked at his daring. "I... I... I can't believe we're doing this! I've only seen *sigbins* in books, or the one time the professor brought one into the Academy to train us on their viciousness." Von's left arm tightened around my waist. "I know I need to get you out of here, but this is incredible. Boston and Bishop won't believe this."

"Who are they?"

"The youngest of us. Twins. Bound for mischief and wrestling with monsters. They'll lose their minds when they hear I got to play with a *sigbin*."

"How come only Lang has bugs on him? Why don't the other people here?"

Von answered without tearing his eyes from the sweet little monster. "Because he's royalty. Royals, important officials and people like that can control bugs, but not everyone. All the citizens of Sakuna used to be able to, but since their sagrado stone was destroyed, some of their magic was lost."

"That's sad." Breath was hard to come by, but I told myself to remain calm. I knew that if I freaked out, Edward would lose his cool. "I can't stay down here much longer," I whispered to Von, not wanting to lose face in front of Lang. Von pressed his cheek to mine to better hear me. The feel of his skin was dangerously addictive. "The air's too thin for me. How are you not feeling this?"

His thumb traced my ribs as his chin hooked onto my shoulder. I could feel his breath on my throat and shivered. "I'm not human, love. I'm Duwende. Let's get out of here, yeah?"

"Yeah, okay. I just... You see how much he loves this, right? He needs me." I sighed, wishing I could play with the puppy a little while longer. I secretly wished I could be held by the beautiful man a little while longer, and blamed my lapse in judgment on the drama of the day. "You want to play fetch, Edward?"

Edward sat up, nuzzling my palm with his snout and snorting at Von. Von nudged the stick toward me, so I picked it up and threw it, grimacing at my weakened throw that only went a few yards. Turns out, oxygen's pretty important. "Ugh. That's embarrassing. I swear, I throw better than that normally."

I watched Edward run after the stick with his janky, disproportioned gait, excited to play instead of kill. People underestimate the importance of play.

Langgam waved off his flabbergasted subjects with a flick of his hand. "Mind the curfew, people. The *sigbin* bows to the Omen, but not to any of you. Keep yourselves locked inside until the curfew lifts." They obeyed immediately, the little boy calling out blessings on me, and his mother shouting out the door tidings of fertility on my womb. I cringed as Von sniggered, pinching my side and earning a jab from my elbow into his gut.

The people didn't seem to despise or totally fear Langgam. I'm guessing he hadn't abducted any of them. With the longing look in a few of the women's eyes, I could tell that they revered him – loved him, even.

I didn't get it.

20

HONEY AND THE HUT

Edward brought me the stick, and I scratched behind his ear. I tossed the toy again, clapping with numbed fingers for Edward when he found it in a matter of seconds.

"Let's go before the *sigbin* changes his mind," Langgam ordered, and then turned to me with a note of wonder in his tone. "Are you really Matruculan?"

"Dude, I've got no idea what that means, but Danny seems to think I am."

Von nodded toward Edward. "It's a creature who can reason with animals. If you were a male, you'd also be able to shapeshift. Your bones are stronger, too. Lots of perks."

"Ah. Of course," I said in all my sage wisdom. "I mean, it's an abused animal. They recognize if you're not there to hurt them." I'd learned it was generally the same with the inmates I worked with.

"I've got one more thing to show you." Langgam turned on his heel and stomped toward the huts.

I muted my internal groan and fought through the pull gravity had on my limbs, forcing a smile at Edward, who whined in concern. My lungs barely constricted as I walked on clumsy legs. I didn't resist Von when he offered his elbow to hold onto. I needed it to stay upright.

Lang led us for two minutes through the mangled forest to a more sizeable hut in a small clearing. The waning suns left little illumination as we entered into the one-room home after him.

I was grateful to not use up my oxygen with the brisk walk anymore. "Sit," I ordered Edward, holding my hand up flat until he obeyed. He tucked his shorter hind legs beneath his body and wagged his mangled long tail behind him. He ground the top of his head into my hip to show me that he loved me. "I love you, too, Edward. Wait here, okay?" Then I dragged my feet into the hut behind Von and shut the door.

"Langgam!" A thinned, older woman shrieked. "Son, what's wrong? Why were you gone so long? Who are... is this the girl? Is this the Omen?" The woman's white hair flowed freely about her shoulders in beautiful, soft waves, cascading forward as she knelt in front of me. I always thought women with white hair were beautiful, and she was no exception. Her brown skin made her hair all the whiter, so that it almost appeared to be glowing.

I leaned heavy on Von again, my oxygen getting too low for comfort. "No, no. Get up. Please!"

Von whispered, "This is what she should do, love. Let her pay you the proper respect."

"I'll not have an old woman on her knees!" I protested, bending down to help her up. I nearly fell myself, but I managed to get us both to stand. "Please don't kneel. I haven't actually done anything worth the fuss."

Her voice was gentle. "Oh, but my Langgam promised to bring hope back to the people, and he brought us you!"

I shook my head, cursing as my knees buckled. My adrenaline ebbed and the muted oxygen inside the hut pressed down on my chest like a weight.

"Whoa! Easy, there." Von caught me before I hit the mud floor and held me upright like a rag doll.

"I have to go back home. I can't breathe down here!"

"Take a break." Von pulled out a chair and lowered me down into it as if I were as fragile as the old woman. My butt was covered in mud and squished on the seat, making me grimace. I felt breakable, and for all his knife-wielding, Von's hands were careful with me. The bark of his voice was a sharp juxtaposition. "Langgam, what's your plan? Suffocate her so your people all die? So *you* die? Do you even have any *baga* root?"

Lang's neck seemed to shrink into his shoulders as he lowered his head in chagrin. "Right. I forgot she was part human."

"Typical Sakuna royalty," Von scoffed. "Take what you

want without researching a thing. Humans die in twenty minutes down here without the *baga* root. She's only lasting longer maybe because she's not a pure human. But you should've been on top of this if you were bent on abducting her."

"Then we have plenty of time. This is important."

"More important than oxygen?" Von asked, irate.

Langgam ignored Von and helped the woman sit in one of the chairs at the small round table. "This is Gerda. She raised me when my father's ways were too one-sided for me to follow." Behind closed doors, Langgam's tensed shoulders and superior tilt to his chin began to relax. He sat down in the sturdy oak chair across the table from me, and Von took the chair to my right, leaning back in it with his arms crossed over his chest in a "try me, punk" kind of way.

I felt like a dummy being the only one in the group who had trouble breathing. Langgam addressed only me, treating Von's seat as if it was empty. "My father is growing desperate. We've run out of food to sustain our people. Sama's offered us rations, but any gift from Sama comes at a heavy price."

"I don't know who the flip Sama is."

Lang reared back, looking up at Von incredulously. "Does she know nothing?"

"Come closer and say that," I dared, though there was no way I could even stand on my own at this point, let alone take on a grown man.

Von snapped his fingers twice. "Moving along."

Lang met my eyes, talking with his hand flat and perpendicular to the table. "The men and women aren't able to work as hard as they need to in the fields or at the mills because they're starving. If things don't change soon, father's going to cut down the weak ones so the food supply's not so diluted."

"You mean like, population control?" I asked, disgusted.

Langgam nodded. "His plan is to start by forcing the pregnant women to swallow the *Patayin* root."

"Are you serious?" Von gasped, and then translated for me. "The *Patayin* root can kill a fetus inside a minute. He's basically forcing all pregnant women to give up their babies."

"Well, that's just going to start an uprising," I ruled, pulling on my knowledge of harsh dictators and their downfalls. I looked around the hut that was basically a wood box. "He can't do that and expect things to get better."

Langgam looked impressed and grateful that he didn't have to spell the inevitable conclusion out for me. "That's right. I've tried reasoning with him, but my brother and sister are louder than I am. It won't stop there, Lady October." He watched my labored breathing and tossed up his hands like he was throwing two Frisbees he was pissed at. "I'm sorry, okay! I forgot humans don't do well down here."

My eyebrow hitched as I tried to maintain some

semblance of control. "Are you raising your voice at me? I don't think you want to do that. Not if you want me cooperative. Honestly. Who taught you politics?"

"I'll make it short. Fetuses are the start. Next will be children under the age of two. Then the prisoners. Then the elderly." He shook his head, his too-large hand resting on Gerda's frail one. "I can't have that. I don't care if you like me or not. I don't care if you don't feel like being an Omen. It's who you are, and Lady Mariang can't sustain the world on her own. You have to help her, or the children die."

I was distraught, my anger melting to confusion as I started to panic. "Don't put this on me! I didn't even know about any of this before yesterday!"

Langgam pounded his fist to the oak table. "You know now! You're the only weapon I have! You and Lady Mariang can save my people in ways that I can't."

Gerda quieted Langgam's fury with a slight lift of her index finger. "Honey, you'll not shout at the poor girl."

It was almost comical that the frail old woman called the forbidding man "honey". I expected him to bellow back something about her insubordination or some flipped-up nonsense, but instead he quieted. "I brought you here so you could see how needed you are – how long we've waited for this, and how many lives depend on you taking up your mantle."

"Okay. I saw it." I gripped the table, the tingling in my fingers traveling up to my wrists. I tried to take in a full breath, but I could only suck down less than half a lung full.

"I'll take you and your Reaper back to Ezra. Just know that soon they'll force the women to give up their children. So whatever learning curve you're hoping for, it doesn't exist."

"Got it. Don't you..." I struggled for breath, staring him down as I slowly suffocated. "Don't you ever abduct... me again... I'll mess you up if you... if you..." My vision started to tunnel, and before I knew it, I was being swept out of my chair and up into Von's lean but muscular arms. For all my fight, I was a toy, limp and wallowing in my humiliation. Bruce Campbell never would've let a man carry him like he was a child.

"Langgam! Take her home this instant, young man. You'll start a war with King Ezra if you bring her back damaged." Gerda was on her feet, cooing over me like I'd seen mothers do on television. She even had a kind smile, like Mrs. Brady. My hazel eyes met her black ones, searching for that maternal loveliness to calm me. They shone with unfettered affection that nearly made me break down in Von's arms. "It's okay, sweetheart. My boy will take you home. Now, mind what you saw here, alright? And don't be afraid of Langgam. He's a good boy. He just gets upset when his people are threatened." She ran her cracked and filthy hands through my hair, and I wanted to plead with her to just get me out of here, but I'd lost my words.

I was beginning to lose my grasp on lucidity when Langgam gripped Von's shoulder and wrapped his other hand under my back to help him support my weight. It was almost a hug, but couldn't have been, since he was such a jerkbutt. Von clutched Langgam's arm so we could all sha-zam out of there together. The sucking sensation pulled my bones upward like the worst kind of Gravitron at the county fair, ripping Mrs. Brady's soothing voice away from me.

21

HOME SWEET NOT-MY-HOUSE

When the stale air of the concrete basement I'd been held in filled my nostrils, I gulped it down like it was the sweetest smell on earth. The sucking sensation threw Von off balance, so he collapsed onto the floor that reformed underneath our feet.

Prince Langgam was ready. His hand underneath me served as a quick tradeoff when Von's knees gave out, shifting me into the muddy arms of the man who'd abducted me for all the right reasons.

I'd not been held much as a child, and certainly never as an adult. Being so high off the ground and positioned like a damsel made me blush with chagrin and temper. I struggled to get down after a few steadying breaths. I heard shouts of "put her down", "let her go", and "what have you done", but I was too weak to extract myself from the strong arms that held me tight. "I returned her just fine," Langgam huffed, setting me down and letting my legs buckle beneath me.

Ezra rushed to my side and helped me to sit up. A hand was rubbing my shoulder while another was bending my head forward between my bent knees to help with my hyperventilation. "Breathe, darling. Just breathe. You're safe here." I wanted all the hands off of me, but they remained in place to support my sagging form. Ezra barked up at Langgam, "The council is starting to assemble upstairs. Make yourself useful; go be diplomatic with them. Get them to calm down and explain that we've found the Omen. I'll deal with you later, when I have the time for a proper debasement."

"She has the sagrado stone," Langgam announced, and Ezra stiffened. "My minions saw her touch it, and she still draws breath. She can end it, Ezra."

Ezra shook his head. "Then perhaps kidnapping our most valuable asset wasn't your best move."

Lang's jaw tightened. "Yes, your majesty."

"Go on, then. I'm afraid if I keep looking at you, I'll... Just go."

I was exhausted and leaned into the arms that radiated safety and warmth, not caring that I ruined Ezra's country club clothing with the mud that coated too much of me. He hugged me, and the kindness was so confusing that I had to cover my mouth to stifle a tearless sob before it escaped. He held me tighter, which almost squeezed a tear right out of me. He smelled like I always imagined a dad would – like sweaters and aftershave. His arms were strong but somehow nonthreatening.

I hated that the second feeling came back into my fingertips, they sought out the shelter Ezra provided. I clung to him. I was afraid of him, sure, but more afraid of someone taking me from him before I could figure out which way was up.

"Told you I'd get us out of there, Peach," Von called from the floor to my left. "Von Vandershot: King of all the Things."

Mason moved to his side and righted his friend, shooting me furtive glances. It was as if Mason wanted to help me, but knew he'd roughed me up too much for me to trust him when I was vulnerable. "Lady October, are you hurt?"

How can you even ask me that? I sucked down my real answer and took a few more breaths before replying with a feeble, "I'm fine. I just want to go home."

"Of course," Ezra crooned, rocking me against him as if I was a child – as if I was *his* child. His voice was soothing, almost like a song of solace that drew me closer to the haven I'd been living for too long without. It was a luxury, and I knew I was being a glutton.

I gently pulled away, grateful I was finally stable enough to sit up without assistance. "I'm getting you all dirty."

Ezra remained beside me on the concrete floor, not

shying away from the muddy mess that my clothes were – the filthy mess that *I* was. "I don't care about the mud. I care about what happened. Where did Prince Langgam take you?"

Von rubbed his temples. "To Sakuna. He wanted to show the new girl what she was working for. He's got a message for her and Mariang and you, I guess," he said to Ezra, finally standing. "King Geon's done waiting. If October doesn't start turning over high numbers soon, they're going to force the pregnant women to eat the *Patayin* root so they all lose their babies. Then if it's still bad, they'll kill all the babies under two. Then the prisoners. Then the elderly. You get the picture. Prince Langgam wanted her to see what was at stake."

Mason was flexing his hands as if to ready himself for a fight in case anyone else showed up to abduct me. "I was caught off my guard. That won't happen again."

I let Ezra pull me up on rubbery legs and leaned on him, despite myself. My voice was quiet as I addressed the men who all wore various shades of the same grave expression. "Look, I'll help however I can, but I'm tapped out for tonight. I'm going home before I have to kill anyone else, take anyone else's soul, or before I get felt up, or abducted again. I can't... This is too much."

Ezra motioned to the stairs. "I insist you rest a bit before you go. There's much to discuss. The heads of the seven nations are assembling upstairs right now. They need to meet you, to know their futures will be secure.

And then there's this matter of the sagrado stone. That needs to be investigated."

"I'm disgusting. I'm not having a sit-down with anyone like this." I had mud up to my hips caking my jeans. Poor Peewee Herman's face was obscured in brown goo on my shirt. "I have to go home and wash up. I'll deal with you all tomorrow."

Ezra shook his head. "I insist you wash up here, if that would make you more comfortable. Von, you clean up, too. Then we can all sit down together and form a plan."

The thought of showering in the stranger's house was unnerving, but so was staining up the perfect interior of Terence the Taurus. "Okay, thanks." My feet were heavy as I moved toward the steps.

I jumped when Von came to my side, wrapping an arm around my waist. He didn't have that playboy bravado this time, but a sincere willingness to help me in my weakened state. I didn't understand why I didn't shove him roughly away, and blamed it on the lack of oxygen impeding higher brain function. "I think I can make it, but thanks."

"I was going to trot upstairs myself. You're merely escorting me. As a matter of fact, I carried you last; it's your turn to hoist me up in your arms."

I blinked up at him, knowing he was helping me to save face. It was sweet. "I'm really fine. Thanks, though. Go figure stuff out with Ezra."

"Alright. Yell if you need anything."

"Will do. And thanks for staying cool down there. You

really did save the day. Von Vandershot: King of all the Things, indeed."

Von softened, sending his smile out to match mine. "Anytime, love."

I swallowed the last of my hesitation to delay showering in a stranger's bathroom and started back up the stairs.

Two. I made it up exactly two more stairs before my knees gave out on me. That's right. I'm a ninja.

Mason and Von ran to help me. I tried to refuse on my newly acquired principle of not accepting assistance from people who dealt in machetes and underworld affairs, but I had little choice in the matter now. The oxygen had been sucked out of me in Sakuna, and my body was still being a wuss about it.

"Easy, now. Let us help you."

"I'm fine. Just clumsy." I tried to army crawl up the steps, but knew that even if I made it all the way up, it would not be enough to save my pride.

Mason's nose crinkled. "What are you... Is it possible anyone's this stubborn?"

This time I didn't resist when Mason reached down and pulled me up. I wanted to, but I didn't have the strength. His arm around my hips supported me while his hand gripping mine guided my path.

"Steady, now," Mason said dubiously as he walked my trembling form up two flights of stairs to a bathroom, where I could lock myself inside.

When I was finally clean enough to breathe without wanting to claw my skin off, I turned the shower off and sighed at the muddied clothing I really didn't have the heart to put back on. A dainty fist knocked on the door as if in answer to my conundrum. "October? October Grace? It's Mariang. I have some clean clothes for you. May I come in?"

"Um, okay. Thanks." I stayed in the shower until she left, though I could tell by her hesitant steps that she wanted to talk to me.

When I was alone again, I stepped out and slipped on a pair of designer jeans with the tags still on in my exact size, underwear still in the package and a fitted green cotton polo that hugged my curves like I was trying to show off, which I wasn't.

I wound my hair up in a messy bun atop my head and slid on the new socks and shoes. My nerves built with every step I took outside of the bathroom door towards the exit. Why did the new clothes fit perfectly? Mariang looked a solid size two, and I was curvier than that. Normally my skin would be crawling at the thought of wearing someone else's clothes, but since they were unworn with the tags on, I saved my freak-out for the big stuff. Like, you know, a man abducting me, my new family tying me to a chair, or the whole soul-reaping extravaganza.

Mariang met me in the hallway and crashed into me with a hug before I could properly brace myself. "We were so worried! We didn't know where he'd taken you! Are you alright? Dad's been yelling at Prince Langgam ever since you got back." She released me just as I was about to hyperventilate at the close contact. "They're all in the conference room. It's one of the few areas the bugs didn't get to during the fight." She didn't need me to comply; she walked knowing that I would follow. For such a dainty person, she possessed a whole lot of power. Before we went into the first floor room that was shut with overlarge double doors, Mariang turned toward me. "I generally bow out of council meetings, but if you need, I'll come in with you."

"What is 'the council'?"

Mariang licked her lips in thought, remembering I knew next to nothing about their world. "It's the rulers of the seven nations, or their delegates, plus other officials who speak for their respective races. They don't care for women sitting at the table, so even though Omens are technically part of the council, I don't attend many meetings. Not everyone gets along. It can be stressful when they start arguing for hours."

"Hours? Oh, jeez. Okay. Thanks for the heads up."

I replayed Ollie's advice to me that had seen me through many an uncertain moment where I'd gotten in over my head. *Keep your head up. Take it slow.*

22

A COUNCIL OF CHILDREN

We were met with cautious eyes, and a quiet hush that fell over the room when we entered. For all the weirdness I'd been introduced to that day, I let out a yelp of shock when I saw the company that stood at our entrance.

Ezra, Danny, Von, Langgam and Mason were there, but there were others who terrified me to my very soul. I tried not to let my nerves show beyond widened eyes and my slight intake of breath, but inside I spluttered a constant stream of *holy crap, holy crap*. Any chance at writing this whole Terraway thing off as a bad dream was obliterated as I took in the members of the council. Sitting at the foot of the table was a creature with the body of a totally ripped man and the head of a horse. No kidding, a horse. And not the majestic Black Beauty kind. This dude had a pure black head with no spots, and a light brown toned body.

His midnight-colored mane was long, and had three thick braids woven through the tresses. He stared at me with his angry black eyes that conveyed emotion like a human. It was the same reverse centaur from the painting in the foyer I'd seen when I'd first walked into the mansion. He'd had a sword in the painting. Judging by this one's scowl, I guessed he wasn't the type to relish sitting in a conference room.

Ezra took the lead, introducing me to each member, starting to his left with the horse guy, and moving clockwise around the long conference table. "Lady October, it's my pleasure to introduce King Kabayo. He rules over Silo, which is where the Tikbalangs reside."

"Hey, man," I offered lamely, feeling like a kid who totally didn't belong at the magical grownup table.

Kabayo snarled, daring me to say something he could cling to as a social faux pas. Given that I had no knowledge of their societal rituals, I swallowed my distress and kept my mouth shut tight, lest I offend him and get... I don't know, whinnied to death or something.

Ezra moved down the line, looking pleased that I hadn't had my head bitten clean off by the horse dude. "This is Queen Sylvia. She's the newly instated ruler of Lumipad. She's a Manas, or a Manananggal."

When no one bothered to explain what the crap a Manas was, I guessed perhaps maybe that was their word for woman, since she was the only other one in attendance. Sylvia was curvy, and clad in a short brown leather dress with frayed edges. She wore tall black combat boots that looked to split the difference between decorative and meaning business. She had pale skin and frizzy red hair pulled back into a high ponytail. When she bowed her head to me in greeting, I jumped when leathery black bat wings unfolded from behind her, draping out from her shoulder blades.

Okay, Manas isn't their word for woman, it's whatever Batgirl Sylvia is. Her chin and forehead jutted out unnaturally, so when she turned to yell at Ezra, her profile almost looked like a half-moon. "I thought you said the Omen was of age. This is a child, Ezra. Children can't be awakened."

I stood straighter, frowning. I didn't even know these people, and already I was being given the label of a useless child. I glanced down at myself, wondering not for the first time what it was about me that screamed fifteen-year-old kid.

Ezra was patient. "Lady October is twenty-two, and has already been awakened. She's well suited to serve out the role of an Omen."

Sylvia wore a tight-lipped expression while she sized me up to see if I'd be an asset or a liability.

Back atcha, girlfriend.

They were all pretty tall, except for a stooped old man with a face like an old yellow potato. *Goblin*, I thought with a grumble. His sparse white hair was slicked back into a ponytail, and his long matching beard was tied similarly below his chin. He had a hump in his back and pointy ears, looking sort of like an old, evil Christmas elf. He eyed me with superior skepticism, as if daring me to be as useless as he'd been predicting. When he opened his mouth, I saw he had no teeth at all. "She's a humanses. I can smells it on her. There's no way she's ones of us."

Ezra stood at attention at the head of the solid wood oval-shaped table. He'd changed into a crisp white dress shirt and navy trousers. His pale lavender and blue striped tie set off his aqua eyes. Ezra possessed the stylishness of a fashionmonger, mixed with the effortless perfection of a man who couldn't have cared less about such things. The combination coupled with his perfect posture made him look positively regal. "Lady October's half Matruculan, and she has already been awakened. So whatever disparaging remarks you have to say about her abilities or my judgment, you can save them for another day, Titus. That you've been invited here to meet her is a courtesy I did not have to extend. I owe the Goblins nothing, especially after two of your kin attacked her earlier this evening."

The old Christmas Elf, er Goblin, shook his gnarled fist in the air. I half expected Titus to threaten to bring Ezra coal for his stocking. "You owes the Goblins the same you owes everyone else who's heres! Just because we aren't starving yets doesn't meanses we like watching the nations dies around us."

My eyes drifted to a military-looking man as Titus and Ezra went back and forth. Judging by the rigid way he stood and the expressionless observation of me, I guessed he was one of those who were always calculating a take-down when he met a new person. He had short, sand-colored hair and trimmed sideburns that framed his classically handsome face. I inhaled sharply when I noticed what could only be described as gills along both sides of his throat, stretching into his black no-frills t-shirt. He nodded to acknowledge me, and I returned the gesture. "Captain Finn Fredo," he said, not ceasing his careful study of me, as if I was the one with the freakishly cool gills. I maintained my stance of not speaking, lest I open my mouth and start a scream that might never stop. Or maybe I'd make a fool of myself by asking if I could poke at his gills to see what they felt like. My crazy-o-meter was a little hard to predict at this point.

For some reason, I felt a tug in my chest that led my head to snap towards Von. Though he appeared silent and professional, I could tell by his narrowed eyes and flared nostrils that he despised Captain Finn on a level that went deeper than "He stole my bike." There was a baser soul-level hatred that I was surprised I could read so easily. I wondered if I could feel his swings because of our Omen-Reaper connection.

I'd never seen a half-horse, half-man in an office setting. Nor had I seen a batgirl with a crescent moon-shaped face, or a soldier with gills. The solid wood floor and the beige walls with the obligatory fichus in the corner made the surreal creatures stand out all the more in their total weirdness.

Lang's flies buzzed in an irritated circle around his head. "We don't have all night for this, Ezra. Let's get started."

Von led me to the nearest chair and sat me down, standing behind me like a guard beside Mason. He had a raised tilt to his chin that dared the others to cast us out from the cool kids meeting he was finally allowed a place at. Though, to be fair, Danny and Von weren't given chairs. They were made to stand, making it clear that they weren't to have a say in things. I didn't love that I'd been given a chair so easily, when I couldn't even name three restaurants in Terraway.

Ezra held up his hands to the others, who quieted as they sat. "Your family's throne isn't represented today, so Mason, would you do the honors and sit in your brother's place to speak for the Hayop nation?"

"I see the nation of Sombi still isn't represented." Mason glared at Ezra, his full lips pursed through his half-inch thick beard. "I gave up my claim to the Hayop throne years ago. Call my brother. Surely he can spare half an hour to shake hands with the new Omen."

"King Carter didn't answer my summons. If you would." Ezra motioned to the empty spot beside Kabayo. When Mason sat down, the horse snorted derisively like a snotty junior higher.

I didn't have amazingly high hopes for the council, since they all seemed to be a little antagonistic.

Ezra was the only one standing. Mariang had entered

silently to take her spot during the introductions. She dragged her chair to sit against the wall with the grace of a delegate bred for keeping her cool in heated political situations. It was as if she was making a point of not joining the table. She would cooperate, but wouldn't participate in such poorly veiled aggression. Danny stood beside her chair, his hand on her shoulder like a sentry.

There was too much don't-you-dare-look-at-me-wrong tension, and I hoped these delightful little meetings wouldn't be a daily thing.

Ezra held up his hands, quieting the murmuring. "I've called you here today to introduce you to the new Omen. She was awakened only yesterday, and I summoned you all first thing. After a few days of adjusting and learning what's expected of her, I fully anticipate things turning around for each of your kingdoms."

Lang stood, pressing his hand to the table to control the meeting. He leaned forward in frustration that Ezra was beginning with the part he already knew. "My minions saw her just yesterday morning with the lost sagrado stone!"

This was apparently a huge deal. Chatter broke out among the ranks, along with gasps and more questions Ezra didn't have an answer to. Captain Finn stood when the horse dude pounded his fist on the table, demanding I get it first thing and "lay it at his feet." *Jag.*

I quirked my eyebrow, not bothering to stand. Ollie's constant wisdom echoed in my ear. *Keep your chin up. Take it slow.* It was good advice to have in a room filled with too many hot heads. "Kabayo, is it? I'd like to know who you think you're talking to. I'm not laying anything at anyone's feet, and you'll calm yourself down about it. There's no use ordering me around like a fool. You don't even know me."

Kabayo's massive nostrils widened as he straightened at my level-toned scolding. "If you knew the king I am, you wouldn't dare speak so boldly."

I waved my hand dismissively, as if his fit throwing was boring to me. "I know enough. Now be a good puppy and sit when you're told. Ezra was talking, not you." I cast Ezra a slight bow of my chin to communicate I was on his side.

Captain Finn's mouth dropped open in amusement, and I saw a flicker of a laugh in Lang's dark eyes. *Whatever.* If Kabayo wanted me to know he was a threat, I had to establish right off the bat that I wouldn't be threatened.

"I've hanged men for less!" Kabayo was tall, brawny and clearly pissed, but aside from the horse head and magical land aspect, I'd met hundreds of him. Entitled men who couldn't be bothered to shut up and play nice. He had to be in charge, but I never had the patience to coddle that kind of attitude when there was actual work to be done.

I tilted my head up at his anger, knowing I'd won, since he had the flaring temper of a child. I crossed my arms over my chest and let a breezy I-friggin'-dare-you smile brush across my lips. "Hanged, eh? Well, that settles it; you're the scariest little pony I've ever seen."

Ezra turned to me after holding up his hands to quiet the room that had quickly devolved into chaos. "Is this true, Lady October? Do you have the sagrado stone?"

Ezra's formal address threw me.

"Um, could someone show me a picture of whatever it is you're looking for? If you're thinking I have some magic rock or something, I'm not aware of it." I kept my chin level, refusing to be intimidated by the seething I could feel coming at me from Kabayo. He was easily seven feet tall and looked like one wrong move from me might make him snap. Not that I'd done anything but, you know, show up and sit down at the table. *The tool.* "I'll look through my stuff when I get home if you can tell me what I'm searching for."

"I can do that." Ezra nodded. "If she does have the stone, then that changes things. We'll need at least a week or two of her Topside, helping Mariang catch up on reaping more souls before she goes under to the different regions."

Finn leaned forward, his knuckles on the table. "Do you understand what this would mean? If she could bring the lost sagrado stone back to the people, we wouldn't need to rely so heavily on the Omens." Excitement lightened Finn's bright green eyes as he sat back in his chair in thought. "This could change everything. What do you need from us? What are you thinking?" He scratched at his flesh-colored gills that appeared soft and flexible. I stared at the oddity with probably impolite fascination.

I had a civilized answer all ready, but when my mouth opened, "You've got gills," popped out. I winced, closed my eyes and hung my head, wishing I could bang my cranium against the table. I could feel the upper hand slipping through my fingers as Mason chuckled under his breath.

Finn narrowed one eye at me, and I could see clearly in that small glimpse that his good looks were just for show. Dude was a killer with very little conscience. I'd seen the same coldness in a good many inmates. His voice lowered as he stared at me with the same size-up I'd fixed Kabayo with. "Yes, and you've got legs."

I looked down, not noticing anything weird about my legs, or his. "That better have been a compliment."

The corners of Finn's full lips curved upward in a sardonic impression of a genuine smile. "Oh, it was."

Out of the corner of my eye, I saw Von stiffen and snarl with distaste. "Captain Finn is second in command of Dagat under King Banak." Von pulled a cigar and lighter out of his pocket, turning the end to evenly heat the tip. "He couldn't get his hands on a good pair of legs unless his king commanded him to."

Finn narrowed his eyes at Von, seeming to weigh some option with which to dismantle Von's perpetual smugness.

Sylvia frowned, her bat wings drooping in time with the corners of her lips. "Could you smoke that thing somewhere else? It's close quarters in here, Duwende."

Von let out a long puff of smoke, unperturbed. "I'm afraid not. See, I'm her Reaper, so I need to be in this meeting. This here cigar keeps me from vamping out and biting all of you."

Sylvia scoffed, looking down her nose at Von like he was scum. "You couldn't turn us. You're no threat. You're only a half-vamp. Almost useful for sport, but not quite. One little trip to Lumipad, and my people would see you turned to your full bestial potential in an hour. You wouldn't be so smug crawling around on all fours like a dog."

"Hey, watch it," I warned her, throwing sisterhood out the door sooner than I'd hoped.

Von touched his tongue to his canine tooth that was slightly longer than his others. "Turn you, Queen Sylvia? Why would I want to do that? No, no. I'd simply lose control and kill you. Can't have the Queen of Lumipad dying in Ezra's house, can we? At least not with so many witnesses roaming about."

Ezra shot Von a look of deep displeasure. "You'll keep your veiled threats contained, son. Have a seat, Queen Sylvia."

The old hunched Goblin redirected the conversation, adding in a snide, "But who should be granted a pieces of the stone? Surely not the Lumipads. They're always in the middles of some uprisings. I barely gets to know the new rulers' nameses anymore, the turnover's so fast." Titus' beady eyes gleamed with greed. "I should get the stone firsts. Goblins have the most magics to protect."

Mason stiffened. "You don't make the rules, old man.

Ezra's in charge, so you'll defer to him and not make things difficult. I live in Sombi, and it matters if it's abandoned to ruin. You live in the dead of heat with the rest of Terraway, but Sombi's turned into a frozen wasteland. It's nearly impossible to get through it if you don't know what you're doing."

"Why should I cares where you lives? What are yous to me? You abandoned your peoples to go hides out in Sombi. Deserters to their thrones mean nothing to me. It's a disgraces you're permitted to sits at the table with us in your brother's stead."

Something in me I didn't recognize stirred protectively when Sylvia had laid into Von, and that same indignation rose up when Titus was snotty to Mason. I didn't understand all the lingo, but I knew a blowhole when I saw one. I pointed my finger at the old Keebler Elf as my upper lip curled in disgust. "You'll watch your mouth, boy. If Ezra wants Mason at this table, you'll accept it, or you can go on back to Hobbitville for all I care."

Finn let out a snigger that he fought unsuccessfully to conceal, shooting me an appreciative look I ignored.

"Boy?" the Goblin guffawed, his overlong lips opening wider than should be possible. "You dares tell me how to speaks to a deserter?"

Mason did not defend himself, but sat back in his chair and took it with what was almost a bored expression. "She can dare tell you whatever she'd like. You're nothing without her and Lady Mariang." Mason narrowed his eyes at Titus and leaned forward to verbally jab at the old Goblin. "I know what kind of a power-hungry, arrogant king you are. I know you tied yourself to your people using the *tahi* charm."

Mariang gasped, but apparently everyone who regularly showed up for council meetings already knew that. I raised my hand. "What the crap is a *tahi* charm?"

Mason's eyes flicked over to me. "It's a binding charm. He blessed himself so that his life is tied to his people. If he eats, all the Goblins are full."

"Oh, well why doesn't every ruler do that then? I mean, if there's a famine and all."

Ezra was patient. "The downside is that if Titus is killed before he can remove the charm, the entire Goblin race dies with him in an instant. It's a very dangerous risk, but in the end, each ruler is free to reign how he or she sees fit."

Titus turned to me and snarled like I was an annoying bug he had to pay respect to. "That's why we should gets a pieces of the stone first. I want to lifts the *tahi* charm so my peoples aren't so at risk of sudden deaths."

I saw Mariang's chest move up and down like she was having trouble breathing properly. Her head began to sway as her body started losing its grip on the perfect posture she'd been maintaining up until that point. Her eyelids were drooping, and she looked utterly exhausted. I felt for the poor girl.

Langgam held up his finger. "The sagrado stone should

be brought to my land first. We're the first ones to suffer when famine strikes. We've lost the most lives, and need the most immediate aid."

Kabayo tossed out his large arm with an accompanying snort of derision. "Are you saying the rest of us haven't watched our *buhay* crops dry up? We haven't seen our people up and die? You're just as entitled as your father. King Geon's never once shown up to a council meeting. Sends you instead. And you know? Shame on me for actually believing you might be different."

"Entitled? Is that how you see me standing up for my people who are at death's door? You know the famine hits us the hardest."

"I know you whine about it the loudest."

Those were fighting words, and Danny and I both recognized the danger brewing when Langgam stood abruptly, knocking his chair back to confront Kabayo. They were on level playing field, as far as musculature went. The tempers were big, swinging like a pendulum, and that was dangerous. If Mariang was really as valuable as everyone said, it wasn't wise to keep her in the room with such volatile people.

I stood and cupped Mariang's elbow, using it to guide her out of her chair. "You're getting out of here," I mumbled, grateful Danny seemed to be on the same page. He took her other arm, and the three of us darted out the door. Mariang's arm was thin, and the nearly translucent skin felt too breakable to be real. I helped Danny walk her up the stairs, perplexed at how light she was and how stiff her movements were. It felt like moving an elderly woman.

"She'll be alright," Danny assured me quietly. "That's how they always get when there's a council meeting called. It's why she usually stays away from them. She doesn't need the excitement, especially if we're going to be training you tomorrow. Just help me get her to her room, yeah?"

"No problem."

Mariang leaned on me. "I'm sorry I'm making you help me. I know you're still on the fence about all this. It's just not good for me to be going all evening."

"You don't need to explain yourself to her," Danny snapped, directing a scowl at me, as if I'd demanded anything of the girl. "It's okay to be tired at eight o'clock at night."

"Still, this isn't what she was expecting. I'd hoped to look stronger to her, and not tip my hand so soon." She cast me a look laced with shame at her feeble body. "I didn't used to be like this."

"It's alright, Mariang. Danny's right; it's late. I was thinking of turning in myself." I helped her turn the corner when we reached the top of the stairs, making sure we didn't go too fast for her. Dread passed over me as I pictured myself in her same weakened state, wondering if Terraway would similarly someday suck the life out of me.

23

THE SOFTER SIDE OF DANNY

Mariang's room had two peach walls and two cream ones, with gold curtains, frames and decorations that bespoke the talents of a pricey interior decorator. Her room was more than twice the size of mine, but it came with the sounds of bickering mythological creatures echoing up from the ground floor through the vents, so that was a definite drawback.

I helped Mariang to her king-sized bed with peach sheets and a cream comforter. The mattress was so soft and large that she looked like she was floating on a sea of sherbet. I couldn't imagine the luxury of sleeping on such a cloud.

"Can you take her shoes off?" Danny asked, pulling back the cover and situating the pillows for her.

I slid off the white ballet flats and peeled off her socks, donning my nurse demeanor so I could muscle past my

OCD and feel her feet. I was a full day off my medication, but Von had been sneaking small touches that shed layers of my neurosis, so I was better at dealing than I'd expected myself to be. "Her feet are ice cold, Danny. Her circulation's not what it should be."

"Yeah, I don't know what to do about that, other than make sure she gets more rest. I can't exactly take her to a doctor. The healers in Terraway haven't done the other Omens before her any favors."

"What kind of medicine do they practice?"

"The kind that gets the most output from the Omen, no matter what the cost. I'll put it to you this way: there were three Omens a few years ago. Two of them died, and the other won't last the year if she keeps up at the rate she's going."

"I'm alright, Danny," Mariang insisted, though her voice was fragile, like very thin glass. "I'm just a little tired, is all."

Danny nodded, though I could tell he was unhappy with how the night was turning out for her. He pulled a sweater out of the dresser drawer and some cream-colored soft pajama pants. "Will this help?" he asked us both.

Mariang nodded and shrugged, not caring what she fell asleep in. I moved to the dresser and guessed at which drawer held socks. "She needs thick socks with no band on them to help keep her feet warm while she sleeps. Are her hands cold?"

"Always. But they're especially icy in the evening,"

Danny answered, relieved to be getting some help. It was the least antagonistic he'd been to me thus far.

"Then she should sleep with gloves on for tonight until I can get a better look at her tomorrow. Sleeping with her legs elevated will help a little." I reached for the doorknob when Mariang started to unbutton her dress.

"Wait," Danny called. "Just let me help her change, and then come back and tell me what else I need to do." I turned to look at them over my shoulder and saw the rare glimpse of pleading soften his Frankenstein monster-like features. "Please."

"Sure. I can help. Call me in when she's decent." I stepped out into the hallway and waited only one minute before Danny came to retrieve me. I heard arguing from the conference room, but most of it was unintelligible.

"You said her legs should be elevated. How much?"

Mariang looked up at me with hopeful eyes, like I might be able to cure her with an aspirin. *Would that I could.* "Here. First lay down and get comfortable." I watched as Danny helped her lay down on the mattress, then I picked up a thick pillow from the head of the bed next to hers and folded it in half. "Now I'm just going to lift your legs and slide this under your knees. Is that uncomfortable?" I cataloged her face for signs of distress that might indicate something more serious in her joints.

"No, but that's Danny's pillow. Can we use a different one?"

I couldn't quite picture the man who'd slapped me

across the face sleeping in the feminine peach room. That little mental image would be one of my favorite things to make me giggle when I needed a boost.

"No," Danny ruled. "If it'll help, use it. I can get a different pillow, no problem."

"You give up too much for me." She reached over and placed her hand on his. "You need to rest, too."

"I feel fine." He slid the thick comforter up to her chest and kissed her lips. Though the kiss was simple, the two of them shuddered, inhaling as if something far more intimate was going on. I wanted to escape the affectionate display, but I put on my best nurse smile and waited patiently. "Now get some sleep. We'll come up with a new plan in the morning, and everything will start looking up, yeah?"

Mariang's voice was quiet, but firm. "You can't put off the inevitable. I appreciate being able to feel my feet and all, but don't go thinking October can save my life. Don't put that on her. We both know I've got barely a year left, if I'm lucky."

Danny closed his eyes as he leaned over to kiss her again, invoking that same sensual shudder from them both. "When you talk like that, it kills me. I'll take care of it. Don't I always? You're not dying if I have anything to say about it."

"Danny bear, it's alright." Her arms were weak, but they managed to loop around his neck when he needed it most.

He kissed her again, and I averted my eyes as I inched

for the door. Nurse or not, there were some things I just couldn't stomach. The public love stuff always made me feel a little queasy. Danny sensed my retreat, so he ended the kiss and turned off the lamp, shutting Mariang in the room for the night.

Danny leaned against the bedroom door in the hallway, closing his worn eyes and sighing at the unending labor of his life. When he finally stood straight, it was with the air of readying himself to fight a bull. "You're a doctor, right?"

"I'm a nurse. Big difference. Like, eons of difference." The doctor I worked under, Brenden, was gracious and trusted me with far more duties than a nurse at a hospital would be given, but it wasn't the same thing has having an M.D. after my name.

"But you can help her?"

"I can try. But she should really be seen by a doctor, don't you think?"

"Sure, but who could she possibly go to? Omens are half from this world and half from Terraway. I don't know anyone qualified for that."

I followed Danny down to the kitchen and washed my hands in the sink three times while he fished a pad of paper and a pen from the drawer. "If it's true that our makeup's different than humans, why hasn't anything weird turned up on my tests? I mean, you all said I'm half human and half Matruculan. Wouldn't my blood be different than a regular person's?"

Danny considered this. "I honestly don't know. The Omens have only ever been treated by Terraway doctors, and it fails every time. Maybe they're more human in nature than anything else."

"I mean, I've had extensive bloodwork done, and I see my general practitioner twice a year. They've never turned up anything weird on me." *Well, not mythologically weird, anyway.*

"Then let's try it the human way. Mariang's mother was part human."

"What's Ezra?" I asked out of idle curiosity.

"Matruculan. Only Matruculan can have children with full humans, but it's difficult for the baby to actually come about."

"What do you mean? Why is it harder for the woman to have a baby if the father's Matruculan?"

"Matruculan men are unnaturally drawn to pregnant women and fetuses. Triggers an animalistic hunger that's hard to control. There've been many who've tried to knock up a human woman in hopes she has a baby who turns out to be an Omen, but they usually end up eating the baby. And then the mother."

My mouth fell open in horror. "Are you kidding me? That's disgusting! Ezra eats babies? And pregnant women?"

Danny rolled his eyes, like I was being dramatic. Like what he'd just said wasn't fodder for the worst kind of horror movie. Bruce Campbell would never dream of starring in a movie with a plot as psychotic as that, I was certain. Danny was unperturbed by my shock. "Of course not. You've met his daughter. He clearly didn't eat her." He furrowed his eyebrows. "I thought you were a doctor. Doctors are supposed to be smart, yeah?"

"Shut your donut hole. What about Mariang's mom?"

"Was hit by a car. Your world killed her, not mine. Not every Matruculan lacks self-control. Non-human-eating Matruculan men exist, but there just aren't all that many out there. Ezra eats a lot of animal meat instead to compensate. It takes more self-control than most have." He sat down on the stool at the freshly scrubbed counter with his pen and paper. "Okay, hit me with whatever you've got that might help Mariang."

I dried off my hands on the towel, going through my mental list aloud. "Okay. She should sleep exactly like that with her legs up, if she can. Tomorrow night she could take a hot bath to stimulate blood flow. Every night, actually. She can go on short walks to get her heart going," I watched Danny write everything down with rapt attention. "Green tea? Do you have any?"

Danny stood from his stool. "I'll pop over to the store and get some right now."

"Easy, tiger. Not much is open right now. It's not a cure-all; it's just something that might help a little bit. If we do enough things that help like, one percent, eventually all that help might start adding up so we can build her health some positive momentum."

"Okay. What else?"

"When she drinks water, make sure it's warm, not cold. Cold water tends to make the blood vessels constrict." I demonstrated by clenching my fist. "And no coffee. No caffeine of any kind. That really doesn't help."

Danny's shoulders deflated. "Oh, that's not going to go over well."

I shrugged. "She doesn't have to do any of these things. They're not a cure. Just little building blocks that might help in small ways."

"I'll take anything at this point." Danny looked utterly spent from the long day and what looked to be a hard life for him. He jerked his head toward the room where all the arguing was coming from. "When you go back in there, don't let them walk all over you. As far as hierarchy goes, the only person more valuable than you is Ezra, since you'll be reporting to him. Don't let them talk over you to shut you up. And don't break eye contact with the Goblin. Titus can sense if you're afraid of him."

"Should I be?"

Danny shuddered. "Oh, yeah. The whole lot of them are absolutely ruthless. That's how they got to where they are now. Goblins didn't used to have a seat on the council, you know. Now they try to run the thing every time. Hold your ground in there. Start off a pawn this early in the game and you'll never shake it."

"Okay. Thanks."

Danny nodded once. "You actually did quite well in

there before. Best get back to it before they start making decisions for you."

"Alright. Thanks, Danny. You know, I was wrong about you. I thought you were the meanest man alive. Now you're mingled somewhere in the top ten."

He snorted and waved me away. "Well, you're still the most annoying person I've ever met. I was spot on about that."

I gave him a sweet little shove off his stool before I stomped toward the conference room, throwing open the door to garner the attention of the bickering creatures.

24

WELCOME TO THE COUNCIL

Upon second thought, I realized banging the door open so hard it hit the wall was probably not the best thing to do. It did get them to shut up long enough to let me take hold of the conversation, though. They were all standing and had been going at their argument since I'd left, accomplishing nothing.

Danny entered behind me, standing in his intimidating way to stare the others down over my shoulder and reinforce my presence there. Mason abandoned his chair and clenched his fists at my side. Von slowly moved to stand on my other side, smoking, as if everyone was just standing around the table drinking beers together. He'd been abducted right alongside me, but apparently it took more than that to truly ruffle him. Von reached his arm out absentmindedly and brushed his knuckles across the back of my neck, absconding with a little of my building nerves.

It was incredible, how he could do that. I fought down my body's strange desire to lean closer to his touch.

I cleared my throat. "Alright, people. If you want me to learn how to be an Omen, you all have to sit down and lower your voices." When no one moved, I reached for my bossy voice I used when an inmate was giving me too much sass, clapping my hands twice. "Do you think I'm speaking metaphorically? Sit down!"

The people around the table obeyed slowly. Finn narrowed his eyes, sizing me up with an edge of hesitation.

A smirk played on Von's lips as he puffed his cigar and clapped his hand on my shoulder. "Those big girl pants look fetching on you, Peach."

I shot Von the only smile I had left, and then turned to the others, lowering my voice to set the tone for an acceptable volume. "Mariang's resting, and I could hear you all the way upstairs. Is that how you treat the person in charge of growing your food? You barge into her house, start yelling like a bunch of children and expect the food to just keep on coming? I hope all that shouting felt good, because it was the last time. That nonsense ends tonight."

Kabayo stood up, his fists on the table as he stared me down with his glassy horse eyes. "I don't know who you think you are, but—"

I snapped my fingers twice to distract him from his tirade. "Sounds like you just volunteered to wash my car, Kabayo."

"I'm not your slave."

"Would you like to be?" I threatened. "If you want me on your side – if you want me to actually start being an Omen and doing what Mariang does so your people can live – you'll sit back down and be civil, like a gentleman. If you can't do that, you can learn some responsibility. Take a lesson on how to behave like an adult by washing my car for me. All raising your voice does is get you big fat nothing from me." I stared him down, daring his anger to be bigger than mine. "I'll wait."

Mason moved closer to my side, posturing like he was there to enforce my presence at the meeting. He'd looked very much like a Viking when I'd first seen him in his furs. Now he was only wearing black pants and a black t-shirt with his sturdy boots, looking like a soldier who didn't need a commander to know the rules. Von merely sucked on the end of his cigar, as if to tell Kabayo that his intimidation tactics were boring us all.

I was trembling inside, but knew I couldn't let the horse-man run the meeting. They were getting nowhere, and I was tired. I placed my fists on the table to mirror Kabayo's body language, not letting it show that the foot and a half he had on me was a huge advantage in his favor.

I couldn't believe it when Kabayo actually sat down, glaring at me as he breathed audibly through his snout. "I hope your vampire eats you in your sleep."

Von removed his cigar from his mouth and bared his modest fangs at Kabayo, hissing.

I straightened. "Thank you for being gracious, Kabayo.

Now since ya'll have been fighting since I left, I hope you don't mind if I straighten a few things out." I held up my finger. "First off, I don't owe anyone here anything. I'm doing this because I care about people dying when I can help them, not because I'm scared of any of you or feel like I work for you. The gravy train could end at any time, so deal. Be on your best behavior around me and Mariang – who also doesn't work for you, by the way." I held up a second finger when Kabayo snorted angrily and Finn crossed his arms over his chest, raising an eyebrow at my gall. "Next off, everyone shut it while Ezra explains what the flip the sagrado stone is."

Ezra inclined his head to me. "Of course. It's a white rock that grants extra stability to Terraway. It makes the magic flow easier, the people healthier and the land richer. It also helps to regulate the suns. There used to be eight sagrado stones – one kept in each land, plus a spare. Over the years, the nations targeted each other's sagrado stones when they would go to battle. Eight stones turned to seven, then six, and so on until they were all destroyed, save for the spare, which was lost long before the battles started. One of the most powerful Kapre named Orson had the spare stone, but someone stole it from him. No one knows whom, but about a century ago, that spare sagrado stone went missing. As the nations warred, they weakened Terraway, not realizing that when one nation fell, we all suffered."

Kabayo pointed his finger at Titus, not in accusation,

but as a threat. "It was the Goblins who set their minds on our destruction. They were the ones who led the battles to steal sagrado stones and destroy them."

Titus hissed, but Ezra continued as if there had been no interruption. "When the last known stone was demolished a few years ago, we began to need Omens to work harder than anyone should've expected them to. There were more back then, so they shared the load, but over time, the land grew harder to work, the magic more distant and the Omens more fragile." He cleared his throat. "If you really are in possession of the lost sagrado stone, it would change a lot for Terraway. It would make it so Mariang and you would only need to reap a person a day to save us all, instead of one per nation per day, plus an extra."

I scratched the back of my hand, wishing I could wash up again. "Oh. Well, that is a big deal, then. And you think I have it, Lang?"

"*Prince Langgam*," the mud man corrected me. "And yes. My minions said they saw it. They even carried back one of their own who touched it and turned to stone as proof. They said it was holding open a door in a pile of garbage."

Bev's hoard. The stone was somewhere in Bev's hoard, propping open a door. My mind flashed to the doorstop that had been in the trailer since before I was born, and I prayed my intake of breath wasn't too noticeable.

Several of the people at the table hissed, but it meant little to me. "Someone want to explain that?"

Ezra fielded my question. "The sagrado stone cannot be touched, except by the Kapre. Kapre were like..." He cast around for something I might understand. "They're like magical giants. If anyone who's not Kapre, or who hasn't been blessed by a Kapre touches it, they turn to stone. As Kapre have been extinct long before any of us were born, it's highly improbable that anyone alive now could touch it without turning to stone."

"And I have this thing? This rock? Good thing I didn't touch it. Being turned to stone would seriously suck." I shuddered at the thought.

Lang crossed his arms over his chest. "But you did touch it. My minions saw it light up when you touched it, and yet you stand before us, not turned to stone."

"But I'm not a magical giant." I glanced down at my stature and frowned. "I mean, clearly that's nowhere in my lineage."

Lang seemed exasperated with my confusion. "I don't care how it's possible; I just know that you did touch it, and here you are. You're the only one who can bring it to the nations, since all the Kapre died off a century ago."

I closed my eyes and tried not to let them see I was upset. "Looks like you all just signed me up for a second job." I turned my head and glanced at Von, whose cigar looked like it might fall out of his mouth with shock. "Super. I guess I'm in."

Lang tapped his fist to his chest twice, like a sort of salute. "Welcome to the council, Lady October."

LAYING DOWN THE LAW

My eyes went wide as Langgam's fist salute was repeated across the room. Each of them stood, dipping their heads in respect to whatever it is I was supposed to be to them.

I turned to give Von a "what the crap" look, but he was doing the same thing, eyes wide with what looked like reverence. I waved off the sincerity from everyone. "Alright, knock it off. I think I liked you all better when you were fighting. I haven't actually done anything to bring peace or whatever to your world, so don't get your hopes that high."

Ezra's voice was quiet, respecting the awe that fell over the room. "If you have the sagrado stone, and if you can touch it without turning to stone yourself, then you can also break it for us. What would happen is that you would travel to the seven nations, break off a piece of the rock and bury it there. As long as the rock stays there, the land will prosper. Then you and Mariang will only have to reap one person a day to keep Terraway afloat."

I pinched the bridge of my nose. "It sounds like the plan will work like this: I can start training to reap or pull or do cartwheels or whatever tomorrow morning. I'll reap as many souls as I can in the next few days so I can build up enough time to go to Lang's world and bring the sagrado stone to his people without more of you all starving."

Murmurs of dissent broke out, and I wondered if that was the right move. Titus' was the first voice to rise above the din. "Why should Sakuna deserves the first pieces?" His bug eyes accused me.

"When Mariang reaps the souls, his land is the last to get fed, which means they're the most desperate."

That's right, I pay attention.

When the Goblin went to open his mouth again, I glared at him, making sure he knew how vicious my wrath would be if he kept being a pain. "And that's how it's going to be. I'll start there and work my way through your world, popping back up whenever we need to refill the soul supply." I frowned. "Though, I don't actually know how easy that part is – the popping in and out of your world."

Not to mention the whole breathing issue.

Lang raised his finger. "I can do it. Only the people here on the council and select officials can transport another person in and out. Some entry gates are a week's trek from one side of the nation to the other, so it'll take some time." Lang stood, his expression tight but sincere. "If you'll let me, I'll escort you through Sakuna, and as much of the rest of Terraway as you need. For putting my father's land first, I owe you to see this through until the end."

This seemed to mollify Titus a little, his big watery eyes blinking twice up at Lang. "Good. I think you shoulds."

"That's what I just said!" Lang growled.

Sylvia broke in with an argumentative tone. "Lumipad is next! Our people are desperate."

Finn scoffed. "Your people are cannibals. Ekeks and Manas add nothing to Terraway."

Sylvia was livid, whirling on Finn. "We have just as much a right to the stone as anyone!"

Finn sat back in his chair, waving her off as if she was a fly who buzzed out of turn. "I wouldn't care if your whole race up and fed on itself, chipping away at your weaker ones until there was nothing left. Extinction doesn't seem like a bad idea for all the problems Lumipad has."

Sylvia stood and grabbed the hilt of her sword. I knew if she drew it, things would go south real fast. My voice was sharp, cutting through the escalating argument. "Finn, knock it off. And Sylvia? I know you don't need to be told not to draw a weapon in Mariang's home. Girlfriend's trying to sleep up there so she can be bright-eyed to serve your world tomorrow. Show some respect." I donned a sweeter tone as I stood. "Thank you for your offer to help me, Lang. Then if that's all, I'll see the rest of you when I cross through your land. Lang, Ezra can keep in touch with you to let you know when we've got enough souls stocked up to where we're ready to leave for Terraway."

This brought about a lot of dissent from the ranks. Everyone had something to say about the sagrado stone. No one could touch it, but no one wanted it out of their sight, either.

I held up my hands to quiet them. I couldn't believe it actually worked – they seemed so attached to their tempers that flared on a dime. "Anyone can come with me to help deliver the stone, but if it's gonna be more bickering, ya'll can stay at home." I slapped my hands together twice. "Now if you don't mind, I'm beat, so I'm turning in." I jerked my thumb toward the door. "Kabayo, don't you even think about coming with us on the journey if you don't personally wash my car before you head home, and I mean right now, mister. If you can't serve, then you can't lead. Plain and simple. Be a good leader. You've yet to show me you're anything more than a donkey with a crown. You heard it here first: I won't work with a jackass."

Kabayo whinnied contemptuously, and stood to tower over me from across the table.

Yeah, that's probably the line I shouldn't have danced over.

Von covered his mouth and chuckled into his hand, coughing to cover his laughter when I narrowed my eyes at him.

"You want to help him?" I challenged.

Von shook his head through his delighted grin at a king being put in his place. "No, ma'am."

I turned to Ezra. "I'm going home now. Do I have to take Von and Mason, or can I just go?"

Ezra looked pleased that I deferred to him. "Let's discuss that out here. Gentlemen," he said to Von and Mason, waving for them to follow.

Ezra wrapped his arm around my shoulder and guided me out of the room. He shut the conference room doors behind us and led me, Mason and Von down the hall to the living room. "That was brilliant!" He kept his voice quiet, but his celebratory joy was obvious on his face. His unfettered smile made him look like a much younger man. "I was worried about them trying to control you, but you handled that beautifully. I must learn to use the camera feature on my phone so I can record King Kabayo washing your car."

Mason sniggered. "Do you think he'll actually do it?"

"He will if he wants to travel with the stone." I offered up a tired smile to the guys. "I'm heading out as soon as Kabayo's done, then."

Ezra straightened, smoothing his tie. "If you could stay here tonight, that would be ideal. You and Mason can stay in Von's room. I'll see about having one of the larger rooms converted for the three of you to share once things settle down."

I pursed my lips so I didn't speak the indignant words I was thinking. "I appreciate the offer, but I don't live here. I have a house all my own, and a brother I want to see. I've gone along with everything else pretty well, but I'm putting my foot down on this one. Until we go to Terraway, I'm sleeping in my own bed."

Ezra looked like he wanted to argue, but nodded with great reluctance. "Okay, if that's your sticking point, I guess there's no use in telling you it's unguarded, and that my house is far safer."

"I've never had my boobs grabbed in my own house," I argued, but then I shook my head and pinched the bridge of my nose. "I'm sorry. You didn't deserve that. It's been a long day. I'll go home and meet you all here in the morning."

Ezra shook his head. "Now it's my turn to put my foot down. Mason and Von are your Reapers now. They sleep where you sleep. They go where you go. I'll be sending Danny tonight so he can train them and make sure they know what they're doing. He can even put charms up around your home to ward off attacks."

"The charms part sounds cool." I scratched at the backs of my hands, wishing the sting would relieve more of the pressure I felt building inside me like a dense gas. "But I live alone, and I like it that way."

"I'm sorry, but that's not an option anymore." Ezra was resolute.

My hackles rose on instinct, but I knew fighting him when I was so tired wouldn't be productive. "They can crash at my place tonight because I'm too beat to argue with you, but we're not done discussing this."

"I look forward to the debate, dear." Ezra motioned to Von. "Pack a bag, son. Mason, you can borrow whatever you need to make yourself comfortable for now. It's time to take October home. Tell Danny he's to make sure her house is secure tonight."

"Yes, sir." Von cast me a sympathetic smile and trotted away with his hands shoved in his pockets, cigar in his teeth.

I swallowed a lump in my throat as I stared down the barrel of unexpected houseguests with no end in sight.

26

DANNY'S TUTORIAL

After Kabayo washed my car and Danny replaced the tire I learned Mason had slashed to keep me there, I tiptoed around the two-inch thick pile of various insects that had croaked on the porch. It wasn't well lit out, so it was hard to find a spot to step on that was not a flipped-up mixture of slick and crunchy. I didn't want to admit that the hordes of lifeless exoskeletons creeped me out.

"I'll drive with her," Danny ruled. "Von can follow us in my car, so I have a way to get home in the morning."

"I'm fine," I said, hopefully not too antagonistically. "Duke out shotgun with your brother. I don't need a chaperone to drive my own car to my own house."

"Then think of me as the one person who'll answer any question you have." Danny opened the passenger door to my car for me.

I consented to getting into the passenger's seat of my own car because I didn't want to have to touch the door handle on the other side. Kabayo had done the bare minimum job of washing Terence the Taurus, and I didn't trust the cleanliness.

Danny slid into the driver's seat, cleaning his hands with a wet wipe from the glovebox I had ready for him. He adjusted the seat, the mirrors and the steering wheel height before he started up the car. I cringed at how much detailing would need to be done now. The bug germs were everywhere – on my steering wheel, on my heater controls, the seatbelt, and the inside of the door. My skin crawled with phantom insects. I was surprised I hadn't had a full-on panic attack yet. So you know, yay me. I guess this pulling thing they did wasn't all talk. If it could help me be more normal, that might not be such a bad thing.

Danny drove onto the freeway with Von and Mason in the car behind us on the empty road. When I didn't speak first, he finally decided to break the silence that had been weighted with too many things that needed saying. "I wasn't trying to kiss you really. I was trying to get the soul out of you before it atrophied. I know what that looks like, and it's not pretty."

I introduced forced vulnerability into my voice. "But... But, I thought you loved me!"

Danny's eyes grew wide before he glanced over at me and saw me smirking. "Hilarious."

"I'm going to take that as a compliment. Under normal circumstances, I am pretty funny."

"Well, it wasn't a compliment. It was sarcasm. Pretty annoying, not pretty funny. Distinction."

"You think I'm pretty, too? Well, you're just the sweetest little cupcake."

He loosened his collar, and I knew I'd succeeded in making him uncomfortable. "Maybe driving you was a bad idea."

"Admitting you're a dummy is the first step to recovery." Yes, that was a little harsh, but I still hadn't totally made my peace with him smacking me across the face, so attitude flare-ups were inevitable.

"Does your mouth come with an off switch?"

"You must've turned it off when you kissed me. Does that happen often? You turning women off with a single kiss?"

I was waiting for the steam to come roiling out of Danny's ears. "Maybe this should be more of a silent road trip."

"Works for me." I looked out the window, taking in the few trees we passed as Danny drove nine miles over the speed limit. "I don't know what I'm supposed to tell Ollie when we get to my house. He's staying with me for a few days. How do I explain the company?"

Danny shrugged, making it clear he couldn't care less about my personal life. "Von and Mason are your Reapers, so they'll be with you around the clock from here on out.

You three will have to come up with a story that works for all of you." He scratched a spot on his elbow and shifted in the seat. "This car's nice. Is it new?"

"It's almost a year old."

"Looks fresh off the lot. Barely a speck of dust in it."

"I detail it once a month."

Danny shot me an appreciative look. "Nice."

I absentmindedly scratched at the skin on the backs of my hands, letting it all sink in. My car smelled faintly of the familiar lavender I wore, and I drew the scent into my lungs in an attempt to calm myself. "Alright. You and Mason can sleep on the pull-out couch tonight. Von can bunk up with Ollie if he can talk Ollie into sharing. Otherwise he can take a sleeping bag on the floor in the living room."

"That won't work."

"Then Von and Mason can sleep on the floor. I've got plenty of sleeping bags." I frowned at Danny. "You know, you can't complain about what I've got to offer when you just spring this whole nonsense on me. Be grateful I'm going along with this at all."

"I mean that at least one of us will stay in your room. It won't do to reinforce protection around your house only to have someone snatch you in the middle of the night out from under our noses."

"What? Jeez! What kind of a world do you live in?"

"The kind where the Terraway royals can show up at

any moment and take you to their world if they think you're stepping a toe out of line."

"I don't like this." My nails raked over the backs of my hands as the anxiety started to grate on my nerves. I'd needed to wash my hands for so long. I fought with my creeping anxiety so my breathing didn't grow too shallow.

"Stop doing that," Danny scolded me, glancing toward my hands. "Von or Mason can help you with that when we get to your house. Plus, if you draw blood, it'll just make things harder on Von, and he's more the take-what's-not-his type of idiot."

"I don't need help. I need to move. I mean, you all clearly can't keep Mariang safe. I don't think bringing more of you into my life is going to help much."

Though I barely knew the guy, I could tell this cut him deep. "Mariang's been abducted twice. One time I wasn't there for. The other I was outnumbered ten to one. The time I wasn't there? I was in the shower. Two rooms away from her for ten minutes, and they snatched her right out from under my nose. So as much as you may not want Von or Mason in your space, trust me that it's necessary." He reached over and touched my hands, retracting at my flinch. "Sorry. Just stop scratching yourself like that. It's weird."

"You don't get to comment on my level of weird. I don't want you touching me. I think I've earned the right to say that." I switched to squeezing my fingers one by one so he didn't feel the need to touch me again. My chin lowered, and I switched to a less antagonistic tone. "I don't want to quit my day job."

Danny chewed on my complaint, taking in the flavor of my mood and digesting it before answering. "You have a new job now. You can't go back to your old one. There's just not enough hours in the day for you to do both. It's tiring work. Being an Omen takes a lot out of you, so you'll need time to rest and recharge from it."

I tugged on my fingertips, my voice quiet. "You don't know how much I love my job, or how hard I work at it. What you're asking me to do? It's mean."

"I've been called worse. And it should show you how bad the situation is in Terraway if we're asking you to give up something that important to you for this."

I scoffed lightly. "You don't care about me or what's important to me. None of you do. I'm a means to an end." I looked out the window and sighed forlornly. "But thanks for pretending it's something nicer than that. You don't have to pretend for me. You slapped me across the face, choked me out and tied me up. I think we're past pretending." I examined my fingernails. "Nice job on the whole choking me out thing. I can't believe I actually lost that one."

"Truth? You almost won. I had to use pulling to get you to calm down. I won't do that again, though. I'm not your Reaper. They're the ones in charge of when to use pulling, and how much from now on." He shot me a wary look. "So, we're cool?"

I raised an eyebrow at him. "Maybe still a day away from cool. I'm entertaining fewer homicidal thoughts concerning your demise, though, so that's a bonus."

Danny's frown tightened. "Alright. Good. Since we don't have to talk about your feelings or whatever, we can move on to the logistics." He gripped the steering wheel like he wished he could strangle it. "Whatever annoyance you, Mason and Von are thinking of being to each other, I'd cut it out now. You're stuck together, so make the best of it."

"I can work on that."

"Mason's great. You'll be safe with him. Von's an okay guard, I guess. Not a great guy, but whatever. He used to be the best big brother in the world – fun on a normal day, terrifyingly vicious when anyone crossed our family. Now he's utterly useless." He glared at the road ahead as if it had insulted his mama. "I can feel when Mariang's upset or happy or tired. It took a while to build up that connection, but it's dead useful. It's nature's way of helping me do my job better. When she was taken while I was in the shower, I felt the tug in my chest and acted as quick as I could. I failed, but point is that I felt it. Von and Mason will start to feel you after a while, too."

I closed my eyes, gulping down my fear at having someone know my inner workings that well. They'd both already made mention of being able to sense my anxiety, and I'd felt their dips on occasion, as well. I kept my voice quiet when I finally opened my mouth. "I don't want that."

Danny was silent for a few beats, respecting the blast of the worst thing he could've said to me. I didn't want anyone knowing how hard simple things were for me. I didn't want anyone knowing me. Even Gabby just thought I was mildly quirky. My best girlfriend knew little of my childhood or the medication I was on to cope with my sometimes crippling OCD.

"Did you want me to pull over so you can talk to Von and Mason? They can help you so you don't freak out."

I shot Danny a look that told him how ludicrous that idea was. "Um, no thanks. They can't help. They're total strangers to me."

"That's where you're wrong." Danny's shoulders relaxed a little as he merged onto the highway I instructed him to take. "They're your Reapers, so they'll be great at taking away small amounts of fear, anxiety, anger – stuff like that. Then you don't have to deal with so much. They don't just take harvested souls and check out. They get you back to zero every night so you can start fresh in the morning."

"No, thanks. I can handle myself just fine. Am I freaking out? No." *Yes.* "Just stay away from my personal life." The new idea that my anxiety would be palpable to someone else was foreign to me. I wasn't sure what to do with that, other than the gleaming option of total denial.

Danny lectured me like an older sibling I didn't ask for. "Being an Omen takes its toll. You'll need your Reapers."

He pointed to the fingers I was still tugging on. "You need them now already."

I tucked my hands under my thighs, and they burned with the desire to be scratched and washed. "No offense to your awesome system, but I don't need strange men to help me deal. I'm fine. See?" I cast up as breezy a smile as I could at him. "Easy-peasy."

Danny shook his head, frustrated with my level of resistance on letting all things unicorn, leprechaun and Omen invade my personal space. "It's intense, the bond between an Omen and her Reaper. Be careful you don't fall too hard. I mean, there's two of them. I don't know how that'll work."

"What are you talking about? How what'll work?"

"I didn't give Mariang the time of day before I became her Reaper, and I said 'I love you' inside the first month after she was awakened. I'm telling you, it's intense. Boot camp for relationships. You're together all the time, and there's something about the whole taking your tension away that's more bonding than anything else. I'm just saying, be careful. Von's not good for you. Or anyone, really."

"Um, not to worry. I don't plan on hooking up with a vampire, or a Viking who's almost a decade older than me." I looked out the window, trying to picture myself next to Mason.

"Before we left, I went up to tell Mariang I was leaving for the night. I felt her getting anxious that I would be gone. Her second abduction was just a few months ago, so she's still a little shaken up."

"Understandable."

"So I held her, and took a little of her fear so she could get some sleep tonight. You, Mason and Von will have to learn how to do that."

I gaped at Danny. "I don't need them to sing me to sleep or whatever. Honestly, that's so embarrassing. I mean, good for the two of you and all, but I don't need that. And what do you do with all that negative emotion? Just suck it up? Because if that's all you do, I can manage that without any help. I'm like, the queen of sucking it up."

Danny sighed, and I could tell he was trying to find the right words to explain second nature things to me. "Reapers are born with the ability to take in an Omen's troubles and get rid of them. Sure, I get upset when I see the toll it all takes on Mariang, but this is different. I can take her upset and make it disappear without any bad effect on me."

"That's so weird. You're like, the ultimate shrink."

Danny offered me half a smile. It looked foreign on his surly face, and disappeared quickly when it realized it didn't belong there. "I suppose that's a good way to put it. The only thing it does to me is make me dreadfully hungry."

"Do you... do you get specifics? Like, can you read her mind? Or is it just a jumbled mess of bad emotions you get rid of?"

Danny scratched his chin as he considered this. "Hard to say. I mean, I know her like the back of my hand because we've been together for years, so a lot of what she's dealing with I know the specifics of because I'm right next to her through it all. But other than that, no. No specifics unless I really look at the mess she hands me. And since it's such a mess, I don't really want to look too closely."

"But you could tell the specifics if you wanted to?"

"I guess. Maybe. But it's a lot like looking into the sun. Why bother with the pain, yeah? I just do my job and let it go. Years of training so I don't have to look at it all too closely."

"But Von doesn't have years of training. Neither does Mason."

"They'll be fine. They'll learn. Von went to the Academy for a few years where they teach Duwende things of that sort. He was kicked out in his last year, so he's fairly well educated. And Mason actually graduated, though that was years ago."

I decided right then and there that I would never need Von or Mason for that service. Suck the flailing soul out of me and keep me from getting abducted, sure, but that's where it ends.

"No other questions? You went all quiet on me."

"How old are you? Von said he's the oldest brother, but you seem much older."

"I get that a lot. I'm twenty-eight. I'm eleven months

younger than Von, so it's quite the draw. Plus, I've had years of actually holding a job. We all thought he was Superman when we were young. He did everything to keep our family afloat after Dad left."

"Oh, I'm sorry."

"Yes, well, after he was kicked out of the Academy, something changed. Couldn't get a job. Couldn't keep a job, so he turned to less respectable means." I could tell he was hinting at something, though I couldn't guess what. "Then he was bitten by an Aswang-turned-vampire, which only made things worse. Vampires don't have a long life expectancy, so Von gave up trying to make something of himself and started debasing himself to revel in what little time he has left." Danny swallowed hard. "Finally Ezra took pity on him and brought him on as a guard. Von's charming, but useless these days. Though I guess not a terrible guard."

I let out a low whistle. "Wow. You must really hate your brother. I can't imagine talking about Ollie like that. What'd he do?"

"You'll learn soon enough. Try counting on him. That's the quickest way to figure out what he's made of."

27

THE MONSTERS I LET IN THE FRONT DOOR

Danny and I drove the rest of the way in silence, with me directing him every now and then until we pulled into the simple three-bedroom ranch on the dead end of Lenoy Avenue that Allie, Ollie and I had bought together a few years ago.

The brown brick home with emerald shutters and matching door had brought me such a sense of contentment walking into it before tonight. But upon sitting in my car and staring at my haven, I dreaded letting the Reapers into my world.

Von parked on the street since there was no room with Ollie's rental car sitting in the garage and Terence the Taurus parked in the driveway. I tugged at my fingers as I gathered my thoughts when Von joined us by sliding into the backseat with his duffel.

"Did you two chum up and decide what to get me for a

Christmas present? It's still a few months away, but good to know you're planning ahead. I like roller coasters. Nothing says 'I love you, Von' quite like a roller coaster. Shouldn't be too troublesome to wrap."

Danny didn't laugh, and I was too nervous to play along in the levity Von tried to introduce. "Where's Mason?" I asked, and then jumped when the very same wolf I'd almost hit when the bugs invaded my car a week ago leapt into the backseat next to Von. "What the crap?" I got out of the car and clicked my fingers. The thick gray coat called out to be stroked, and I wondered how the wolf had found my home. "Come on, baby. Out you go."

Von sniggered. "I keep forgetting you know nothing about our world. Mason's a Matruculan. It means he can shapeshift. He thought it might be easier if you only had to explain bringing an animal home instead of taking a thirty-one-year-old bloke into your bed." He jerked his thumb to Mason. "He said you've already met him in his wolf form."

I bristled and got back into the car so we could talk more, feeling like a dummy that I hadn't put that together. I mean, Fantasy Fiction 101 would demand I know that every wolf in the world is clearly a werewolf or shapeshifter of some sort. I felt woefully behind on my magical education. "I don't know what to say to that. I mean, it's crazy cool you're a shapeshifter, Mason." I turned to face him and get a good look at my new dog under the car's cabin light. I reached out and scratched behind his ears, smiling when he burrowed the top of his head into my palm. "Thanks for being a dog. That does make it a little easier."

Mason sneezed in my direction, as if in answer.

Danny spoke for him. "Mason's a wolf, not a dog. Can you seriously not tell the difference? He's a giant gray wolf."

I frowned at Danny. "No, he's not. If you want me to tell Ollie I'm bringing a pet home, how well do you think a wolf's going to go over? You'd be safer as a Viking." I turned to Mason, taking in his slate eyes that almost seemed to glow. "You're a dog, chief."

Mason sat his hindquarters on the backseat and sighed his compliance.

"So, my brother's inside. He came into town just for a few days because Bev wanted us to meet her new guy. You have to figure out how to explain that you're here and staying the night."

Von shrugged. "Easy. We hooked up at Ezra's when you came back to get your car fixed, and you fell head over heels for me. And oh, have you met my dog? He's a rare breed from England."

"Charming as you are, Ollie would never buy that. I don't fall head over heels."

"Fine, then we're just hooking up for the night."

I sighed, rubbing the stress from my forehead. "I'm a virgin, Von. I don't invite strange men to stay the night at my house. The point is to avoid looking suspicious, not draw attention to the freak show."

Danny unbuckled his seatbelt when Ollie came stomping out of the front door. My brother flung open my car door with bare feet, wild eyes, a disheveled white undershirt and black sweatpants he wore as pajamas. "Where have you been? I've been calling you for hours! I almost called the cops to report you missing. Don't do that to me!"

I sucked in a deep breath before I extracted myself from the car and was pulled into Ollie's arms. "I'm fine, Ollie. My car was having problems, so Danny and Von fixed it for me. Then they followed me home to make sure I got here safe. Took a little longer than expected."

When I squirmed to get out of Ollie's arms, he held me tighter. That was one of the good things about Ollie. He knew when not to listen to me. "I don't care if you want to be hugged or not. I was worried! Call if you're going to be this late. Ezra said it was just a flat tire. It's nearly ten o'clock! How could it have possibly taken this long? You got the flat yesterday night."

"Two flat tires, one spare. They went out and got me a new tire, though." I tapped the one Danny had taken off of his car with the heel of my shoe.

I wanted to get away from the restrictive hug that threatened too many emotions to burst out of me, but I relented, holding my breath until the flood of feeling passed. I hadn't meant to worry my brother. It had been so long since anyone in the state lines had worried about me. I indulged him in the hug I knew he needed so he could feel better about his hours of fretting. He stiffened when Mason trotted out of the backseat. "Um, what's that? Is that a wolf?"

"No," Danny, Von and I all answered together, which wasn't suspicious sounding at all, I'm sure.

I rolled back my shoulders, feigning ease. "It's my new dog. Just got him today. Thought I'd surprise you. He's already housebroken, too," I warned Mason by way of a loaded hint.

"Whoa, seriously? That's a huge decision. I had no idea you were even thinking about getting a dog." Ollie reached down and patted the top of Mason's head. "Aw, that's a good boy. Man, I miss Sandy." He looked up at Von. "Our neighbor's dog growing up was amazing. What's this one's name?"

"Mason," I answered, and then closed my eyes and smacked myself in the forehead. I should've given him a name like Fido or something that was clearly not a person. Ollie merely smiled, not noticing the weirdness, thank goodness.

Danny got out of the car, bags slung over his shoulder. He stood tall and addressed Ollie with a firm handshake, man to man. "It was my fault. I had a dreadful time getting the new tire on. I'll take her car in tomorrow morning to make sure it's done right, first thing."

Ollie examined all four of my tires. "October knows how to change her own tires."

I scrambled for a plausible excuse. "The rims bent a little, though. It took a while to get everything set."

"Well, they look fine now. I can take it in tomorrow to make sure everything's okay. You all can go on home. Thanks for getting her here safely. Really do appreciate it."

Danny looked at me, unwilling to sew any more stitches into the web of lies. I butted my head to Ollie's shoulder. "It's fine. They can stay. It's too late to drive back anyway. I don't want them falling asleep on the road. Come on in, guys."

I could tell Ollie wanted to argue further against me inviting strange men to stay over, but since it was my house now, he could only protest so much without crossing the line into being overbearing.

"I almost called Bev," Ollie told me quietly.

I quirked my eyebrow at him. "I can't imagine what you hoped to accomplish by doing that."

"You scared me, kid."

"I'm fine, as I always am."

When I first walked inside, there were already signs that someone else was living there who was not me. The beige carpet had man-sized foot indentations from Ollie's circling as he waited for me. There was a bowl and a spoon in the sink just sitting there.

I mean, just sitting there. *Unwashed.* Growing bacteria.

The two maroon silk throw pillows on the tan couch

were lying around haphazardly, as if they didn't know where their proper place was (on the left side, propped up and fluffed evenly, obviously). The remotes were strewn about on the coffee table, which had fingerprints on the glass and a watermark from a cup Ollie had no doubt forgotten to put on a coaster.

When the others came in through the front door, I tried not to screech, "Take off your shoes!" to the two newbies, but failed miserably, making them both flinch.

Von laughed, and then looked at me incredulously, his eyebrow raised. "Oh, you're serious? Okay. Calm down, Grandmother."

Ollie poured me a glass of water. "You look shaken up. What's going on?"

I took a grateful sip, letting the water cleanse my tired insides. "Car troubles always sit badly with me. I bought the car new so I wouldn't have to deal with repairs this early on. Just a bummer, is all."

"You could've called me. I would've come in a second." He lowered his voice. "But I'm proud of you for sleeping in a place that wasn't yours. That's some real progress."

I lowered my chin, hoping the guys hadn't overheard that little tidbit. Yes, I like my own bed. My room is perfect, just the way I want it. Other beds? I couldn't even fathom the germs that might be crawling on sheets I hadn't washed myself.

I noticed the taupe curtains on either side of the picture window on the front of the house were not hanging as they had been when I'd vacuumed them three days ago. "You don't have to worry about me, Ollie. I was lucky to be at Ezra's when it happened, so no big deal. I'm just overly tired." I finished my water and set to washing my glass and the few dishes in the sink. "Guys, you can hit the shower if you need. I'll take the last shower, and then I'm going to bed."

Danny slapped his brother on the back. "You first, Von. That was a long drive. Need to stretch my legs." He shot Von a knowing look, and I guessed he was doing a check of my property to make sure no evil trolls, leprechauns, or gremlins were lurking about.

Von hoisted his duffel over his shoulder and strode into the bathroom. Von didn't walk; he strutted like the cocky son-of-a-biscuit he was, casting me a flirty smirk on his way to the bathroom Ollie pointed him to.

Ollie stood next to me, his butt leaning against the counter as he watched me wash the dishes while my new dog stood sentry at my feet. "They packed overnight bags? Why? Were they expecting to stay here?"

I shrugged, fishing for a nugget of truth so I didn't have to lie too badly. "Ezra's weird. He's taking this new stepdad thing to the extreme. Didn't think it was right to send me home by myself after the car stuff. Sweet, but he thinks I'm twelve."

"Well, you look about twelve." Ollie chewed on his lip. "Huh. I guess I can't fault the guy for being too nice, even if it is a little overbearing. What do you make of him?"

"You nailed it right. Overbearing. Too nice. Wants us to like him so Bev stays around."

He lowered his voice conspiratorially, his eyebrow raised as he hopped up to sit on the counter next to the sink so we could speak face-to-face. "Can we talk about that for a minute? He seemed so nervous around us, like Bev's this great prize. Do you think he's seen her place?"

I suppressed a shudder at the thought of the hoard. I couldn't picture Ezra in all of his perfectly pressed country club-ness slow dancing in the mountains of filth with her. "No. I know he hasn't. And she's your mama. Be respectful."

Ollie ignored my scolding, as he always did in matters concerning Bev. "I almost feel like we should warn him. On the other hand, having someone take her off your hands might be good for you."

I don't know why his simple words hit me so hard, but suddenly I was overcome with a blanket of depression that weighed me down. My shoulders slumped and my chin lowered. Bev used to be my biggest struggle, but now I'd be dealing with death every day. I rinsed the last dish, washed my hands three times and dried them off on the soft taupe terrycloth towel that hung over the oven's handle. I couldn't say everything I wanted to, for fear of all the crazy spewing out onto my brother like uncontrollable vomit. "I missed you, Ollie."

"Oh, kid. You have no idea." He hopped off the counter

and opened his arms in an invitation to hide out from whatever storms were chasing after me.

Before I could stop myself, I threw my body into Ollie's arms, squeezing him tight for a few beats before letting go and retreating to my bedroom before he could say a word.

When he knocked on the door to my bedroom, I collected myself. "October, you alright?"

"I'm fine. Just a long night. I guess we'll have to schedule the *Nightmare on Elm Street* marathon for another night. I'm beat."

"You're just saying that because you want yet another *Evil Dead* marathon instead."

I shrugged. "Bruce Campbell's just plain better than any other horror movie star out there. Face the facts."

Ollie smiled with his hands in his pockets as he leaned on the doorjamb. I could tell that he was tired. "Sleep tight, kid. I'll be in my room if you need anything. Call me if the monsters come and get'cha."

If only.

I nodded, wishing Ollie could save me from the monsters I'd let in the front door.

28

SHARING MY HAVEN

lue was supposed to be a calming color. That's what I'd read, anyway. My bedroom had two dusky blue walls and two eggshell-colored walls. My white comforter with blue stitching matched my sheets and pillowcases perfectly. My queen-sized bed hadn't been disturbed, nor had the white carpet or the closet, which was still shut tight. My blue and taupe curtains were hanging as they should, and my lamp hadn't been bothered. The few items on my nightstand were each in their proper right angle like beautiful little soldiers that never spun out of control.

In my perfect bedroom, everything was as it should be, and that simple fact lowered my blood pressure a noticeable amount. Ollie's mantra of *life is messy, and that's okay* only worked because I had this unmessed utopia to come home to.

When I heard Von emerge from the bathroom five minutes later, I grabbed my purple pajama pants, matching shirt and green hoodie, a new towel, and everything I needed to scrub this horrible weekend from my skin so I could start fresh in the morning. Though I'd showered at Ezra's, I felt like I needed a second scrub-down.

Mason had been waiting right outside the bedroom, giving me a narrow-eyed glower that I'd shut him out. I shrugged an apology to him. "You can't go into the bedroom until you wipe your paws off. I'm serious. My bedroom is my sanctuary."

Mason obeyed, moving to the mat at the front door before going into the bedroom I prayed he wouldn't shed all over.

I passed Von in the hallway, whose shirtless form drew my eyes, despite my wariness of all things in his bizarre universe. Upon shutting myself in the taupe and pea green bathroom, my anxiety began to climb once again. Von had thrown his used towel on the floor, there were a few black hairs in the sink, too many water drops on the counter to number, and a toothpaste gob still in the sink he hadn't bothered to wash all the way down. I set to work cleaning my bathroom before I cleaned myself. I didn't always have to do it this way, but then I didn't usually have three strangers crashing at my place while my brother was in town.

My hands and wrists stung when I finally stepped into

the shower and began washing them. Now that Danny wasn't there to watch my every move, I scratched the back of my hands to my heart's content, relishing the small release it gave me. Every inch of my body needed to be scrubbed thoroughly, and by the time I'd washed myself the usual three times, I'd run out of hot water and was shivering under the spray.

The backs of my hands were bloody, but I didn't care. I rinsed them in the sink when I got out of the shower, and then pulled out my first aid kit and dabbed at the wounds. I wrapped my wrists again, knowing I looked like a suicide survivor. I was glad I'd chosen long sleeves to sleep in that night.

When I emerged from the bathroom, I heard shouts of male camaraderie coming from the living room down the hall. Von and Ollie were in the middle of a game of poker, and Ollie was winning like a brat. "Oh, these chips look good stacked next to my untouched ones over here."

Von grinned, leaning back on the couch and messing up my pillows. "Keep laughing, college boy. I'll trounce you on the next hand."

I hid my hands in the pockets of my purple flannel pajama pants. I saw Danny surreptitiously checking the locks on the windows and understood that Von was the distraction, while Danny tightened up any loose ends to secure my house. I grimaced when I realized I'd taken too long a shower. "Sorry, Danny. I used up the last of the hot water. Totally thoughtless of me. You might want to wait a little bit before washing up."

"I don't mind." He picked up his duffel and walked toward the bathroom, stopping at my side on the way to whisper to me. "After Ollie turns in, I'll take the couch, and Von will sneak into your room. Mason's already there. Lock the door, and I'll see you all in the morning."

"There's no way out of this?" I asked forlornly. It was my last desperate attempt to get him to tell me this was all some horrible practical joke.

Danny paused, but didn't soften. I'm not sure he was capable. "Not even a little. If there was, I would've gotten Mariang out long ago."

I nodded, not looking forward to sharing my unmessed haven with the strangers. I moved to the linen closet, pulling out several blankets and a spare pillow for the guys. There was a slight draft in the living room, so I left the warmest blanket on the arm of the couch with a pillow for Danny. I kissed Ollie on the top of his hair before turning in with a blanket to be laid on the floor for Von and Mason to share. "Night, Ollie. I'm glad you're back."

"Me too. I've got a few things to take care of in the morning. People to see tomorrow during the day. Can we have a movie night tomorrow? You working late?"

"I'll be home tomorrow night. See you and Bruce Campbell then."

"Looking forward to it, kiddo." Ollie sat straighter and pulled out an envelope from his pocket. "Oh, I brought in the mail for you today. Judge sends his love. Must've hand delivered it, since there wasn't a stamp on it."

My spine straightened with new purpose. "Give me that nonsense." I snatched the letter from his hand and ripped it open. My eyebrows furrowed as I quickly read the contents, my frown pronouncing itself as I skimmed the end. "I swear, I've never had anyone make such a fuss over something so small."

"It's not small. You saved T's life. Judge and Darius McCray can't look after their brother while he's in prison. You being there gives them peace of mind."

"That's not why I did it. And it's been months. It shouldn't be this big a deal." I held up the letter as proof. "Now he wants to give me his boat for a weekend? What am I possibly going to do with a boat?"

Ollie shrugged. "You know this would all be over if you just accepted one of his gifts and forgave him. It's been fifteen years, October. This beef you have with him is long moldy."

I scoffed. "Judge disrespected you, Ollie, and he abandoned me. I've got another fifteen years' worth of anger stored up for what he did to us. The time for ridiculous gifts was back then. I don't need a thing from him." I drew my thumb across my throat to show where my loyalties lay. "Plus, all of his gifts are either stolen or come from drug money. It would look bad if I'm seen taking favors from his little empire."

"Maybe it was little when Judge started this years ago,

but it's not so little now. Take the weekend with the boat. I've gotten over it all. You should, too."

"Hello, you know I can't even swim. Plus, then Judge wins. Then he thinks I'm for sale, that I can be bought off with toys, which is not the case."

Von watched our exchange curiously. "Who's this now?"

Ollie answered as I moved into the kitchen. I discreetly popped a small white pill in my mouth to cover over the one I'd missed, and got out a metal bowl. I placed the letter inside and put a lighter to it, watching the offer burn. Then I got out a pen and paper and wrote Judge my billionth "no, thank you" note.

Dear Judge,

Thank you for the offer to take your boat out. As I've told you before, the restrictions of my job are clear that I can't accept gifts from family members of inmates. Please stop sending me stuff. Nice of you, but I only did my job. I'm not supposed to let inmates get hurt on my watch. I would've intervened even if it hadn't been Terence. You had your chance to help Ollie, Allie and me years ago, and you turned your back on us. I don't want your gifts now. I'd rather drown than take a ride on your stupid boat.

Also, tell Darius that his older brother is too stubborn for his own good, and he should stay away from you. Enclosed you'll find the ashes of your offer. You can sprinkle them with the others I've sent back. Make yourself a little collection.

-October

I WAITED FOR THE ASHES TO COOL, AND THEN SWEPT THEM into a Ziploc bag, which was sealed and then folded into the envelope.

Von was chuckling when I came out to place the stamped envelope in our mailbox. "That's brilliant. He really offered to buy you a car?"

I glowered at Ollie for telling Von that little tidbit. "I was already buying a car for myself when he offered. I don't need a drug lord with a selective conscience to do me any favors."

I bid the boys goodnight and then disappeared into my bedroom. I straightened out one of the spare blankets on a spot on the white carpet near my dresser, but really the guys had their pick of the floor. I had zero clutter and nothing taking up space other than my bed, a cherry wood nightstand and matching dresser.

And a giant gray wolf. I jumped when he came out from the other side of the bed, startling me. Mason stared up at me from the center of the room expectantly. I shoved my hands into my flannel pockets, feeling totally unbalanced with a wolf in my room who was actually a man. I kept my eyes on my feet as I struggled to figure out how to make this awful day seem kosher. "Um, do you need anything before I turn in?" I whispered.

Mason could sense my discomfort and took pity on me. He moved to my side and nudged my leg towards the bed.

I smiled. "Okay, okay. Let me know if you need another blanket for the floor. Sometimes it gets drafty." I laid down in the center of the bed, but then hissed when he hopped up next to me. "Get down! Down, boy." I clicked my fingers as if he were a real dog before I remembered myself. "You can't sleep in bed with me. You and Von can share the floor."

Mason lowered his snout and let out a low growl that started in his throat and filtered out through closed teeth.

"Don't you try that nonsense on me. This is my house. My bed. I'm the only one who gets to be intimidating in here. You get to be the obedient puppy everyone loves. That's your only job."

Mason's answer was to flop down on the mattress and rest his head on the pillow next to mine. Then he closed his eyes, feigning sleep.

"You are such a lousy faker. I know you're awake, and I know you can hear me." I leaned closer to glare at him, but he surprised me by licking my cheek. I squealed and giggled despite myself, wiping off the slobber on the comforter I knew I'd have to wash in the morning. "Oh, fine. You can stay just this once." I reached over and stroked his fur, then recalled that beneath the wolf was an actual person. "I'm sorry. Am I allowed to do that?"

Mason responded by leaning into the touch, inching his nose closer to mine. I buried my fingers in his soft, luxurious gray fur and watched his tension dissipate as his eyes closed again.

Since there weren't any other humans in the room to hear my confession, I whispered into the dark, "I killed someone. That Tanga woman? I've never killed anyone before, but I murdered her. Like, actual murder."

Mason licked my chin in understanding. He'd killed her too, though something told me murdering wasn't all that earthshattering for him, Viking as he was.

"I don't know what to do with that. It feels... I killed someone," I admitted again, ashamed at the person I now was. Maybe I could've gotten off on it being self-defense, since Tanga attacked me and tried to abduct me, but it wouldn't change the fact that someone had died, and I'd been the guilty one with the shiv this time.

Mason let out a sympathetic whine, resting his maw against my face to nuzzle me, to pet me in his own way to return the favor. I wasn't sure what to make of human Mason, but wolf-Mason totally got me.

"You've had a rough day too, huh." My heart melted a little when Mason moved his body closer to mine in answer. "You didn't mean to link up with me. Do you have family you're leaving behind to do this whole reaping thing?"

Mason shook his head and leaned into my touch as I scratched under his chin, craving the closeness of contact behind closed doors.

"Ah. Well, whatever life you're leaving behind to do this thing, I'm sorry you had to give it up. It's not fair to you. I didn't mean for any of it to happen."

Mason rolled onto his side and pushed his back into my stomach. I'd always wanted a puppy, but Ollie and Allie had said no. Then when I lived in the house by myself, I knew I wouldn't be home enough to make it fair for the puppy. But I wanted one. Oh, how I wanted the eyes that always loved me and the tail that never stopped wagging when he saw me. For this one night, I got my wish. Despite the craziness of the last two days, a smile played across my lips at the gift I'd been granted. I wrapped my arm around my new dog and scratched his tummy, spooning the puppy and burying my face in his fur. I didn't care about the germs; I was content in the cuddle.

"Could you do me a favor? Could you make sure Von doesn't eat me in my sleep?" I tried to pass it off as a blasé joke, but Mason sensed my unease. He licked my cheek in answer. I pulled up my white comforter over us and snuggled into the warmth. "Goodnight, Mason. Sweet dreams."

It took longer than I would've liked, but eventually I fell asleep, knowing the morning would bring more questions and fewer things I wanted to be part of.

MY NEW BODY PILLOW

I hadn't been this comfortable in ages. Usually I tossed and turned in my sleep, but despite the awful days previous, I awoke fully rested and feeling like I'd slept ten hours, though I knew from the hardly there dawn peeking under the drawn curtains, it had only been a handful.

I stretched and yawned as my eyes closed again. I turned and cuddled up to my body pillow that was warmer than it usually was, and molded to my curves easier. It smelled like a dream and felt like a man.

"Boy, do you sleep like the dead," commented a voice much too close for comfort.

My eyes flew open and I gasped. My body pillow had been thrown on the floor, and my right arm and leg were currently wrapped around Von while wolf-Mason laid on the bed at my back. "What are you doing?!" I whisper-shouted at him, retracting and sitting up. Embarrassment colored my cheeks and anger laced through my words when I saw Von was bare-chested and taking up half the bed like he owned it.

"What?"

"Why are you in my bed?" I motioned to the floor. "Didn't you see the blanket I laid out for you?"

Von scoffed and reached over me to pet Mason, who was stretching on my other side. "I thought that was a joke. I don't sleep on the floor, love."

I shoved him lightly to get up. "Go sneak out and lay down in the living room before Ollie wakes up and finds you stayed in here last night! Go! Or turn into a bat or whatever vampires do at night."

"Half-vampire," he corrected me.

"Fine, whatever. Turn into half a bat, then. Just go!"

Von chuckled at my chagrin, taking in my flustered demeanor as he stretched his muscular arms toward the headboard, looking like a smutty pin-up model for women to drool over. I refused to drool. "You make the most adorable noises when you sleep, you know." He closed his eyes in imitation of me and gave off little "hmm" and "oh" noises. "And for the record, I slid into the bed on my own side. You're the one who couldn't stay off me. Not that I minded, and not that I blame you." He motioned to his sculpted abs and lean, muscular form.

I was flummoxed, my cheeks pink. My hands flew out, gesturing to the mattress that he was still sprawled out on like he owned the place. "For the record, this whole bed is my side. You don't sleep in it with me. I live alone, and I don't need you horning in on my space."

"Who's Beto?" Von asked, his grin turning evil at my horror. "You were having some good dreams about Beto last night. I'm not offended. I mean, we barely know each other, but if you could work in an occasional, 'Von, you're so big and strong', that would do wonders for my ego."

"And your ego seems to be suffering so much. Get out! I'm not explaining you to Ollie."

Von frowned, picking up a pillow and kneeling on the bed, his naked chest staring me in the face. "Let me ask you something. So what if Ollie thinks we're hooking up? He's your brother. Does he really want you to die alone?"

I swallowed hard at the notion that I'd come to terms with when Ollie moved to New York. I had resigned myself to the fact that I probably would die alone, but it still hurt to think about and have thrown in my face first thing in the morning. "Of course not, but I'm not like that. I don't take random guys home. He still thinks I'm dating his old best friend. I haven't had the nerve to tell him we broke it off yet."

"Did Beto move on to greener pastures?"

My face soured. "What makes you assume he dumped me? *I* ended things with Beto, but I was avoiding the lecture from Ollie until the last possible moment. He can get a little long-winded when he's worked up."

Von stretched his arms over his head again, smirking

when my eyes were drawn to his sculpted torso. "Ollie's a bit overprotective, then?"

"He's fine. Look, I like you just fine. We're cool. But I don't want you in my business, and definitely not in my bed." I tried to look away from his hard body, but my guilty eyes kept springing back to his abdomen like they were on a tether. "Would you put on a shirt already, Hasselhoff?!"

Von stuck his finger in his mouth and pulled it out, as if testing the direction of the wind. "Yep. Too much sexual tension between us. Sure, I'll put on a shirt. I wouldn't want to get you all hot and bothered."

"Just go. Please, Von. This whole thing is weird enough without waking up to a stranger in my bed." I jabbed my finger to the door.

Von held up his hands in surrender, shoving a navy t-shirt over his head that matched his green flannels in a thrown-together sort of way. "Whatever you say, Peach." He winked at me before he left.

I went to get changed, but remembered Mason was a man, despite his gray fur. "Okay, you've got to go, too. I need to get dressed."

Mason nodded and moved toward the door, but stopped by my side to rub his torso against my leg. I softened, wishing he was a real dog as I knelt down and hugged him. His head looped over my shoulder, reminding me of the therapy dog I'd had to go to sessions with as a teenager. I had a hard time making physical contact with peers and adults, but I always had a hug and a treat for that dog. I'm not sure why my germ phobia or distant demeanor were null and void when it came to animals, but I took the contact where I could get it and squeezed Mason around the neck. "Thanks for staying with me last night. You were right. You shouldn't have to sleep on the floor. And thanks for not letting Von eat me in my sleep."

Mason licked my cheek and leaned the top of his head into my hand for one more scratch before giving me my privacy. Mason's simple touch made me feel instantly lighter, and I wondered if he'd done his pulling thing on me to take away my anxiety.

I threw on jeans and a comfortable pink t-shirt with my black long-sleeved zip-up hoodie. I padded out to the kitchen in my socks. Danny was already rummaging through my fridge, pulling out things at random.

My best sleep ever fended off the unhappiness I felt at having my stuff rearranged in the fridge. "Looking for something?" I asked Danny.

He shut the fridge and leaned on the counter. "I'm starving, so I know Von and Mason are dying, too. Not to eat you out of house and home, but it's a side effect of taking in your baggage. I only took in Mariang's normal amount, but Von told me he and Mason were pulling rubbish from you all night while you slept." He scratched his head. "Von's better than I thought if he's already pulling from you while he's sleeping. Usually you have to have done it a few months before you can make it a subconscious thing." He stiffened with a stern frown. "Don't tell him I said that, yeah? It'll make him even cockier if he knows I think he's doing well, and he's at the maximum level of insufferable as it is."

"What?" My nose crinkled. "He didn't pull anything from me. I didn't tell him to do that."

"You didn't have to, and you shouldn't stop him. He's doing his job and finally being an adult. Better late than never. And I didn't know Mason could do that in his animal form, but he did brilliantly. He's out catching squirrels now. He's starving."

I took out the carton of eggs, knowing I could add some leftover Thai food I'd cooked two days ago to make the spread go farther. "Is that how it works with you and Mariang? Can you pull from her right now?"

Danny shook his head, taking out the orange juice and drinking from the carton. I nearly puked, making a mental note to buy a fresh container. "No. We sleep in the same bed, so a lot of work's done while we're resting. Easiest that way. You have to be touching for them to pull the bad stuff out of you."

Von came out of the bathroom and strutted toward us with the proudest smile on his face. "You two talking about what a brilliant Reaper I am? Because you should be. I know how hard it is to do what I did last night."

I held up my hands to the brothers. "Look, I don't need to be handled. I don't need for you to sneak into my bed and pull stuff out of me while I sleep. Everything crashed down this weekend, and I'm fine. See? Still in one piece."

Von turned to his brother as if I hadn't spoken. "I'm ravenous. Like, could eat a whole cow and drink a whole person by myself. Is that normal?"

"Yeah. Stick with the cow, though. You'll feel more of it for the first month or so. She's got a lot of buildup. Whatever craziness that's stored up over time in her will take more than a night to pull out. Mason's out there eating everything he can get his paws on." Danny handed him the orange juice, and Von sipped out of the carton. The same carton Danny had just drank out of.

"Use a glass! Gross!" I exclaimed, the ickiness crawling under my collar and making me itch. I scratched the back of my hand as I shoved past Von to grab a glass from the cupboard.

"See what I mean?" Danny said to his brother.

Von took the glass I handed him, set it down on the counter, and then stood taller while he started chugging the juice straight from the carton as if to challenge me, palming my face with his free hand.

I finally succeeded in batting his arm away. "You two can go out for breakfast. I'm not making you any, and since you haven't been housebroken, you can find your meals outside in the wild, where you belong."

"Huh. How come it didn't work that time?" Von asked his brother. "I tried to pull the crazy out of her, but it didn't work. I mean, look at that cute little scowl." He thumbed my cheek, laughing when I swatted at his hand.

So it was palpable now. I was crazy, and Von could see it, plain as day. I don't know why this hit me as a new low.

Danny took the orange juice and shoved it back in the fridge – on the wrong shelf with the label not facing the front. You know, like a barbarian. "She has to let you take it from her, or she has to be unconscious. Your best bet with this one is to wait till she's asleep, or wait until you take a soul from her. Suck a little harder, and a little of her madness will go out with it."

"I'm not crazy," I argued, knowing I sounded like a kid trying to hide muddy fingers behind her back while swearing she hadn't been outside all day. "This is my house. I have every right to not want your mouth on my jug."

"Dirty! Come on, pigtails. Have a seat." He pointed to the quaint dining area in the corner of the kitchen. "I'll make us breakfast."

"She doesn't have enough food for all of us." Danny fished his keys out of his pocket. "I'll pick up something for you, Von. Mariang's on her way. Try not to kill each other, kids."

30

MY NEW DOG, AND BEV'S OLD TRICKS

I had a routine for cleaning my house. First I did my bedroom, since that hardly took any time at all. Then I did the living room and the two spare bedrooms, and I saved the kitchen for last before detailing my car. This morning everything took twice as long. My sheets had to be washed since Von and a wolf had slept in them. Von had thrown his dirty clothes in a pile on the floor in the corner of my room, so I vacuumed the whole house twice, just in case.

Von and Danny ate more than I could've imagined. Danny alone consumed five egg and ham breakfast sandwiches from the nearest fast food joint, four glasses of orange juice, five large orders of fries, seven hash browns, three egg burritos and two fruit and yogurt cups. Von and Mason ate double what Danny did, sharing one egg sandwich grudgingly when Ollie awoke and grabbed a sandwich off the table before jumping in the shower to start his day. Ollie was a classic long showerer, which gave the others free rein to talk as loud as they wanted about any number of Omen-related topics.

Mariang arrived a few seconds after Ollie disappeared into the shower. She looked at the spread on the kitchen table and gasped. "Oh, did you really take that much from me? Danny, I'm sorry. I didn't realize I was that upset."

Danny motioned her over and laced his fingers through her frail ones. I noticed them both relax a degree as he pulled some anxiety from her. Though he was calming her by pulling, it looked as if the motion soothed him, as well. "No. Most of this is for Von and Mason." He jerked his thumb toward me. "The new one's got a lot of baggage to sift through."

I glowered at Danny. "Shut your donut hole about my baggage, dude. Not cool."

Mariang kissed Von's temple, standing between the two brothers at the table while Mason contented himself eating from a plate on the floor at my feet. "You alright?"

Von pounded the hand without food in it to his chest. "Are you kidding me? I'm the master! Did it all in my sleep."

Mariang was clearly impressed. "Wow! Good for you. You're a natural. Not that I'm surprised. You're good at everything you put your mind to."

Danny didn't look up as he laced acidity into the morning just to remind us all that he was still on Team I-Hate-Von. "I guess prostitutes make the best Pullers."

My face twisted as I glared at Danny for throwing such a wicked curveball out of left field. "What are you talking about? No one in this room is a prostitute."

Danny motioned to his brother, whose smile subdued. "Our very own Von was. Ezra pulled him out of the gutter to work doing security at the mansion."

Von kept his chin level, refusing to be shamed. I knew that stiff upper lip and feigned serenity. I wore the same expression to keep my sanity when Bev was around. Von gave me an apologetic nod. "That's me. Pay by the hour for a glimpse at what I've got. But you get me for free, love. I won't open a tab for you."

Maybe I should've been offended by his crappy joke, but I knew Von was trying to breeze over the blight. I brushed a calm smile onto my face, just to show Danny that he didn't have the power over our morning, and to show Von that he was still welcome in my home. "Man, you must be absolutely filthy rich, if that's how you made money." That brought about a scoff from Danny, and a short laugh from Von, who clapped at my compliment. "And Danny, stop being a tool. You're stirring things up that are best left private." I cleared my throat and nodded when Von mouthed his thanks to me. "We were talking about Von doing his pulling thing in his sleep, and what a great job he did. See? He sucked most of the murderous rage out of me, so now I only want to pound on you a medium amount, Danny."

Mariang's eyebrows were so high, they almost disappeared into her hair. "That's very difficult to do. Danny didn't learn how until weeks after I was awakened." She visibly shrank at casting a disparaging remark on Danny's stellar abilities. "Of course, he does it seamlessly now. Must be a Vandershot brother thing."

Von leaned his head to Mariang's side in brotherly affection. "See? Someone still believes in me. Take note, Danny old boy."

"And you didn't need to feed at all?"

"No." His nose scrunched. "Actually, I'm fine. Her scrapes are still pretty raw, but I didn't bite her even a little."

I shuddered, but Mariang threw her arms around Von's neck indulgently. "I'm so proud of you! See? Ezra was right. You can hold onto your humanity, no problem. It just takes a little practice. I brought you some honey and a blood bag."

"Aw, you love me. Give me some sugar, sugar." He leaned his cheek out, grinning when she gave him a sweet peck on his roguish dimple.

"Of course I do. What's not to love?"

Mason laid his furry body atop my feet to warm them while he ate, and I felt a portion of my irritation drain out of me like a gentle drip from a leaky faucet. When he wolfed down everything on his plate (wolfed down! I'm funny), I snaked a breakfast sandwich from Von, unwrapped it and handed it under the table to Mason, scratching behind his ears and kissing the top of his head. "There you go, baby. Are you still hungry?"

Mariang bit back a goofy smile while Von chuckled in his suggestive way that always made it sound like he was thinking about something dirty.

"What?" I asked them.

Mariang shook her head, but Von had no qualms speaking his mind. "You just called Mason 'baby'. He's like, almost a decade older than you and a seasoned warrior. He's Matruculan. Those are some of the strongest creatures in Terraway, and you just called him 'baby'. I really want you to repeat the whole scene when he's a man again." He bit into his sandwich and grinned.

Mason growled irritably at Von, but returned to his sandwich otherwise unperturbed. He maintained his position of laying on my feet, ensuring either that he didn't think I was being a freak, or that he forgave me for being one. Either way, I really kinda loved my new dog.

Danny surreptitiously eyed my every fidget, so to compensate, I moved slower as the others ate. How I wished I could've spent my weekend with my brother, but he was going off with his friends, and I was starting a new career in death.

When the doorbell rang, I expected Gabby and geared myself up for a stream of lies to spew at her. I knew I would have to explain why I went from being a hermit she had to drag out of the house to go to bars and clubs, to hosting two new guys, a wolf and an almost sister here.

Mason accompanied me like a shadow as I moved through the immaculate house to the living room. I flung open the door, but didn't find my spunky BFF. Instead, I was greeted by Bev, who had a smile and a box full of junk. "Hi, honey pie. I was just in the neighborhood and thought I'd stop by to visit." She gasped when she saw Mason. "Is that a wolf?"

"Oh, no. It's my new dog. Looks like a wolf, though, right? That's why I got him. His name's Mason."

"Oh, he's so cute! Does he have a bed? We have to go shopping for a new doggie bed."

I bit my lower lip before speaking. "No thanks, Bev. He sleeps in my bed with me. That's real sweet of you to offer." Mason inched closer and brushed his side up against my leg. That same slow drip started up again, and I felt the tension that usually peaked when Bev came over lessen by the slightest degree.

"And look! I found two garage sales on the way over. Isn't this great?" She pointed to a lamp with tiny seashells on the sides. She motioned to the car in the driveway with her chin. "Do you have company? I would've did my hair if I'd known you had people over." Her blonde do was usually coifed higher, but she wasn't out of sorts by any means. Bev never left the house looking anything less than ready to have her picture taken, should the occasion arise.

I closed my eyes when Danny skulked over. "Good morning, Ms. Reese."

Bev almost dropped her box of crap; she was so surprised to see Ezra's daughter's special friend at my house. Her voice moved up an octave and her tone turned syrupy, with an extra layer of her southern lilt. "Danny? Well, color me surprised. What're you doing here with my October Grace?"

"We got to talking, and she offered to show us the town."

"Well, I'll be. You're being friendly? You're making nice with my fiancé's family? Good for you, honey pie! I knew you had it in you. Here, can you hold onto this for me? Mind you store it somewhere safe, now." She shoved the box into my arms and pulled out an imaginary ball from her pocket and showed it to Mason. "Here, boy. Fetch!" She flung the fake ball across the living room.

Mason looked up at me with a bored expression before trotting off after the nothing he guessed he was supposed to find in the corner.

My hands burned with the sting of germs and dust that radiated off the box I knew I didn't want in my house. "No, Bev. You know the rules." I lowered my voice, but there was no hiding my words from Danny, who was standing right next to me. I tried to hand the box back to her, but she breezed past me to see who else was over. I was shaking inside, afraid they would see my childhood for what it was – a giant mess. I didn't want to cause a scene, but Bev and I had rules. I let her come visit, and she agreed not to bring anything over to store in my house.

Bev was the life of the party. She had that way about her. You could say five words, and she had a million hilarious stories that would have even the most stalwart person laughing their socks off. Bev entertained while I took the box of junk to her car, shoving it in the backseat atop several layers of fast food wrappers, maggots, clothing and other things that had been things once upon a time, but had since fallen into disrepair.

I tried not to let my heart break, as it always did when I thought about my mama driving around in such inhumane conditions. I wanted to clean her car – I never stopped wanting to clean up her life – but knew that she would beat me something awful if I threw out even a wrapper.

"What are you doing?" came Ollie's low voice from over my shoulder.

"Jeez! You scared me. Hey, Ollie. I'm just putting Bev's stuff back in her car."

His expression was composed, but his posture was rigid with displeasure as his damp auburn hair dripped down into his folded collar. I saw Mason trot out the door to watch our exchange from the front porch. "Do you let her do this? What about the rules?"

"I don't *let* her bring stuff over, but sometimes she tries to sneak stuff in. I always put it back in her car before she leaves." I scratched the back of my neck under my ponytail. "I didn't want to tell you."

"How long?" Ollie snapped the rubber band on his wrist that he always wore. It was part of his Anger Management sessions. The smack of the rubber was supposed to remind him not to lose his temper. These days it had about a fifty percent success rate of centering him, which was a vast improvement from a few years ago.

"How long has Bev been trying to sneak stuff into our house? Since you left. I never let her, though, so it's no big deal."

"No big deal? We'll see about that." Ollie turned on his heel, his takedown face in full swing. "Bev!" he barked as he reached the house.

I scampered behind him with Mason on my heels, not wanting them to get in a fight during the few days I had with him. "No, Ollie! It's fine! I can handle it!"

Ollie stomped inside, cutting right into Bev's bit about the motorcycle that almost killed her on her first ride, and the officer who saved her life. She'd managed to talk her way into having the cop drive her to motorcycle safety classes that weekend. It was a good story, but Ollie was in no mood. "Bev, a word. Outside, right now."

"Oliver! Everyone, isn't my son so handsome? I mean, just look at his haircut."

"Outside, Bev." Bev tried to laugh him off, but Ollie

raised his voice to draw the attention of everyone in the room. "Now!"

I flinched at the bark in him that only Bev ever brought out.

Her mascaraed eyes sharpened and lasered in on her son with a hint of loathing. "Excuse me, kids. I'll be right back. It seems someone left his manners in New York."

As my brother marched Bev past me out onto the porch, I wrung my hands together. "Ollie, it's fine! I've got it under control! Ollie, don't!"

Ollie slammed the door shut behind him and Bev, but I could make out shouting on the porch that I hoped was unintelligible to the others. They were all gawking at me like guppies with their mouths hanging open.

I had a hard time finding my voice, and when I did, it was the mousy version. "I... um, so when do ya'll want to leave? Now's good for me. Like, *right* now."

Mariang was the only one with enough grace in her to appropriately word what they were all thinking. "October, is everything alright? Oliver seemed a bit upset."

I tried to swallow, but my mouth was too dry. "I, uh, everything's fine. Just a little family stuff. Nothing to talk about." I flinched when Bev's voice rose above Ollie's. She didn't like it when Ollie stood up to her. She didn't much like it when anyone did. That's how I learned to get her to not hate me so much; I stopped standing up to her so overtly. "So, can you pack that food up? We should leave. Like, now if we can. Super now. Five minutes ago, now."

Danny huffed. "Von, do you need a manual? She needs you to pull this family drama from her. Look at what she's doing to her hands!" He pointed to my fingers that were scratching the back of my left hand. I hadn't even realized I was doing it. "Whenever she does that, it means you're not doing your job. Have you ever seen Mariang bite her nails? No! Because I do my job."

"I'm fine! Jeez!" I exclaimed as Von stood, shoving half an egg sandwich in his mouth. I held up my hands to Von and Mason, who were closing in on me like I needed to be handled. "Let's just go. I don't need you to do that pulling thing. Family stuff's nothing new, and it's not a big deal. Ollie and Bev just have to get into it every now and then. He hasn't seen her for a few years, so they're overdue."

Ollie flung the door open, ignoring our audience as he fumed in my direction. "Never again. That'll never happen again. I had a talk with her, and she won't pressure you like that anymore. If she does, I want you to tell me first thing."

"I'm fine, Ollie. I told you I could handle it."

He smacked the back of his hand into his palm for emphasis. "Throwing her junk back in her car before she leaves isn't handling it. It's cleaning up after her, which you're not allowed to do!"

My hands flew out in frustration and hurt. "Don't yell at me!" Ollie loved me, and was only ever nasty when it was on the backlash of a fight with Bev.

Mason growled as he moved to my side, brushing against my leg and stripping a layer of stress from me.

Ollie took a breath, his hands up in surrender. "Fine. Sorry. I just don't like it when she does that." He pointed to the floor to punctuate his point. "This is *our* house. We worked for every square foot. Bev doesn't get an inch of it. Not one single inch. You know the damage she can do with an inch."

I lowered my voice, hoping the separation between the kitchen and the entrance was enough so the others didn't hear our conversation. "Look, I appreciate it, but the thing is, you're gone. You live in New York, and I deal with Bev. It sucks, but I'm fine. You yelling doesn't actually solve anything."

Ollie and I glared at each other, locked in our usual stalemate. He didn't like Bev around me, and I didn't like either of them telling me what to do. "I won't abandon our mama. Don't make me be someone I'm not. This is me, Ollie. Love me this way."

"She abandoned you from day one. She hasn't earned you taking care of her."

I straightened, letting Ollie know he wouldn't win this. "Love can't be earned. I love, and that defines *me*; it's not contingent on Bev's list of good or bad deeds. This is me," I repeated in earnest. "Love me this way!"

Finally Ollie deflated, and I followed suit. "I'm being a jerk to you, and the whole point was to help you with her. I do love you, whatever way you are. We've got a lot to catch up on." He turned and motioned me toward his room, so I followed. He pulled on a green hoodie from his suitcase, zipping it up as he spoke. He was so pressed and Wall-Street-looking for work, but he always made me smile when he came home for a break from the grind in his street clothes. "Can we make some time to talk tonight? I've got a few things I want to run by you."

"Sure. Anything important?"

He ducked his head almost apologetically. "Kind of. Tonight?"

I nodded, bumping the crown of my head to his chest before exiting out into the kitchen. Ollie waved his goodbye and left the house after Bev skidded down the driveway, and with him he took about twenty percent of my nerves.

With a determined look, Von took a step toward me, but I backed away. "Please don't do your pulling thing on me. I'm fine. We're strictly business here, so let's get to it." I narrowed my eyes at Mason. "That means you, too, pup. I felt you pull something just then when Ollie was yelling. I can handle it."

Danny rolled his eyes at me. "You're being stubborn. Their job is to help you. You have no idea the kind of stress you're walking into, so it's best you have a clean slate."

"I said I'm fine. If I get the urge to spontaneously burst into tears, I'll let you know," I lied. I shoved my feet into my purple tennis shoes that had three white stripes climbing up the sides. They were comfortable, good for standing on your feet all day, and felt like a second skin I didn't have to question. They were exactly what I needed to make sure I didn't let myself get too swept away from myself by Terraway.

I opened the front door like a bellman, ushering each of them out into the early morning sunshine. My stomach was in knots, but my chin was high, and hopefully my weak spots were invisible.

31

FIRST DAY ON THE DEATH JOB

"*R*eally? You want me to do it now? I thought this was more of a training day. I think I should watch you reap another person before I dive in." I was whispering to Mariang outside Room 207 of St. John's Hospital. We were in the terminal ward, and the atmosphere was a mixture of a holy hush and utterly grim. Ezra had swung by to pick up Mason and take him shopping so he had non-Viking attire to sport around town, leaving me to work with Von.

"You feel the tug in your stomach, right?"

"Yeah. I think so." Either that or I was hungry.

"Then when we go in, hand him the note and make sure to touch his hand."

I'd skimmed the note Mariang had given to the three people we'd visited already. It was a "you can do it" kind of sentiment that was a total lie. Everyone we visited would die within twenty-four hours no matter what we did. I was there so their souls didn't go to waste. It felt icky and in the worst kind of taste. I was the Grim Reaper's opening act, and I was expected to go onstage in Room 207 with a smile.

Von's hand found my back. "You good, Peach?" The four of us were an awkward group to enter into a small hospital room. This time it would just be Von and me, and I wasn't sure I was ready.

I wasn't sure I'd ever be ready, really.

I went into the unadorned room with Von. The grim atmosphere reeked of impending death and an overly full adult diaper. The white walls felt sterile, but not in the comforting way where you knew everything was clean. They felt like a siren blaring out at the old man in his steel bar bed, warning him not to go to sleep, for it would surely be his last. He had to be at least in his late eighties, with a long chin and sallow skin that was yellowed with jaundice.

I had the note in my shaking hand, ready to give it to him as my excuse for barging in on his last day on earth. There was no need though; his eyes were closed, and he didn't even stir when the door clicked behind us.

"Go ahead," Von whispered. "Do it!"

"Don't rush me!" I shot back, overthinking the smallest movements. I knew I needed to touch him and will the soul toward me, but I was punking out.

"What are you waiting for?"

"Just... I just need you to give me a minute." I bit my lip and reached for the elderly man's arm. It was devoid of the necessary moisture to keep it looking life-like. The papery skin creased when I touched it, and didn't bounce back when I moved my hand up toward his elbow. I couldn't feel the cold, but then I wasn't focusing either.

"Hurry along, now. We don't want to wake him. This is the best scenario for your first time, so do your thing."

"I have no idea what I'm doing here! I can't feel the cold. Maybe I picked the wrong room." Now that there was a face to the job, I had a hard time doing it. Being a nurse meant saving people, not standing next to them while they slowly withered away. Not trying to fix the old man went against all my natural instincts.

"You're stalling, you adorable little chicken. Mariang said this is the bloke. You want I should motivate you?" He pinched my side, making me yelp, and I worried he would wake the old man.

"Would you knock it off? I'm a grown woman. I don't even remember the last time someone tried to tickle me."

"Was it the last time you were being a big, fat coward?"

I shot him a withering look. "Here's a tip on women from me to you: Don't call us fat."

"I didn't mean actual fat. You know you're a pixie." He pinched both my sides this time, making my eyes bulge. I fought my way through a giggle while I squirmed. My irritation started to give way to borderline affection. It's as if Von understood my hang-ups and decided to waltz right through them with a big old grin.

I slapped his hands away, sharing half a smile with him

that I didn't understand. I'd been freaking out just a second ago, and now we were laughing. "Get your paws off my danger zone. Men lose fingers if they trespass."

"Maybe you need to let a few men trespass from time to time. Might help you calm down."

I stepped back with as much of a glare as I could muster through the levity. "Next time I need dating advice, I'll hit you up. I'm good for now. I'm not really the dating type."

"Ah. You're the marrying type, then?"

My cheeks pinked. "Jeez! Obviously not. I'm the working type. I don't have time for much dating."

"Could've fooled me. You've been putting off your job for the past few minutes, begging me to dance with you instead."

"What?" Before I could work up a proper retort, Von had me in his arms. He spun me around the hospital room to an old Rat Pack tune he hummed, while my legs fell into step with his. I had always been a terrible dancer, but in that moment, somehow I was able to follow along without stepping on his toes.

After a few beats, I forgot my frustration and gave in to the fun. I hadn't danced with a guy in ages, and even when I had, I'd been too nervous to really enjoy the thrill of it. Von's smile gleamed at me, loving watching me let go and have fun as he enjoyed the dance himself. He was lithe and graceful, and I was just trying to keep up, looking down at his feet to make sure I didn't step out of turn.

"Don't look down. Look at me. I won't lead where you can't follow." His smile had the hint of a promise to it that stuck in me like a friendship I wouldn't be ready to throw away anytime soon.

"Promise?" I asked, though there was a hint of insecurity poking through my smile. "I've never been much good at this."

"You've had the wrong partners, then. You're a natural." He slowed the dance from a lively ditty to a tender sway, his footwork easier to follow as I tried to keep my eyes locked on his. The smiles between us grew to something sweeter, kinder than a mere laugh. His dimples drew me closer to his chest as he waltzed us around the hospital room.

"This is nicer than I thought. Just don't dip me."

Von smirked. "You really shouldn't have said that." My eyes widened as I clung to him, my fingernails digging into his hand and arm when Von dipped me backward. My neck was stiff, and I knew from his laugh that I looked nothing like the women did in the movies. He leaned in, whispering in my ear, "Let go, *hani*. I won't let you fall."

"Promise?" My eyes asked a myriad of things I was too chicken to put a voice to. Trust wasn't a strong suit of mine – even worse than dancing, if you can imagine. But Von's smile had the hint of a vow to it that made me choose to muscle through my resistance and give trusting him a try. Slowly, my fingers loosened their death grip on him one by one, my neck relaxing as my head fell back where it was supposed to be. My curls dangled, succumbing to gravity as they danced and twirled more gracefully than I ever could.

Von looked down on me, his eyes taking in my rare moment of total trust. "Beautiful," he murmured. Then he cleared his throat. "How much would you hate me right now if I dropped you?"

"Nine."

"Yikes. That sounds painful. Best not be careless with this one, then." He slowly brought me back up, kissing the knuckles on the hand that was still resting in his. My stomach did a flip-flop that I scolded my hormones for. "Now that we've had our dance, I think it's time to pretend we're responsible adults and do our job, yeah?"

I gulped, remembering why we were here. Our clasped hands dangled between us, reminding me that I didn't have to be alone in this new life. His slow drip of pulling made something as simple as handholding possible for me, and I adored him for the small gift that was actually a big deal. "I think I'm ready now. Thanks for that."

"Anytime, November."

"Could you do me a favor? Please don't tell Danny I froze on the job."

The dimple in his left cheek became my new best friend when he smirked at me. "I don't know what you're talking about. It's me what needed a few extra minutes to ready myself." He pulled out a bottle of honey from his black jacket inside pocket, flipped open the top with his thumb and started sucking on it. "So much blood in this place."

"You doing alright?" I reached out, wanting to touch his arm to assure him that I believed in him – that he could control his cravings, even when surrounded by temptation. I retracted my hand, unsure if Von was crawling in germs or not. Normally people not in my family were for sure crawling in germs, but I couldn't tell with Von.

It was as if Von understood my limitations, and was a decent enough guy not to take offense. His hand found the small of my back, so we were connected through this inaugural moment. Strangers as we were, there was a comfort I felt around Von that warred with my desire to claw the skin off my hands and run from human contact. "Thanks for worrying about me. I'm holding on just fine. Now it's your turn to be brave."

I cleared my throat and brushed the arm of the old man who was obviously heavily medicated, since he hadn't woken for our song and dance. I closed my eyes and breathed in deep. The next breath was deeper, and then I felt the cold. It was as if the chill had been awakened at my presence and was peeking its little head at me like a dog looking for its master. I stroked the puppy and he came to me, resting under my hand until I grabbed him by the scruff of the neck and pulled him gently from his home.

The second the soul left the man and went completely into me, I felt the same mixture of ice and knives in my veins as I had when Tanga's life escaped into my palm. The freeze was painful, lighting my nerves up with a kind of arctic fire I couldn't escape. It climbed all through me like a thousand tiny freezing spiders that were aiming for my heart like a race toward cardiac arrest.

I breathed through the horror that made me want to run like a crazy person and find the hottest shower imaginable. I clung to the bar on the old man's bed, willing it to keep me centered and upright.

Von's hand was on my shoulder, and on instinct I shrugged it off. "I'm trying to help you," he insisted, keeping his voice gentle. "You have to let me take it."

"I c-can't! It's stuck!"

Von flew out the door and returned with a barrel-chested Danny. He looked as if he was gearing up for a fist-fight, and not, you know, a conversation.

Danny pried my hands off the bar, and I could feel how stiff they were from the cold that bit at me on the inside. "Look at me," Danny commanded in a firm whisper.

Even my eyeballs felt stiff from the ice I couldn't chase away, but somehow I obeyed. "I'm f-freaking out!"

"Don't be stubborn. You're going to take the cold, ball it up like a wad of paper and feed it to Von. That's how this works. You keep it inside you for too long, your skin will start to turn like Mariang's. Is that what you want?"

I reached for Von, but the movement was as ungraceful as a zombie. He met me halfway, holding onto my hands and inhaling in time with my exhale. Finally I let go of the cold that had me tied up in knots. The sensation of the soul leaving me was like a thousand spiders scurrying away from me in droves, running through my veins and leaving my natural warmth behind as they trailed through my palms and into Von's. The heat was a relief like none other, melting into my body like hot fondue chocolate and rolling through me with deliciousness I couldn't quantify. So deep was my body's elation at letting go of the cold, that my knees buckled. Von caught me before I hit the floor, and carried my limp form toward the chair by the side of the bed. He sat me right next to the old man I'd just helped to die peacefully when his hour was finally up.

Von sank into the chair with me across his lap, my eyes shut. My head lolled on his shoulder, and when he combed his fingers through the small curls at the base of my neck, I nearly drooled on him. He traced the curve of my face, watching as my eyelashes fluttered like a hummingbird against his finger.

"This is why you should've let them take a little stress off your plate this morning. It hits you hard when you get too much buildup."

Von waved off Danny's lecture, since I could barely keep my head up at the moment. Von's voice was rich, like the best kind of British radio DJ who you didn't care what they said, so long as they kept on talking. "What did you and Oliver fight about this morning?"

The heat and the comfort were heady. My body felt like warm taffy that Von was able to mold, making my rigid parts pliable again. I hadn't sat on a man's lap since

Ollie and Allie had taken me to the mall to see Santa Claus. I'd been five, and even back then I thought I was a little too old for such things. "Just sibling stuff. Nothing big."

His lips tickled my ear. "I know you're lying. I can feel how stressed you are. It's coming off you in waves."

I moaned pornographically. "That feels..."

His lips trespassed, capturing my earlobe and giving it a slight tug. "What did you fight about?"

"Bev. We only ever fight about Bev."

"What about her?"

"So warm," I cooed, burrowing myself into his body, relishing the embrace. I couldn't remember my reasons for fending it off. I couldn't feel the sting of Bev, or the loneliness I usually wore like a cloak. I felt warm, chocolatey nothing, and it was heavenly. "This is..."

Danny's tone was sharp. "That's enough. Up, Von. You're pulling too hard. It's making her forget herself. That's not the goal."

Von stroked the side of my cheek, and I leaned into the touch as heat from his thumb radiated through my face. "She's got rubbish buried deep, Danny. Give me a few more minutes. Look at how much she loves this. She needs me."

Suddenly I was lifted from the warmth and found myself in Danny's arms. Lucidity started coming back to me, and my face turned crimson. "Oh, no. I didn't mean to... Don't you ever let me do that again!" I tried to struggle away from Danny's grip, but my knees were too weak to carry me without crapping out.

Danny righted me and offered his arm, leading me out into the deserted hallway. He deposited me into a spare wheelchair at the end of the hall before he whirled on Von. "What were you thinking? You have a long road ahead with her. What you just did? Unacceptable. You have to get her to trust you, Von. You have to get her to want to give you her secrets. Ripping that out of her? Look what you did. Typical Von. Big personality bursts through the door, doesn't look to see who he's clobbered in the process. You used to be responsible, but this? You can't be a fool any longer. You're just as bad as the Reapers who ripped through all the other Omens, took what they wanted and made them useless!"

Von was incredulous and hyper dramatic, his gestures big and wide. "Oh, am I? Am I a date rapist? Is that where we're taking this? Come on, Danny. She's stubborn as a mule. No way were we going to meet our quota going this slow."

My head hung, and not just because it was a chore to lift it. Von was right; I was too stubborn, and it would mean I might suck at this job if I couldn't learn to work with him like I needed to. It had taken me a few months to trust Doctor Brenden; I guessed we wouldn't have that same grace period with reaping.

"You shouldn't have signed on for the job if you couldn't handle the work. That's your problem. You don't know how to work anymore! What happened to you? What happened to the big brother that raised us? It's all about shortcuts with you now. You think just because your life is shortened now that you're a half-vamp, you're allowed to take the easy road."

"Dealing with you's a full-time gig!"

Danny shoved Von, who scowled, though I could tell he was inches away from shoving his younger brother back.

Mariang squeaked as she wheeled me away from the dueling pistols and turned a corner. She stopped and knelt in front of me, slapping my cheeks to liven me up. "You alright? Were you able to get the soul out of the gentleman in 207? Did it work?"

I blinked at her and nodded slowly. "Does it always feel like this?"

"No. Von sucked much too hard. He's new at this. He didn't mean to. You'll get a rhythm down. Don't you worry. Danny's setting him straight. It takes more than doing it once to get it right. This is all part of the learning curve. Plus, Von's on edge because this is a hospital, and no doubt he can smell the blood at every turn."

Danny stomped toward us and jerked my chin up toward the light. He pried open my eyelid and grumbled to Von, who sidled up beside him. "Do you see this?" Danny said to Von in accusation. "Her pupils are completely dilated. You took too much out of her at once. Now she's useless! Think, Von. Think for once in your life."

Von's eyebrows pushed together in concern as he stared at my dazed expression. "Easy, Danny. I didn't go through all the courses you took. I'm learning here, too. Instead of yelling like a wanker, how about you teach me how to not lobotomize her next time, yeah?"

Danny jerked the wheelchair in the opposite direction, wheeling me down to a room Mariang indicated on her left. "In here. This should wake her up a little."

Von knocked politely before taking me from Danny and wheeling me inside. A woman, who was not quite as old as the elderly man, but a stone's throw from her late eighties, was hooked up to several machines. She was breathing steadily as the equipment beeped at a predictable rhythm. Von picked up my limp hand and placed it on hers. The bone beneath was frail, and the soul was easy to find. She must've been only minutes from death, as opposed to half a day away from it.

The freezing sensation revived me like I was crashing through the ice, submerged in the arctic. It took my breath away, jerking my chin upright and making my arms and legs prick with that painful stab that had taken me over before.

"Now gently take it from her in layers," Danny instructed his older brother. "You were yanking the soul from her before. Pull it slowly."

Von's large hands reached down from behind my wheelchair and cupped my cheeks, massaging my face as he searched for the cold. This time the removal was gentle, like a carefully threaded needle. The warmth took its time moving through me, like slow-moving molasses that replaced the utter subzero with a gradually building heat. The relief didn't deflate me into a puddle this time around, and I felt a little more myself.

My breathing evened out, and I was able to sit upright on my own, feeling pleasantly toasty instead of frozen or roiling with chocolatey heat.

Danny checked my eyes, and I batted his hand away from my face. "That's better. Do it like that, and you're fine. Same thing when you're just pulling normal stress from her. Gentle. Slow. You can't take shortcuts, or you'll wreck everything, like you always do."

"You missed your calling. With sweet talk like that, you should've gotten a gig writing holiday cards. She's fine. I'm brilliant. Tell me how amazing I am to've done it perfect on my first official day. Come on. You know you're taking back a few of those 'you'll never amount to anything' speeches."

Danny harrumphed and pushed past Von toward the hallway.

Von crouched down in front of me, examining my forlorn and confused face the way a doctor would. "Watching Danny be wrong about anything is one of my great joys in life. That he was wrong about me being a loser? So much the better."

"You're not a loser," Mariang assured him, her hand on his arm.

"Aw, thanks little sis." He grinned, sending her after Danny. "You alright, November?"

I swallowed, debating between being pissed off and relieved I wasn't at their mercy anymore. I opted for nodding, which felt more neutral than a tongue-lashing or voicing my total anxiety that Von could control me so easily.

"Good. We'll figure it out, alright? Our people need this to work, and I need not to be the screw-up anymore. Not many jobs out there for a vampire who refuses to transition. No one will hire me because they're afraid I'll go mental on the job and eat every human in sight. Can you be patient for a few days until we find a good rhythm? I need this, November."

I leaned forward in the wheelchair, resting my elbows on my knees and covering my despondent expression with my hands. "This is my life now? This is what I get?"

Von was still kneeling, but when his hand brushed over my shoulder to comfort me, I stiffened. He paused, but kept his hand where it was. "Don't worry. I'm not pulling a ton from you. Just practicing peeling back the layers. Is that alright?"

I wanted to say no, but something told me we needed the practice so he didn't lay me out again like he'd done before. "Okay, but only a little, and just for practice. Please don't ever do what you did before again. I don't want to be that person."

"What person?"

"The girl who sits on men's laps and loses herself when a hot guy whispers in her ear. I'm not that girl, so don't try to make me be. I'm giving up enough for this; don't make me give up myself."

Von studied my face and then nodded slowly. "I am sorry for that. I'm learning, and I did it wrong. Now that I know it was too much, I'll not pull that hard again. Let's get past the learning curve, and then I promise you can trust me. No more sitting on men's laps for you. In fact, if I see you on a bloke's lap at any point in time, I'll know something nefarious is going on, and I'll come in, guns blazing."

"Actual guns? That's some promise." I looked around the hospital room, registering that the fancy equipment was far more sophisticated than the stuff we had to work with at the prison. I swallowed hard, opting for blatant honesty. "I don't like this. Being touched. Being here. The whole thing."

Von took his hand away, his messy black hair shifting as he tilted his head to examine my state. "Okay. You don't like being touched, but I'm not sure how to work around that. I mean, contact's the only way to take the soul from you. I know you're not over the moon about the idea of pulling, but this is a stressful job, and you'll need it done regularly." He pursed his lips in thought. "You have to help me do my job better. I'm trying here, but if you don't tell me what sets you off, you're just going to walk around angry, and I'm going to get frustrated or fired. Then Danny wins. We can't have that."

"Yeah. He's kind of a tool." Anxiety crept up inside me, strangling me around the throat as I spoke, forcing my words to come out in a pinched whisper. I curled my fingers into fists. "I don't like this."

"I'm doing my best not to touch your hands so much. Is it helping? I noticed you don't like that kind of contact in particular."

I looked into his blue eye and his gold eye with an intense level of gratitude for the considerations he had to make just to work with me. "Thanks. Thanks for not... just thanks. I know I'm being difficult. This whole thing is... and I'm not... So, thanks."

"No problem. You know, I can make it so maybe you don't have to wash your hands as much. If you let me know when you're starting to go off, I can pull a layer from you. Maybe that'll help you stop scratching your hands. Then I won't have to walk around smelling hints of your blood all day long."

At mention of my tick, I wanted to gouge a rivulet down the back of my hand, but I resisted, gripping my elbows to hold myself in a hug I wished I didn't need. "You noticed that?"

Von drew his pursed lips to the side. "You don't like that I noticed. That's understandable. I can help you, love."

I didn't have words, so I stuck to nodding. I was grateful, wary and filled with hope that someone might actually be able to help me find the roadmap to normal.

Von lifted me out of the wheelchair slowly, gripping

only my elbows. He took great care not to touch my hands, which was a kindness I couldn't quantify. As I rose, a newfound respect started to bloom between us. He walked next to me, his hand on my elbow in case I needed to lean on him while my legs tried to find their stability.

When we emerged from the hospital room, Mariang and Danny visibly relaxed at my mobile body and Von's non-antagonistic demeanor.

I met Mariang's hopeful gaze and nodded. "Bring on the next victim," I announced.

NOT A COUPLE

Twenty almost stiffs later, Mariang could barely form sentences, and I needed help climbing the stairs, though I'd done fifteen reaps, and she'd made it through only five.

My job up until this had been quite physical, and I was in good shape. I could run a 5K without keeling over or complaining. I was trim, but I could still body-slam a hefty inmate if they got out of control. I was a big fan of using their weight against them.

Still, this death-culling thing was no joke. I had a little energy left long after Mariang begged Danny for a break, so I racked up the additional souls while she rested in her wheelchair, looking every bit as despondent as I had when I'd been confined to mine.

"I really don't know how you're doing this," Danny

commented to me with what could only be described as admiration. "I didn't think it was possible for one Omen to do that many reapings in a day. I mean, Mariang needs to do eight a day, and she's shot by the end of it if we make it that far, which we usually don't. How have you done fifteen and you're still upright?"

"Beginner's luck?" I guessed. I felt queasy and tired, and when seven o'clock hit, I wanted to go home.

Danny carried Mariang through the parking lot to my car, but I categorically refused when Von uncomfortably offered up the same car-side service. My words came out labored, like I was on my way to tipsy. "I'm fine. Just a little tired. And for the record, you will never, ever carry me to my car. Thanks for the offer, though."

"Anyone ever tell you you're an utter joy when you're beat?"

"Only every day. Quit distracting me with all your yammering. I'm trying to make it to the car." My chest was heaving, and my feet were heavy as bricks. My stomach churned like I'd eaten something past its expiration date. The car looked like it was a million miles away, so when Von offered me his elbow to hold, I took it as a last resort, leaning heavily on him as my clumsy feet stumbled drunkenly toward Terence the Taurus.

Von opened the door to the backseat and let out Mason, who was more than happy to see us after Ezra had dropped him off. He wagged his tail and nuzzled my leg, circling me like a sweet puppy should. Von lowered me into the back like I was a fragile old woman, and in that moment, I felt exactly that.

The ride home was spent with Danny grilling Von on the different things he could've done to take a little of the death residue off me for tomorrow's shift. Mason laid his head in my lap, gazing up at me with slate wolf eyes that told me he was bummed to've missed out on the action. "How are you holding up, October?" Danny called back to me.

"I'm fine," I lied. My eyes were shut as my head leaned on the back of the seat. Von was a respectable distance from me on my other side, sucking the honey out of a second bottle, and alternating with a drag from the blood bag Ezra had stashed in a small cooler for him. I appreciated the nonintrusive way he occasionally reached over to rub my forearm. With Mason lying partially in my lap, it was a double shot of the good stuff. My heart rate started to inch toward normal again, and the agony in my stomach slowly faded to a tolerable level.

"It won't be this hard every day. You'll get the hang of it. Now that there are two of you, we can start building up a stockpile of souls, so everyone down in Terraway can start getting a little stronger. After a few months, you won't have to take so many souls." Danny gripped the steering wheel, uncomfortable at the next words that tumbled out of his mouth. "I'm real proud of you, kid. I mean it. I've never even heard of an Omen taking in that many souls in a single day. It was kind of incredible to watch."

I ducked my head to hide from the sincerity. "Um, thanks, Danny. Now that I've got the hang of it, I'm sure I'll be able to do more tomorrow." My phone rang from inside my purse, and it dawned on me that I'd not had my phone on me all day, since I'd locked my bag in the car. "Oh, man! That's Ollie. He's probably freaking out. Can you hand me my purse, Mariang?"

"Sure." She handed the purple messenger bag to me with unsteady fingers. "Everything alright?"

My fingers were clumsy, but I managed to locate the phone before the last ring. "Ollie? I'm almost home."

I heard loud music and a crowd in the background as Ollie shouted into the phone. "Did you do this?" he asked too loudly for me to hold the device to my ear.

"Do what?"

"Invite the whole crew over? I didn't know you were planning a surprise party. You're the best sister a guy could ask for."

I groaned inwardly. "No. That's all Gabby. I guess technically, *she's* the best sister ever, so you know, think twice about hooking up with her tonight." I thought back to Ollie's last visit, and their subsequent heartbreak after much dramatic back and forth. Gabby was good to him, but Ollie was a Reese. We had trust issues and an aversion to being known. "Can of worms, my friend. Can of worms."

"I can't hear you," he lied.

"Do not let Gabby spend the night. Hey! I know you can hear me. You're a masochist!" I shouted into the phone, hoping he heard my chuckle above the din.

"Coming home soon?"

"Yeah. Keep everyone out of my room, okay?"

"They know the rules."

We hung up, and I checked my phone to find that I had three missed calls. One was from Ollie, one from Gabby, and another from an unknown number. I checked my voicemail and heard Ezra's British lilt lending itself to my ear. "October Grace? It's Ezra Manaul. I'm calling to let you know two Duwende guards will be stopping by to increase the security around your house tomorrow. I hope this isn't too much an imposition. I trust you're having a splendid first day on the job. Keep me posted. Happy to help however I can." I hung up and tossed my phone in my purse carelessly.

Von whistled. "You're trippy. I can feel you going up and down. Your brother calls, you're up. But whatever he said brought you down. Then the message you listened to brought you further down. Girls have a lot going on that us blokes just plain don't."

I batted my eyelashes at him and spoke in my most condescending southern tone. "Your views on gender studies fascinate me. I simply must take notes. Tell me, how do you feel about the color pink?"

"On you? Anything'd look just fine." He winked at me.

Yesterday I might've debated between blanching and blushing. Tonight, after the long day I'd endured seeing people on the brink of death? Von was great comic relief. I was tired, so my southern hint started peeking out more from the Midwestern accent Allie, Ollie and I always tried to keep firmly locked in place. "Oh, you like dressing me up in all sorts of colors. I'll have to get you a pink shirt to match mine. Then no one'll be able to tell us apart."

Von was unfazed by the threat, smiling that I'd finally cottoned onto his offbeat brand of humor. "I'd be dashing in a pink shirt."

Mariang cast us a weak smile from the passenger's seat. "You could be one of those delightful couples that always match."

Without grace, I cut through the levity. "We are *not* a couple."

Von scoffed, clearly offended. "You jumped on that awfully quick. I'm fairly certain I should be offended. What's so wrong about being with me? I'd like to know how you think you can do better than this." He motioned to his amazingly sculpted form and churlish half-smile.

I glanced out the window, picking out a pedestrian at random. "That one there. See? I just did better. Or that one. Or him. Or that guy if he pulled up his pants. Or that guy."

"He's at least seventy!" Von chuckled at my dig. "Tough crowd. It's just as well. I'm meeting up with some of my mates tonight. Perhaps they can cheer me up from such blatant rejection."

Danny gripped the steering wheel. "Any chance you felt like telling me you were planning on ditching your job? Did you make arrangements to have someone watch her house while you go off with God only knows who? Did you even discuss this with Mason?"

Von shifted in his seat. "You're staying the night. So's Mason. No point in both of us being a bore." He craned his head toward me. "You need a babysitter, love?"

I blanched. "No. I've been living on my own or with Ollie and Allie since I was eleven. Ezra called and said he was sending over two guards to watch the house or whatever tomorrow. I'm fine. Go get some with whatever woman's got the lowest standards. Blow off some steam. It was a long day."

With a grin I couldn't help but find adorable, Von leaned over and kissed my cheek, shocking me with the unexpected sweetness to answer my slam. "You're the best work wife a man could ask for. I'll be back by dawn."

"We start work at seven, right? Just be back by then." I returned his smile as I scrubbed his kiss off my cheek, enjoying the relaxed look on him. His shoulders were rolled back and his face was devoid of the toils of the day. Death was no big deal to him, and that somehow gave me permission to not let myself get too upset about the lives I'd witnessed breathe some of their last breaths.

He held out his fist to mine, and I realized that he was

meeting my neurosis halfway. I didn't like high-fives or handshakes, so he was buddying it up with me by using a fist-bump. It was the best fist-bump I'd had in a long time. Only people who truly knew me did that, and though Von wasn't one of those people, it was nice that he was trying. I mouthed my thanks to him, and he nodded once with a modest smile.

I cleared my throat. "So my best friend is Gabby, and she's throwing a surprise welcome-home-for-the-week party for my brother with all our friends. You guys are welcome to stay, but you don't have to. Just try to tone down the Death Omen talk. And don't mention me leaving my job. You're just Bev's fiancé's daughter, the boyfriend and the brother, come to hang for the weekend. Plus my new dog." I brushed my tired fingers through Mason's luxurious gray fur.

"We have to stop for food first," Danny ruled. "I'm starving, so I know Von's hungry. And you two only ate fruit this afternoon."

I shrugged. "Just drop me at home, then. I'm not hungry."

Mariang answered for Danny. "It's part of Omen work. Your stomach's always a little queasy. You're never hungry, so you have to start reminding yourself to eat. The job is hard, so you can't let yourself get too weak." She cleared her throat. "The souls are a sort of poison to your system, which is why it's important they leave your body as soon as possible. But there's always that sick feeling that comes from being poisoned over and over."

I began to understand why Mariang was so rail thin. I had a healthy amount of curves and muscle, and didn't relish giving up either. Though I couldn't fathom eating anything, I resolved to work my way through one meal, at least.

33

BEST WORK WIFE EVER

"I've never seen anyone cut their burger with a fork and knife," Danny commented with a mouth full of beef.

Mariang and I took small bites while the guys seemed to be in contest with each other to see how many half-pound burgers they could swallow whole. We'd snuck Mason in past the hostess. He was laying over my feet and consuming burgers cooked rare by the truckload underneath the table in our back corner booth.

I cut myself another piece, chewing only enough to be able to choke it down so I didn't punk out. I was halfway through the burger, and I felt like I was going to barf. "Yeah? Well I've never seen anyone eat three pounds of beef in one sitting. Does it really make you that hungry?"

Von belched in answer. "It's like I can't eat fast enough. I'm going to have to hit the gym hard after this."

Danny shook his head. "No need to compensate. Your metabolism's running high now. Just taking the soul from her does that." Danny slapped his massive bicep. "If her security's threatened, your body will start compensating by developing muscle more easily to keep her safe."

Von straightened. "Stand back, mates, I'm the total package."

I pointed to a waitress who'd been eyeing Von since we walked in. "Dude, waitress at four o'clock concurs. That'll be an easy number to pick up if you're interested." The dark-haired mid-thirties beauty was sneaking looks at his mischievous smile, but was too polite to ask for his number, seeing as how we looked like we were on a double date. Thought I'd throw the girl a bone.

Von raised his arms in victory. "If I wasn't about to go hit on that girl, I'd kiss you square on the mouth. Best work wife ever! Cheers, darling."

I gave him a fist-bump and a grin. "You've got burger grease on your chin. Not sexy." I handed him a spare napkin.

He wiped his face and cast me a dazzling grin. "Better?"

"Almost handsome."

"Oh, you." He batted his hand at me, feigning coyness as he slid out of the booth to go work his magic on the waitress. Girlfriend wouldn't know what hit her; Von was just as charming as he was handsome.

Mariang watched me pick at my burger as the sun set through the window. "You don't have to do that, you know.

Pretend it doesn't bother you that Von's not interested in settling down."

I chewed carefully as I thought through my response. "It doesn't bother me. Why would that be an issue? I work with lots of men at the prison. None of them are interested in settling down with me, either. Von and I are coworkers."

"Maybe Mason, then?"

My eyes widened at the awkward line of questioning. I felt Mason shift against my feet uncomfortably. "I'm thinking there are at least ten other topics more relevant to everyone here. Let's switch to one of those, shall we?"

Mariang was quiet for a few beats while Danny debased himself in his seventh giant burger, moaning gluttonously. When she finally spoke, it was with a mousy voice I had a hard time hearing. "You don't get along with your mother."

I swallowed, and though I hadn't finished my burger, I knew I couldn't stomach another bite if this was the road we were headed down. "I've learned that I can get along with just about anybody. Bev and I do alright."

"My mother was killed in a car crash when I was a baby. I've had a lot of time to dream up what I'd like in a stepmum if Dad ever remarried." She stopped talking, letting the words hang between us as if daring me to react to them so she could judge how much to get her hopes up with Bev. "What do you think of her?"

"Bev's the life of the party. She's always up to go shopping, so feel free to bond with her over that. She's very popular. She can be nice." I chose my words carefully. "If she's ever not, I want you to tell me about it first thing, and I'll handle it." I wasn't sure why I felt oddly protective of Mariang. Perhaps it was her slight figure, or her waif-like complexion. Her gentle way made me want to keep her far from Bev, who was often hurtful to people without thick skin. I didn't want Mariang to have to grow the tough outer layer I wore like armor around Bev. I made purposeful eye contact with Danny, and he nodded in understanding. "Bev will be over the moon to get to know you better, I'm sure. She really likes Ezra."

Mariang's aqua eyes grew large. "Dad's quite taken with her. I've never seen him so happy. He laughs now. It had been a while before he started his phone calls and dates with Bev." She twisted her napkin nervously, and like a pro, Danny reached out and stroked the back of her hand, taking a small amount of nerves from her as she spoke. "You and Ollie don't call her 'mother' most of the time. What should I call her?"

"I guess that's between you and Bev. Um, how much do you and your dad know about our family situation?" I had to ask. I mean, the sweet girl was tiptoeing around dynamite, asking me if it would make a pretty sparkle.

"That your father left when you were young, and that she raised you all by herself while working as a receptionist for a real estate office."

That can be the truth. Close enough. I scratched the backs of my hands under the table as I ignored the scabbed-over wound I didn't like talking about. "Cool. That's good."

Mason paused his ravenous meat-fest to nuzzle his nose into my shin.

"But it's not the truth?"

I pushed my plate away. "I think I'm full. You guys about ready? Want me to tell them to slaughter another cow to go?" I asked Danny, who was studying me as he chewed.

"Mariang deserves to know what she's getting thrown into. Ezra deserves to know, too."

"True enough. But don't I deserve a little privacy?"

Danny looked me square in the face and replied with a succinct, "No."

I sighed, balling up my napkin after I dabbed at my lips. "Look, I'm letting you all stay in my house. I'm talking about normal stuff just fine. Not for nothing, but I just met you all a couple days ago. Don't forget that." I turned to Mariang, my voice softening. "Look, if you want to get to know Bev, that's good. You totally should know your new mama. You two will probably get along great." It was the truth. No matter how much I tried, overlooked and smiled, Bev would always despise me. I didn't blame her for hating me. I was a souvenir from her one-night stand.

"Why do I get the feeling something's very off with your situation?" Danny asked, challenging me.

"I'm all done. I'll wait in the car until you guys are ready to go." And just like that, I shut the door on the conversation.

34

LIFE OF THE PARTY

I groaned internally at the crowd gathered in my average-sized home. There would be a parade of germs infesting my safe place, and I would have to just get over it. *Life is messy, and that's okay.* Germs in my home were the cost I had to pay in order to have friends in my life, so I made the concession with a forced smile. The regular crew was only eight of us, but there were twelve cars parked on the street.

This was a homecoming for Ollie, so I put on my best look-at-me-I'm-social smile as I walked through the garage door. I reminded myself that if not for these impromptu parties where my friends tried to force me to be more social, I would have no life at all outside of work. It was their way of being nice to me, making sure I didn't hermitize myself until the end of time. The kindness felt like medicine I wished I didn't need to choke down, but knew I probably should.

There were coasters not being used under the red plastic cups that held Gabby's famous punch. The pungent beverage served as both a party-starter and a fire-starter. She bounded up to me in her short skirt and wrapped me in a tight hug I reminded myself I had to enjoy if I was going to appear normal. Marcus had the heel of his boot on my glass coffee table. Only Gabby, Ollie and Beto had taken off their shoes.

Beto. I expected him to be there, but seeing him in my house made me introvert afresh. He caught my eye and smiled in his casual we-didn't-just-break-up-again way, and I gave him a two-fingered salute. Mason was quickly descended upon by four women who fawned over his gorgeous fur, their cleavage on full display to him as they bent over. It was his lucky day, the dirty dog.

Excited cries of, "What breed is he? He looks like a wolf!" and "When did you get a pet?" greeted me from my girlfriends. They were enraptured by him, and rightly so; wolf-Mason was gorgeous.

Katrina lifted her cup to me in a hearty "cheers" that was echoed around the living room. "Bait's here, guys!"

I hated that they called me Bait. They were all around Ollie's age, which was eight years older than me, so I had always been the official jailbait, even though I was twenty-two now.

"It's been too long, kiddo!" Jordan and Nick rushed me

like the beer-chugging frat guys they would never stop being, even at thirty. With silly grins on their faces, they crushed me between their bodies.

"Not today, guys," I protested to no avail. I was still a little queasy, and didn't relish the suffocating squeeze.

"But you're my favorite dessert!" Nick countered. "I haven't had an October sandwich cookie in weeks!" Nick reached around me and hugged Jordan, who was pressed up against my other side, squishing me too tight. The affection was innocent and sweet, but I silently prayed for the friendliness to be over as I faked a laugh I'm sure nobody bought. They double hugged me in what felt like a slow, public death while I tried not to hyperventilate.

Mason growled, his hackles rising at my discomfort. I don't know why it made me feel better, knowing someone got how uncomfortable this whole thing was for me. My friends had known me for ages, and Mason only a few days, yet he understood me better than they did. Even Ollie never intervened at these parties; he thought the baptism by fire way of being around all his friends might someday shake me out of my hermit routine. It was a sweet theory.

"Hey, guys. How's it going?" Once Nick and Jordan released me, I ran my fingers through Mason's fur to assure him I was fine, and that this was all normal. He rubbed his side to my leg, standing sentry so the guys would think twice before trying that again.

I had to put in a solid show of being social for Ollie's

sake. I knew it hurt him when I hid in my bedroom during parties. I made polite chitchat while Danny and Mariang stood in the doorway with wide eyes, surveying the scene.

Von pumped his fist in the air in time with the eighties rock music Gabby always insisted upon, despite the current decade. "I didn't know you were awesome, November!" Then he called over to Rachel, my red-headed friend who was always quick to hit on the new guy, "You there! Something's wrong with this party if I've been here a whole minute and I don't have a drink in my hand."

Rachel gleamed at the fresh meat I'd brought home for the kill, and poured him a drink that I'd learned to muscle my way through long ago.

Ten minutes later, Von and Rachel were making eyes and flirting on my couch. Marcus tried to insert himself into the mix. He was halfway to a state of drunkenness that usually took him two hours to devolve into. I wondered how long they'd all been here.

So long as everyone obeyed my solitary rule of staying out of my bedroom, they could do what they wanted with the rest of the house. I'd made my peace with it long ago. The parties gave me a valid excuse to scrub the house from top to bottom. Ollie worried when I went on a cleaning binge for "no good reason," so at least I got something out of the night, too.

Gabby took it upon herself to bring the party together for a grand moment that always began with her standing on my coffee table. There was a reason I was never the one to invite them all to hang out at my house, and toe-prints on my coffee table were only one of them. "Everyone, I have a few things I'd like to say in honor of our dear friend, Oliver James Reese."

Ollie grinned through a few hoots at him being middle named by the girl he'd never been able to shake.

She raised her bangled, mocha-colored hands to reclaim the attention. She was always good at that. "Ollie left us for bigger and better things in New York, and after five long years of searching for something more exciting than what we could give him, he's decided at long last to come back home where he belongs!" She jumped off the table and wrapped her long arms and legs around Ollie, who kissed her in public – a thing he only did if he was caught by surprise. The house exploded in hoots and cheers and good-natured jabs.

My mouth hung open in shock. Ollie had only told me that he was coming back for a few days. I had no clue he'd even been thinking about moving home. I mean, he'd mentioned things at work were getting stressful, but I hadn't realized it was that bad.

He pulled his face back from Gabby's devouring lips to cast me an apologetic look that he hadn't talked to me first.

I nodded, thunderstruck. My chest felt tight that Ollie had kept something this big from me. I plastered on my smile as I skirted around the living room, accidentally bumping into three of my friends before I slipped into the safety of my bedroom.

Before I could lock the door, it opened. "Hey, October."

I turned to find Beto with that same familiar smile on his face. Mason sneaked in behind him and made to lie down in the corner of my room, feigning sleep.

Beto had black hair, brown skin and a round face that was friendly to everyone. His jeans were faded and his flannel shirt was untucked. While everyone in the world felt much taller than I was, Beto had only an inch on me, which had been nice when we were dating in our constant loop of on-again and off-again. He leaned against the wall to take a breather from the noise of the party.

"Hey, Beto. How's it going?"

"Oh, you know. Gabby." He explained his presence in my home with a shrug. "Nice to see you. You're looking good."

"You, too."

I didn't feel the need to fill the silence, since he was the one with something to say. I gave him a few seconds to work up to whatever it was that had him shoving his hands in his pockets – a thing he did when he was nervous. My special casual guy was eight years older than me, so it was always a surprise when I made him nervous. "So, I don't know if this is something I'm supposed to tell you or not, but in case it is, here you go. Jessica and I've been hanging out a lot, and it just started to turn into something." He watched my face for a reaction, so I vowed not to give him anything more than the color draining from my face. "I didn't want you to hear it from anyone else."

"Oh. Well, thanks for the heads up, I guess. Good for you. She's great." She *was* great. She was currently in my living room laughing at one of Nick's "hilarious" jokes. I'd known her for years. The girls in our group did dinner and a movie once a month, and at the last one three weeks ago, she hadn't said anything about hooking up with Beto. I guessed that it must've been only a few days they'd been flirting. "That's great, Beto. Happy for you both. And thanks again for the heads up."

He kept his brown eyes averted, addressing the wall behind me instead of my face. "Yeah, I just got tired of waiting for you. If it was right, it would've happened by now, you know?"

I nodded, guessing I should've seen this coming. Really I can't believe he'd stuck around as long as he had. He'd always wanted to be exclusive and move forward onto more serious things, but I hadn't wanted that. I wasn't built for it. I'd kept him on hold for too long, and now I'd lost him. "Sounds logical."

"Cool. Jessica's been freaking out for like, two months. She thinks you're going to hate her."

"I don't hate her." My nose wrinkled. "Wait, two months? You've been together for two months? Beto, we broke it off, what? A month and a half ago?"

He cleared his throat. "Yeah. There was a little overlap."

I was shocked, though maybe I shouldn't have been. Maybe I should've known better. Maybe I shouldn't have gotten as close as I did to Beto, which was still never close enough for him to be happy. "What do you want me to say to that?"

Beto shrugged, his hands in his pockets. "I don't expect you'll say anything. If you loved me, you'd get upset and tell me where I could go, but you don't, so I know you'll be alright. I hurt your pride, not your heart."

I kept my glower to myself and swallowed down the anger that rose up in me. "I actually came in here to change, so I'm guessing your girlfriend would want you out there with her."

"That's a nail on the head, then." He touched his forehead in mild frustration, letting the politeness die between us so we could be real for a second. "Were you ever even a little serious about me? Was something more ever going to be in the cards for us?"

"Honestly, Beto. You come in here, tell me you cheated on me with my friend, and because I don't scream at you like you deserve, I didn't..."

"You can't even say you loved me in a hypothetical situation! See? That's what I'm talking about."

"I don't deserve this," I muttered, shaking my head. Instead of leaving, Beto closed the gap between us and wrapped me in a hug. I stiffened on instinct, but softened after a few seconds. Beto knew it took me a few seconds, and he gave them to me graciously, never taking offense. Now he had a real girlfriend who probably never hesitated with a hug. Come to think of it, Jessica wasn't much of a hesitator, so I guessed Beto was far happier than he'd ever been with me.

He exhaled as we squeezed each other. "I still love you, kid, even if you never loved me. I think about us all the time." "Kid" was my other fabulous nickname. I wasn't sure which one I hated more: Bait or kid. At least Beto had stopped calling me Bait when we were together. Bonus.

"I'm guessing you probably shouldn't say stuff like that to me anymore. New girlfriend and all. And maybe don't hug me." I shrugged out of his embrace, realizing that him cheating on me meant I didn't have to make myself be softer around him anymore.

Beto's thin lips hardened in a tight line. "Fine. I didn't mean to hurt you, you know."

"Yeah, you did. You could've broken it off and then gone for her, but you had us both. Grade-A assjack behavior, and you know it."

"Whatever you think, I didn't mean for it to get messy." And just like that, Beto kissed me goodbye. It was a closed-mouth peck that brushed my lips, but it was laced with the final farewell I'd more than deserved. I wanted to push him away, but knew my violent tendencies weren't my most mature qualities. I could feel Beto's germs now, festering on my mouth where he'd kissed me. I'd worked hard to erase the amoebas that coated him when we'd first started dating, but now all that progress was lost.

After Beto left, I sat on my bed and just stared at the wall for a solid three minutes. I willed the waves of emotion to die down so I could show my face to Jessica without tearstains marking up the happiness I was supposed to pull out of thin air for her. Two months meant two movie nights we'd gone to with her having been with Beto the whole time. I felt like such a child for missing him, and for saying so at that first movie night to the girls after our last breakup. They'd been sympathetic, but now I knew it was pity. I'd never had much of a stomach for being pitied.

Mason hopped up onto the bed and laid down next to me, his head in my lap. I could feel that slow trickle of negative emotion draining, and was grateful for the boost. I was so much younger than any of my friends. It made things like crying not an option. Mason picked his head up and licked my cheek. "Thanks, buddy. You're a good boy." I buried my face into his fur. We both sighed contentedly when he looped his nose over my shoulder and my arms encircled him. "It's fine," I assured us. "It's all fine. Beto should be with someone who can make him happy. Aside from the relationship stacking, he's a good guy. I'm really fine."

Mason snorted his objection, and I giggled softly.

"Yeah, that was a lie, but I'm trying, here. Don't tell anyone, okay? Totally embarrassing to be cheated on."

Mason nuzzled the top of his head to my forehead, and I knew that he got me. He understood the pride that ran deeper than the hurt of the moment.

35

HELLO OLLIE, GOODBYE BETO

Mariang and Danny let themselves into my room a few minutes later, breaking us out of our reverie. Mariang gave a startled, "Oh! I'm sorry. I didn't realize you two were..." She sounded like she'd caught Mason and me in the middle of a naked tryst.

"Is Oliver staying here?" Danny asked without preamble. "Because if he is, we have to decide whether or not you want him brought in on all this."

Mason hopped down from the bed and sat at attention next to my feet. I blinked at the two, trying to force my brain to form words that made sense. "I... um..."

Mariang sat on my bed next to me. "Your friends seem lovely. So fun and positively delightful. I adore Jessica and Gabby."

I pulled on my fingers as I nodded. "They're great.

Gabby will love you for sure. She's my closest friend here. Super up for anything, and real nice."

"I told Von to get his arse in here. Lazy, good for nothing…" Danny ducked out of the room with Mason, leaving me with Mariang.

She bumped her shoulder to mine. "What was that guy doing in here? Are you two dating?"

Mariang was sweet. She was doing such a good job at making an effort with me, and I was a mute bump on a log. I sat up straighter and smiled at her. "No. We used to date, but he's seeing Jessica now, actually."

Mariang's face soured. "Oh. Really? Isn't that uncomfortable? Her dating your ex-boyfriend?"

I kept my smile in place, though all I wanted out of life was to hide somewhere in my shame and take a nap. "Beto was never my boyfriend. We just dated on and off. They're better together. No big deal."

"Oh. Are any of those guys out there your boyfriend?"

"No. I only ever dated Beto, and that's long over. I work a lot, so I don't have a ton of time for a social life. Gabby brings the social life to me when I get too preoccupied. She's good like that."

"The prison keeps you that busy?"

"Yeah. I work a lot of overtime. Not a ton of people want my job, so I go from the men's facility to the women's whenever they have extra hours."

"How much did you work?"

Did. That one hit me hard. I would have to put in my

two weeks, and was dreading it. "Ten to twelve hour days, six days a week. I took this weekend off to spend with Ollie. Not much time for a boyfriend. Probably similar to the hours we're going to be working doing the death thing."

Danny shoved Von into the bedroom, and Mason followed behind. Danny locked the five of us in with a frown. "If you'd come up for air for two seconds, you'd know that our situation is changing. If Oliver's staying here, we have to decide if it's worth it to tell him every-thing, or if we can hide it easy enough."

Von was still coming out of his horny flirty haze, but he tried to be in the conversation. "You want to weigh in, Peach?"

"I don't know what Ollie's situation is. I don't have a clue why he's moving home. I just found out when you all did."

"Will he be living here?" Danny asked, his arms crossed over his chest.

"I would assume so. I mean, it's *our* house. Ollie, Allie and I bought it together and shared it until they moved. I'm not asking him to live somewhere else, if that's what you're getting at."

"Okay. Find out the details tonight, and we can make a plan in the morning, yeah?" Danny reached for Mariang, and I saw her take a deeper breath at the contact he offered. "Come on. You haven't eaten enough. Mason?

Von? I could use some help checking the perimeter. Too many bodies moving about; I don't like it."

They all left, and I slumped on the bed, indulging in a few minutes to collect myself. A few minutes gave way to ten, and I found myself lying down on my pillow when the door cracked open and shut again.

36

BABY BIRD

"November," Von whispered. "I think I'm going to take off with your friend, Katrina."

I picked up my head to glance back at Von over my shoulder, but didn't otherwise get up from my bed to greet him. "I thought you were chatting up Rachel."

"Yeah, she called me 'honey' halfway through. Too relationshippy, so I jumped ship. I was thinking of going home with Katrina. That alright?"

"Totally cool, so long as you don't vamp out on her. Katrina's kind of the queen bee of the group. She likes to take the new guys for a test drive first. I can't believe Rachel actually got first crack at you and blew her chance."

"You make me sound like a baseball card." I couldn't tell if Von sounded amused or mildly offended.

"To them, that's exactly what you are. Enjoy being the shiny new toy."

"Oh, I intend to enjoy every bit of Katrina tonight."

"See you at seven tomorrow morning." I rolled over, expecting him to leave when my back was to him.

I didn't anticipate him sitting on the bed next to me, resting against my oak headboard as he resituated the spare pillow at his back. He ran his hand over my shoulder, and I could feel a small amount of my melancholy lifting. "Danny practically feeds Mariang like she's a baby bird. Am I supposed to do that for you?"

"How about you don't ask me ludicrous questions, and I won't have to think up a clever way to tell you to never, ever suggest that idea to me again."

"Okay, good. I mean, they've got their whole connection thing going strong, and more power to them, but I don't want to have to keep track of how often a girl eats."

"You're off the hook. Thanks for this, though. It's been a day. And don't tell Danny I needed it. He seems like a gloater." Von's hand on my shoulder felt right in a way no one's ever had before. It must've been the whole Omen-Reaper connection thing.

Von let silence fall for a few beats before speaking quietly. "Danny told you I used to work as a prostitute. You aren't curious about that? You haven't been treating me any different today. I was expecting to be the leper."

"Do you want me to ask you about it?"

"No. I don't like people knowing, but it seems to be the first thing my brother mentions."

"Danny's a tool. If you want to talk to me about it, you

can. But I'm not going to press you about something you didn't even tell me in the first place. It's your business. I'm here when you need to talk, and even if you don't."

"Thanks." Von seemed relieved, exhaling tension I didn't realize he'd been carrying around. "This party's stressing you out, yeah? Doesn't really seem like your friends know you all that well."

I didn't know what to say to that, so I nodded. "I'm eight years younger than all of them, so they're not really sure what to do with me. They love Ollie and Allie, and I come with the package."

"They seem to like you well enough." Von slid down on the mattress next to me, his hand brushing from my shoulder to my hip and back again as he spooned me. I normally didn't go for the whole cuddling thing, but the pulling was a relief I couldn't afford to brush off. I deflated, letting out a tired sigh I'd been keeping in for who knows how long.

"Thanks. I'm fine. You don't have to baby bird me. They'll go home around two. They always do."

"Danny will be here, so if you need anything, ask him for one of Mariang's worms. Mason, too."

I sniggered, but then quickly bit off anything that could be construed as mocking Mariang. "For the record, I like her a lot. But yeah, they're intense."

"Oh, make no mistake, I love her. I'm on the fence about my brother, but Mariang's an absolute gem. A sister if I ever had one."

"Do you have any sisters?" I knew next to nothing about the guy stroking my hip.

"Just brothers. Six of us."

"Holy crap! Seriously? Your mother must be amazing to keep up with all of you." I relaxed into him as his body curled around mine. Beto had tried spooning me a few times, but I couldn't unwind, so I always found a reason to get up and leave a few minutes into the snuggle. The slow drip of my sadness was steadily leaking out of me and into Von, and though I didn't know him all that well, I was glad he was there.

"Mum's a saint, that's for sure. When you meet her, be sure to tell her and all my brothers what a brilliant Death Reaper I am. I mean, really ham it up and sell it to the cheap seats."

"How about, 'Mrs. Von's Mom, how you gave birth to such a wonderful boy is beyond me. Tell me the wisdom of your ways so I can take notes on how to raise such a responsible, kind, and well-mannered young man.'"

"Perfect. If you could add in something about my strong jawline, I'd be grateful."

"Making a mental note as we speak."

"Speaking of which, I haven't called them in a couple days. The natives get restless if they don't have their big brother to answer to. Give the twins a good ear-bashing just for the fun of it." He pulled out his phone and hit one of the speed dials.

I laughed through my nose. "Oh, yes. I'm sure you're

terrifying when you're crossed. You probably throw out all kinds of bottom drawer words like 'poppycock' and 'balderdash'."

"I'm perfectly terrifying when I need to be, love." His hand rested on my hip while he waited for the call to connect. It was wrong how right his hand felt there – how easy it was all coming.

"Hey, Boston. How badly did you miss your dear old brother? ...Oh yeah? Up yours, too." Von laughed and settled into some mildly crude banter with his brother that relaxed him as his thumb mindlessly stroked the curve from my hip to my waist. When Von switched to talking to the next brother, his tone shifted from trash-talking antagonizer to normal older brother. "Pulling's not so bad. I'm hungry all the time, but I get to stare at a fiery little crumpet all day long, so there's nothing to complain about. ...Oh yes, very pretty. A ten if ever I saw one." We shared a sweet smile when I rolled onto my back to shoot up a look of gratitude at him for the compliment. I mean, pretty? The only compliments I usually got were about my work ethic, or gross ones about my body that weren't worth repeating. He talked with Boston's twin named Bishop a few more minutes about Omen work before putting his brother on hold so he could talk to me. "Have to use the bathroom. Entertain Bishop for me for a minute?"

My eyes widened that he was letting me into his world so easily and without any request on my end. I mean, so far they'd been infiltrating my world with no reciprocation expected. I carefully took Von's phone and wiped it off, making sure to hold it half an inch from my face so I didn't get his mouth or ear germs on me. Ears were not always the cleanest area on a person, and I couldn't be sure about Von's. Von watched me with eyebrows furrowed as he stood next to the bed. "Hello, this is October."

"Truly? You're the new Omen? Lady October, it's an honor." The voice on the other end sounded like a more polite version of Von, though that wasn't saying much.

"Oh, none of that 'Lady October' nonsense. You're Von's brother. With how much time I'll be spending with him during the work day, I'm sure we'll be old friends in no time." I caught Von's smile that told me how grateful he was that I was making an effort with his family. I waved him out of the room so he could use the bathroom.

"Friends with the new Omen? Wicked." Bishop called over his shoulder to his brother. "Eh, Bos? I'm friends with the new Omen. That's right. Now who's the king of the flat?"

"You can tell him I said you sounded taller than him, too, if that helps secure your 'king of the flat' position."

"Now I really like you," Bishop laughed. "What's it like, breaking into a new job like that? Mariang always talks about how exhausted the whole thing leaves her. That you, too?"

"I would say that it's a breeze, but I'm talking to you from my bed, so I guess exhausting's a good word for it."

"Von mentioned that you didn't know anything about Terraway before this. How's that settling?"

"Oh, you know, it's not. I have no idea what I'm doing or which magical creature's going to fart on me next."

Bishop snorted through his laugh at my unexpected joke. "Here's hoping it's not Von."

"From your lips to God's ears, dude."

Bishop sounded like he was given to smiling without needing a piano to fall on someone else's head to enjoy a good laugh. "You sound like an American, 'dude'."

I waved my hand around in the air. "We're wasting valuable time, here. Von's in the other room. Give me the dirt on him. Something I can use as leverage when he starts being a pain."

"He hasn't started yet? You must be very pretty, then."

I rolled my eyes with an "Oh, brother" smirk while he thought for a second.

"He hates lighting his cigars with matches. Has a whole rant about the leaves not burning as evenly or some poppycock."

I buttoned my lips through my slight giggle that Bishop had used the word "poppycock". "Is that so?"

"He only uses a lighter, so if he's being a pain, nick his and watch him get mad as a bag of ferrets."

"This is good. You're starting to become my favorite of Von's brothers. Though, you've only got Danny for competition so far."

"Oh, his paintings. He keeps a boring one on his easel,

but what he's really working on is behind it. He doesn't like people to see his paintings, not the unfinished ones, anyways."

"Decoy paintings. Got it. Keep them coming."

Bishop's voice turned wistful. "Von paints these perfect portraits, you know. I mean, not just how the person looks in a photograph, but how they look to him. He did one of me and one of Boston for Mum to hang in the hallway when we moved out. We're identical, but the portraits of us are somehow totally different. It's unreal."

Bishop talked for a few more minutes about the differences in the details of the two portraits until Von came back, sliding into the bed with me. He was on his side, propped up on his elbow and staring down at my supine form while I laughed at Bishop's jokes and told a few of my own. Von's palm rested across my stomach, which was way more intimate than I'd been expecting, but I much preferred that to him touching my hand. I don't know why my stomach seemed to purr for his touch, but unbidden swirls of sensation rose up where his hand lay. "Okay, Von's getting impatient. Here's your brother back."

I wiped off the phone again before I handed it to him. Though I hadn't put my face on it, my germs had been near enough. Von chatted for a few minutes after rolling me onto my side again so he could spoon me and pull out my stress while he caught up with his twin brothers. When he hung up, he set the phone behind him on my nightstand and curled his arm around my stomach again, giving the butterflies something to flutter around. "Sorry. That took longer than I thought."

"It's fine. I like hearing you be happy. Much better than you being smarmy to deflect, or polite when Danny runs you down. You love your brothers."

"I do." He was thoughtful a few beats as he lightly rubbed my arm, turning the soothing touch into a gentle massage. "Do you take anything for your OCD?"

"Does that fall under the baby bird category? I think it might."

"Bollocks. You're right. I'm sorry. I'm just having a difficult time getting a read on it. Sometimes you're completely normal, and other times I see how hindered you are. It feels like it comes and goes. I always thought OCD made your ticks non-negotiable, but sometimes yours are gone completely. I don't understand."

I bit down on my lower lip at the fact that I wasn't doing a perfect job at fending off the crazy. "I'm amazing at faking normal. I do my best to keep myself functional. Sometimes I hit it on the nose, and other times I couldn't find normal with a roadmap." My voice quieted with the admission I didn't want to make. "The pulling thing you and Mason do seems to be helping."

Von stroked my navel, making my eyelashes flutter involuntarily. "This Omen-Reaper bond is no joke. Sorry if I'm hovering. It just feels better when I'm near you." He buried his face in the pillow. "I'm truly not making a pass at you. That came out all wrong. I just meant that I finally understand why Danny gets anxious if he's away from Mariang too long. I think I'm calming myself down more than I am you. Push me off the bed if I'm a bother. I honestly don't understand what I'm doing anymore."

I waited a few beats to make sure his stammering was over. "No, I get it. If you could do me a favor and not be close in public, though, I'd appreciate it. I'm not... I don't... This right here? Not normal for me, and I don't want my friends to think I'm throwing myself at the new hottie, or that any of the guys out there are welcome to come lie next to me in my bed. My bedroom is off-limits to them. This is my one safe place, and I don't like them in it." Maybe that was mean, but it was the only thing I insisted on.

"I completely understand. I don't want Katrina thinking I'm going to hold her like this tonight, either. Unrealistic expectations. You're turning me from a sex king into a cuddler, and I'd rather keep that little secret behind closed doors."

I reached behind me and stroked his cheek, proud of myself for ignoring the germs. "Well, for what it's worth, you look like the type to go all night, Cuddle King. I'll keep this part of you all to myself any day."

He kissed the back of my shoulder, sending goose-bumps down my spine. "What were we talking about? Right, your OCD."

"It's fine. It's manageable. I made it through all that mud in Terraway, didn't I?" I sighed, relaxing into the cuddle he was very free with. "Look, everyone out there calls me either kid or Bait. If you want this to work, you can't treat me like I'm a child. I've got enough of that going on. I can handle myself and take my own meds."

"Understood." He sniggered softly and started rubbing my bicep with gentle fingers and steady pressure. "Bait. That's brilliant."

I reached for an abrupt change of topic. "By the way, Katrina's thing is to steal one pair of underwear from each guy she sleeps with to add to her collection. Hope you brought a spare."

"Ah. A challenge. Thanks for the heads up."

"That feels awesome, by the way," I said of the massage. I'd never had one before, and though my natural distrust of touch ran deep, Von was learning whatever loophole existed that let the therapeutic contact be possible for me. Despite everything, I was grateful for him in that moment. "I'll be sure to send an A-plus rating to your supervisor or whoever."

"You're like, a ball of tension."

"I'm fine."

"Do you have a dollar?" he asked.

"Sure, but not for you. Why?"

"I'm buying you a jar. Every time you say 'I'm fine', you have to put a dollar in the Denial Jar."

"That goes double for you every time you say something sleazy."

"Are you having a laugh? Nobody's that rich." We chuckled together, and I felt infinitely better than I had before he laid down with me. "You think you'll be able to sleep tonight?"

"That's the thing about nighttime. I'll be fine."

He squeezed my hip as he pressed another kiss to the back of my shoulder, and I smiled, despite myself, as goosebumps broke out on my arms. "That's two dollars, love."

37

DREAM GUY IN PARIS

Ollie and Gabby spent the night in his room. I donated my bed to Danny and Mariang, who looked like they needed about a week of sleep. Since Allie's old room had been converted into an office, that left me and Mason with the living room, which was where I wanted to be anyway. My friends were nice, but they were pigs. I wouldn't have been able to sleep knowing the state they'd left my house in. I scrubbed, dusted, washed and organized until four in the morning, when I finally gave in to my exhaustion. The carpet needed a good vacuuming and probably a deep cleaning, but that would have to wait until morning so I didn't wake the house.

Mason woke up from the sofa he'd been snoozing on, shooting me a look of scolding with his wolfy eyes. I'd pretended to fall asleep on the couch a while ago, waiting for him to doze off before I went back to my housework. "Don't look at me like that. If I don't clean the house, no one will." He responded by nudging me toward the couch, corralling me like a sheepdog. "Alright, alright. I was finished anyway."

I debated sleeping on the couch, but opted for the soft carpet of the living room instead. I draped a blanket on the floor and laid down. As much as I didn't want to sleep on the floor of my own house, it tugged at my heart that Mason was worlds away from his home, and probably could use the comfort of someplace soft to rest his head. The Omen-Reaper bond was setting itself in deep, so much that I could feel small forlorn swings of Mason missing his home.

Mason placed his paw on the couch in confusion. "There's not enough room on the sofa for the both of us. You can have the couch tonight. It's softer than the floor," I explained, pulling a throw pillow down to rest my head on. I expected Mason to hop up on the couch, but he surprised me by worming his head under my arm. He gave my face a few licks and rolled on his back, telling me that he'd rather sleep with me on the floor than alone in a more comfortable place. My arm stretched across to rub his tummy, and just as it had been with Von when we'd laid in bed together, something in me clicked – felt right – now that Mason was near. We both sighed contentedly at the contact. I tried not to examine the oddity too thoroughly as

I pressed my face into his luxurious fur just to get a little closer. "Mm, so cozy. This is nice."

He responded by licking my cheek and grinding his head to mine to ensure there wasn't a millimeter of space between us. I couldn't help but love my new dog.

My eyelids didn't need any coercion to close. I was content to sleep on the floor with all the feet germs if I had my teddy bear with me. I nuzzled my face in Mason's neck and breathed more peacefully than I had in hours.

My dream was mundane, but since life had been so surreal, I welcomed watching two squirrels share an acorn at the base of the Eiffel Tower. I'd always wanted to go to Paris, but there were more important things to do than traveling. "I've got my whole life to see the world," I told the squirrels, who chittered at me like they knew better.

"Your whole life, eh?" a man in my dream asked from behind me.

I looked up, squinting through the sun's rays that lit the thirty-something man from behind like an angel. He had white-blond hair and a mouthful of gleaming straight teeth. "Oh, hi." I didn't know what to say to the pretty guy who was clearly a figment of my imagination. I usually conjured up the tall, dark hair and handsome type in my dreams. Ian Somerhalder couldn't get enough of me in my dream life. This was a new one, for sure. I usually didn't need to banter with dream guys, either. They thought I was pretty, and I let them think it, not needing many words to get down and dirty.

Don't judge me. It's a friggin' dream, no doubt brought on by my usual daily routine of solitude and celibacy.

I was surprised when blond guy sat down next to me in the short grass that had been freshly mowed. "Do you come here a lot?" he asked.

I laughed at the "Come here often" pickup line I didn't think I would put in my dream of my own volition. "Not usually. I wanted somewhere very far away tonight."

"Far from where?"

"From my house."

He brushed his shoulder to mine, and I let him. "Where's your house?"

"Not here. I don't have to think about there right now. I've got squirrels and a tower. What more could a girl want?"

"I was just wondering that exact thing. What do you want?"

"More of this. It gets me through until I find something real." I leaned into his side, my hand playing with the buttons on his white dress shirt.

Yes, I was being forward, but this was a dream guy. He was my distraction, so I let myself be distracted from the drama of the past few days. He had a dimple in his square chin that grew more pronounced with my simple seduction.

"I can be real." He looked like he was debating something, but smiled when his thumb made the decision and landed on my cheek. He seemed surprised when I leaned into his touch, like he'd been starved for simple contact. My dream guys weren't usually so unsure of themselves.

He relaxed when I dragged my lips against his thumb. His wide smile curled the corners of his lips like a Cheshire cat as he breathed, "This is going to be easier than I thought."

WELCOME TO BEV'S HOUSE

What felt like ten minutes later, my eyes opened again, and it was already morning time. Ollie and Gabby would sleep in, but Danny was on task, rising early to start his day with the first shower. I said goodbye to my dreamy makeout buddy and kissed the side of Mason's muzzle when he stirred. "Go back to sleep, baby." I took the second shower while Danny dressed and started to make breakfast for himself and Mariang.

Danny and I moved soundlessly around the kitchen, cracking eggs and shoving bread in the toaster. Neither of us preferred to speak in the morning, so we actually got along fairly well. We chewed in silence while he leafed through the paper and I read a medical journal that updated weekly on my Kindle. It was nice, actually. Danny and I got along just fine when we didn't need to risk talking and pissing the other one off. Mason moseyed in and laid on my feet, making me feel the perfect amount of cozy and relaxed. I was starting to come around on this whole pulling business.

When seven o'clock hit, Mariang, Danny and I were fed, dressed and ready to go, but Von was still gone. "Let's just go," I said. "I'll shadow you today. Learn instead of do. Von can meet us when he wakes up."

Danny was livid after checking his phone and finding a text from Von there. "Of course this is how he treats the most prestigious job our kind can get. Of course he flakes the first week in. He's saying something came up, and we should start without him. He'll call when he can meet us." He put his hand on his forehead. "Mason, you're up. You'll need to turn human for today, which means a shower and normal Topsider clothing. We'll grab the stone first, and then reap as many souls as we can."

Mason scampered into the bathroom with one of the shopping bags he'd bought with Ezra, but returned with a whine.

"Do you know how to work the shower?" I asked, bending down to kiss his cheek and give him a good scratch behind the ears. I trotted to the bathroom and turned on the faucet for him, testing the temperature. I closed the door behind me as I walked out of the bathroom, giving him the privacy to mutate back into a human (or Matruculan. Or wizard. Or whatever).

Danny was still shoving his face with food when Mason emerged from the bathroom, fully human and fully clothed. I probably shouldn't have been bummed that my dog was gone. Mason wore a pair of nice, dark blue jeans and a white polo shirt, his seven long dreads pulled back with a leather lace to reveal his half inch-long caramel beard and piercing slate eyes.

As Mason slid on his black steel-toed boots, I pulled up a mental list of everything I'd done to wolf-Mason that would be totally inappropriate now that he was a person. I'd ran my hands through his hair, spooned him, let him kiss my face, called him "baby", kissed his neck and stroked his belly. My face turned crimson on that last one. I snatched up my keys and all but ran toward the garage.

Mason blocked me, his gray eyes kind but firm. "Now that I'm human again, I need to look at your hands."

"Come again?"

"The scrapes on your hands. I need to dress the wounds you keep giving yourself. Make sure they'll heal properly."

"I'm fine. We should get going."

Mason moved to the bathroom and held open the door, giving me a stern look that left no room for arguing.

My shoulders slumped. "Yeah, okay. But not here and not now. Ollie could wake up any second, and I don't want to explain you to him. I'll take the first aid kid with us, and you can take a look when we get where we're going."

When the four of us got into my car, I left a large gap in the backseat between Mason and me that was hopefully big enough to hold all my embarrassment. He'd seen Beto dump me. He'd hugged me in his wolfy way. I couldn't look at him; I was so ashamed.

I directed Danny to Bev's trailer park, noting the familiar knot in my gut that twisted as we reached the entrance. "Park in the guest lot. I'll walk from here."

"Is it far?"

"Not too."

"Then show me which one's her house, and I'll drive us there."

"No."

Danny looked at me in the rearview mirror, dropping Mariang's hand he'd been holding the whole drive. "No? What makes you think we'll just wing it with something as big as the lost sagrado stone on the line? Prince Langgam knows where your mum's house is. He followed you there before. I'll drive this car off a cliff before I let his dad get his slimy hands on the stone. We do this together, October. That's the only way of it."

"No. This is *my* mama's house. *My* stupid magic rock. My call."

Danny turned around in his seat to face me. "You think you can be stubborn? Wait until the heads of the nations get impatient. You don't want us in your childhood home? I think you don't want Prince Langgam's bugs crawling all over it. I think you don't want to explain King Kabayo to the neighbors."

I closed my eyes and leaned my head back in defeat. "I hate you so much right now." I sighed through my anxiety, which was ping-ponging around inside me. "Fine. But you all stay outside. I'm serious. You pretty much moved into my house and I didn't get a say in it. You don't get to see where I grew up."

"You don't get to put your foot down about anything anymore." Danny held tight to his bossy personality, which was made worse by Von's disappearing act. It was like because Von went rogue, Danny expected we all would.

Mariang placed her hand on Danny's. "Danny, be nice. How would you feel if strangers invaded your space? This is her childhood home. It's sacred. Probably full of happy memories she doesn't want tarnished with Terraway's drama."

Mariang was sweet. Wrong, but sweet. "It's not that. Thanks, though. I..." The air was suddenly too thick to pull in a full breath. I could smell the garbage as I pointed Danny to the street I'd ridden my rusty bike down too many times to count. I scratched at the backs of my hands as my chest heaved. "I'll just go in and grab it. I'm pretty sure I know which rock you're talking about. I..." I shook my head when Mariang turned around in her seat to put her hand on my knee. "Please don't come in with me! Please don't make me show you where I lived!"

"Whoa. Danny, something big's coming off her." Mason said as he touched my back.

"You think?" Danny's eyebrows were furrowed, making the square shape of his head look more like the monster of

Frankenstein than usual. "October, what's the problem? Why are you being like this?"

"I'm freaking out! Mariang can't come inside. She's used to the mansion and a servant, and this isn't…"

"Oh, October. I don't care about any of that. Please don't think me a snob."

I thought about all the sharp edges, the unsafe places to walk, the maggots and the mold corrupting such a sweet and pure girl. "It's not safe for her inside. You care about her safety? She stays here."

"Okay, now I'm worried." Danny gripped the steering wheel as he parked in the space outside of Bev's trailer. "Do I need to phone for more Duwendes? Do we need more security or something?"

I shook my head as it hung low, my elbows resting on my knees as I tried to steady my breath. "Please don't make me do this. Please, Danny. I've been a good soldier, learning the ropes. Didn't I do a good job yesterday?"

"You were incredible yesterday."

"Please just give me this."

Danny watched me scrape at my hands in utter confusion. "If it's not safe for Mariang, I can take that into consideration. She can stay locked in the car while Mason and I go in with you." He held up his hands when I cast him what I'm sure was my most pitiful expression. "Look, it's the best I can do. We need this rock, but we also need you in one piece. I can't let you out of my sight until we're more caught up. We got a decent head start yesterday with all those extra souls. You're doing real good, kid. But I can't slack off on the job now. This is important."

I was glad Bev wasn't home. I knew she would be answering phones at the real estate office, so at least there was one less issue to deal with.

Danny and Mason got out of the car, but my feet were frozen to the floor. Mason walked around the car and cracked the door for me so he could kneel in the opening. His eyes were filled with compassion I didn't want to feel. "Hey. What are we about to walk in on? You're making me nervous." He rubbed my forearms, and I felt that steady trickle of the tension starting to release, but it was like a pinprick on the bottom of a swimming pool. It barely made a dent in the angst that had me by the throat.

"Please don't make me do this," I begged in a whisper. "This isn't me. I'm not this place. I escaped Bev and her trailer. I got out. I don't want to show you how bad it all was. You won't understand that it's a sickness. You'll judge her and me, and I don't need that in my life."

Mason's hands were firm but gentle as he pulled me out of the car, ignoring my noise of distress. My movements were stiff and hesitant, but his were fluid. He tapped his finger under my chin so I had to look up into his compassionate and discerning eyes. "You're really that afraid?"

"That's the thing about being pushed to the end of your rope."

Mason's mouth drew to the side beneath his short

beard as he looked me over. "Listen to me. I can tell when people are at the end of their rope. I've got a sixth sense about it. It's one of the things that made me a good ruler, once upon a time." His finger under my chin pulled me closer, like a fish on a lure. My heart rate began to pick up speed as I let myself be drawn closer. His voice was low and steady, while I was aflutter. "You, my October, are not at the end of your rope. You've got miles of rope before someone like you's defeated." He thumbed my lower lip, and my eyelashes fluttered shut through the swoon that utterly confused me. He smelled like pine and patchouli, and very, very masculine.

I could feel his breath on my nose. His voice lowered to a barely audible command between us. "And you can stop avoiding me. If you love me in my wolf form, you can do better than barely look at me when I'm a man. We're the same animal." He brought my face forward and kissed my cheek. My blood pounded around the spot his lips caressed. It was nothing like Von's flirty remarks he doled out like party favors. Mason's lips on my cheek had intent. Intent that made me want to draw closer instead of pull back, which was an entirely new concept for me. "There's nothing in there that'll make me run away from my duty to you, so let's get on with it. I'm by your side."

I gulped when his hand drifted from my chin down my side to wrap around my hips. It was boyfriendy, and I wasn't sure how I felt about that. I heard a low growl to my left, and knew my favorite pit bull was watching from his yard. Sandy didn't much like strangers.

"Okay. Thanks." I extracted myself from the closeness and popped the trunk. I pulled out a pair of my hospital gloves from the box, offering some to the men. "You'll want them. Trust me." I tucked my pants into my socks, wishing Sandy would come out from his yard to greet me with a quick moral support snuggle. He was watching from beside his house, his body half shrouded in shadow so he could growl and unnerve the newcomers.

They each took a pair of hospital gloves while exchanging wary looks. "This is necessary?" Danny inquired, flummoxed.

I didn't answer, but whirled on them before I took another step. "I want your word that you won't talk about what you see in here. I mean it. Not to Ezra especially."

Danny wasn't in the mood to be bossed around. "You don't get to lay down any kind of rules."

"I just did. Ezra finds out about this, and I stop reaping today. You two decide how many people in Terraway get fed. I won't ruin the best thing that's ever happened to Bev."

Mason held up his hands. "Okay. That's fine. We can keep what we see to ourselves."

With my heart pounding, I moved forward to the house, unlocking the front door and saying a quick prayer that somehow the maggots had magically cleaned up the mess in my sleep.

39

WITNESSES TO BEV'S MADNESS

I didn't glance behind me to see Danny or Mason's reaction. I didn't want to see the looks of horror. "Stay back," I warned. I conjured up the image of my favorite horror movie star to move through the mess with me. Imaginary Bruce Campbell and I stepped carefully through the chaos, and not once did he judge me. Bruce knew that sometimes life got messy, and he was always cool. "You don't know how to maneuver the mess. Certain spots are dodgy. Some of the rats ate away at the flooring, and the cat urine's soaked through too much to be sturdy if you don't know where to step. I don't want you falling through, so just stay where you are."

I could hear the shock and revulsion in Danny's voice. "October, we'll call for help. This is too much to sort through in a day."

"If I find the rock in here, can you tell by looking if it's the right one?"

"Of course." Danny's voice was responsive, but I could tell he was still taking it in, letting the waves of horror-laced astonishment crash over him. "How did you live in this?"

"Very carefully."

"And Bev lives here? This is how Ezra's fiancée lives?"

"Yup." I heard something shift behind me. "Be careful, guys. Seriously. Just stand in the entrance. Bev can tell if you move her stuff. She'll beat me something awful if she finds out I've been touching her 'special things', so do me a solid and stay put."

Mason's reply was sharp. "Your mother beats you?"

I winced at my slip. "Not so much anymore. I know how to defend myself, so she doesn't get too many hits in. It's fine."

"How can she find anything in this? October, the rubbish is piled to the ceiling! It's an actual wall of trash! What is she keeping it for?" Danny was indignant, and I couldn't blame him. He was witnessing Bev's madness for the first time; I couldn't calculate how blown his perception of our family must be as he gaped at the chaos. "This is a sickness. I mean, I can't wrap my mind around it all. Oh! It's a dead rat."

Mason sniffed the air. "I'm pretty sure I can smell a few dead rats. A few live ones, too. And so many cats. Too many. Your mother really lives here?"

"How could you let your mum live like this?" Danny balked.

I straightened and turned, which was a dangerous thing to do. I was almost to the other end of the main room and saw them through the walls of brightly colored and broken stuff. "Are you joking? *Let* her? Listen up, mansion boy, Bev does what she wants. She didn't want me, Ollie or Allie here, so she inched us out until there wasn't any more space for us. I'm the only one who comes once a week to take her out of this Hellhole! There *is* no helping her. There's no way out except to run, which is exactly what Ollie and Allie did. This is who Bev is, and I can't change her."

Danny was still taking it all in. "Does she not have a trash bin to throw things out in? I'll buy her one, if that's the problem."

"Don't you dare touch so much as a tin can, Danny. I mean it. These are all Bev's 'special things'. She'll know if something's been touched or removed."

"No, no. No, no. You can't let Ezra's fiancée live like this. This place isn't fit for a human."

My indignation built into anger that directed itself at Danny like a dragon who'd been pushed one too many times. "We're seriously back on you thinking I 'let' Bev do anything? You think she listens to me at all? I was born into this mess! My crib was a busted up laundry basket with sharp plastic edges. My toys were whatever Ollie and Allie could make me out of old boxes and cans!"

I pointed to a dollhouse I knew the guys couldn't see from their vantage point, but I sure as anything knew where it was buried. The pink shutters blinked out at me through the jumble of old newspapers and ratty, frayed towels. "Do you see that? It's a dollhouse I wasn't allowed to play with because these are all Bev's 'special things'!" Tears were pricking my eyes, and I was angry with each of them for betraying me as they slid down my cheeks. "You want to know why we *let* her live like this? Because she kicked us out! I was eleven and homeless. You want to know why? You want to guess what we did to deserve that, rich boy?"

"I'm sorry." The worst part is that Danny actually did sound contrite, but it was too little too late. I never talked about Bev and the whole mess, but the second that latch opened, a whole mansion worth of garbage came spilling out of my mouth.

"Ollie threw out a bag of old hangers because he found out Allie was using them to cut herself. The hangers were Bev's 'special things', so the three of us were kicked out. We had nothing! We had nowhere to go. I was eleven years old and living in a tent in the woods until Ollie found us a place. But thank God that Bev's *special things* were safe." Tears were streaming down my face now, and I was glad there was no way the guys could reach me through the narrow tunnels. "But I still come to visit the woman who never loved me, and never took care of me. You know why? Because I'm crazy, too! I'm a bucket of damage, and if I had a daughter, I'd want her to take pity on me even when I didn't deserve it. So I take Bev out once a week. That's how I can live with myself and still get a weekly dose of hating myself." I slapped my hands together. "Package deal."

"You come back to this every week? Why?" Mason asked, confused.

"Because I don't want her to die in this hoard! No matter what, she's my mama. You're supposed to love your mama, and take care of her when she can't take care of herself. Bev hasn't been able to take care of herself since before I was born. I've been able to take care of myself since before I hit puberty. That makes me the adult, so she's my responsibility."

Mason shook his head with a downward tilt to his chin. "The parent's supposed to take care of the child. Not the other way around."

I swiped my sleeve across my face to gather up my angry tears. "But she can't, so I get what I get. I can take care of her, at least as much as she'll let me. I can take her out once a week so she gets fresh air and fresh food. I can keep her alive until... until she... until she gets better someday."

Danny shook his head, and through his furrowed eyebrows, I saw that stupid pity I'd avoided like the plague. "You don't get better from this."

"You think it doesn't kill me that my mama lives like this? That every day she chooses this over her kids?"

I crawled through one of the more narrow spaces,

ignoring Danny's apologies and Mason's pleas for me to come back. I found the white rock that rested in Bev's room in the doorway across from her mirror and jerked it up, accidentally moving a few things in the process I knew Bev would notice. When I picked up the rock, it lit up like a cheap toy. It had never felt like a wizarding tool before, and even now, it still looked like a dirty old doorstop. I wasn't sure if this was the thing they needed, but I prayed it was, just so I hadn't spilled my innards for nothing.

40

KING MASON: ZOMBIE SLAYER

The drive was silent. I mean, utterly silent. Danny had called Ezra when Mason and I got into the car, speaking to him in quiet tones before he got in. I listened carefully, confirming that he didn't say a word about the state of the trailer, only informing him that we'd secured the stone.

Even so, I knew I'd ruined it. The one good thing that had actually happened to Bev, and I was taking it away. They wouldn't look at her the same. They wouldn't laugh at her jokes as easily, and she needed that. Bev drew confidence from other people adoring her, and I was now the person who took that away. I didn't want to take good things away from Bev.

Mason drew me into his side midway through the drive. He was unused to cars, so his other hand gripped the door, like he was afraid of being catapulted into the stratosphere. I knew he had to hold me or touch me in some way. I was his job. However, in that car ride, his arm felt protective. It had been a long time since I'd been protected and felt that supreme level of solidarity.

The rock, apparently, was in fact, the lost sagrado stone, and it remained tucked in the trunk as we drove to the nearest camping store to buy a sturdy bag to seal it in so it didn't turn anyone to stone. I didn't even get out of the car, allowing Danny and Mariang the space to go shopping without us.

"October?"

"No," I warned, still dangerously close to another tearful outburst.

Mason respected my need to not talk about it, and I in turn respected him for granting me that courtesy.

"You like me better as a wolf," he observed. I could tell he was watching my face.

"It's not you. It's me. I'm not all that great with people."

"Neither am I." He cast me a furtive glance, as if debating how much to let his guard down, now that they'd barreled through my privacy fence. "How much do you know about me?"

I pfft'd. "You're crazy strong. Can twist a spine like nobody's business. You're Matruculan, but I'm only kind of sure what that means. You don't like sleeping on the floor, and you like your meat rare. That's about it, chief. Kind of uncool to make me show you Bev's house when I know next to nothing about you. My own friends have never even seen that."

Mason's hand migrated from cupping my shoulder to gently stroking it, pulling out a portion of my anxiety as he held me closer. I don't know at what point it was that I stopped being allergic to all the touching that went down between an Omen and her Pullers, but I found I didn't hate the closeness. "You're right. That is unfair. Do you want to know my baggage, since we made you show us yours?"

"That'd be a good place to start." I settled more comfortably into his side, grateful he was willing to help level the playing field a little. He was taller than me, like Von was (and everyone else, for that matter), but his bulk was thicker, more solid with hardened muscles. Yet somehow, he was still comfortable to lean against, even though I didn't have much practice with tenderness like this. "Where'd you grow up?"

"In Terraway in a nation called Hayop. I'm the king's firstborn. I imagine people called me far worse things than 'mansion boy'. I was sheltered and spoiled."

"I probably shouldn't have said that to Danny. I'll apologize."

"Danny's one of my best friends. He won't let you apologize for that. We were wrong to make you take us in."

"We were talking about you," I reminded him. I could tell he was uncomfortable with his too-long legs cramped in the backseat. "I'm sorry. I'm crowding you. Here. Stretch out a little." I tried to pull away, but Mason's arm around me tightened.

"I'm alright. I like you near me. I don't actually get a lot of this." He cast me half a smirk. "I don't suppose I could ask you to rub my stomach like you did last night?"

I didn't need a mirror to know my cheeks were crimson. "Yeah. Sorry about that. I've just always wanted a dog. I guess I got carried away with the fantasy."

The corner of his mouth lifted, making him look impossibly more handsome with the slight tease on his lips. "So I'm your fantasy?"

Apparently there was a whole shade deeper than crimson my face had the ability of turning. I blushed furiously, ducking my head. "I didn't mean it like that, and you know it."

Mason reached over his body and lifted my hand, resting it on his toned stomach. "I wasn't kidding."

I tucked back into his side just so he couldn't see the rose color in my cheeks as my fingers lightly dragged up and down above his navel. "Tell me a story, chief."

Mason closed his eyes and leaned his chin atop my head, contented with my simple touch that reeked of inexperience. "When war came to our land, Father was too wary of the battle to go out and fight in it, so in an act of desperation, he gave me his crown and sent me to oversee the soldiers. I'd never been to battle before, though I'd been trained extensively in the palace." He cleared his throat. "War is not the same as sparring with your shield bearer, who I watched die trying to protect me."

"That's awful. I'm sorry, Mason. I've never gone to war before. Sounds pretty scarring." The only wars I'd seen were of the undead apocalypse variety, and Bruce Campbell was always the king of those movies. I imagined the real thing must be a touch more difficult than good old Bruce made it seem, with all of his dashing flawlessness.

"It was scarring, in the best and worst of ways. I saw my father's men die one after the other for days. Then I was taken and tortured for sport." He paused to swallow the lump of agony I could tell this admission cost him.

My hand snaked around his abdomen, wrapping him in a hug I could tell he needed. I'd never been great at giving or receiving hugs, but for some reason I didn't question every move so much with Mason or Von. I needed, and he gave. He needed, and I was starting to give.

The tempo of my heart picked up to a thrumming I didn't recognize as I felt one of his needs come through our strange connection and zap me in the conscience. I strangled the chicken inside of me as I reached up and pressed my lips to his cheek, nuzzling my nose into his short beard. He smelled of pine and a faint hint of patchouli, which as it turns out, isn't such a bad combination when paired with a handsome, brawny man. "I'm sorry that happened to you. Do you want to tell me about it?"

Mason squeezed me, sucking in a long, audible breath

that sounded like he'd been drowning before that brush of my lips to his cheek pulled him to fresh air. He cleared his throat and continued. "You... That... It feels very different when I'm not a wolf, though I appreciate those kisses, too."

I kissed his cheek again, knowing he needed it when he wet his lips with obvious desire. I was playing on the furthest edge of my daring, and I found that I liked the empowering rush that flooded me. I could make a tortured prince feel alive again with a kiss. It felt like the simplest kind of fairytale, and while I'd never put much stock in those, I was starting to see the appeal. "Keep telling me your story. How'd you escape?"

"Danny and Von. They found me after my father's men had given up the search. They and their younger brothers killed a great many Goblins to get to me; I still don't know how they managed it. The Vandershot boys are good like that. Most people get frustrated with Danny's stubborn nature, Von's recklessness, but I'd never been more grateful. They got me out when I was halfway dead."

Mason's cheek rested on my forehead as I leaned my head on his shoulder. The unfamiliar desire to kiss his lips rose up in me, but I fended it off as fiercely as I could, knowing I couldn't kiss my coworker and still respect myself. Though, I didn't think rubbing his stomach, cuddling up to him or pressing my lips to his cheek would pass any sort of corporate scrutiny, either. "I'm glad you made it out of there."

His thumb was dragging up and down the length of my

arm, and he spoke as if he was very far away. "I came back to find my father's land utterly pillaged, and my wife murdered."

I stiffened, not sure if I should pull away. I'd never been snuggled up to someone else's husband before, dead or alive, and didn't know all the rules.

"Kara hadn't been given a proper burial, so she migrated to Sombi. I followed her there."

"Wait, I missed a step. How did she go to Sombi if she was dead?"

"In our land, when we die, our bodies reanimate if not buried correctly."

"Come again? Reanimate?" That was my cue to pull away. The moment my skin parted from his, I felt bereft somehow, and out of sorts. "Sorry. If your wife's somehow still alive, I don't think she'd like me cozying up to you like this." I inched to the far side of the backseat from him, embarrassed at how thoroughly I'd let my guard down. The guilt and confusion tore at me as I wrestled with the foreign desire to go back to his solid embrace. "Oh! I was rubbing your belly. I'm sorry! I'll talk to her and tell her it was all my fault. I'll sit in the front seat. Mariang can trade."

Mason chuckled, though I couldn't see what could possibly be funny about the situation. "She passed away years ago. Her body reanimated, like our kind do if not buried, and she migrated to Sombi. Her body's a shell. She wasn't inside of it anymore. She's not alive, just her body can move."

My nose scrunched. "Like a zombie?"

"I don't know what that word means. You'll have to ask Danny. We call them Amalanhigs. There's something in our dead that are drawn to Sombi. Perhaps it's the snowy woods they prefer hiding in, or the arctic temperatures to keep their carcasses from rotting so quickly. The undead have no language, no real will other than to drink blood and eat organs. Like Von, if he started feeding to his heart's content and transitioned. That's why his self-control is most important if he's to stay alive."

"What? Please tell me you're making this up."

"Why would I make up such a horrible story? I followed my wife there to put her to rest." He punched his chest. "Stabbed her through the heart and buried her face-down, how it's supposed to be done."

I blinked at him, my mouth agape. "You stabbed your wife through the heart?"

"And buried her. I wouldn't have her sucking the blood of innocents, peeling their skin off so she could eat it. She wouldn't want her body used to murder people. The Amalanhigs can't control themselves. They don't recognize individuals, only blood and organs. They're the only race that's thriving with the famine hitting so hard. More and more bodies are migrating to Sombi. They're fed on by the others as soon as they cross over. It's sad, really. The dead feeding on the dead." He took stock of the distance between us and motioned me toward him. "I'm not telling you these things to scare you away from me. You showed us your cuts. I promised to show you mine. If we're going to make a solid team, we can't have secrets."

"Well, I'm not giving up all my secrets just yet."

"Neither am I. But this is a good place to start. It's all common knowledge about me anyway." He laid his hand out on the seat. "Please. I don't know what it is about you, but I like you near me."

I inched back to his side, feeling so very right mixed with a tinge of wrong at being so close to him. His arm wrapped around me, and I felt him exhale, as if the touch that was supposed to be relaxing to me was also soothing him. I guess that's the funny thing about touch when you do it right. "So you buried your wife the way she needed. You took care of her the way she would've wanted. Then what?"

"I saw the land for what it was – a breeding ground for danger everyone was ignoring. The Amalanhigs, or – what did you call them?"

"Zombies."

"Yes, the zombies are drawn from all over Terraway to Sombi. Their numbers are growing constantly because of the famine. Soon there'll to be too many, and they'll hunt out more prey – live prey from surrounding nations. So I did what I thought was right. I abdicated my claim on the throne of my people in Hayop, and took up residence in Sombi's frozen forest. I kill zombies during the night when they're most active, and sleep during the day. I'm making a dent in the population, but it's not what it needs to be. The famine's too widespread. Too many of us are dying. That's why I'm here with you. I'll serve Terraway however it needs me to, but I worry about the zombie population multiplying, left unchecked as it is." He squeezed me like I was special to him, though I knew I was projecting. I had to be; we barely knew each other. Mason cleared his throat. "But this is a much better plan. With a second Omen, fewer people will die, which means fewer zombies. My conscience is clear at having abandoned the residents of Sombi to their devices for this, but it's a big change for me – living Topside, and with a woman, no less. I've been hunting alone in the frozen woods for a long time."

"No one went with you to Sombi?"

"No one. Oh, Danny would've, but his duty's to Mari-ang. Von might've, but he went through sort of a downward spiral shortly after that. He still hasn't completely bounced back from it. I'm the only person with a heartbeat in the land. They feed off each other mostly, and animals. I use my heartbeat and the blood in my veins to lure them into traps and kill them, giving my kin and the other beings in Terraway a proper burial when they need it."

I pulled away so I could face him, turning in my seat so my knee rested on the side of his leg. "Mason, that is without a doubt the most noble, honorable and heroic thing I've ever heard." Mason was trying to save all of Terraway by thanklessly taking out the garbage, when he could've been sitting on a throne, eating peeled grapes. He was Bruce Campbell, incarnate. I couldn't think of anything better.

Mason turned to me, taken aback. "Are you serious?"

"Giving up your title to take care of your wife when she couldn't take care of herself? Knight in shining armor if I ever saw one."

He cast me a bashful sidelong smile. "That's not how people see it in Terraway. I'm a deserter to the throne. I lost my wife and lost my mind, abandoning civilization to live with the undead. There are even rumors that I keep my wife's body locked up so I can be with her, even though she's not her."

I grimaced. "Oh, that's not cool. Yeah, necrophilia would be a hard rumor to shake."

Mason motioned to his body and then flipped his hands out like a magic trick finale. "So that's my baggage. Now we're even. You don't have to hate us for making you let us into your mother's home anymore."

"I guess not."

He was quiet for a few beats. "Where did you even sleep? It was hard to stand without feeling like things were going to start falling on us."

"Ollie and Allie sealed off the smallest bedroom when Bev started stacking her special things in our room. We knew it was a matter of time before we were edged out. Our room was perfectly clean. Nearly empty of clutter. We squeezed in a bunk bed. Allie had the top bunk, and Ollie took the bottom. I slept with whoever felt like sharing that night." I was scratching the backs of my hands, but that was par for the course. I almost didn't even feel the sting that usually helped to center me or vent off a little of my anxiety. Though my scratching was normal for angst-riddled conversations, I began to wonder if I wanted it to be normal. If maybe someday I wouldn't need to hurt myself so much just to fake blending in.

41

NOT ORLANDO BLOOM, CHRISTMAS OR KEEBLER

Mason closed his eyes and pursed his lips, unhappy with himself as he leaned against the door of my car's backseat. "No wonder you didn't want us sharing your bed. I can sleep on the floor. I was being selfish. It'd just been so long since I'd slept in a bed with a woman. I was wrong to make you take me in."

I waved off his apology. "It's fine now. I have a big bed, and it actually wasn't bad to share the space with you." I paused when Mason pulled my calf out to rest across his lap. He started rubbing the muscle there, and I felt that dripping of my tension leaking out that made it possible for me to continue with the emotional nudity. "Thanks. That feels like the best kind of amazing."

"Of course. You would do the same for me. You just did when you kissed my cheek."

I dipped my chin to hide my chagrin. "Yeah, but you do that cool pulling thing. I can't do that for you."

"Oh, *hani*. Yes, you do." His expression was filled with appreciation for our budding connection, and I echoed his soft smile. "Go on. I want to know more."

I swallowed as I dug back into the muck of the past that always seemed too near the present, no matter how often I tried to bat it away. "I don't know what set it all off – Ollie still won't tell me. One day Ollie came home with some wood and nails, and he hammered the bedroom door shut. He even got that builder's foam and sprayed the space under the door to seal it so the bugs couldn't get in. Allie cried all night long while I held her." I paused, recalling my sister's pinched expression of emotional turmoil while I'd done my best to give her a safe place to fall apart. "It was rough. I hate it when Allie cries."

"I can imagine."

"We got in and out through the window, which Allie put a lock on that only we had keys to. She was scared after that, but I never found out why. I just knew that something broke my sister, and Ollie and I couldn't fix it."

I "mm'd" at the delicious feel of a man's hands massaging my calf. I couldn't believe the vast difference this whole pulling thing did for me. A week ago, I never would've debated letting someone touch me so thoroughly, but here I was, relaxing further with every stroke. I didn't even care about the germs I knew were still there. Mason's touch was giving goodness to me, not taking from me. I couldn't feel anything but content with him.

I was leaning back against the door, my eyelids fluttering shut when Mason started just above my kneecap and pulled downward with steady pressure befitting a masseur. My heart was fluttering at the supreme intimacy that was well out of my zone of experience. "That feels incredible, by the way."

"Good. It's going to be a long day of Omen work. It's best to start the day with no stress. It was poor planning on our parts to push for finding the rock this morning."

I was about to say something snarky, but the door I was leaning on popped open, sending me tumbling backward into the mid-morning air. I caught myself on the door before I hit the pavement, but my victory was short-lived. "Gives it to me!" a creaky old voice yelled.

I was yanked out from under my arms onto the blacktop of the parking lot, shrieking at the intrusion of the wrinkly and smelly Goblin King. Titus was surprisingly stronger and more limber than I would've guessed. Sneaky Christmas Elf.

Mason was a blur that leapt over me and tackled my attacker, turning them both into a mess of limbs as I struggled to stand. Mason was far stronger than the Goblin King, but he howled and dropped him, recoiling as he shook his hands like they were on fire. "Hot! Dirty trick, that is! Go back to Terraway, Titus!"

"Like I'd really give yous the two seconds it would takes

for yous to tear my head offs. I can't best Matruculan strength, but I've gots a few tricks up my sleeveses." Titus pulled back the beige gauzy sleeve of his robe as if gearing up to pull out a rabbit. He watched me with his giant eyes that had a hint of play mixed in with the malice. "I needs the rock for my peoples first!" His hunched body and crackly skin made him look like a fight would be out of the question, but as soon as Mason lunged again, Titus pushed at the air with a flick of his hand. "Lift theses, strong man." I watched in horror as Mason's hands grew so heavy that when they hit the blacktop, they actually cracked it. Mason struggled against the injustice. With muscle-straining effort, he actually managed to lift them off the ground, but was unable to put them to much use.

"October, run!" Mason shouted.

Titus sneered at me. "Do it, and I'll snaps his thick necks. I know you's got a spare Duwende."

I held up my hands, the debate to give Titus the stone plain on my face. "You'll let Mason go if I give you the rock?"

Mason met my eyes with panic. "No! You can't let him have it! He'll keep the whole thing for his people, and no one else will stand a chance! Goblins only care about their race. They don't care about the whole of Terraway. They're the reason we're down to one stone. They stole and destroyed the others, experimenting with dark magic."

Titus clicked his knobby fingers, and Mason's lips glued shut. My guard was rendered mute as he struggled with his hands that weighed more than I could guess. I didn't know how heavy something had to be to put a bowling ball-sized dent in blacktop. Mason was built like a pro wrestler.

Titus' bug eyes gleamed with delight and greed. He spoke so only I could hear him, keeping his threats from Mason. "Good girl. Yes, I'll lets him go if you gives it to me. Gives it to me, or I'll hurt you worse than he can."

I got the sense that Titus was referring to some higher darker power I'd yet to be introduced to. My face screwed up like I'd eaten a pack of Sour Patch Kids. "Dude, is this your idea of politics? I'm already unhappy with you because you couldn't keep your people in line. Fergo and the jag who felt me up got a swift death for crossing us, and this is how you're petitioning for a favor? Weak, Titus. Totally weak."

Titus smiled – a twisted, crooked line that split his wrinkled old potato face and somehow made him look more sinister. "Goblins aren't the ones to crosses. We's got magic you don't wants to messes with. Gives me the stone now, or I'll sends my men after Mason and Von."

"You'll keep your claws off Mason and Von. Leave them alone. I'll give the stone to you. Jeez. Relax your balls, man." I did my best to maintain a façade of calm through Mason's muted protests.

"There are organses they don't needs, you know. I could takes out Mason's spleen and he could still do his jobs. I could takes a number of things from him if you don't cooperates." Titus' voice cracked with delight. "Ezra's looking into upping your securities as we speaks. You're a smart girls. Yous has to know anyone can be boughts. Sama's trying to get the other kings to get the stone to gives it to him, but Goblins are smarters! We keeps it for ourselves. Then we be the ones Terraway comes to for aid." He raised a megalomaniacal finger in triumph.

"Who the crap is Sama, and why is everyone so up in arms about this d-bag?"

Titus' eyes bulged. "Sama's the greats immortal king without a crowns. It's because of his rations the famines hasn't killed us all. Some of the other kings are willing to turns their crowns over to him if he'll takes care of their land. But Goblins never surrenders!" His eyes bulged with the confidence of a madman. "Hurry, girl."

"Dude, chill. It's a heavy rock." I feigned exasperation so he didn't see my fingers trembling with rage at being threatened.

"Sama wants to controls you, but I got here firsts! You'll do as I say until your last breaths, or I'll have one of my spics do away with one of your Reapers altogethers." When I didn't move, Titus' voice lowered, his giant eyes glinting with unconcealed malice. "Lady Mariang's on her last legs. If Ezra stands in my ways – if he sends Danny after me to steals back the sagrado stone, I'll starts in on their non-vital organs. I'll do it, girl. I could feeds them to Sylvia's people. They're always hungries for more meat. Danny would survives just fine with only one kidney, but

Lady Mariang? I shudders to think what would happen if she caught a mere colds."

I was shaking with red-hot rage on the inside, but knew it was important for me to shrug like this was all boring to me. "Like I want to trek across the whole of Terraway lugging this thing around. Save me the hassle. It's in the trunk." I ignored Mason's look of utter betrayal and shock as I popped the trunk. "Here. I've got a grocery bag you can put it in so you don't touch it." I dumped out the spare set of shoes I kept in my bag for changing into at work and slid the white flimsy plastic over the top of the rock.

Titus was next to me, a lust-filled cackle busting out from his lips at the sight of the rock that lit up at my touch. He was a ball of gleaming lust; the covetous energy was practically radiating off of him as he rose up on his toes. "That's it! That's the lost sagrado stone! Finally we can lives how we were meants to! Puts it in the bag, girl! Hurry!"

"Chill out. I'm doing it." Mason's unintelligible moans tugged at my heart, and I prayed my hands didn't tremble and give me away. Mason was a good man, and I couldn't just stand idly by and let Titus use him to control me. Mason was too strong to be abused like that. The world needed more selfless people like him in it. I wouldn't let Titus take away one of the few good ones.

Danny's voice couldn't have been more perfectly timed. "Titus! Get away from her!" His feet pounded the pavement behind me, and I waited for Titus to jinx Danny in a similar way he'd gotten Mason.

As if in slow motion, Titus turned his head and sneered in Danny's direction. He raised his hand to snap his fingers so he could inflict whatever damage he felt like on my own personal Frankenstein monster.

Titus was distracted, and I was ready. Both hands on the stone, I hoisted it up and bashed the old man in the skull with it. I knew that even if it wasn't the magical tool that turned anyone who wasn't me into stone, it was still a heavy rock I could do significant damage with.

Titus fell to the pavement, crumpling like an old sheet on a summer's day as it drifted off the laundry line. He reached for me drunkenly, but I was a woman possessed. I dropped to my knees and cracked him in the skull again, this time hitting my rock atop gray slate that was hard to break, but not impossible.

There were too many people in my life who stepped on others to get what they wanted. Jessica, who stepped on me by dating Beto while we were still together. The kids in elementary school, who made up a rhyme to make fun of me called "Filthy February". The inmates, who tried to scare me while I was treating them. Bev, every single time I let my guard down.

I was tired of being stepped on.

Titus didn't care about his world. He cared that he got his peeled grapes while the rest of Terraway starved.

I brought the glowing weapon down over and over again until Mason's voice found me in my madness. "October, stop! He's dead. He's dead. Put the stone down."

I smashed a few more times on autopilot, not noticing that Titus' head was almost completely turned into a pile of scattered pebbles.

Danny slid the backpack he'd just purchased from the outdoor supply store toward me with wide eyes, his hands up to display their innocence. "Okay, kid. Just put the stone into the backpack so we don't accidentally turn into that." He pointed to what was left of Titus, and I gasped in terror at the irreparable damage I'd done.

Mason's hands and mouth were back to normal. His palm was covering his mouth in horror as he took in the carnage. "They're tied with the *tahi* charm. Titus tied himself to the entire Goblin nation!"

It took a solid three seconds for his words to take meaning. The color drained from my face when it hit me. "You don't mean... I didn't just kill a whole race of people. I only killed Titus." I said "only" like it wasn't the worst thing a person could do, to kill another.

Mariang's shock and dread were contagious as she came out from where she'd been hiding in the store's exit, her expression mirroring itself onto me at the awful thing I'd done. "Oh, what are we going to do? They'll sentence her, Danny! She'll be locked up or executed for sure!"

Danny's shock melted into a hard look to cover over his disbelief. "No. October can't be executed. If she is, all of Terraway will keep starving to death. You know Omens are untouchable. But this... A whole nation gone."

Then it dawned on me: Titus wasn't the monster; I was.

I stumbled back until my butt bumped the car. "Oh! What did I do? How did... I just... He went after Mason and I just snapped!"

"It's alright, just put the stone away and everything will be fine." Danny's tone was the steady one of an officer talking down a shooter.

I was the shooter. I was the danger. I was the criminal. I'd stepped on Titus, and he would never get back up to fight the stink off another day.

Terraway was already changing me. First I'd murdered Tanga, and now a whole nation. I was supposed to bring life and stability to their world, but instead I'd brought genocide and destruction.

Danny jerked his head toward the car, but gave me a wide berth. "Come on, kid. We've got to go straight to Ezra and see what's to be done from here."

It was in that moment I knew that of all the monsters I'd met in Terraway, I was the worst one.

Love the book?
Leave a review!

42

TREMBLE

Enjoy a free preview of *Tremble*,
book two in the *Terraway* series.

Mariang cried the whole way to the mansion. Her cooing sniffles were the only sounds as we walked inside and awaited my doom. I didn't want to think about the fact that I'd just murdered the Goblin King, Titus. Each time I closed my eyes longer than a blink, I saw his wrinkled Christmas Elf body turning to stone and crushing into pebbles when I'd lost my mind after he'd threatened Mason.

My head hung as I waited outside the conference room at Ezra's mansion. I guess Ezra was going to be my stepdad when he married Bev, but in this capacity, he was my boss.

I'd just screwed up royally my first week on the job. Instead of reaping enough souls to feed the nations of Terraway, I'd managed to wipe out one-seventh of their nations in a single blow. Titus had tied himself to his people, connecting his life with all the Goblins in Terraway. It had been a solid plan to survive a famine – if he ate, none of the Goblins starved.

I don't think Titus counted on a fight when he crossed me.

Ezra opened the door to the conference room with a closed expression, ushering me inside. I gasped at the remnants of Titus' body that had been shoved in the corner next to the fichus. The statue that had mere hours ago been a living, breathing being was still intact from the neck down – solid stone though it was. One leg was raised higher than the other, and his arm was outstretched, frozen as it reached out to snatch at the stone, or at me. I backed away, my heels skidding on the short carpet as anxiety brimmed in me at the evidence of my madness.

Mason's hand on my back was supposed to be reassuring, but I'm not sure anything could've calmed me enough to make me forget I'd just slaughtered an entire people in one go. I kept my head down, accepting whatever sentence the council of Terraway had for me.

My hands were shaking as I scratched at the skin on the backs of them. I didn't bother sitting at the long oval-shaped polished wood table. My insides felt hollow and painted in a thin layer of white coldness that had nothing to do with the chill I got from reaping.

Mason sat in his chair, patting the one next to him that had been selected for me. I stood, knowing I didn't deserve a seat at the cool kids' table after what I'd done. Kabayo, Captain Finn, Sylvia and Langgam all stared at me with a new kind of curious fascination that was mingled with a wary watch-out-for-that-one;-she's-nuts looks.

I was sorely missing Von, who still hadn't shown up for work. They would lock me up for sure, and I wouldn't even be able to say goodbye to him.

The worst was that I wouldn't be able to explain things to Ollie. I'd just disappear in some Terraway jail, separated from my big brother, who would never be the same. He'd think I'd abandoned him, like our sister Allie had done to us.

Ezra and I were the only ones standing. I lowered my chin when he took the floor to start my private hearing. "We've been discussing at length how to handle this situation, and have come to the conclusion that your involvement in this should be kept secret, Lady October."

My head whipped up to gaze at Ezra, but I didn't say a word.

"It's in the best interest of Terraway to let Titus' arrogance of tying himself to his people, as if he were immortal, stand as a lesson not to dabble in such things. He was foolish, and now he and his people are dead. Who did it doesn't matter at this point. What matters is that no other kings feel tempted to bind themselves to their people in the same way."

My mouth fell open in shock. It wasn't until Ezra's verdict that I glanced up and took in the casual demeanor of everyone on the council. Kabayo was leaning back, his black horse head mildly interested as he tapped his fingertips on the arm of his chair. Captain Finn had his hands folded across his stomach, his left combat boot crossed over his right knee. He had a calm look about him, like he was watching the whole thing on television on a Sunday afternoon. Even Sylvia, the woman with a crescent-shaped face and bat-like enhancements only wore an expression of mild concern.

Like I was there for a traffic violation. Like I hadn't just murdered a whole race of people.

Ezra waved his hand in my direction. "You can carry on about your day, then. That's all. Just keep this to yourselves the next time you're in Terraway."

My head whipped from one end of the table to the other, my somber expression mutating into indignation. "No! Are you kidding me with this? I just murdered probably thousands of people!"

Kabayo raised his finger to correct me. "Tens of thousands. And Goblins aren't people; they're a plague. Good riddance to the whole of them."

Prince Langgam wasn't even interested in the conversation, but played with one of the cockroaches as it skittered up his muddy arm. "Is the meeting over yet?"

I glowered at Lang. "I'm smack in the middle of talking, you jag."

Finn quirked an eyebrow at my outburst. "Do you want us to hang you? Then where would we be? Even with the Goblins taken off the list of creatures the souls you reap have to fuel, Terraway will still starve without a healthy Omen. Lady Mariang can't keep up with the demand anymore." Finn inclined his head apologetically to Ezra out of respect for speaking disparagingly about his daughter.

Kabayo stood, as if the whole meeting was adjourned. "Frankly, you only did what everyone in this room wishes they could get away with. Goblins have been stealing food from the neighboring lands when they don't actually need it, since they were tied to Titus. Every time one of our horses takes ill, it's from some Goblin's curse."

I tried to picture the reverse centaur standing before me actually riding on a horse, but it was too weird a visual. I cleared my throat to address the room as an equal. "You all should be ashamed of yourselves. I killed baby Goblins who didn't even have a chance to change their people for the better. I killed the good people as well as the bad. You can't let me off the hook for this. It's not right."

Sylvia eyed Titus' stone body warily. "There's no such thing as a good Goblin. None that I've seen, anyway. They all grow up the same – greedy and sneaky."

Mason's hand on my arm was gently trying to tell me to shut up and be grateful, but I ignored him. I leaned my knuckles down on the table, resolute in my conviction. "No. I won't help a world that has no checks and balances. No one's above the law, not even the people in this room. I mean it. I'm not leaving until I'm punished in some way."

Ezra softened, pinching the bridge of his nose. "What would you have me do? If I throw you in jail, it only punishes the people of Terraway who continue to starve."

My eyes met Ezra's with no hint of optimism or peace. "I just committed genocide. I hope you understand that. I don't care if the Goblins were a people worth saving. On your payroll is a mass murderer. Don't you dare tell me you can go to sleep with that on your conscience." I shook my head at Ezra. "I'm a correctional nurse. I believe in the justice system. Know me a little bit, Ezra."

Captain Finn's smile told me that no matter how insistent I was, they weren't going to take this as seriously as they should. "Kabayo, why don't you take the new Omen down to your prison? Let her look around at how many cells were opened up when the Goblins turned to stone."

"More than half. The statues are being moved to the palace garden right now, actually."

"No one's above the law," I argued, furious. "That's the whole point of having a law! I mean, honestly!"

Prince Langgam stood, and several dozen cockroaches skittered across his shoulders and trailed down his mud-streaked arms. "Are we done here? I've got to get back."

"No, we're not done! You can't let me do this with no repercussions."

Captain Finn scratched the gills on his neck and stood. His short blond hair was ruffled on the left, and I wondered if he ever worried about things like bedhead. He was wearing that same cocky smile that had a hint of cruelty to it as he stared across the table at me. "Expect a shipment of gold from King Banak in the morning, expressing his gratitude. You've done Terraway a great favor, Lady October."

I jabbed my finger in his direction, livid that this was all a joke to them. "Don't you smile at me. Don't you dare smile about this."

Kabayo bowed slightly to Ezra, and then to me, chuckling at my indignation. "She wants to be punished? Take away her dessert, Ezra. No cake for a whole day." He extended his hand to shake mine, but I refused, sniffing at the offensive offer. Kabayo shook Mason's hand instead, and then vanished before my eyes. I jumped, and then remembered the kings and important blowhards all had enhancements that allowed them to transport their bodies between worlds on a dime.

Sylvia inclined her head to me. "We've been trying to ward off the Goblins for months now, but they keep encroaching on our territory. Thank you for helping us." She placed her hand on the table and met my eyes with sincerity I couldn't shrug off. "Truly."

"But I didn't..." I tried to protest, but no one was listening.

Sylvia and Captain Finn vanished, and then Lang

followed suit after he walked behind my chair and squeezed my shoulder.

Mason exhaled when it was just Danny, Ezra and me with him in the conference room. "We got lucky there." Then he craned his neck up at me with a scolding expression from where he still sat at the table. "Are you trying to get yourself killed? Take the pardon and run next time."

"Are you kidding me with this? This is wrong, Mason. You should know that a country's leaders should have to follow the same rules as its citizens."

Danny's arms were crossed over his chest. "I can't believe you're upset about getting off without punishment. You're just trying to be difficult."

"Hello, I work at a prison! I see every day that checks and balances matter. I know in my heart that I belong in jail on death row. I killed a man in cold blood just because he..." My eyes fell on Mason before they closed to shut out the world for a few seconds.

Mason stood, his hand rubbing circles into the middle of my back. "You thought Titus was going to kill me. I can't tell if you were right, but I know you did what you had to do. It was Titus' fault for tying himself to his people with the *tahi* charm. We all warned him of the danger."

"Don't," I warned quietly. "Don't you let me off the hook, too." Mason's body was warm and inviting. I don't know why I felt the tug of a magnet in my gut, but it drew me to him so I could wrap myself in his comfort.

For three whole seconds I breathed, inhaling the relief

of his calming presence that smelled like patchouli and grown man.

I stiffened when his hand trailed to the small of my back. It was such an intimate space on my body, but the alarms weren't because his hand felt wrong there – my hackles rose because his touch felt all too right. I didn't deserve comfort, and I was taking it like a glutton. I pushed Mason back and stomped out of the room, running down to the basement where the cell I knew I deserved was waiting for me.

Read *Tremble* and continue with
the next book in the *Terraway* series.